Cover design by Red Cape Graphic Design

Any Which Way but South Wales

Book Two

David Owain Hughes

Foreword
Richard Ayre

I first met David Owain Hughes at a Guy N Smith convention, a couple of years ago. My impression of him was of a mild mannered, bearded, bespectacled fella, who seemed very friendly. This was confirmed later on that same evening where we bonded over a curry and a round of drunken dancing in a pub in Knighton, the village where the meet up takes place every year. We became firm friends straight away.

At that point, I only knew Dave as a horror writer; and pretty full on horror too. We have since become stablemates in two Darkwater Syndicate publications: *Shadows and Teeth Volume Three* and *Postcards from the Void.* With both of these publications, we helped each other out with the stories we had forwarded. This has now become the norm, and Dave asked me to have a look at his first crime noir novel *South by Southwest Wales*, before he sent it to Darkwater. If you're reading this, then you'll know it has since been published and was declared one of 'The best reads of 2018' recently. High praise indeed.

And well-deserved praise. What Dave accomplished with that novel was something difficult to do: He created an instant modern hero, Samson Valentine.

Samson is a wonderful creation. A man who lives in the wrong time. He really should have been around in 1940's Chicago, but instead lives in modern day Cardiff, although he still wears his Fedora hat and raincoat with panache, spouting out Bogartesque dialogue, like calling everyone he meets a 'Palooka' (love it). He is a good man in a world gone bad. A true 'hero' if ever there was one.

However, this could have led to a cartoon-like character without the skills of Dave and the back story we get about Samson. When we first meet him, he is as down as a man can be. He has lost not one, but two wives to cancer, he is seen as a joke by the local thugs and the police force, and he's living his life in the bottom of a whiskey bottle. His only sanctuary is a jazz bar where he spends his time drinking to such an extent that he starts to believe he is actually living in a strange, 1940's Chicago era city. Things are looking pretty bleak for him.

But of course, he is Samson Valentine and he's not going to let a little thing like alcoholism and fantasy get in his way. Even though he is a broken man, Samson solves the crime, sorts out the corruption in the police force and becomes the triumphant hero we all know he is.

So when Dave told me he was working on a sequel to *South by Southwest Wales*, I was really interested to know where he would go with it. And, boy, was I impressed.

The character of Samson has developed massively in *Any Which Way but South Wales*. He's on the wagon, on the ball, and on the case. Now seen as a very useful ally by the newly appointed and squeaky clean police chief, Samson is engaged in busting heads, still trying to find and bring to justice the elusive gang boss, XRay from the first novel. Samson has cleaned up. He's stopped drinking, and instead of smoking endless cigarillos, he has instead taken to nibbling on breadsticks, and there are some wonderful scenes of him doing just this whilst muttering words of wisdom to some poor sap he's just taken apart in the name of justice.

But he has his hands full. There is a serial killer on the loose in his city, and Sam is going to need all his cunning and gumption to find 'The Widower Maker' before he strikes once more.

Any Which Way but South Wales is what *South by Southwest Wales* is: a modern classic. Two fast-paced, hugely enjoyable stories with a central character who is much more complex and three dimensional than he would have been in the hands of a lesser writer.

Take off your raincoat and hat, loosen your tie, put some 40s jazz on the turntable and sit in that pool of light from the shaded chintz lamp. Take a sip of your favourite single malt and get stuck into this story.

I promise you. You'll be up all night.

Chapter 1

Samson's mind was clear. The clearest it had been in months, *years* even, maybe, but it wasn't perfect. Not yet, anyway. But he was getting there, thanks to the good people at the hospital. However, there were things Samson did know for sure: he lived and worked in Cardiff, Wales, not Chicago, USA; that his wives were dead and had only been a figment of his imagination brought on by alcohol abuse, stress, and anxiety.

Had me all jingle-brained, he thought, looking through his binoculars that were trained on a dilapidated flophouse. His mark was somewhere inside.

Samson now had a firm grip on who he was and what he wanted out of life. For the first time in a while, he was living. Furthermore, he was back in the gym, hitting the bag and pumping iron, going on dates, had dropped two stone in weight, and kicked the booze and smokes.

Samson was, for the most part, he hoped, in complete control.

He still dressed, talked and acted like a hardboiled P.I. from a decade long past, because it was a part of his make-up, his charm, and it was an aspect that would remain.

I made sure the headshrinkers left that chunk of my psyche alone.

Samson, fancying he saw his man leave the dive

before him, moved his head

to the left, but it wasn't him.

Damn. How much longer? My backside has gone to sleep.

Admittedly, it took duration for the croakers, nurses and therapists to drum reality into Samson's conk after he checked himself into a rehab clinic. And it wasn't easy for him to open up, either; he wouldn't, no, *couldn't*, speak about his problems, his 'feelings', as *they* put it.

I'm not a muffin, he'd thought.

***

"Men don't chin about such emotional tosh, Doc. They deal with it and soldier on, just like a good trooper," Samson spoke, lighting a cigarillo.

"Then why are you here, Sam? You want help, don't you? You came to us, remember? How long do you want to play these games? We're wasting precious time…"

"*Come on, Sam, you* can *do this*!" Angie encouraged. "*You've come a long way in the past year or so. Push a little further, and harder, like I know you can.*"

"Okay, babe," he answered absentmindedly.

"Excuse me, Sam?"

"Oh, I wasn't—nothing, Doc." The quack, looking concerned and confused, didn't have time to respond. "I guess I *could* try flapping to you and your staff if you think it would help. What have I got to lose?"

The doctor smiled. "Nothing, of course."

"*Well done, honey. Proud of you.*"

Sam, through fear of looking dizzy, didn't acknowledge Angie this time. "When do we start?"

"Immediately."

"Doc?"

"Yes, Samson?"

"I'm no loony tune. I—it-it's been a difficult few years, and—"

"It's okay, Sam," the doctor said, resting a hand on Samson's arm. "I'm not here to judge, but to make you feel better. Come, let's begin."

***

That conversation had taken place four months ago—three weeks into his stint at rehab—with his treatment lasting a further month afterwards. Whilst undergoing his therapy sessions and a series of drugs and tests, he'd been advised to cut back on his smoking.

"Jeepers, Doc, can't a fella have one vice to his flea-bitten name? I never said I was schooling to be a monk."

"No, but it'll help improve your fitness and sharpen your mind. I'm not asking you to quit fully—although I'd advise it in due course—just shorten your intake."

"First I had to stop the jorum of skee and now the smokes? And I thought bumping my gums to the headshrinkers would be the hardest part," Samson admitted.

"The *what* of skee?"

"Jorum. It means booze, Doc."

"Right, I see. Anyway, please try your best with the cigars, Sam," the doctor said, scribbling in his pad.

Much to Samson's surprise, he was able to go from fifteen a day to ten, and then five. But by God did he *need* that five, and it wasn't until after rehab and he'd joined a local gym that he was able to give up the stogies completely.

***

Breadsticks. They were my answer. Them, and a whole load of wheezing after smacking a punching bag around and lifting weights at Paul's boxing club, Samson thought, continuing to eye the lank joint, his peepers pressed firmly to his binoculars.

As he watched, Samson slipped a hand inside his trench coat's upper breast pocket and dug out a plain-flavoured breadstick. He began to chew on it.

Yeah, these things sure do help keep the cravings at bay. Although, it was getting to be that he didn't miss smoking at all. *Hopefully, in a few weeks, I can quit eating these things and stop making a bloody mess and racket.*

A laugh escaped him as he swept the binoculars back the other way, spotting a gang of hooded teenagers. His guts flip-flopped. They were pushing around a couple of young girls who couldn't have been more than thirteen or fourteen.

Samson adjusted the focus and noticed the

‘children' were being held in place; one of them appeared to have a knife jammed in the small of her back. The thugs, four in total, looked anxious, as they threw nervous glances left and right.

“The goddamn pissants are—”

Two large, brutish men, one with a flat nose, the other sporting a buzz cut, approached the small gang and engaged them in conversation.

Samson momentarily took his eyes off them to peek over his shoulder. It appeared the bozos had arrived by car, and there was a third, a driver, sat behind the wheel, the engine idling.

“I’ll just wait for the berries and canaries to exchange hands before dropping a dime on these clowns.” Samson’s hand reached for the mike belonging to his CB, which he’d installed in his car last year, and put it to his mouth in readiness.

He licked his lips, his eyes glued to the hatchet-men. “Come on, come on, what are you waiting for?” He shook his head. “I can’t believe they’re selling underage girls in broad daylight. It makes me want to retch.” His grip tightened on the binoculars. He wanted nothing more than to show those ‘men’ what he’d been practising at Paul’s – particularly his speedball skills. “If I wasn’t busy—”

Money exchanged hands and the girls dressed to look like whore-ish women were shoved into the paws of the older thugs, who should have known better. When Samson was positive the guys were headed back towards the car he thought was theirs, he called it in.

“Your days are marked, palookas.”

In the distance, sirens wailed, and a smiled stretched across Samson’s face.

“My first week back on the job sure has been interesting,” he muttered, turning his eyes back to the building he’d been watching. Everything seemed quiet.

Hope I didn’t miss something.

Close by, tyres came to a screeching halt. Doors opened and slammed shut.

“*Police*! Down on the ground!” Samson heard from his right. He looked, noticing the gang of youths being apprehended. To his left, the buyers were trying to make a quick getaway, but squad cars sealed off their escape route.

“It would seem you hop-heads aren’t going anywhere.” Samson laughed, pulling another breadstick from his coat pocket. “Yeah, what a week...”

***

The eighteen months or so after the showdown at Cardiff docks with XRay’s goons—which had ended with Samson checking himself into rehab—had been smooth sailing.

With the biggest case of his life cracked, superior thugs caged, nuclear warhead codes seized, the hierarchy of the police force probed and shaken down, the city cleaned up, and his private eye business flourishing once more, Samson had turned everything around.

Hell, he'd even kicked the booze and shifted Angie from his mind.

And, with business coming through his door in spades, Samson had thought it would keep him and his mind busy forever, and for that, he was sure he could continue walking the straight line he'd started upon. Also, when a new chief of police took over, Gary Broadbank, who wanted Samson working closer to the police, his workload increased tenfold.

Together, Samson and Broadbank kept the streets clean and safe.

Then, roughly fifteen months into sobriety and straightforwardness—two things Samson wasn't familiar with—loneliness kicked in. And, even though he had Steve at the Jazz Hole and Alice at the coffee shop, it wasn't enough to stop the slip from happening.

Being clear-headed all day, every day, like being intoxicated twenty-four seven, became sheer hell. When he wasn't working, he was cooped up in his flat, listening to blues or stalking the streets at the dead of night.

He became a different kind of lost, emptiness set in, and it wasn't long before he took to the booze again. At the beginning, it was a stray glass here and there to help take the edge off reality. Soon enough, though, the odd belt of whiskey became bottles at a time, and Angie returned, bringing with her anxiety, grief, and a whole host of other problems.

Samson managed to realise he was reverting back to his pit of despair—and, not wanting his business to unravel—Samson suspended everything and checked himself into the drying out tank. He knew it was that or nothing, the decision vital, and thought he might be able to see off his demons once and for all.

***

Yeah, it was a tough time, he thought, lowering the binoculars. There was no sign of his target. *I knew I'd have to let a lot of personal stuff out of the bag to unknowns. Still, it was worth—*

Samson's thoughts derailed when he saw his mark poke his head around the building's front door. He looked shifty, his peepers scanning his surroundings. Samson raised the binoculars and drank the man in.

"Peek-a-boo, I see you, palooka." The man's dubious, twitchy movements drew a smile across Samson's face. "You've got a date with destiny, jug-head."

When the man moved away from the door, his body exposed, Samson saw the briefcase he was holding, which was handcuffed to his wrist.

"Excellent."

The mark walked away from the building and hurried down the street as fast as his short legs would carry him. Samson started his car and went after him at a snail's pace until the chap cut down a smog-filled alley.

Samson parked his car at the kerb, killed the engine and got out. He left his camera behind, but made sure he had his cuffs. *I have all I need on this guy to take him downtown and throw his punk backside in the caboose.*

Samson jogged after his perpetrator, making sure his fedora was pushed down tight on his head, and entered the alley. Up ahead, Samson saw the man disappear beyond tendrils of smoke. He clenched his jaw.

Damn it, he's getting away.

From all around him sounds assaulted his ears from the businesses' back entryways and yards. Chefs' knives made machine gun-like sounds as they chopped vegetables on cutting boards, the soft hubbub of voices, fork trucks beeped and whined, and gas pipes hissed and groaned. Somewhere close by, Samson heard water trickling against the floor.

He didn't hang around long enough to inspect his surroundings. Samson chased after his target, feeling the fittest he had been in years.

Can't remember the last time I ran a palooka down with such ease, but what in the hell's got him so spooked, anyway? He's making a drop, that's what; maybe he's worried about a tail.

When the mist cleared, Samson saw he was at a dead-end, a wall blocked his progress. He stood, turned a circle, and tried to figure out where the man had gone. At this section of the alley, there appeared to be no businesses or doors to flats. There was nowhere to hide.

"What *the*—?!"

Gas burped from a pipe to his side and erupted from a drain close to his feet. The stench forced

Samson to cover his nose and mouth with a kerchief he kept in the breast pocket of his jacket.

All week I've been tailing this wanker, and as I'm about to glom him, he does a Great Gatsby on me!

The thought made him smile, for it was an inside joke between him and Alice.

"The Gatsby was a magician, right?" she asked him in all seriousness one evening before he'd checked into rehab. "I mean, with a name like that, what else *could* he have been?"

Samson had almost choked on the pie she'd served him, having to wash it down with a sip of coffee. "You need to read more classics, kid," he retorted, not answering her question.

Such a nice, wholesome—

"Well, well, well, if it ain't the hero *dick* from two years ago."

Samson turned his head, slowly, to the sound of the voice coming from behind him.

"Thought you had me trapped like a rat in a corner, eh, Valentine? Guess I'm smarter than you think."

Before Samson could fully turn, something hard smacked against the backs of his legs, taking him to his knees. He yelled, his hands slapping against the ground, stopping him from tipping over.

"End of the line, fuckface."

Got to be two of them – The Brain and The Brawn, Samson thought.

"I had you pegged from the moment you started following me, Valentine. Broadbank needs to find himself some better help, am I right boys?"

Maybe three...

Samson heard the bat—or whatever it was—cut through the air. He ducked, and the bludgeoning instrument clonked against an industrial-sized bin.

"*Argh*!" the hatchet-man man called out, dropping his weapon.

The canny P.I. rolled, turned, and got to his feet cat-like, as a second, shoddily dressed bruno came at him with a piece of lead piping; his movements were slow and pitiful. Sweat covered his brow.

"*You*—" the fat, out of shape goon grunted.

Again, Samson ducked the sweeping attack and put all his weight behind a right jab. His knuckles ploughed into the tubby yob's guts and propelled him backwards. He tumbled out of sight, the air wheezing out of him like a trampled-on bagpipe.

The initial goon had his weapon back in his hand, which was the butt of a pool cue. It slashed at Samson's face, missing his nose by inches, and smacked against the ground. Samson stepped on it and launched a left hook at the man's jaw, cracking it clean off its hinges.

He went down hard and fast—lights out—and some broken teeth surfed out of his mouth on a wave of blood.

"Holy shit!" The Brain backed away slowly. Hands up.

"You're going downtown, mook." Samson clubbed his open hand with the cue. "But are you going quietly, that's the question?" The look in The Brain's eye told Samson everything he needed to know. "Don't even think—"

The Brain turned on his heel and dashed up the mouth of the alley, his form quickly lost within the smoke that continued to billow from broken pipes, manholes, and shops.

"*Halt*!" Samson ordered and took off in pursuit. He burst out of the alley's entrance and looked left and right, spotting The Brain as he disappeared out of sight.

Damn. This should have been a simple bust.

Undeterred, Samson ran after the man, surprised by how fast he could shift. Up ahead, he saw The Brain push and shoulder-barge people out of his way, with some bowled into the road. Car horns blared, whilst other vehicles skidded and slammed on their brakes.

Drivers yelled out of their windows.

Now and then, The Brain threw a glance over his shoulder.

Yeah, I'm right here, weasel.

The chase continued for another four blocks, with The Brain hurdling, ducking, weaving and diving over vehicles and people alike. At one point, the man rolled over a car bonnet, cracking the windshield.

"You fucking lunatic!" the bloke behind the wheel screamed.

Samson, more level-headed, skirted his obstacles, which did little to slow him.

The Brain was now hobbling, and within seconds, Samson was close enough to be able to dive on him. His superior weight shoved The Brain up against a fruit and vegetable stand, with both cop and robber toppling over it, pulling cabbages and other greens onto themselves.

"You're under arrest, meathead."

"*No*!" The Brain tried scrabbling away from Samson's grip, but the P.I. was fast in slipping his cuffs on him and hoisting him off the floor.

"It's the big house for you, sunshine."

"You'll pay for this, pig." He thrashed, and tried kicking and biting Samson. "This is brutality."

"Tell it to the fella with the funny wig." Samson twisted the man's arm, relishing the clicking sound that released from the shoulder area. "A prison cell's too good for the likes of you, scumbag." He looked down at the man's briefcase. "I'm sure that's filled with plenty of incriminating evidence."

"F-fuck *you*!" The Brain spat.

Samson smiled as he hauled the yelling man up the street and back to his car.

Within fifteen minutes, he had him down at the station.

Chapter 2

"Thanks, Samson," a uniformed officer said, "but I can take him from here."

"No problem," Samson said.

"Come on, punk," the copper addressed The Brain, grabbing him by his arm and dragging him towards a set of stairs leading down to the holding cells.

"I'm going to get you, *Valentine*!" The Brain threatened.

"I'll look forward to it, friend." Samson dipped his hand into his coat pocket for a breadstick, only to find they were all smashed.

Damn it. That must have happened when I fell over the greengrocer's stand. I'll get more on my way home.

Samson turned to leave when someone called him.

"Ah, just the man. Sam, can I have a word, please?"

"Hey, Broadbank." Samson faced the chief with a smile and an extended hand.

The chief took the proffered mitt and shook it. "I see you pinched Ross Outright, AKA, The Brain."

"Yeah, and I handed all my gathered evidence over to your desk sergeant. Also, his case is filled with incriminating evidence."

Broadbank clapped a hand to Samson's shoulder. "I knew bringing you in was the right thing to do,

Sam. That dirty bastard was involved in child po—"

"I'd rather not talk about the particulars."

"That's fair enough. Hey, and thanks for the tip-off regarding that gang selling those girls – it seems they were connected to The Brain."

"A job well done, eh?" Samson smiled.

"My boys are upstairs with them now – it seems they're part of XRay's corporation."

"I'm surprised they opened their yaps, if that's the case…"

Broadbank nodded. "They spilt their guts in return for protection, Sam. You've put a huge dent in a key operation. XRay could stand to lose millions."

"Noggins will roll, so you best keep a close eye on your prisoners, Broadbank. We don't want them rubbed out before they can grass."

"I'm all over it, Sam. Thanks."

"My pleasure, babe."

Broadbank chuckled. "I'll have something else for you to work on in a few days, Sam. Until then, it's goodbye."

Samson nodded and then strolled towards the building's exit. "Good stuff. You have my number, so call when you need me," he said over his shoulder. "Bye, Broadbank."

Outside, Samson breathed deep, the air clean.

"Such a nice afternoon."

He started walking, having decided to leave his car where it was.

Whilst I'm in this part of the city, why not head over to see Alice? I could have a catch up with her and then with Steve, before heading home.

He hadn't seen either since leaving rehab.

Then *his* name bounced to mind, almost souring Samson's stroll.

XRay. It didn't take long for that palooka to muscle his way back into the city, did it?

According to Broadbank, who'd filled Samson in on everything the day he'd left the hospital, XRay had brought his operation back to Cardiff as soon as Samson was gone.

"It only took him a couple of weeks to get a hold on the city with his poisonous ventures and hired hands," Broadbank said. "I think he thought you weren't coming back, Sam. Hell, I didn't. You were in a bad place."

"You can't keep a good dick down," Samson retorted, winking. "I've been in worse ways and situations before, Broadbank, trust me."

Within a month, some of XRay's goons were out of the caboose and walking the streets again. Samson was informed that Ziggy was back running his 'shitshow' of an arcade and that Big O had returned to operating the Green Baize.

Samson was yet to see all this for himself.

Apparently, XRay had pulled strings to get his thugs released from her Majesty's pleasure early. Others, like Davis, who'd enraged their crime overlord with their failure, weren't so lucky. Davis, along with several others, started flushing up dead on the inside. Their throats cut.

"It comes with the vocation," Samson tittered.

"Any ideas who this XRay character of yours is, Sam?" Broadbank asked.

"None. But sooner or later, the cat will slip, and we'll be there to catch him!"

Of that, Samson was confident.

A crime figure of his size can't hide forever, and it'll be a glorious day when I march him down to the clubhouse in shiny bracelets.

***

He slipped his hands inside his trouser pockets and whistled as he walked. The birds were singing in the trees and there wasn't a cloud in the sky. All about him, people whizzed around the busy shopping centre, oblivious to the dangers that lurked; dangers that were held back only by the light of day, Samson, and the good ol' boys who marched the beat.

That was another thing Samson praised Broadbank for; ever since he'd taken control, there were a lot more coppers walking the streets.

The city was reasonably safe.

If XRay waited for me to disappear, then he knows I'm capable of dismantling his operations and organisation, and soon enough, he's going to know I'm back where I belong. Things could get hairy.

He shook the notion from his mind. It was bad enough Ziggy and Big O were back on the streets. A shiver glided down his back, and the hair on the nape of his neck stood on edge.

They'll have to get up early to catch this worm.

Besides, Samson wasn't looking to step on XRay's toes yet—even though the capture of The Brain and the girl-pushing gang was sure to annoy him—as he was fresh out of rehab and trying to re-establish his private eye business. Sure, if work involving XRay came his way via Broadbank further down the line, then he'd gladly take it on. Until then, Samson would fill his working days with personal cases.

The Brain and his team was a fluke. It's not like I knew *they were a part of XRay's mob.*

Samson stopped at a corner shop and bought breadsticks. He opened the box, dug one out and stuck it in his gob. He then put the rest in his coat pocket, thinking he needed to get something solid to keep them in, like a tin of sorts.

He munched as he strolled, his mind wandering.

Didn't I take a number from a possible client before checking in to the booby hatch?

His memory served him correctly.

A few days before Samson had sought help, he'd taken a call from a local contractor looking for someone to help him catch his business partner red-handed.

"I believe he's skimming and/or pumping business cash into private ventures, drugs, and strippers, Mr Valentine. If it continues, it will ruin everything he and I have worked hard for. Me, more so."

Samson had refused the job. "I'm un—taking time away. I won't be around for a few months. If you're still looking for someone when I return, I'll be happy to—"

"It might be *too* late by then. Please, can't you take this one job before you go? I'm told you're the best."

Samson had been firm with the man and disconnected.

I'm sure I stored his number. I'll have a search for it when I get back. A job like that will keep me busy for a few weeks.

With that in mind, Samson felt good to think he might have something he could sink his teeth into immediately.

When he rounded the next corner, Alice's parents' coffee shop came into view, and a smile pulled across his face. His throat was dry, and his stomach rumbled.

Hopefully, they'll have some elderberry pie fresh out of the oven.

He walked into the shop and noticed Alice was stood behind the counter, pouring a coffee, her back to him. Samson went up to Alice and stood directly behind her.

"Excuse me, miss—"

"*Samson*!" she squealed, turning to face him. Her face lit up. "Oh, my God – it *is* you!" Alice rushed around the counter, ploughed into him and threw her skinny arms around his large frame, her hands far from touching.

"*Oph*!" he puffed, pretending to be winded. "Slow down, palooka."

"Oh, I've missed you," she squeezed.

"Same, kid. Listen, you don't happen to have any of that pie, do you?"

"Yeah, of course," she said, pulling away from him, her eyes wet.

His heart missed a beat. "Didn't think you'd see me again, eh?"

She wiped her cheeks. "Just, you know—I was worried about you. You were acting funny. Talking to people that weren't there."

"Well, that was the old me. I'm as right as rain now, toots. How about less gaggling and more serving? I mean, what's a guy got to do to get some food and a mug of coffee around these parts?" he smiled, giving her a wink.

"Sure, sure!" She went back behind the counter and finished what she was doing. "Let me get this order over to those people in the corner and I'll be right with you, Sam. Go and take a seat," she smiled.

He nodded.

In between his heroics and second fall from grace, Samson had spent a lot of time in Alice's presence, and not just here at the coffee shop. They'd grown a strong, strictly platonic relationship, much like father and daughter, and had done things together when they weren't working: walks through the park, trips to the cinema, bowling, etc.

Alice had been good for him and would be again. She was a calming force. The day he'd told her he was going away for a spell because of his mental health issues had been hard. She'd cried and held him fiercely.

"Will you be okay?"

"Hey, I'm off for help. I'm not dying," he teased.

"Can I visit?" she snivelled.

"Not where I'm going, no, but I'll call. And as soon as I get out, I'll come and see you. Promise."

Samson took up a corner booth by the window and scanned a local rag that had been left on the table. The headline on the front page read "*Organised Crime Back to Peak*!" Beneath it, Samson saw his name in print, whereby the writer was asking, '*Where's your* super *P.I. now*?!'

His hands balled into fists.

Samson had to grit his teeth and stop himself from lashing out.

"Hey, mister, I've got a bone to pick with you," Alice laughed, placing his pie and coffee down on the table and breaking his chain of thought.

"*Hmm*?" he looked up at her.

"In the time you've been away, I've read *The Great Gatsby*. He *wasn't* a magician."

"No, you're right, he wasn't. He was a millionaire with an obsession for the beautiful former debutante, Daisy Buchanan. It's also a tale about the roaring twenties that errs on the side of caution regarding the American Dream," he smiled, cutting a piece of lukewarm pie off the hunk that sat on a small plate.

"But you—"

"I didn't lead you to believe anything. I let you assume he was a magic man, toots. It gave me a giggle."

"*Ooh*, you utter rotter, Samson Valentine."

***

Once he'd finished eating, Samson hung around a while to chat, before giving his well-wishes to Alice's parents and heading out the door.

"I'll be in touch via the blower. We'll set something up, Alice."

And then he was gone, striding down the main street towards Steve's bar, the new and improved Jazz Hole.

Wonder if he's made further improvements? Samson thought, removing a breadstick from his coat pocket. *I sure was glad he turned it into an authentic 40s style jazz bar. It looked snappy.*

Samson guided his bulk through the crowds of shoppers and grinned to himself. It was good to be back in Cardiff – to be home and clear-minded.

No more mental slips or relapses. This is it. This is the brand spanking new Samson, so the palooka bad guys better watch their step.

In front, up ahead, Samson saw roving twosomes of boys in blue. Some were moving homeless people along, others dealt with youths who were drunk and causing noise pollution.

The streets definitely aren't as safe as they were, he thought, *but we'll get there. However, now that there are more patrols, there does seem to be less violent crime and theft during the daytime. Broadbank's a good man, and he knows his job.*

Samson polished off the last of his breadstick and cut down an alley that headed alongside the Taff's riverbank. The backstreets were clear of children sniffing glue and drinking, and gangs causing mayhem by spraying graffiti and dealing terrorism to the good people of Cardiff.

When he popped out of the back street, Samson found he could see Steve's pub in the near distance, and a horrible thought crashed through his mind.

What if I'm tempted to take a drink? It could ruin all my hard work.

Samson shook his head. No, he knew his darkest days were behind him.

***

"Well, if it isn't the toughest P.I. this side of Chicago," Steve said with a silly smile plastered all over his face. He was stood behind the bar. "How have you been, Sam? Come, sit down, ya dirty rat." The barman winked, pointing at a stool.

The place was quiet.

Not surprising, considering the time, Samson thought.

"Never felt better, Steve. How's the ol' gin joint doing, fella?"

"*Ha*! You haven't changed a bit."

Samson took up the seat and asked for a drink. "Virgin Mary, please."

"Well, maybe you have, slightly." Steve's smile grew as he drummed the top of the bar with his fingers before moving away to make Samson's poison. "Off the sauce *completely*?"

Samson nodded, removed a breadstick and stuck it in his mouth. "The smokes too, baby."

"Impressive. They your substitute?" he chuckled.

Samson nodded as his drink was set down in front of him. "Yeah, tasty." Both men laughed. "You're looking well, Steve." Samson eyed his friend and found the scars on the man's face when he turned towards the light.

"Ah, they were mere scratches."

"Yeah, and the goons who tied you up and assaulted you were a couple of weak sisters."

For the next few hours they caught up on what was new and what had been happening whilst Samson had been away. After that, and four Virgin Marys later, Samson bid Steve farewell and headed back to his car.

***

When he arrived at his apartment complex, he was relieved to see the doorway clear of trouble. He remembered what it was like at his old place, with the homeless and thugs hanging around at all hours.

Glad to see they haven't moved in whilst I was away on The Brain case. Then again, I would have spotted them before now, wouldn't I? Besides, they never really hung out at this building, did they? He couldn't recall. His mind was exhausted. *God, that stakeout was long.*

Every now and then, his anxiety returned – something his doctor had reassured him would fade in time.

"Go home, settle down and try not to take on too much work to begin with, Sam," his doctor had ordered.

Samson took a deep breath, opened the door, and walked inside. The lobby was cool. A lift opened its doors as if on cue, but he ignored it, favouring the stairs to his apartment.

When he got to the landing with his keys in hand, Samson again froze as he studied his front door – flashbacks from when he found the note in his letterbox seized a hold of him.

He took a deep, trembling breath.

That was my old apartment. Remember, you've been home a week and nothing's happened.

After closing his eyes, Samson steadied himself and counted to three.

It wasn't like this before rehab. What's changed? Dry? No smoking? The body is cleansing itself, that's all. He shook his head. *Just spooked, I guess. I need to spend a few days holed up, doing nothing. Familiarise myself with my surroundings.*

He let out a huff and walked towards his flat. Samson inserted the key in the lock, disengaged the bolts and pushed the door inwards, half expecting Bogart, his Corgi, to be right there waiting for him.

"Here, boy," he whistled, crossing the threshold. "Bogart?" He closed the door and heard the dog whining from somewhere within the flat. "Dumb mutt, have you shut yourself in the bathroom again?" When Samson walked towards the room in question, a board creaked from behind him. He turned, catching a swift-moving reflection in the darkened television screen. "Jesus," he muttered, getting his hands up, but not fast enough.

A garrotte wrapped around his throat, trapping four of Samson's fingers beneath the wire, which prevented his attacker from throttling the life out of him.

"Welcome home, Valentine," the assassin grunted. "Mr Lovell sends his well-wishes!"

"*Uch*!" Samson coughed, tugging at the wire, his body thrashing.

Both men stumbled around the flat, knocking things over and bouncing off walls and various pieces of furniture. Trinkets smashed, chairs broke.

Got to stay upright! Samson tried not to panic and breathed the best he could. His eyes made rapid movements in search of something he could use, and then the pressure around his throat intensified. The back of his head was pinned to his assailant's chest.

Samson could feel blood trickling from his throat and neck.

With his free arm, he shot it forward and pistoned it backwards with all the force he could muster. His elbow smashed into the man's guts with driving force, knocking him off-kilter, but not dislodging his hold.

"*Bastard*!" the man hissed through clenched teeth. "I'll kill you." He reapplied the pressure twofold. "How do you like that, *pig*?"

Samson gasped, held his breath, and tried three more times with his elbow, all in quick succession.

Thump, thump, thump.

"Ugh-*argh*!"

Samson was free—the assassin had fallen away—and he collapsed over a chair and held his throat.

"*Jesus*!" he wheezed, his eyes glassed over. From behind, he heard the sound of tumbling. Samson turned on his heel to see the bruno take a spill over his easy chair, and he was slow in getting back to his feet.

The man was squat and round. "You're going to pay for that," the dapper button man said, pocketing the garrotte and producing a hunting knife with an eight-inch blade. The steel gleamed from hilt to tip. "Gonna look you in the eye as I turn it in your guts," he whispered.

As Samson searched for something he could use to protect himself with, the assassin bull-charged him, with the knife out in front like a lance.

"*Argh*!"

Samson picked up his small, round coffee table and held it at arm's length. The blade stabbed through it, trapping it there. The P.I. turned the piece of furniture, twisting the man's hand and popping something in his wrist.

The assassin gasped.

Samson shoved the table with all his might, propelling the guy backwards, who swung his uninjured fist, missing.

"Get…" he growled. "*Off*!" He kicked Samson in the shin, causing the P.I. to drop the table, which was then thrown to one side by the hatchet-man. The knife was still embedded in it.

The bruno rugby-tackled Samson and shoved him into the kitchen. The table and chairs there were bowled out of the way. Both men went to the ground and rolled about the small space. Each of them went for a spilt implement, with the thug's fingertips brushing against a butcher's cleaver.

Samson brought a plate down on the man's head, followed by another, dazing him. The peeper then got a booted foot to the fella's chest and shoved him backwards, into the living room, where he tripped over his own feet and struck his head against a cabinet.

But he wasn't out of the game. He shook his head and attempted to stand.

He doesn't know when to quit, Samson thought, getting to his feet and charging at the man. He hit the attacker square in the chest with the flats of his hands, driving him through the window.

Glass erupted.

The goon screamed as he dropped the eight floors to the bottom, his body smashing through the soft roof of a parked sports car.

More screams followed.

By the time Samson got to the window to see for himself, a large crowd had gathered. Some were looking up at him, pointing, whilst others were taking pictures of the dead man in the car with its windows blown out. Glass sprinkled the pavement.

Samson put his back to the wall, steadied himself, took a few deep breaths, and walked to his phone.

Yeah, hell of a week, he thought.

"Desk sergeant," he said into the phone's receiver. "Could you please put me through to Broadbank? Yes, right away. I'll hold. Thanks."

Chapter 3

It took Broadbank less than twenty minutes to arrive on the scene with a handful of officers, cordon the area off, and delegate duties to his people – most of whom were holding the crowd back and stopping the press from getting close.

"They're goddamn vultures," he told Samson, "with their lights, cameras, and questions. If it was up to me, the media would be banned from stepping anywhere near a crime scene." He dragged on the last of his cigarette before flicking the butt to the gutter. As he blew the smoke free, he spoke again. "Any idea *who* he was?" Broadbank jacked a thumb towards the car.

Samson shook his head. He was holding a breadstick. "No," he said, his voice barely audible. Purple bruising encircled his neck and he rubbed it. "He did mention a name, though."

"I'm all ears."

"Lovell," Samson croaked. "The tag doesn't ring a bell, but I'm assuming it was him who sent that mook to give me the big sleep."

"*Richard* Lovell?"

"I didn't catch a first name, chief."

"If it's the Lovell I'm thinking of, then you knew his brother—uh—*personally*, shall we say…"

"Keep flappin' your yap, Broadbank. Who *are* the Lovell brothers?"

"I believe Richard's sibling went by the name

Alligator."

"The clown who ran an outfit comprised of thugs and hoodlums in the southwest area?"

Broadbank nodded. "This could be retaliation."

"If it is, why leave it so long?" Samson asked himself, mostly.

"Could be a number of reasons, I guess."

"Yeah, but they had months to hit my snooze button before I went away, Broadbank. *Months*."

"Maybe they wanted to make sure your guard was well and truly down before pouncing? Who knows how these punks' minds work? Anyway, if I was you, I'd start watching my back. I can post coppers for your protection?"

Samson shook his head and chuckled. "Your officers have enough to worry about. I'll be fine."

Both men's attention was drawn to the wrecked car when they heard the paramedics discussing the best way to remove the body.

"Through the roof, or out one of the unbuckled doors?" the female asked.

"Neither. From the boot, I think – it'll be easier."

The woman nodded, ducked her head inside the car via the driver's side window and did something unseen. The vehicle's boot popped open and lifted skyward in a slow, lazy motion. With better access to the deceased, the male paramedic was able to begin the removal process.

"Oh, Jesus," he said. "Looks like his head was ripped off in the fall…"

At that point, Samson and Broadbank turned away.

"Listen, Broadbank, I'm going to hit the gym to clear my noggin whilst you and your team do your mop-up mission."

Broadbank nodded, popped a fresh smoke in his mouth and waved Samson off, who headed back to his flat.

***

Inside, Samson let Bogart out of the bedroom and fussed over him.

"Who's a good palooka? Yes, you are." The dog licked his face, hands, and all the exposed skin he could find in his frantic display of affection. "Ha! I'm pretty happy to see you too, meathead. How about we head to the park for an hour later, eh? See if we can find you a dame to get dizzy over."

Samson gave the dog's head a ruffle before standing and going to the smashed window. He poked his head out and saw Broadbank and Co. below. The ambulance had gone, the crushed car was being towed away, and the streets were starting to die down of spectators. However, reporters still lurked.

"Bloody vultures," he muttered, leaning back. "What am I going to do about this window?" Samson noted the time – it was gone three p.m. "It's worth a shot."

Samson picked up the phone, dialled a local glazier and was told someone would be with him in a couple of days. He wrote the particulars down and hung up.

"Guess I'll have to board her up for now."

He went downstairs, left the building, went around back to the bins and sought out a few scraps of wood big enough to plug the gap in his window. With the timber tucked under his arm, Samson returned to his flat and dug out his hammer and nails.

He was about to slam the final few nails home when a thought hit him.

How did he get in here? His guts knotted.

Samson walked to the front door and inspected it.

"How did I miss this?" He slapped his thigh with an open hand. The lock had been jimmied, with a portion of the wood around it splintered. Shavings littered the carpet. He turned the key in the lock, securing the door.

Sloppiness can get a fool killed. I need to get my head out of the clouds, especially if Lovell is planning to send more button men my way.

"I better get someone to have a proper peep at this thing," he tutted, rattling the door in its frame by tugging on the handle. It felt flimsy.

Shaking his head, he returned to the window to finish up.

When he was done, Samson went into the kitchen and called Bogart. He put fresh water and food down for the mutt before entering his bedroom to grab his gym gear and sports bag.

An hour of pounding the bag and lifting some weights will get my thoughts in order.

Samson said goodbye to Bogart as he left.

***

Thirty minutes later, with his suit, hat, and trench coat hung up in a locker, Samson was at Paul's boxing gym breaking a sweat. He bit down hard on his gum shield as he gave the heavy bag a combination of powerful lefts and rights, making the weighted implement swing with force.

"*Urgh*!" he grunted, following through with a jab.

Feels good to get the shoulders rolling, he thought, stalking the bag and growling with effort. *Gonna knock its stuffing out*.

The last time Samson had donned boxing gloves was when he'd been in the police force, and the army before that, which is where his fondness for the sport had come from. He'd been strong-armed into it by his drill sergeant, who'd caught Samson brawling with two cadets older than him.

***

"I saw what you did to those lads, boy," he yelled at Samson. "Your fists are like hammers and I want you to put them to proper use. You'll join our boxing squad."

"But—"

"*Quiet*! You fucking maggot."

"Yes, *sir*!"

"With you on our side, we might be able to whip those navy boys once and for all. After your training today, you'll report to Sergeant Tomos over at the gym. Do I make myself crystal, boy?"

Samson had taken to the sport like a fish to water, finding he couldn't get enough of it. He not only helped beat the navy, but he won multiple ribbons and cups whilst serving with the armed forces.

After his career was done in the army, Samson continued his boxing, alongside his police job. And, just like in his army days, he took part in many competitions and charity events. At one point, he'd even thought about taking himself semi-professional.

"I might fight pro one day," he'd joshed with one of the other beat coppers.

***

Yeah, that would have been something, he thought, stepping away from the bag and mopping his brow with the towel he had draped across his shoulders. Samson then ambled over to the bench where he'd placed his water bottle and upended it to his mouth, taking a hearty gulp.

"*Agh*! That hit the spot."

He recapped the bottle and replaced it on the seat. He then hit the rope for ten minutes before taking on the speedball. When he was finished, he lifted some weights before moving to the pool to soak his aching body, his workout done.

By the time Samson got home, the good ol' boys had gone. So, too, had the civilians and the roving packs of reporters. The only thing left to suggest there had been an altercation was the small amount of broken glass and specks of blood.

Samson looked up at his window.

Hell of a way to snuff it.

He then turned and looked at the sky. The sun was still reasonably high, and a fair amount of heat and light was left in the day.

Plenty of time to take Bogart for that walk.

***

Samson, with Bogart on his leash, led the hound out of the built-up area and to the park that was a few miles' walk from his home.

That bozo thought he could clip me and make a clean sneak, Samson thought, looking down at his furry friend. *Alligator; why, after all this time*? He shook his head. It wasn't worth thinking about. *If Lovell is going to come for me, then come for me he will, especially when he finds out his current assassin is being fitted for a Chicago overcoat. I'll have to be extra careful until I can work this mess out.*

Moving crossed his mind, but he'd have none of it. To Samson, that would be like admitting defeat and looking like a weak sister. No, there was no running. Hell, hiding wasn't going to be possible, anyway.

They'd soon flush me out by finding someone willing to talk for some tiger milk or a box of smokes.

Bogart stopped to do his business, but Samson kept walking, lost in his thoughts, until the dog whined.

"Sorry, fella."

With the mutt's doings scooped and deposited, Samson moved on, giving the pooch another look.

***

"Take in a pet, Samson," his doctor suggested.

"Like a koala bear?" the P.I. answered, half out of his mind on medication.

"Ha! Maybe something a little less… err… *exotic*?"

The thought of that addled conversation made Samson laugh as he coaxed the sniffing Bogart along the pavement in readiness to cross the road. Up ahead, the park was in sight.

It should be quiet at this time of day.

Then, out of the blue, Samson had a frightening urge to look over his shoulder. Terror settled in his guts and sweat broke along his brow. There was nobody there – no hitters in trilbies with Tommy guns, or hatchet-men with broken bottles or knifes gunning for him.

He then checked the road before stepping off the kerb.

There were no speeding, vintage mob cars hurtling towards him with gunmen hanging out their windows, or any such vehicles powering his way to mow him down.

"There are no mobsters," he told himself. "Not like that, anyway."

Samson removed a breadstick from his coat pocket and gnawed on it.

Bogart looked up, licking his chops, so Samson dropped a bit of his snack into the hound's mouth.

"Good lad."

After making sure both ways were clear, Samson marched himself and Bogart to the other side of the road and entered the park. The sun had almost set. Once they were beyond the park's metal gates, Samson removed the dog's lead and let Bogart run free, noticing there were no small children or mothers pushing prams.

Samson liked this time of day, when busy had burned itself out and most people were behind closed doors; off the streets and out of his hair.

As he strolled along the grass, Samson picked up a stick from off the leaf-scattered ground and teased Bogart with it, finally throwing it when his companion kept leaping at his trousers with his muddy paws.

"Fetch, boy."

A warmth spread through him as he watched his hairy friend dash along the park.

***

"Not sure I'll have the time to feed goldfish or clean out a rabbit's hutch, Doc. I'm a working P.I., which means I'm out of the house most days."

"Then I suggest you *make* time, Samson. I'm

sure the great Humphrey Bogart had the occasional holiday and reprieve from his work."

"It's possible, I guess."

***

The suggestion, which Samson had put into effect as soon as he'd returned home, turned out to be an instant blessing. It not only gave him more focus and took the steam out of his anxiety and depression, but made his life a lot more fun and interesting.

At night, if he felt like a stroll, he had Bogart to take with him for company. Also, Samson didn't find it odd that he kept conversations with his pooch.

"Hell, if that Prince of ours can talk to his plants on a daily basis, then me yapping to a mutt isn't so crazy. Besides, the doc told me I'm not, so there. Just had a lot of things going on, that's all," he'd told himself. "I'm a 'well-adjusted individual'."

Bogart returned the stick at his master's feet and chased his tail, letting out a few short, sharp barks every so often.

"Okay, okay, you crazy hoocha-poocha." Samson bent, retrieved the partly-chewed stick, and hurled it as far into the distance as possible. When the dog disappeared out of sight, Samson, having noted a bench close by, removed his jacket and placed it on the spray-painted seat along with his fedora.

The P.I. parked his rear.

Never thought having an animal in my life would be so beneficial. Not only is he helping me keep fit, but also my mind sane. It's clear, not clouded.

Bogart dashed back to him with his jaws wrapped fiercely around the stick. His tongue bobbed and slobber sprayed.

"Drop, fella," Samson commanded, and the dog did as he was told. Samson stood, threw it, and returned to his seat. The sun was at his back, warming his skin through his shirt. A sweat broke across the nape of his neck.

Hell, I never saw myself as an animal person.

"Why don't we get a dog, Sam…?" Angie suggested.

For the briefest of moments, Samson thought his wife was back, but he knew she wasn't. It was just a memory.

"…You know, to help fill the void?"

The poor woman had wanted children more than anything. He took a deep breath, shoved the thought aside and stood. *I can't look back. It's time to press forward. I'm not sure who said it, but 'Get busy living, or get busy dying' has a lot of truth to it.*

Samson put his hat on and threw his coat over his shoulder. Before Bogart could turn, pick up the stick, and make his way back towards his master, Samson walked in the pooch's direction. The Corgi, busy sniffing a tree stump with wild daffodils growing around it, was oblivious to Samson's approach.

I would have liked a couple of Samsons or Samsonettes running around the place myself. But it wasn't to be.

"Here, boy," Samson whistled. "Here, Bogart."

The dog looked over its shoulder with a confused expression on his face.

"Stupid mutt," Samson laughed, patting his thigh. "Come on, this way."

Samson skirted a bench and strolled towards the park's bandstand. Back a few years ago, even at this time of day, teenage gang members would have been seen loitering here, but not so much nowadays. However, they were here in essence. Their tags, marks, and art plastered the old wooden structure that had knots and chunks of wood knocked out of it here and there. It reminded Samson of a veteran heavyweight with most of his teeth missing.

"I think they stopped repainting this thing ten years ago," Samson muttered, tugging on one of the support beams. "Probably riddled with woodworm."

***

"Make love to me, Samson," Claire said, a fresh memory flooding his mind. Some of this stuff he hadn't thought about in years. The alcohol had numbed him. "Come on, right here, under the bandstand." She bit her lip as a flash of excited electricity shot through her eyes.

"Why, Mrs Valentine, I thought you were a *lady*?"

"Who told you that?" she whispered in his ear. "Don't you just hate vicious rumours?"

"But you're in your best and I'll be late back to

work. I couldn't very well show up in a—"

"*Shh*! Come and wrinkle my clothes." She drew him close, kissed him deep, and held him as if her life depended on it.

***

The smile lingered on his face as he walked around the bandstand and sought out their carved initials.

"You always were a minx, babe."

Samson traced the marks in the wood with the tips of his fingers, the last of the foggy recollection clearing.

He would have thought such reminiscences as this, and of missed opportunities with Angie, would have brought tears, anxiety and all the rest of it to him, but it didn't. In fact, it did the opposite. Samson felt he could finally open up his box of treasured moments whenever he wanted to, without folding on an emotional level. The doctor had said unleashing such thoughts would be good for him.

Yeah, remembering is good, not bad.

"Purge the soul, Samson. Let it all out, big guy," the doctor had said.

The best part about being able to reach back into his emotional past was that it didn't trigger the need to hammer whiskey down his neck.

I was so foolish. I could have lost it all. Hell, I very nearly did. Maybe I should send XRay some flowers with a thank you card? After all, it was his mess that got me on the road to recovery.

A hearty laugh escaped Samson, but it was cut

short when a youth of maybe fifteen shoved past from behind, pushing him out of the way.

"*Hey*, palooka, watch where you're going."

But the boy didn't stop.

Up ahead, Samson saw another couple of teenaged boys standing around with their phones out, and the lad who'd barged by joined them.

"What the hell are those hop-heads up to?"

With annoyance, Samson called his dog and marched over to where the thugs had congregated.

No goddamn respect for anyone, the little pissants. Had I been an old lady, he no doubt would have tried snatching my purse as he railroaded me out of the way.

As he neared, Samson noticed the three of them were giggling and looking down at the ground. Their mobiles flashed.

They're taking pictures?

"Hey. What's the big idea, punks?"

"Oh, shit, look out," one of the boys said, tapping his mates on the shoulder after seeing Samson's approach.

"Police," Samson alerted.

"Let's get out of here," a second teen said.

Samson couldn't see their faces thanks to the dimming sun and the scarves they wore around their faces.

"Come back here," Samson demanded, thinking about giving chase, but they were out of sight before the thought had cemented. "Damn it. What the hell were they up to?"

He ambled over to the spot where they'd been

stood and looked about.

I don't see—

"Sweet *Jesus*!"

There, in the mud, on a slight incline, was the naked body of a middle-aged woman. She was lying on her back with an article stuffed in her mouth; on closer inspection, Samson found it to be a necklace of pearl beads. She'd been beaten black and blue, and the marks around her neck suggested strangulation.

His head swam, and the smell of her decomposing body filled his nostrils.

Samson backed away.

Those sick wankers were taking pictures of her.

Smalls flies made a disturbing halo around his head.

After shaking them away he looked at her again, spotting words carved in her flesh - a sentence.

"'Eat the Fucking Rich...'" Samson couldn't bring himself to utter the last word, which was 'Cunts'. "What does that vileness mean?"

Then he saw bite marks on her thighs and arms. There was flesh missing.

"A wild animal? No, it links to the words."

Samson removed gloves from his pocket and slipped them on. Before bending over and rolling her onto her stomach, he spotted money stuffed in her vagina. Then, with the woman on her stomach, he found more beads in her anus, and her hands were tied behind her back with zip ties. So, too, were her ankles.

Mob-related?

He thought about it for a moment longer, thinking it wouldn't hurt to write down some of the particulars, such as the articles in her orifices, the words, how she lay, etc. Samson removed a small pad and pencil from the inside of his coat and scribbled.

When he was finished, he replaced the notebook and examined the body further.

He found nothing under her fingernails.

No sign of a struggle.

He then felt the back of her head and discovered an unnatural lump there. *Hit her from behind? Whoever did this to her, did it in a secluded spot before dumping her here.*

Samson stood up, pocketed his gloves and leashed his dog. He then headed out of the park to find a payphone.

"Broadbank, please. Yes, I'll hold..."

Chapter 4

Samson awoke—an empty bottle of whisky rolling off his lap—to the sound of thumps and thuds. Heartbeats crashed in his chest like waves against a rock face, and a lump which tasted of fear lodged in his throat, trapping a scream.

"Jesus *H.*" He leapt out of his easy chair and scrabbled along the ground in search of the spilt liquor container. Samson grabbed it by its neck and clubbed his open hand. "Who's there? Speak up."

Samson did a one-ninety on the spot, eyeing the shadowed nooks and crannies within his flat, even though morning sun poured through his open, yet slanted, blinds.

"Sing up, or do you fancy winding up like your chum they scraped off the pavement, eh? I have no problem in sending more of your kind to the morgue."

More thuds.

Samson faced his front door, fancying the sounds were coming from beyond it. He walked over to it and placed his eye to the peephole. There were people moving around in the hallway.

"*Huh,*" he laughed, looking at the bottle in his hand. "In hindsight, I'd have been better off with a knife, or a rolling pin from the kitchen. This thing's a reminder of darker days."

Dark, yes, but gloriously rich with victory at the same time.

The bottle—emptied weeks before his stint in rehab—had been the first thing to cross his field of vision when searching for something sturdy to defend himself with. *I have to be prepared – I can't have them catch me in my kingdom with my drawers down.*

"A fat lot of use you are, *meathead*," he said, staring down at Bogart. The mutt, who'd been in and out of sleep by the side of Samson's chair, looked up at his master with dopey eyes and yawned. "A fine good ol' boy you'd make, lazy. We could have been murdered in our sleep."

Bogart put his head back on his paws and closed his eyes.

Great.

Samson put the bottle down on the sideboard and ran his hands through his moist hair. He looked at his chair and let the memories of last night wash over him. He'd returned from a long walk, drained a jug of freshly prepared Virgin Mary whilst listening to jazz in his seat, and drifted off to sleep. For the past couple of nights—ever since the surprise thug—he'd slept in the living room, thinking it safer.

I'd hear someone trying to break in.

The sight of Broadbank's pale face came to him, along with the man's first words upon seeing the body in the park.

"You think it's gang related, Sam?"

The thought made icy circles in his guts.

With a shake of his head, Samson turned back to the door and looked through the spy hole again.

There were more than two people out there shifting around and talking.

He put his hand to the security chain and slipped it off before turning the key in the new lock, disengaging the bolts with a firm clack. Before pulling the door wide, Samson checked himself. He was still in his shirt and trousers, his hat and jacket amiss.

"What a disgrace," he tusked to himself. "What with me being a man of the law, too." He slipped his braces over his shoulders and opened up. Samson stood there, barefoot, eyeing two brutes—one fella white, the other black—dressed in the same-coloured coveralls with the words Morrissey's Movers etched on their backs. They had weightlifting belts of sorts strapped around their waists and were wrestling a sofa through the door to the apartment opposite.

I didn't even realise Mr Jenkins had moved out.

"Hi. Mr Valentine?" a small, sweet voice asked.

Samson looked to his left to find a short, petite woman of roughly his age standing there holding her hand out towards him.

"Who's asking?" he smiled, taking her hand whilst admiring her well-groomed and lengthy nails.

"Sorry," she laughed, slapping her forehead with the flat of her other hand. "I'm pretty dizzy at times. My name's Lisa Dennings. Miss, and it looks like we're going to be neighbours."

"How did you know *my* name?"

"Suspicious cat, ain't ya?" Lisa beamed, taking her shook hand back.

"A fellow can't be too careful around these parts, toots."

"It says it right there, Poirot," she said, pointing at the tag beneath his doorbell.

"Yeah, I was just testing ya, kitty-cat," he winked.

"I like you. You talk funny."

"'A 'Ha-ha' kind of funny?"

"No, but I can't put my finger on it. Maybe you'd like to come over for a coffee this morning, you know, once you've found your socks and I've discovered my jar of Kenco?" Lisa strolled towards the beefcakes manhandling her furniture. "How about it, boys – coffee?" She put her hands to their shoulders.

Samson smiled. He'd instantly liked her, too. *A real livewire,* he thought, catching himself gazing at her pert backside. He averted his eyes, his cheeks flushing. *Thank heavens she has her back to me.*

"That would do the trick just fine, Miss D," the white man said.

"Please, call me Lisa, chaps," she instructed, slipping her lath-like frame past them and into her flat. "Oh, Valentine, you don't happen to have any sugar do you, sugar?" she laughed, popping her head back out the door, her face planted in between the burly removal men.

Samson nodded, lost for words.

"Then bring a cupful with you, there's a dear."

"Yes, ma'am."

The men looked over their shoulders at him.

"I think you're in there, son, if you play your

cards right," the black man said, nodding and winking in a sly way, as though he and Samson were in on a joke.

Not much of a way to speak about a muffin, he thought, keeping his yap firmly closed. He smiled, turned, and closed his door.

Wait, no, I can't go for a coffee... date? No, no, no. It's a get-to-know-your-neighbour type of thingy, fool, not a—

Samson opened the door again and spoke to the men who were desperately trying to ram Dennings' sofa through her doorway without breaking something.

"Could you tell the lady I have to grab a shower and get myself ready for work before popping over, please, chaps?"

"We look like your secretary, old-timer?" the white one asked.

"Hey, no need to be rude, man," his mate said. "Of course, it's no—"

"That's okay, Sam," Lisa said from somewhere behind the prize bozos. "Come when you're ready – don't forget the sugar."

Samson couldn't help but smile as he turned and went back inside.

Knock it off. She's just being friendly.

Still, he couldn't wipe the stupid grin from off his face.

As he made his way across the living room to the kitchen, after making sure the front door was bolted, Samson happened to look out his window and spot a police car parked across the way.

Three good ol' boys occupied the vehicle.

"Huh," Samson huffed. "Well, I'll be a monkey's uncle, Broadbank. You went and posted guards anyway." He eyed the three boys in blue and felt for them. They were yawning, and their body language spoke in a listless tongue. "I'll sort you guys out with some joe."

***

After he'd showered and dressed in clean duds—a crisp white shirt, brown slacks, fresh tie, and jacket—Samson slipped into his shoes, adorned his trench coat and fedora and headed out the door and across the hallway with a cup of sugar in hand.

Hope she doesn't mind it being brown.

The gorillas in the hallway were nowhere to be seen, and the door to Dennings' flat was closed. Samson wrapped on the wood three times, lightly.

"Come. It's open."

Samson pushed at the door and entered. "Want me to lock it?" he asked from the jamb.

"Why, isn't it safe here?"

He was about to tell her about the body in the park, then remembered the police hadn't released any details yet. They were sitting on it.

"We don't want to cause panic," had been Broadbank's words.

Samson had agreed.

"It's perfectly safe." He lied, of course, but told himself it was only a white one. "Do you think inviting strange men over for morning coffee is the *safest* thing you can do?" Samson walked deeper into the home and found himself in the living room. The layout was much different from his place. "Where—"

"I'm in the kitchen."

Samson noted pillars of cardboard boxes, upended furniture, wrapped paintings/pictures, and piles of trinkets he thought would never fit inside a mansion, let alone a box-sized apartment such as this.

"Jeepers," he muttered, averting his eyes from her packed possessions.

"Sorry?"

"Nothing." Samson headed in the direction of slamming doors and rattling cutlery. When he found her, she was unloading boxes of dried goods.

"Ah-ha, got ya, sucker," Lisa said, hauling the coffee from its hiding place. "I feared I wouldn't have found it on time, leading you over her on a wild goose chase."

"Oh, that would have been fine, ma'am." Samson removed his hat, his hair slicked. "It's nice to get to know the people around you."

"Yes, but I didn't want you thinking I'd lured you over here for…"

He felt his face heat.

"…Well, I don't know what, I suppose," she chuckled, proceeding to fill the kettle and setting it to boil. "I know we introduced ourselves earlier in the passageway, but I felt it was rushed and a little awkward. Lisa extended her arm. "I'm *Miss* Lisa Dennings."

Samson smiled. *She's a quirky one, alright.*

He took her offered hand in his and shook it with grace. "I'm pleased to make your acquaintance, Miss Dennings. I'm Samson Valentine, but my friends call me Sam or Val, and I won't hold either against you," he winked.

They both laughed.

"Well, isn't this a pip."

He eyed her, liking her old-school manner and debonair attitude. For the first time, he noticed her fancy attire, chic hairdo, and grandiose jewellery. Her earrings winked at him, her smile blinding.

"I guess you could say that, doll. Is brown sugar golden by your standards?" He beamed. "I'd sure hate to disappoint the little lady."

"Yes, fine." She took it from him and filled the prepped mugs. "What are those flasks in aid of, Val?"

"Oh," he said, holding up the pair of Thermoses. "Got a couple of colleagues pulling a nightshift across the street, so I thought I'd take them some joe. You know, warm their bellies and freshen their peepers."

"You sure have a way with words, Val."

"I get that a lot."

She poured the boiled water over the contents in their mugs, stirred, and added milk as she did so. "Here you go, precious," Lisa said, handing him one of the coffees.

"That accent of yours. You're not from around these parts, are you?"

Lisa blew on her drink, took a sip, and set it

aside. "I'm from Rhyl, North Wales. I divorced my husband of twenty years after I caught him screwing the paper*boy*."

"*Wow*, that's a new one," Samson admitted, taking a gulp of coffee.

"Do you have asbestos guts or something?"

He smiled. "Get it while it's hot, right?"

"That's what my husband used to say," Lisa admitted, pokerfaced.

"Oh, listen, I didn't—"

"Ha. I'm playing with you, Val." Lisa reached out and patted his guts with the back of her hand. "You're too easy. Keep taking the bait like that and I'll be riding you from now until doomsday."

"Excuse me? Oh… I—never mind."

She gave him a confused look. "Anyway, he begged for a second chance, but I'd have none of it. Turns out it wasn't just the paperboy he was sticking it to, but others. My mother always warned me about my taste in men."

"Why here, you seem like a lady of wealth? If you wanted to get out, why not head thousands of miles away?"

"Inquisitive, aren't you?"

"I'm a snoop, it's my job, ma'am."

"Oh?"

"Yeah, a private investigator, and I'm guessing your ex-fella was a drinker and/or a beater," he said, drawing a breadstick from his coat pocket. This elicited a smile from her. "They help with my cravings. I've kicked the smokes."

"I see. And yes, he was prone to taking a few

drinks and his fists to my face, but that's enough of my morbid old tosh, Val. Tell me about your job. It must be exciting."

He took another hit of coffee and replaced his mug. "I wouldn't want to cripple you with boredom," he stated.

"I'm sure—"

A friendly jingle and rumble from Samson's pocket cut her dead.

"What the?" Samson said, looking around him before realising it was his mobile phone. He smiled and tutted and hauled the device out of his trousers pocket. "I swear I'll never get used to this dingus."

"A *what*?"

"Valentine," he said into the phone. "Start flapping, pal. *Broadbank*? Can't you call my house blower like normal folk? You did? Well, I'm at a neighbour's. What's up? I didn't think we were meeting until midday? *Two* more? That's bad. Are they in the same style as the first? They are? Then you know what that could mean, Broadbank…"

Cardiff may have a... serial killer... on the loose, he thought, ignoring Broadbank's chatter.

Samson was trembling. The city had never, in all its history, ever faced such a threat.

If that's the case, then we'll need to snuff this problem out immediately. We? *Do I want any part in such a case at this moment in time? What happened to taking it easy?*

"…Look, I don't want any involvement in such a job, Broadbank. I'm trying—yeah, you know that—to rebuild my business. I only want small stuff at the moment. You want me to what?" Samson huffed, rubbed his forehead and blew air out of his mouth in a defeated way. "Okay, okay – give me thirty minutes and I'll be there."

Samson terminated the call and pocketed his mobile.

"I have to dash," he said, draining the last of his coffee and placing his mug in the kitchen sink. "This was good. Maybe we could do it again sometime?" He hadn't meant to follow the former sentences with the latter. Samson blushed.

I basically asked her on a da— He couldn't think it. *No, it sounded friendly, right*?

Lisa smiled and touched a hand to his, which held his hat. "I'd love that. Say, what time do you get off tonight? I can cook us a meal and we could swap war stories. You know, in a getting-to-know-your-neighbour type of way," she winked, a laugh escaping her.

You have great moxie, kiddo. At first, he was hesitant to accept. *It's only dinner, for Pete's sake.*

"How's about I call by around seven?"

"Sounds good."

"Do I need to bring anything?"

"Such as?"

He shook his head, forgetting he was off the sauce. "Nothing, forget I mentioned it. Seven, then?"

She nodded, he left.

***

After Samson departed his apartment block, he crossed the road and headed straight toward the good ol' boys assigned to keep him from ending up in a Chicago overcoat or concrete boots.

To him, they looked young – fresh out of academy young.

Poor sods, stuck here guarding an old fart like me when all they probably want to be doing is seeing some action out on the streets.

"Morning, fellas," Samson beamed. "Got some coffee for ya." He held the flasks up and shook them.

Two out of the three men stood slumped against their patrol car, their shirts un-tucked, and their vests askew.

"Thank you, sir," one of them said, taking the flasks from Samson. "This is very kind of you."

"You boys been here all night?"

"Yes, sir," the chap behind the wheel answered, and then yawned.

"See anything?"

"Quieter than a grave out here," the third cop informed him.

Samson nodded. "Thanks, and keep up the good work."

"We will," the driver assured.

"Two words of advice: Broadbank is a stickler for neatness, so I'd straighten your uniforms before he drops by out of nowhere. Second of all: you stick out like sore thumbs. You should park up that side street over there," Samson advised whilst pointing. "You'll still be able to see my apartment block."

The slumped coppers rallied themselves and the driver started the engine.

Samson smiled, drew a breadstick, and crossed the road to his car. By the time he'd fired up his engine and looked back, he saw the young cops parking behind a flatbed van in the street Samson had suggested.

That's good, he thought, pulling off.

***

Twenty minutes later, with Lisa well and truly on his mind, Samson pulled into the police station's car park, got out, locked his vehicle, and walked inside. The place was a hive of activity, with a rippling hubbub assaulting his ears: ringing phones, talking officers, yelling suspects in handcuffs, fights and struggles and the rush of coppers and higher-ranking men and women as they came and went.

Samson felt caught in the eye of a storm.

"Valentine," someone called over the noise.

Samson noticed it was the desk sergeant. "Yes?"

"Broadbank's in his office, and he's eagerly awaiting you."

Samson made his way to the chief's kingdom and passed pleasantries with a few of the serving men and women he'd become friendly with. When he arrived at the door and knocked, announcing his arrival, Samson was summoned inside.

"Get in here, Sam."

He didn't need telling twice.

"We've got a shitstorm on our hands, and the

media are going to take this to town."

"What have I missed?"

"You know that first stiff you discovered in the park?"

"Aye, what about her?"

"She *was* the wife of a rather influential lawyer, Samson."

"Oh?"

"The husband went to the papers and blabbed. The stupid son-of-a-bitch even offered up a reward, like some kind of vigilante. Can you believe that? The rich think they can do as they please. I'll have no such justice in this city. Not on my watch, goddamn it." He slammed his hairy, meaty paw down on his desk. A cup rattled. Pens rolled.

"He told the rags he was offering money for information alone?"

Broadbank nodded. "Also, word on the street is he's putting cash out to any hitter, thug, or user that brings him the head of this would-be serial killer the papers have dubbed 'The Widower Maker'."

"That's not good at all, them hyping it up to be the work of a serial killer. Jesus. What made *them* think that?"

"You know how the media like to cause a panic, Sam, but we both know it's the case at this point."

"Yes, but you could have done with the press being out of this for as long as possible. Some serial killers love the limelight, Broadbank. You've got your work cut—"

"That's why I need you on this with me, *us*, Sam."

The P.I. was shaking his head. “It’s not going to happen, sorry.”

The chief sighed. “I don’t think you have much choice, Sam.” Broadbank placed photos on his desk in front of Samson. “These are shots of the latest dead women. I think you’ll find you know one of them.”

Samson got his eyes closer to the images and gasped. “Oh, no,” he groaned, collapsing into the chair behind him.

Chapter 5

If ever he'd felt like a drink, now was the time.

Samson had left Broadbank's office in a daze, as though he *had* been on the booze; his guts flip-flopped, and his head had spun. Even now, as he lay stretched out in his easy chair, with soft jazz playing, Samson was finding it hard to get his noggin and guts to cool it.

The music did nothing to soothe him.

Why? *Why* her? *Why, damn it?* He blamed himself, of course.

Another *I couldn't protect.*

Samson feared his mind would snap, and he was thankful there was no liquor around the place.

I could go down to the corner shop... No, get a hold of yourself, man.

Tears threatened.

He sat with the lights off, his thoughts a scrambled mess. After seeing the pictures of the dead women splayed out in front of him, and the information about the woman he'd known had sunk in, Samson had agreed to join Broadbank's task force.

***

"We need to bring this bastard to justice, Samson, and fast."

"Three in five nights… Jesus."

It was sobering, yet he felt punch-drunk.

"They've taken their murderous virginity, Samson, and there's no knowing what the person or persons are now capable of."

Of course, he knew the chief was right. And, back in the day, when Samson had been sharp, he would have been all over this case like flies on the proverbial cow pat.

He was weak. Hell, he wasn't even as good as he was before rehab.

"I'm nowhere near my best, Broadbank," he admitted. "Not even a little."

"You took down the scum selling child sex and porn easily enough."

"They were a couple of thick-headed dopes and youths from broken homes. Any desperado could have handled them. But this," he said, holding up one of the photos close to his face, "is a whole different ball game. There's no knowing how lethal this berserko is, Broadbank. Tangling with him or her could give me a one-way ticket to the bone collector's place."

One of the images on Broadbank's desk depicted a woman of around middle-age, much like the lawyer's wife, and the similarities didn't end there. She, a Mrs Crutchview, had jewellery inserted in her vagina along with the words '*Eat the Fucking Rich Cunts*' etched into her body. Chunks of her flesh had also been taken.

"You think he… *eats* it, Sam?"

Samson could only stare in disbelief. "I—" He couldn't finish.

"Mrs Crutchview. You recognise the name?"

Samson did, but only of recent. "Mayor's wife, correct?" Broadbank nodded. "Jesus. He hasn't been in office that long, has he?"

"Eight months or so."

"I thought as much. I was drying out on the inside when I saw his mug on the picture box."

"You know her, too, right?" Broadbank pointed at the second set of photos.

Samson felt bile rise in his throat. He closed his eyes and nodded.

"Where the hell do we start, Sam?"

"I need to go home, mull it over," he breathed out and looked at the chief. "I'll give you a tinkle on the blower tomorrow. Mind if I take this information home with me?"

"Go ahead, I have other copies." Broadbank left it at that. "Speak soon."

Samson gathered up what he wanted, unable to look at the images of the woman he knew, and left.

Before heading home however, Samson had spent a few hours walking around the city to clear his head, sat in the park to feed the birds, and grabbed a bite to eat.

***

After letting himself in, he'd pressed play on his CD player, removed his hat, coat and jacket, grabbed the ice-cold jug of pre-mixed Virgin Mary from out of the fridge and slumped in his chair.

"What was she doing around here? I told her to

get as far away as possible. Why? *Why*?" Samson slammed a fist against the side of his chair and slugged some cocktail, which did little to take the edge off his mood.

Maybe he *has something to do with all this*? he thought, bringing to mind XRay. *Or perhaps it was that Lovell ape*? *No, what on earth would Lovell gain from going after her? She did nothing to him. And XRay? Well, she did double-cross him and help me take his organisation down.*

Samson hammered his chair again, got to his feet, and startled Bogart in the process.

"Sorry, fella," he said, making his way over to the dining room table where he'd tossed the file containing the photos and information he'd bagged at Broadbank's office.

Upon opening the manila folder, he was greeted with the blown-up shots of Mrs Crutchview. Samson thumbed them out of the way and dug out the snaps of the second corpse. He held them up in front of him, finally able to view them, and expelled air through his nostrils in a noisy fashion.

"Goddamn it. And what's become of—"

There was a shallow knock at his door.

Samson looked over his shoulder, and his gaze landed on the empty bottle. He was about to step over to it and pick it up when a voice called out.

"Val, are you home?"

Damn. Lisa.

"Val?" she pushed, which was followed by more feeble raps.

Not tonight, he thought. *Hell, I can't be rude and*

ignore her, either. That would never do.

When he heard her footsteps drawing away in the hallway, he rushed to the door and opened it. "Lisa?"

She turned back, about to walk through her open front door, and he noticed she was dressed to the nines.

Damn, she went all out. I hope my tongue doesn't roll out when I open my flapper.

"I'm sorry, I'm a right boob – our da—get-together slipped my mind. Forgive me?"

"It's quite alright, Val. You don't know me from Adam, and there I was, forcing my company upon you like some stalker."

Samson chuckled. "Huh, no, it's not like that at all, toots. It's been a rough day at the office. I found out a close friend of mine has been snuffed out."

"Oh, no? You're not talking about that woman they found in the park a few nights ago, are you?"

He steadied himself before opening his trap. "No—"

"It's related? Another murder? Is it true what they're saying on the TV, that there's a serial killer loose in the city?" Her voice reached fever-pitch.

"Shh, Lisa, please. Keep your noise down. I—look, can we do this another night, possibly tomorrow?"

"I guess," she looked dejected, her bottom lip pouted.

What's this dame's deal? She's just seeking companionship in a new city, that's all, nothing sinister here, jar-head.

"Actually, you know what – I could do with the company right now."

"Sure," Lisa perked. "I would have hated feeding your half of my meal to the stray dogs out back."

He laughed again. "Let me get cleaned up and I'll be right over. Shall we say twenty minutes?" She nodded. "Good. See you shortly."

Samson went inside and headed towards the bathroom.

I must be bonkers going over there – my mind is in no fit state. It's going ga-ga. The more he thought about XRay being behind her murder, the more it made sense. *Maybe I'll start with some of his punks around the city tomorrow. See if I can dig up some dirt.*

The photos caught in his eyesight as he passed them.

Poor Roxie. She didn't deserve it.

Then another thought occurred to him as he eyed her pictures. She didn't fit the profile of the other dead women. Sure, he'd given her money, but not enough to be classed as 'wealthy' or 'stinking rich'.

What was her connection in all this?

Samson looked through the photos of Roxie. Like the other women, she too had missing flesh, articles stuffed in various orifices, and the words carved into her body.

She was a pro-skirt, nothing more. And what was she doing back here? That questioned plagued, no, needled him. *Was Charlie with her*? *Had she planned on visiting me*? Samson looked up at the clock. He'd wasted ten minutes out of the twenty he'd promised Lisa. He huffed. *I really could have done with staying in and thinking all this through. Broadbank's going to want some form of an update from me tomorrow.*

He shook his head, left the kitchen, and got in the shower.

***

When he left his apartment, he saw Lisa's door was standing open in readiness for him. In his hands, he held a couple of bottles of Virgin Mary.

I hope she likes the stuff. It's been a while since a muffin asked me to chow.

An inviting waft of food drifted from within her flat, setting his stomach off rumbling.

Easy, boy.

He hadn't eaten much that day.

"Knock-knock," Samson said, pushing the door wide and popping his head around it. "Anyone home?"

"Come on in, Val. I'll be dishing up soon."

"Sorry, I'm a bit later than I said. I got held up."

"That's okay, hun. With your job, I'm not surprised."

He walked into the main room and she greeted him with a smile.

Wow, he thought, seeing her better in the light.

The dress she wore sparkled. It also hugged her body with ferocity and was short enough to show off most of her thighs, which were covered in nude-coloured tights.

What a knock-out.

Lisa looked down at herself, then up at Samson. "Is there something wrong with me?"

He shook his head. "Quite the opposite. Virgin?"

She blushed, her mouth forming a perfect O.

"*Mary*, that is," Samson smiled, holding up the bottles of the pre-mixed cocktail.

"Ha-ha, you're the devil, Val. I'd love one. You'll find some glasses in one of the boxes above the washing machine. Excuse the mess."

"Nonsense, gal – you've only just moved in. It's to be expected."

"Thank you," Lisa mouthed.

"Will I find a corkscrew in the same place?" She nodded. "Great, I'll be back in two shakes of a lamb's tail, dear. Why don't you sit your pretty little self down, ma'am?"

Her blush was back. "I'll do that, but dinner won't be long."

"Long enough for us to have a non-alcoholic aperitif, surely?"

"Should be."

"What's cooking? Smells delicious," he said, rooting through her boxes to try and unearth glasses. As he rummaged, he found the corkscrew. "Well, that's something, I suppose," he muttered.

"There's a joint of beef in the oven, which I'll be serving with fresh vegetables and new potatoes."

Samson whistled. "Sounds good enough to… well, *eat*," he laughed, uncorking one of the bottles. After placing the skewered plug to one side, Samson went in search of the glasses. "Where on—

”

The phone attached to the wall caught his attention. There was a sticky note stuck to the receiver, and he couldn't help but snoop.

That appears to be a telephone number. What's that word above—

"Boss," he said aloud.

"Pardon?"

"Er… I can't seem to find the glasses," he shook his head, laughed and discarded what he'd seen. *Probably something to do with a possible job she has lined up.* His hands, deep inside a box, clutched onto something cold and solid. "Ah-*ha*!"

Samson removed a couple of mismatched glasses from their depths and swilled them under the cold tap.

The number attached to the phone caught his eye again.

"What is it you used to do, Lisa? For work, I mean."

"Reporter."

"Looking to do the same kind of thing here in Cardiff?"

"No need. I already have a job."

"Oh?" he prodded, knowing this was not chit-chatting any longer. Not for him, at least. *I'm too suspicious for my own good. Hey, I'm a peeper – it pays to be over cautious.*

"The rag I was working for has a sister paper here in Cardiff, and my editor was only too happy to have me come join their team. She knew all about the hell I was going through with my husband."

“Palooka kept pestering you, eh?” Samson entered the living room with a cocktail apiece, the incompatible glasses giving her a smile. “Best I could find, sorry.”

She waved her hand. “After I filed for divorce and threw him out, he hounded and hounded me. Not even the restraining orders deterred him. And, after several trips to the hospital later, I’d finally had enough. I packed, picked up, and left.”

“Only your editor knows where you went?”

Lisa nodded. “And before you ask, yes, she’s more than trustworthy. Stella will take my whereabouts to her grave.”

“Friends like that don’t come around often.”

Lisa took her offered drink and had a sip. “No, they don’t,” she smiled. “Hopefully we’ll become like that, Val.”

“Well, we’re off to a good start, wouldn’t you say?”

***

Over dinner they conversed about past jobs, lovers, homes, places they’d been/moved to and everything in between, leaving Samson amazed at how at ease she made him feel.

Glad I came, now, he thought.

He opened up about his wives—something the doctor had encouraged he do around people—and his battles with mental health issues and drink. It all spilt out of him. By the end of the evening, he felt regenerated, having forgotten about the murders and

Roxie. No, that wasn't true. The images of Roxie's dead, naked body arranged on a small hill located close to city hall had clawed away at the back of his brain all evening.

When he got up to leave, he knew it would all come crashing down on him as soon as he entered his flat.

Still, the evening had been a welcome reprieve.

What would I have done otherwise, sat in my flat and moped like a soft-headed clown?

***

"Well, goodnight, Lisa," Samson said, donning his hat and pulling his overcoat on. He turned to face her.

"Is the getup necessary?" she smiled. A titter followed. "You're only across the hall.

"Are you getting wise, lady?" She held her hands up in mock surprise. "If you are, I'll haul you downtown and have you thrown in the slammer." He screwed one eye closed and scrutinised her.

"I'll be good, if you promise to be a fair cop, Columbo?"

They laughed like naughty schoolchildren.

"This was fun," he admitted.

"You seem shocked by having such a good time."

"I guess I am. It's been a tough few years, and I—"

She touched a hand to his arm. "I understand, I've been there, remember?"

He gave her a stiff nod. "Well, g'night."

"Night, Val."

When she closed the door he stayed there, turned, and pressed his back to the wall. He needed a few minutes to process the evening before facing the files and photos that awaited him in the darkness of his flat.

Lisa's a special one, alright, and there's no point standing out here all night like a night watchman.

Samson was about to push off the wall when shrill ringing from within Lisa's apartment stopped him.

"No, let's give her some—"

"You need to give me more time," he heard her say, stopping him dead in his tracks. His heartbeat increased. She sounded distressed. "Please. You must. It's not as simple as you think."

Samson felt ashamed for having his ear pressed to her door. *It sounds like her ex is still giving her some grief. Maybe I can help her out by putting weight on him, or offering up some chin music.*

But he knew he could only intervene if she allowed it.

He pushed away from her door.

Lisa knows where I am if she needs me, he thought, crossing the hallway to his door and slipping his key into the lock.

After entering, Samson removed his coat and hat and placed them on the stand behind the door. When he turned, his eyes fell on the documents and pictures that lay strewn across his living room table.

A sigh escaped him.

Should I pore over them for a little, or hit the sack?

It was gone midnight.

Samson stretched, yawned and decided to make himself a coffee.

Might as well let the food go down first, or I'll never be able to sleep.

As he set the kettle to boil, his home phone started ringing. "Who could that be?" He left the kitchen and crossed the living room to where his phone sat on a sideboard. "Someone jangling about a job, maybe… At this hour, though? Must be urgent—*hello*?" he said into the receiver. "Normal folk are trying to get some sleep. This better—"

"Mr Valentine?"

"Yeah, who wants to know?"

"I believe you met with one of my associates a couple of days ago."

"The button man?"

"Excuse me?"

"The gorilla who tried to strangle me," Samson clarified.

"Hmm, yes."

"Well, it sure is swell to be talking to the big bad Lovell."

"This will be the first and *last* time, I hope."

"Why do you get others to do your dirty work, pal? Why don't you come down here and see me like a man?" Samson felt his grip intensify on the receiver, thinking he would crush it to dust. His jaw tensed.

"Did you get my message?"

"What would that be, jug-head? You sent him to put me six feet under, right? Because after his attempt, he didn't do a whole lot of yapping, only screaming. What's the matter, annoyed I got your brother killed? Or are you squirming over the fact I almost closed your operation down? Come on, out with it, clown. I've bigger fish to fry—"

The man on the other end of the phone laughed. "You're so colourful and animated, Mr Valentine. I don't want you dead, unlike the cops who *were* guarding your apartment complex—you're too much fun—I just want you gone from the city and out of the south, for good. Go and chase bad guys elsewhere. God only knows there are enough of them in the world through and through."

"What have you done to those officers?"

"I've had them *removed*, shall we say."

"You—"

"Save your energy, Mr Valentine."

He could be lying, Samson thought. *Keep your cool.*

"What was your man doing here if he wasn't meant to kill me, Lovell – scare me?"

"Yes."

"Could have fooled me."

"It was only a scare tactic, to get you moving along, much like tonight's will be. You like playing gangsters, right?"

"What—" The line disconnected. "Hello? *Hello*? Goddamn that son of a…" Samson slammed the receiver into its cradle, curbing his temper.

The sudden squeal of angry tyres from out on the

street somewhere filled his head. Doors opened and thumped shut. He crossed to the window and saw half-a-dozen men down there with Tommy guns pointed towards him.

"*Jesus*! Chopper squad!" he yelled.

Samson dove to the ground as the first wave of bullets ripped through his windows. Pottery, china, books, cups and plates and the TV set were riddled. Glass popped and exploded, which rained down around Samson as he crawled along the living room floor.

Get to the bathroom…

Ammunition stitched the walls close to his head, pummelled the sofa, and sliced the stuffing from the cushions.

The firing seemed to go on for hours, days even, with no sign of stopping.

When Samson got to the bathroom, he rushed inside, closed the door and flopped into the bath. He was confident he was safe. Beyond the door, he could hear his flat being torn asunder by hot showers of lead.

My mobile.

He patted down his trouser pockets and found the device he thought would have been the bane of his life. Samson opened the small phone, found Broadbank's personal number and hit dial.

It was answered after the fifth ring. The man sounded groggy. "Sam, do you have any—"

"Shut up and listen, fool. I've got bozos here with automatic weapons, and they are turning my much-adored abode into a goddamn colander."

***

Forty minutes after the shooting, Samson was now stood outside his apartment block looking up at his home.

He shook his head. "Turned it into Swiss cheese!"

"We'll get 'em, Sam," Broadbank insisted.

The three guards posted on the street to take care of Samson had been murdered, their car shot up.

"You're damn tootin' we will, Broadbank."

All around them, behind the police lines, Samson's neighbours stood watching. *Thankfully, nobody within the building had been harmed. But where's Lisa? Surely she heard the shooting?*

"It was definitely Lovell on the phone?"

"There's nothing wrong with my lugs, chief. I want that pig in a pen."

"Look, why don't you stay with me tonight, eh? Then, in the morning, I'll sort you out with some fresh digs courtesy of the police department."

"Nah, I'll be fine. It's only a few broken windows and a couple of chipped plates and some china."

"You're sure?"

"Positive." Samson sighed.

"You should consider relocating though, Sam. When they realise you're not going to leave the city, they'll try for you again."

"Let 'em, see what they get. Besides, I have a serial killer to find."

"You could work the case from outside the city, no big deal."

Samson waved Broadbank off. "I'll speak with you in the morning," he said, heading back inside. When he got to his flat, he looked over at Lisa's door and considered knocking.

Where is she?

***

Samson had spent some time covering the shot-out windows with plastic bags before slumping in his chair, and it didn't take long for sleep to claim him.

A few hours later, he was awoken by the sound of knocking.

For a moment, he lay there in the darkness and listened, his heartrate out of control. In between the knocks, the bags across the windows flapped in response.

Maybe they went away? *No respecting hitman would announce his presence.*

He was about to investigate when the knocking started again.

Broadbank checking to see if I'm okay? *Lisa, maybe*?

"Sam?" a thin voice asked. The person sounded upset.

Jesus, Lisa's been hurt.

Samson threw his blanket aside and got out of his chair. Airing on the side of caution, he looked through the peephole, half expecting to gaze down the muzzle of a silenced revolver, but he wasn't.

Is that a child?

He opened the door and gasped. "*Charlie*?!"

She looked up at him. "I didn't know where to go, or who to turn to. Please, will you help me?"

Samson took her in and locked the door.

Chapter 6

He zigzagged the scissors in a slow, methodical method, savouring the sound it made as it sliced through the thin newspaper. Ever since the press had started printing stories about him, he'd begun collecting the clippings and filing them in a scrapbook entitled *Treasured Memories*.

He was hunkered over a workbench in his apartment, somewhere in the guts of the city. Outside his single, low-level window, people of the night walked by. Some were headed to work, he guessed, whilst others went to and from bars.

Somewhere in the background of his hovel, someone was singing about an angel of the city on his TV.

He liked the night.

I own it.

His smile revealed white, perfect teeth.

The headline on that day's rag read "*Widower Maker Totals Three.*" On another paper, one he'd already dismantled, the journalist likened his grisly killings to that of Kenneth Alessio Bianchi and his cousin, Angelo Buono – The Hillside Stranglers; the pair terrorised the streets of Los Angles from 1977-78. They, like The Widower Maker, dumped their victims on raised ground for the whole world to see their humiliation.

He liked that accolade.

His smile widened. He licked his lips.

"Unlike them, I *won't* get caught."

If the press hadn't started giving him attention, due to lack of information from the police, then he would have kicked things up by sending them taunting letters. As it happens, the husband of his first victim had helped him along in that department.

"*Idiot.* Why do rich men think they can buy, sell, and destroy everything with their paper god? 'And then I came home, the woman who married the fool who wished for gold'," he said, quoting the famous poem. "Money won't stop me from completing my mission – to rid the world of the worst sinners; the greedy."

With his trusty knife, rope, and bag full of scream-provoking implements, The Widower Maker was determined to cut the city open. He wanted to fill its culverts, nooks and crannies with its life-force, and to drown the 'stinking rich' in the process.

He shook his head, clearing the thoughts as he worked away in a pool of light cast by his lamp, building his memories.

To his left was a note—an envelope lay by its side with the *Cardiff Times'* address jotted on it—which read:

You call me The widower maker. A thing of evil.; A destroyer of good, life, and all things that make you pure. You say I'm an imp of mass destruction.; a cool calculated and heinous thing.;

a beast with a beastly heat. Youre quick with the words but I'm quicker with the knife. Do you think you can stop me? Catch me? Ha-ha-ha!!!

Im not any of these things you call me. I am the opposite. I've been sent from a divine force to rid you of greed. Of affluence in all its forms.

I. am. your. Saviour. And you shall kneel and cower in my bloody and vengeful wake.

You are to release this note in your rag. Front page. Or I shall cast out the blood of a young, rich child.

The letter had come from a raging heart and a head full of screaming nightmares. He didn't care that it made little sense, only that it would help strike fear into the hearts of those who read it.

His threat was a promise.

If he didn't see his words make the front page, then his already sought out victim would turn up dead like the others.

He stopped cutting, put the scissors down, and went to the telescope he had set up close to the window. It was angled upwards, and when he looked through the spy hole, he could see a little girl sat in her bedroom opposite.

"Playing dollies and tea parties," he muttered. Again, he licked his lips.

There was no sexual malice involved in his crimes, for he saw fornication as a disgusting act. It sickened him. So, too, did the thought of touching his penis, and whenever he needed to urinate, ejaculate or shower, he would use gloves.

No. They would not find any trace of such deviance on his victims, unlike the Hillside Stranglers', who raped most, if not all, of their prey.

However, he'd make sure the pretty little thing before him, with blonde pigtails and a smattering of freckles, would scream and beg for her life. And he would strip her, slowly, and cut his words into her ripe skin before ending her short life and snacking on her rich skin.

At that thought, he looked at the set of fake, vampire-like dentures he had swimming in a jar close by.

Custom made, he thought, *and just right for gnawing through flesh.*

He put his eye back to the telescope.

"You look so happy in your ivory tower. Careful, though, because someone might start throwing rocks at you soon, little princess."

He pulled away and went back to his work. Carefully, he turned over the fresh clipping and applied paste to its back before sticking it in his scrapbook. So far, he had a dozen or so memories made up of headlines, by-lines, and articles.

"*Mmm,*" he groaned, closing the book and pressing his weight on it. When enough time had lapsed, he placed it to one side and stood from his chair.

He felt like a walk.

Prey picking?

No, he didn't need to do that. He already had his next victim lined up, who lived right around the corner from him, thanks to his pal Hatchy.

Maybe I could go and see her? Take some photos on my phone and send them to Hatchy. Yes, sounds like a good idea.

The Widower Maker liked watching his prey as they went about their daily routine, thinking they had enough time left to get everything done, oblivious to the fact that one day soon he'd be along to snuff them out.

"They're as delicate as a flame in the wind," he uttered. Yes, the thought of seeing her excited him.

He grabbed his keys from off the hook by the door and headed out into the neon-lit night. The city was alive, as though it was the middle of the day, with noise and colour, people rushing and dashing, coming and going.

A stomach-growling smell from a nearby hotdog stand stuffed his nostrils. He stopped, bought one, applied mustard, paid, and moved on. At the newspaper shack, he idled, admiring the headlines splashed across the lesser-known rags and gossip and girly magazines.

He was everywhere, and the terror that engulfed him from those around him was palpable. He gazed at strangers who looked at other strangers, including him, in a dirty, distrusting way. It made him smile on the inside.

There are so many people still going about their nightly routines like they don't care. Well, I'll soon put a stop to that. I won't be happy until the streets are dead at night. Ha. Dead.

He stuffed a piece of hotdog bun into his mouth,

stifling a further laugh, as garnish dribbled. As he licked it away, a young businesswoman passed him by, shooting him a look of disdain, which he played on. He smiled and flapped his tongue at her. When she scuttled off, whimpering, he laughed and choked down more of his meal.

People are definitely rattled. I can see it in their eyes.

He'd previously observed that the city had never been that much of a warm, welcoming place. Still, people, strangers, did occasionally stop and chat, give a polite nod or friendly 'Good morning' to one another. However, since his reign of terror had begun, he'd noticed a big shift in people's attitude, even though most seemed to be walking around in a blasé way.

That thin, trusting thread of common decency between everyday folk on the streets had changed: they couldn't look at each other, let alone smile or part with a few sociable words.

They knew a wolf walked amongst them, and it was amusing for him to watch them squirm. Soon, a curfew would be set in place, of that he was sure.

I'm the biggest news this rat hole of a city has ever known. I'll put Wales on the map.

After stuffing the last of the hotdog into his mouth, he placed the empty wrapper into a bin.

I can't bloody abide people who litter and leave their mess everywhere. Like that arsehole last night.

***

Whilst walking around by the train station, The Widower Maker witnessed a man throw his empty burger box onto the floor. He saw red and almost caught up with the bloke and stuck his knife through his eyeball.

But he remained strong, knowing he had a job to do, which couldn't be done from the inside of a prison cell. And so, to dampen his rage, he strolled around the back of an off-licence close by and found what he wanted; a passed-out wino hugging an empty bottle of spirits.

With a blind, snarling rage, he snatched the spent receptacle from the man and smashed it over his head with glee.

"Have. You. No. Fucking. Respect. For. Yourself?" he said with gritted teeth, as he stamped on the man's head repeatedly, before kicking him in the stomach and face until the anger burned out of him.

Blood mixed with vomit pooled around his feet.

At that point, he stopped lashing out, stepped back, and took a few deep breaths. His hands were shaking, his body trembling. When he looked at the man, he couldn't tell if he was still breathing, and then he heard drunken voices from around the corner.

He ran, savouring the shrieks of those who discovered the homeless man that lay in a twisted puddle of spew and blood.

***

The mere thought of the incident warmed him, making his insides fuzzy, and then his heart missed a beat when he realised he was approaching his next target's house. She was outside, unloading her car of shopping bags—the front door to her house stood open—her children disappearing inside.

"Tell your father to come and give me a hand, please," she called after them.

He didn't hear their response as he got closer, his full attention on her, as he watched her heave the bags out of her car and place them on the pavement.

I'm almost too close, he thought, stopping by a tree and leaning against it. *But that's part of the thrill, right, being within touching distance*?

He felt exhilarated. Alive.

The woman's husband came outdoors and they exchanged greetings and kisses. It turned his guts.

Ah, the fat, greedy banker; *the man who likes to take, take, take and give nothing back to society. Well, not to worry, Mr Big Shot. Your wife will pay with her blood, covering your debut.*

If there was one thing he detested about people with money, it was those born into it.

Most of them have hearts of lead.

He continued to watch as the couple proceeded inside their home with the shopping.

It must be the butler's night off. How noble of you, Mr Big Shot, he thought, all the while snapping photos with his phone and sending them to Hatchy.

The wife, taking up the rear, halted at the front door and turned. She looked across the street to where he was stood, but didn't see him.

A flicker of electricity—which started in his guts—flashed through his heart, and the hairs at the nape of his neck stood on end.

Does she know she's being watched? Impossible. It's the recent spate of killings that has her spooked.

For the briefest of moments, he could have sworn she was staring him dead in the eye, and the pleasure was beyond words. He shivered, pocketed his phone, and zipped his coat up to his chin.

He wanted her at his mercy right now, but knew he couldn't.

You'll keep, Catherine.

The front door was closed, shutting him out. He felt nothing but loss and was tempted to cross the road and peek through their living room window.

No, don't push—

"Fuck it," he said, eyeing the street up and down, which was deserted. He climbed the few steps to her porch and risked a look through her window. Catherine and her husband were in the kitchen, emptying the bags of shopping and putting the food away.

Happy families indeed.

And then things turned amorous, the children nowhere in sight, as Mr Big Shot put his arms around his wife's waist and planted his face in her neck. She slapped at him and said something. They both laughed.

The Widower Maker's jaw tightened, but the thought of how he would destroy this family of wealth and power eased his flaring rage.

A smile was born of temper. He turned from the window, walked down the steps, and left the street the way he'd come.

"Soon, my delicious Catherine, soon," he muttered, strolling out of sight.

Chapter 7

"I have money, Mr Valentine. Enough, I hope, which was a part of the gift—"

"Wow, wow, kiddo. Slow down," Samson said, putting his hands to the girl's shoulders.

"I-I—" She pulled away, tears spilt from her eyes, and she collapsed against the door she'd walked through. Charlie slid down it and pulled her knees to her chin. She hugged herself, face buried between her thighs. "It's over, all of it," she sobbed.

Samson looked down at her. He was frozen, unsure of what to do. Adults he could deal with: men and women. But minors? He hadn't the foggiest. He constructed and deconstructed sentences in his head; "Things will work out fine, you'll see." "It's a shame what happened to your mother, kid – she was a swell gal." "I'll nail the palooka that did this, you'll see." "I'm here for you, Charlie."

It all sounded empty and meaningless.

Lame, even.

Samson, for the first time in a while, was lost for words and out of his league.

"I'm sorry," he started with, getting down on his haunches.

I'm tactful, always have been.

A lump developed in his throat and tears threatened when he thought about how Roxie appeared in the images on his table.

The photos! I need to move them.

Samson looked over his shoulder and saw them, along with the police reports. He turned back to the teen and placed his hands on hers, which rested on her knees.

"It would be disrespectful of me to take money from you, Charlie. Besides, I want to see the pissant who hurt your mum thrown in jail."

She slowly lifted her head, her eyes were glazed over, and fresh tears spilt down her cheeks. "You know?"

He nodded. "News got to me this afternoon, kid."

"But how, you're not a policeman?"

"I'm working in close relation with them these days, and as soon as I saw your mother had been—" Samson looked away, unable to finish.

"Murdered. It's okay, you can say it." Charlie pulled a hand away from his and used the back of it to dry her face. "Have there been others?" she asked, sniffling.

How much do I part with?

He nodded. "I can't go into too much detail with you, Charlie. It's…" He gazed into her eyes. He sighed. "There have been three killings so far, counting your mum, and from what I can tell they're all connected. Same MO."

"So it's true a second woman was found with my mother?"

"It's looking that way, but I can't see the correlation between Roxie and the other women."

"What do you mean?"

"It seems our local snooze man is offing wealthy women, or women who have come from money. I.E. – rich, influential husbands, mammies or daddies. Your mother was neither, right? Sorry to be so blunt."

Charlie shook her head, sniffed and wiped away a few stray tears. "Don't be silly, Mr Valentine."

"Sam, please."

"Sam. Right. My mother was a prostitute and my dad left when I was little. He was a common thief. There's never, *ever* been money, only what you so generously gave mum and me upon us escaping."

"And I was only too glad to help."

"Thing is, we never left the city…"

That was a bombshell he'd not been expecting. He reeled, and Charlie noticed.

"*What*? How could she have been so reckless? So careless, after everything we went through?"

"*Hey*." Charlie yanked her other hand from his and got to her feet.

Sam did the same. "Sorry, I—"

"You never let me finish, did you?" She fiercely jabbed a finger into his chest. "You think she was like all the rest, don't you? A dumb, empty-headed whore who *fucked* guys for money."

"Charlie, I'd never think that about Roxie."

"Then what the hell are you getting at? Maybe coming here was a mistake." She turned, grabbed the doorknob, and opened up. Before she could walk out of Samson's flat, Samson caught her by the arm and pulled her back in, locking the door in the process.

"Are you ga-ga, gal? If anyone saw you coming here, someone who knows who you and I are, we'll both be pushing up daisies, capiche?"

"Leave me alone." Charlie wriggled in his grip and kicked him in the shin.

"Ugh," he grunted, clenching his teeth. He hauled the youngster across the room, who couldn't have weighed more than eight stone soaking wet, and shoved her into his easy chair. "Now you listen to me, child. I loved your mother, she was a close, personal friend of mine, and there was nothing I wanted more than to see you and her get out of this apple; to flourish, after spreading your wings."

Charlie slapped his finger out of her face. "We never left because we were stopped, *idiot*!"

"Wh—what?"

"By two uniformed men. Cops."

Samson stepped back and examined her.

Was she lying?

"Go on."

"They said they were friends of yours, and that you'd requested to see us once more before we went away. We didn't—we followed them like sheep."

"What did they do?" Samson was almost too scared to let the question leave his mouth.

"Nothing, apart from take us to *him*."

"XRay?" His mouth formed a perfect O.

"Yes, and then they separated us. When I saw my mother next, they'd beaten her bloody and broken her spirit. She was forced to stay and take up work on the streets again. XRay told her that if she didn't, he'd let his perverts have their way with me for months on end before killing me."

Samson swallowed hard. "Then?" he pressed, not that he wanted to endure any more information, but knew he had to have the *full* story.

Charlie's head dropped. "She agreed. What choice did she have?"

"Roxie was a fine lady and would have died to protect you. Go on."

"After mum buckled, XRay put her to work that night, and it wasn't long before I, too, was forced to walk the—"

"*Pig*!" Samson smashed both of his fists down onto the chair's arms. He then turned and walked over to the door.

If only I was at Paul's now. I'd knock the damn stuffing out of his—hang on…

"You've *been* to XRay's main hideout?"

She nodded. Her lips trembled and her body shook.

"Hey, hey, I'm sorry." Samson got down on one knee in front of the youngster and held her hands in his. "As long as I'm around, nobody walking this spinning ball will harm a single hair on your head, kiddo. And if they try, they best bring an army with them."

"I know you were close to mum, that you're upset about the news, and I shouldn't have gone off on you as I did."

"Forget it, honestly. It just came as a massive shock, knowing you never left the city."

"He-he made her his bride."

"XRay *married* your mother?"

"Again, she was pushed into it by him using me as a bargaining chip."

His nostrils flared. "Hang on. Let me get this as straight as a poker face. You're telling me he put you *both* to work as pro-skirts, and then married your mother?"

Charlie nodded. "My mother also worked his clubs."

"Clubs?"

"Strip joints. She worked the poles and stages. Sometimes, if he was feeling generous, he'd allow mum to cover the tills or the bar."

"Jesus."

"There's something else. They were childhood sweethearts and close friends."

"Holy smoke," he gasped, staggering backwards. "Roxie never mentioned that to me."

"She was ashamed of it and swore me to secrecy. I'm only telling you now because I want to see you either kill, or catch the bastard."

He wanted to tell her to kerb her vile language, but he didn't dare.

Poor thing. God only knows what horrors she's seen and been through.

As if reading his mind, she opened up further. "They beat and humiliated me, with one guy liking to put his cigarettes out on my bare flesh." Her chin trembled.

Samson felt his face flush. He wrapped his arms around her and held her close to his chest. "You're safe now, Charlie, but I've got some questions for you," he said, holding her tighter. "If he was married to your mother, why would he want her killed? He loved her, right? Besides which, you were both doing as you were told."

"I didn't stick around long enough to ask. As soon as I heard about her death, I hauled arse out of his hideout."

"But do you know of a reason why he'd want to harm her?" he pressed, pulling away from her.

She nodded, wiping snot from her upper lip. "I think so. Two nights before she turned up dead, we'd tried to make a run for it."

"Okay."

"XRay had warned us from the start, that if we ever tried to escape him, he'd kill us."

"Jesus," he muttered. "Do you think you'd know how to get back to his hangout?"

"I could try, but I fled in a hurry."

"What about when you were coming and going for work?"

She shook her head. "We girls were always blindfolded whilst being escorted on and off the property."

"Palooka's got brains, I'll give him that much. I'm starting to think he had the other women killed, too, to make it look like the work of a serial killer."

"But why?"

"Excuse me?"

"Why would XRay go through so much bother? He buys and sells and kills people for fun."

"Could be a number of reasons, I guess. For one, by making it look like the work of a serial killer, he knows it would keep the police busy for months, maybe a few years on end, and would hope for me to be tied up in it, too. Me, the biggest thorn in his side; XRay knows I'll be gunning for him sooner or later."

"That's a valid point."

"Ha. Are you a peeper in training? I might need a sidekick on this one."

Charlie looked at him with red-rimmed eyes. "I don't think I'd be much good to you, Sam."

He ruffled her hair. "Stashing you somewhere safe would be for the best, now, anyway. We can't be seen together."

"I can't stay *here*?"

"Definitely not."

Charlie got up and looked around. "Why—what in the hell happened to your flat?"

"Goons with machine guns, kid."

"XRay?"

He shook his head. "No."

"Then shouldn't we *both* go underground in that case?"

"I'm not running scared from any hop-head. No thin-as-paper, tin-pot gangster is going to hustle me out of town."

Charlie smiled at him. "I-I love you, Sam, for everything you did for me and mum, and for what I know you'll do."

"Come on, let's get you someplace safe."

Charlie walked over to Samson, about to embrace him, when she saw the photos on the table in her peripheral vision. She went to them. "Oh,

God."

"Damn it. I didn't want you seeing those. If only I'd known you were coming, I would have put everything away. I am so sorry."

Charlie turned and buried her face in his chest. "Look at what he *did* to my mother!" she wailed.

"I know, and I'll right it." Samson stroked her back and soothed her.

"Where are you taking me?"

"Somewhere I know you'll be as fine as if you were with me."

"That man who owns the bar?"

"No, I think I've put Steve through enough. Come on, you'll see."

***

Samson was glad for the cover of darkness.

He stood in the doorway to his apartment block and quickly poked his head around the corner and looked to his left and then right.

The streets were quiet, dead in fact, and the traffic was light.

Before turning to go back inside to fetch Charlie from the foyer, he scanned the parked cars, most of which were covered in an orange hue from off the streetlights, to see if he could see anyone sitting within the shadowed vehicles.

His skin crawled. A shiver inched down his back and nestled in his guts. Ice-vipers gnawed at his innards.

Samson craned his neck this way and that.

There doesn't appear to be any dangers in the darkness, but one can never be too careful.

Satisfied nobody was watching, Samson opened the door to the apartment block and stepped inside.

"Come on, it's now or never."

"You're sure it's safe?"

"I wouldn't bet my shirt on it, but I'm pretty sure." He held his hand out. "I'll have a better gauge on things once we're moving."

"And you're positive we can't just take your car?"

"Yes, I am. If someone is tailing us, then I'll have a healthier chance of losing them on foot and getting you to safety."

"If you can't trust a shrewd P.I., then who can you trust, right?" she muttered.

He smiled and then nodded. "True. Now come on, let's beat it."

On the streets, without the protection of the walls around him, Samson felt the nip of the three a.m. air.

"Warm enough?" he asked her.

"Yes, thanks."

As they walked and talked, Samson kept looking over his shoulder, and all around him, to see if anyone might be following.

If they are, they're good, he thought, not spotting anyone.

"I like it at this hour," she admitted. "And I'm thankful that Cardiff isn't a big city. After the small hours kick in, it goes dead."

"Yes, same here, kid. And you're right – Cardiff

is a nice-sized apple. Any bigger, and it would be tough to police. We have it lucky."

"It scares me to think there could be a serial killer running amok, and not just a cardboard gangster trying to throw his weight around by inserting false fear."

"False?"

"Yeah. I mean, how much fear did XRay have to begin with? Loads. Everyone knows who he is and what he does. He is a seen danger. But by making us all believe there's a serial killer creeping around in the shadows, and lurking in our parks and bushes, and tapping on our back-room windows is weird."

"So what makes it false?"

"Him. If XRay is behind it, then it's a lie. It's a false fear, even if it is odd."

"A pretty damn good one at that, if you ask me, because if any more snoozers turn up naked atop our city hills, then there's going to be mass panic."

"I don't think there's much to worry about, since speaking with you. It's pretty clear-cut XRay's behind it, right?"

"All evidence seems to be leading that way. Tomorrow, I'm off into the city to see if I can shake down some of his crooks," Samson said.

"Good luck. His most trusted crew members would rather die before uttering a word."

"I can be very persuasive," he said, removing a breadstick from his pocket. "Would you like one?"

"I'm sure you can, and no, thanks." She sidled up to him and locked her arm around his.

As they entered the heart of the city, the seedier

it became: people were shooting up in doorways, others were having rough, loud sex, whilst some fought, swore, and drank themselves stupid.

There were too many to move on or threaten with arrest. Besides, Samson had an important mission to carry out. To get his charge to his 'safe house'.

The filth looked at him, now he was in the belly of the beast, and he knew there would be trouble.

"Oink," someone said.

Others laughed.

"Don't look at them," Samson warned Charlie.

"Fucking pig bastard," another yelled, hurling a bottle that shot over Samson's head and obliterated before him.

He turned on his heel. "Why don't you lot amscray, before I bring the boys in blue this way and have you all taken down to the clubhouse."

Most of the delinquents hiding in the darkness fell silent.

"Well, what do you say, palookas, fancy a trip downtown?" Samson produced his cuffs, which had been given to him by Broadbank, along with a few powers he didn't have previously. "Aren't my bracelets pretty?"

"Hey, it's cool, man," a woman said, staggering. "We don't want no trouble, see."

"Yeah, easy," a fella sporting a Mohawk whined.

"When I come back this way in an hour, you lot best be gone." Samson stepped up to the boy, towered over him, and jabbed a finger in his chest. "Now apologise, son, like I know you're going to.

It's not nice to scare little girls. Or do you like that sort of thing?"

The winos and druggies who were gathered at the punk's back drifted away.

"S-sorry, love."

Samson put a hand to the lad's cheek and patted it gently. "Good boy."

***

Thirty minutes later, Samson and Charlie entered onto the street where Alice's café stood.

"Where are we going, Sam? I just want to stay with you."

"You'll be fine, trust me. But before we go there, I need to make sure there's no bozo on our tail. Okay?"

Charlie nodded.

"If you start to think we're walking in funny directions, it's for that reason, okay?"

"I trust you."

They strolled by Alice's shop, went down a side street, and ducked behind a bin.

"Keep quiet," he instructed.

When nobody came after them, Samson knew it was safe to move. They took a turn down an alley and stopped before an abandoned, boarded-up shop. "Here you go," he said, nice and loud.

"*Here*?"

Rats squawked, scurried, and clawed at the boards over the building's windows.

"Yep."

Samson pricked his ears, fancying he heard something.

Footsteps. Not far back.

He put his arm around Charlie and pulled her closer to a car that had been burned out and left for dead.

They're getting closer.

When he heard a whoosh of air and a grunt of effort from behind him, Samson pushed Charlie aside and ducked. The giant at his back flew forward, his fist leading the way, and he punched out the driver's side window of the stalled vehicle.

"*Argh*!" the man screamed, retracting his busted hand. Blood pumped, he crumpled to the floor and applied pressure to the wrist of his destroyed paw.

"There's no time for pointless questions right now, because I've got a job to do, but I'm coming back for you, you hear, hatchet-man? Boy, you must be about the dumbest, heaviest-footed son of a gun out of Knucklehead's Ville." Samson snapped one cuff to the guy's wrecked hand and the other to the car's door handle. "I'll want all you've got to tell me when I return, lad. Come on, Charlie, let's go."

The man grunted and snarled. "You're dead, man. *Dead*."

"Pipe down and cool off, clown – you're going to need your energy."

"H-how—"

"I got lucky," Samson answered Charlie. He then put his arm around her and led her out onto the main street.

Ten minutes later, they were inside Alice's shop.

***

Alice was behind the counter, hunched over a magazine, looking bored.

That's soon going to change, he thought, stepping up to her with Charlie behind him.

"One mug of joe, please," he beamed down at Alice.

"Sam!" Alice snapped her head up with a grin on her face.

"Listen, I have a huge favour to ask of you and your family."

"Oh-oh, this sounds like it could be expensive, am I right?"

"Hey, enough with the smart mouth, young lady, yeah?"

Alice laughed. "I'm pretty much head honcho around here nowadays, so shoot. What do you need?"

"I'd like you to keep this young muffin out of harm's way. Think you could do that for ol' Sam?" Samson stepped aside, revealing Charlie. "She's got the mob on her back. They—"

"Killed my mother," Charlie said.

"Oh, God." Alice stepped from around the counter and hugged Charlie. "You poor thing. How long for, Sam? Not that it matters."

"A few weeks. Maybe she can work to earn her keep?"

"No problem. Leave it with me."

"You have my mobile number. If anyone suspicious comes around or anything happens, call immediately, day or night. I'll be back in a few days to check in on you all."

Alice nodded.

"Sam, please..." Charlie pleaded, holding onto his coat sleeve.

"You'll be perfectly safe with these fine people. With the mob also on my back, it's not sane or safe for you stay close to me."

"They're gunning for you *again*?" Alice smiled.

"Watch the lip, toots, or I'll bust you."

Alice beamed. "Don't worry about us. I have plenty of frying pans lying around..."

They both chuckled and then parted ways.

When Samson exited the shop, fat droplets of rain started to fall. He lifted the lapels of his trench coat and headed for the alley that held his prisoner. When he got back to the abandoned car, he wasn't shocked to see the man gone, along with the car's door handle.

Chapter 8

Samson was sat in his easy chair, waiting for his alarm to sound. When he'd arrived home at four a.m., he'd collapsed into his beloved seat and tried to sleep but couldn't. He'd been too wired, with too many unanswered questions swirling around inside his head.

He put a hand to his face and scratched at the stubble on his chin and neck. He yawned, his eyes burning.

Got no time to sleep now, he thought. *I've got a lot to do today.*

Samson slapped a hand to his thighs, got up, and looked at the time – it was pushing ten o'clock. *I need to be at the station.*

He headed to the bathroom, stripped, got in the shower and shaved. Once he was done, he balled his clothes up and threw them into the washing machine as he made his way into the bedroom to dress.

After downing a cup of black coffee with enough sugar to sink a post, he was out the door and into the city. As he drifted in between the crowds of shoppers, Samson couldn't help but think, and smirk, at the thought of how The Widower Maker hadn't dampened Cardiff's economy.

People will always shop until they drop, no matter what. Let's just pray the dropping isn't literal, though.

He sniggered and munched on a breadstick. His breakfast.

Just how much info am I willing to give Broadbank? he thought, remembering Charlie's safety. The events involving XRay the last time around had him distrusting those about him. *The thug has a lot of people in his pocket. Can I afford to expose the source of my information? It would put her in a whole heap of brown sticky stuff if her name and whereabouts were leaked.*

But, deep down, he knew he could trust Broadbank.

The man's been nothing but straight with me. Hell, he's practically made me a lawman.

It wasn't strictly a case of trust, though, was it? No, not really. What if the chief got picked up by XRay's goons because they thought he knew more than he actually did? If so, could Broadbank survive a licking and keep his mouth closed?

Samson wasn't sure.

Steve blabbed, remember?

Samson knew the barman hadn't meant to talk. *A lot of good men would have done the same in his situation. But would XRay be so bold as to kidnap the chief of police and rough him up?*

No, Samson couldn't see that, but he wouldn't put anything past XRay.

I'll see how I feel about things once I lay my peepers on Broadbank. Not only that, I tend to work cases better when it's only me privy to certain, sensitive info.

When he finished the breadstick, he produced

another and started on that one. Up ahead, a saxophone busker was piping out a haunting rendition of *Boys of Summer*. The young musician had a medium-sized crowd gathered around him, and Samson couldn't help but stop and throw a handful of spare coins into the lad's open instrument case.

I wish I had more clock to burn, he thought, heading away from the sax player. Before Samson was out of earshot, the musician started belting out a chilling version of *Runaway Train*.

It cooled Samson's blood. His hairs stood on end.

Boy's good, really *good.*

He passed the Jazz Hole and decided against stopping to check on Steve.

Maybe later.

As he walked, his mind reverted back to the conversation he'd had with Charlie. Was he sure XRay would do such a thing as make people think a serial killer was on the loose? Sure, he'd come up with a few good reasons as to why he would, but now that he'd slept on it, all three hours, he wasn't so sure.

Kill his wife in a rage, yes, but carve her up and throw her out on the streets to be discovered in such a way?

He mulled that thought over.

No matter which way he looked at it, it was an important lead, and the first real solid clue he had to work with.

And then another thought struck him.

What if it's a spurned hatchet-man? Someone who'd been loyal to the el capitano and had been exiled for some reason or another? A stool pigeon? Nah, they're usually weak sisters – pissants who are scared of their own shadows. A hitter? A professional button man? A serious heavy who wasn't paid for a job?

Samson wasn't convinced.

What about Lovell? I know I dismissed it at first, but the thug from the west is out for revenge against me... What's stopping him from going after XRay, too?

Again, he wasn't so sure. If that was the case, why would Lovell kill two other women?

It doesn't make sense. Maybe it is just coincidence Roxie was killed by a serial killer. I mean, XRay fits the picture, right? Roxie was, after all, ball and chained to a wealthy man. Perhaps the psycho is putting down women who belong to good and *bad men.*

His mind was awash with questions, answers, and half-baked ideas.

Good *guys, that's a laugh.*

After going through the notes on the husbands of the two dead women, Samson had found them anything *but* clean. Not only were they skimming money from the companies they worked for, but they also had their fingers in many dirty little pies. The one, the first husband, a lawyer, had a river of dirty cash rolling into his bank account from thrown cases.

He also had his stubby, greasy digits in drugs,

prostitution and all sorts, he thought. *The pig was even robbing charities he was meant to be sponsoring.*

The second husband, the mayor, was worse.

It was found out that he had shares in corrupt, underground organisations that fed pounds to paedophile rings in Europe.

Makes my guts flip. At least both bozos are in the big house, and they won't see the light of day anytime soon. Especially if the hatchet-men they were supporting with their wealth and public stature have hitters on the inside.

That pleasant thought brought a smile to Samson's face.

Is it possible, then, that The Widower Maker is killing women who were married to just bad men?

He pondered this possibility.

Like a warped Robin Hood. He'll be shooting apples off people's heads next. Wait, wasn't that William Tell?

Samson drew another breadstick, promising himself it would be his last.

Let's wait and see if Broadbank has any new thoughts.

***

Another fifteen minutes of strolling and Samson found himself entering the police station.

He walked up to the desk sergeant and said he was there to see the chief.

"He's in his office – you know where, right? I'll

sign you in."

Samson nodded and walked off.

He'd been told by Broadbank that he didn't need to alert them to his presence every time he dropped in, but Samson liked doing things by the book, no matter how mundane the task.

What's the point in doing something if you're not going to do it properly? That's the problem with folks these days – they take the shortcut every time.

He knocked on Broadbank's door and waited to be summoned.

"*Come*!" the chief demanded.

Samson opened up, strolled in, and sat in one of the comfy chairs opposite Broadbank's desk. The chief was on the phone, a worried look crumpled his face.

"I'll get my best down to you right away, sir." Broadbank wrote something on the pad in front of him. "Shall we say," he looked at his watch, "within the next thirty minutes? Yes, okay. Bye." He hung up and addressed Samson, "Damn, am I glad to see you."

"Trouble in paradise?"

"Phone hasn't stopped ringing all morning."

"Leads?"

"Could be a few, yeah."

"Who was that? The prime minister?"

"Enough of the jokes, Sam, yeah? This killer is making my balls ache."

"Got anything for me to go on?"

"You can have this." Broadbank tore the paper from the pad and gave it to the P.I. "Get on that."

Samson looked at the note. "Jameson?"

"He's the editor-in-chief down at the *Times*. They've received a signed letter from The Widower Maker, but they think it might be a hoax."

"Okay, sounds promising."

"What about you, anything to share? Did the notes tell you much?"

Samson looked the chief in the eye and a mental image of Charlie appeared before him. "Not really, no, but I do have some leads to follow. A possible witness, too, but I'd like to keep it close to my chest for now, if that's all the same to you?"

"Trust issues?" Broadbank smiled.

"Call it what you like, princess."

"Fine, have it your way."

"The *best* you have, hey?" Samson flapped the piece of paper at Broadbank.

"What did you want me to tell him, that I was in the process of sending a halfwit his way?"

Both men laughed, and then Samson left.

Public transport had always bothered him.

Buses, trains, taxies – they all smell worse than the inside of a boxer's jockstrap.

Had he known he'd be taking a trip to the other side of town, Samson would have brought his car.

Can't be helped, I suppose.

The bus rolled to a stop and a little old lady pushed by him, stepping on his toes in the process.

"An 'Excuse me' would have been nice," Samson told her.

She didn't acknowledge him.

Think they own the damn place.

Three more stops down the line and it was his turn to get off.

Thankful to be rid of the sour stink and herky-jerky movements, Samson breathed in the city air, not that it was much better.

Goddamn daily traffic jams are poisoning this place. This apple's core is rotting.

He straightened his tie and readjusted his fedora before moving down the street. It had been a long time since he'd visited the building block that housed the city's tabloids.

It took him less than five minutes to get there.

Ashton House, it read on the gold-plated placard affixed to the wall by the side of the door. Samson pushed the buzzer and a voice spoke through the intercom.

"What's your business, please?"

"Hi ma'am, I'm here to see Mr Jameson. I'm with the police department."

"Thank you. I'll buzz you in."

A second later the door sounded and Samson was able to step inside.

"This way, Inspector, please," came the same voice that had crackled through the intercom when he moved into a box-sized room. A receptionist peered at him over her half-moon glasses. "Name?" she tusked. "So I can sign you in."

"Valentine, ma'am. Samson."

She raised an eyebrow and gave him the once over. "Charmed to meet you, I'm sure." She scribbled in a heavy-looking book and spoke into an intercom. "Mr Jameson, the police are here to see you."

"Send them in, please," a voice replied with swiftness.

"Please, won't you, Mr Valentine?" she said, pointing to a door behind her.

He put his thumb and forefinger to the rim of his hat and tipped it. *No point in being as rude as her,* he thought, *old goat that she is*.

Upon walking through the door he'd been directed to, Samson found he was in the middle of a busy office. People whizzed by him, whilst others spoke on their phones with such rapidity that it made his head spin.

The noise and buzz within the room was crushing.

"Where can I find Jameson?" Samson asked a young boy holding a tray filled with hot drinks and a pencil stuck behind his ear.

"Third door on your left, sir," he said without stopping.

Stuff this environment, Samson thought, seeking out the editor's office.

"Get in here," Jameson bellowed when Samson rapped on the man's door.

"P.I. Valentine, Mr Jameson," Samson confirmed, extending his hand to the fat editor, who had an even rounder cigar jabbed in his gob.

"*P.I.*? Great, so the police send me a wannabe copper when I'm up to my neck in serial killer shit. Charming. He told me he was sending his best, not some errand boy."

Samson kept his cool and smiled. "With all due respect, *sir*, I am the best there is, and I'm currently working with the police on this case."

The man's face softened. "Look, I'm sorry. It's been a stressful morning."

"I can certainly appreciate that, and I'm sure it's not every day you get such…*correspondence*."

"As a matter of fact, you'd be surprised. Sit, please," Jameson growled. "What's the name, son?"

Son?

"Valentine, friend. Samson."

"Huh. Sounds like a name you'd find in one of those hardboiled pulp novels."

"Can I see the letter?"

Jameson slid the note across the desk. "As I was saying, you'd be surprised. We've had multiple bomb threats, terror scares, perverts, weirdos, and strung-out flunkies of all kinds sending us stuff on a regular basis. And *all* have turned out to be harmless, Valentine. However, *this* is a first. Nowadays, we don't take them seriously. Still, I thought someone from the police department should see it, especially with what's happened. What do you make of it?"

Samson couldn't help but smile on the inside at how the note had been constructed from letters cut out of magazines and newspapers.

This guy is straight off the silver screen, Samson thought.

"I'd say he's watched one too many flicks of a disturbing nature."

"So you think it's genuine?"

Samson didn't respond. He was too busy reading the last of the note. "It says here that he wanted you to run it in this morning's paper. Front page. Did you?"

Jameson looked at Samson with his mouth open, and then belly-laughed. "Hell no I didn't. I can't go giving front page to every Tom, Dick and Harry loony-toon who wants to send us wind-up notes. And why on earth would you want crackpots like that to get limelight? That's what they crave."

"But you know we have a serial killer on the loose. What if this *is* genuine? The husband of the first muffin who bit the big one came to you, remember? And you were quite happy to write articles on that, weren't you, and on the other deaths that followed? I'd call that pandering to the 'crackpots', wouldn't you?"

Rage brewed in Samson's guts.

"You can't just waltz in here and start playing the big I am, damn it."

"We better hope the threat at the bottom of this letter *is* a hoax, hadn't we, sweetheart?"

"Oh, come off it. I've had over a hundred threats since I've been in charge, and I'm not giving pages to nutters."

Samson turned his back to leave, feeling he was about to do something he would regret. "Thanks for your time."

***

Before hitting the mean streets of Cardiff to shake

down a couple of XRay's known affiliates, Samson dropped back to Broadbank to give him the letter and to make a copy for himself.

"Get this to your boys at the lab. See if they can lift anything from it, but I'm guessing there are more fingerprints on it than they have at Scotland Yard," Samson said, handing over the evidence.

"The forensic boys and girls are clever bastards, mind. They could detect a fart in a hurricane."

"Thanks for the image, chief." Samson turned to leave.

"Where are you going now?"

"To catch the bad guys, of course. Why, are you heading to the doughnut shop?" Samson left the office before Broadbank had a chance to respond.

***

Samson walked into the city. His first destination was the Green Baize.

"Go see me ol' pal Big O."

Samson took a breadstick out of his coat pocket, realised he only had three left and stuffed it into his mouth as he approached the pool hall.

The noise coming from inside the joint was deafening. So, too, was the raucous laughter and chatter. Cigarette smoke billowed out from open windows and Samson caught a hint of weed.

It irritated him, and he coughed.

"Vile," he croaked, putting a hand to the door's handle and yanking on it.

A cloud encircled him as he marched down the

hallway and into the bar area. He saw Big O serving a few bikers, but nobody seemed to notice Samson. If they did, they didn't care.

When Samson took a step closer to the big pub owner, Big O looked up as though he knew he was being watched, and his mismatch-coloured eyes fell on the P.I.

"*Pig*!" he warned, slipping out the back door.

Two bikers turned on Samson, with one bringing out a knife. Samson, who was ever the quick thinker, grabbed a pint off a nearby table and swished it into the armed fella's face.

"*Ugh*!" the biker choked.

This gave Samson time to hit the blade out of the man's hand, which skittered across the spit and sawdust-covered floor.

"Step aside," he told the other. "Or I'll take you boys in for obstructing an officer of the law."

When they let him pass without a fuss, Samson hot-footed after Big O. He went through the door the barman had entered and gave chase. Above, he could hear heavy footfalls, and doors opened and slammed.

Only the guilty run, he thought, finding a set of steps. He climbed them and searched every room until he came across one with an open window that had a set of steel steps outside it.

Samson dashed onto the staircase that was attached to the side of the building and found Big O close to the bottom. He rushed down the rusted stairway, jumping most of the steps, in his hot pursuit.

Those weekly sessions at the gym sure are paying off.

He didn't break a sweat nor stride as he closed the gap on Big O.

"Give it up, scumbag. What are you so scared of?" Samson yelled, reaching a hand out but missing O's shoulder by inches.

"Get off me, man. I ain't done anything."

"You've gone and done plenty, fella."

Big O rounded a corner and almost tripped over a couple of vegetable crates that were outside a greengrocer's; he elbow-shoved people out of his way, including a small boy on a skateboard, as he made his getaway.

Samson stopped and helped the youngster out of the gutter before continuing the chase.

"*Stop*!" he demanded.

Big O sprinted across the busy road, avoiding traffic like he was involved in an unholy game of dodgeball, and made it to the other side unscathed.

Samson went after him but stayed on his side of the road until he saw a natural gap in the traffic before crossing. When he got there, he saw Big O run into Saint David's shopping centre.

"For a big man, you can shift."

Samson crashed through the shop's doors and saw Big O riding the escalator to the next floor.

"I've got you now," he grinned, stepping onto the moving floor. Unlike the people around him, Samson charged up it, yelling his apologies as he barged through and past.

"Hey, ya big oaf," a lady cried.

He got to the second floor and looked both ways and all-around him before he spotted Big O, who vanished into a strip club called Daisy Dukes.

"Great." Undeterred, Samson entered the far from classy joint.

The coloured lights in the place were dazzling, and Samson had to shield his eyes in order to see. Big O was nowhere to be found.

He came here for a reason, I know it.

Samson ambled through the establishment and couldn't locate a rear exit. He shuffled to the bar, not looking at the nude girls on stage, and asked for Big O.

"I think he just came in," the young girl serving said. Her nametag read Jade. "I'll call the office. Who shall I say is here?"

"That's okay, I'd like to surprise the potty-mouthed palooka," Samson said as he turned from Jade and walked away.

"Sir, you can't go back there unauthorised. Sir. *Sir?*"

He ignored her and continued his journey, knowing she was probably on the phone to her boss in the office to warn him and his goons of his presence.

"And please welcome to the stage the lovely Porsche, people. Come on and give this lovely Southern English girl a warm, Welsh round of applause," the compere's voice boomed over the speakers.

The place erupted in wolf-whistles, claps, hoots and howls, and some bloke propping up the bar yelled vulgarity and promises of all night sex. Samson gave him a death glare as he walked by, but said nothing. His mind was focused on more important things at hand.

Big O has come running to one of his hierarchy, he thought and jogged up the three steps that lead to a door he shouldered open. He walked through it and was greeted by more steps. He took them and came face-to-face with yet another door. This one, however, was marked with a single word: 'Manager'.

Samson raised his foot, about to kick the door apart, when it opened, revealing a sliver of darkness from beyond its depths.

"No need for such destruction, Mr Valentine. Please, won't you step into my parlour?"

Said the spider to the fly…

The door opened some more, and a pink-purple neon light spilt out, splashing across Samson's face. He stepped close, spotting a large man sat in a shadowed corner; only the outline of his body could be seen. On either side of him stood two extremely pretty women with tight bodies; they wore next to nothing, their modesty on display, but they didn't seem to mind.

Samson walked in.

"Where's O, and who are you, jug-head?"

"Always with the hero talk, huh?" The shadowed man pulled a cigar out of his mouth and blew smoke into the room. "I thought you might have had a hunch as to who I am. Nothing? *Really*?"

"Enough games, pal. Do you run this joint?"

"I run the whole show, Mr Valentine. I'm the elusive XRay."

"You—"

The door was slammed shut at Samson's back and he was coshed over the head. His world slanted and turned black.

Chapter 9

He spied the pretty little blonde-headed princess in her dress-up clothes as she played hostess at her dolly's tea party. She circled her seated Barbies and Cindies and Groovy Girls and Lalaloopsies with a fake teapot and a plastic plate filled with mock sandwiches and toy cakes that looked good enough to eat.

Sat at the head of the table was a brown teddy bear in the form of a dog; a black patch covered its right eye.

The Widower Maker couldn't help but smile as he watched on, her mouth moving, and he ached to know the dialogue of her game.

"It's going to be a real shame cutting you up, honey," he muttered, continuing to watch the child prance amongst her playthings with a silly, somewhat slanted, grin on her face. "But if the media isn't going to start taking me seriously, then I'm going to have to *make* them."

He gritted his teeth and looked at his copy of today's *Cardiff Times*—which lay by his side—and the front page told a story of scandal and mayhem within one of the major political parties.

I was good enough for the front page of your trashy rag when the bodies were discovered, but not now I've reached out with a letter. Shame on you – you've cost a small child their life.

Someone else entered the girl's room, and so he

moved the telescope to get a better look at them. It was her mother. After they'd exchanged words, her mum left with a smile on her face.

She was probably laying down the law. Lights out in ten minutes, he thought, glancing at the clock on his wall. It was approaching eight p.m.

When the girl proceeded to undress, he pulled away from the telescope and decided to check through the equipment he'd prepared for that evening's venture: rope, flashlight, lock-picking tools, holdall, a small club (which he planned to use to stun the parents), gloves, and a balaclava.

"I seem to have everything."

He got up from the stool he was sat on and moved to the other side of his large, one room flat, where he kept a table with wrist and ankle straps attached to it. He unbuckled the restraints and fastened them back up to test them; this was a check he liked to carry out at least three times a day on the day he knew he was bringing a victim home. Once he was happy, he set the table in place.

"Everything seems to be in working order." Before stepping away, however, he made sure the leather cuffs weren't frayed or worn. "I wouldn't want one of my delicate little angels slipping a hand or foot free, now would I?" he chuckled as he yanked on the restraints and grunted with the effort.

Satisfied, he moved back to the telescope and had another peep. The child was now wearing her princess pyjamas and cuddling the stuffed dog with an eye patch. Her parents were also in the room, and they took turns in giving their only child a kiss on the cheek before her dad lifted her up and carried her to bed.

The mother exited the room.

With the child tucked in, the father removed a book from the bookcase and knelt by his girl's bedside.

The Widower Maker watched until the father stepped away, turned the light off, and left the room, closing the door behind him.

"Excellent," he whispered, licking his lips. He moved into his kitchenette to prep a light meal consisting of fresh salad, a bottle of water and a slice of lemon.

As he ate, he watched the news and hoped to see some coverage regarding himself, but there was none.

A lick of anger ignited in the nucleus of his guts.

I'm being ignored. Do they hope I'll go away or do something rash, like reveal my identity, because of it? Fools. He spent a few minutes channel-hopping in the hope of finding something, anything, but nothing cropped up. *It doesn't matter. Soon the world will sit up, pay attention, and quiver in the very shadows of their own homes.*

He put the TV remote to one side, smiled, and got to his feet. After depositing his plate in the sink and his empty bottle in the bin, he went to the closet-sized washroom in the corner of the flat and started the shower.

Whilst the water gushed, he went back to the telescope and trained it on the lower windows of the house. Just like previous nights, the parents were sat in front of their television in the family room.

"Come nine-thirty, ten, they'll be wrapped up in bed. He works early mornings down at the government buildings," he uttered, "and she's just a kept, spoiled, and pampered queen."

He glanced at the clock.

Eight-thirty.

Plenty of time just yet.

He returned to the shower, the water a perfect temperature, and stepped beneath the rays after slipping into a pair of rubber gloves. Before washing, he shaved away the day's worth of stubble on his neck, face, arms and legs and pubic region and made sure his head was silky-smooth.

He hated hair, always had, and even shaved his eyebrows clean and kept his nose hairs to a minimum. Every month he booked himself into a beauty salon and got his 'Sack, back and crack' done.

Such dirty stuff.

On top of keeping his hygiene tip-top, he also made sure his body remained rock hard. Fast food and junk, like chocolate and sweets, were kept to a minimum. Alcohol was a no-no.

The fat slobs of this planet are a tragedy to us all, he thought, lathering his body with a soap product that hadn't been tested on animals; he found such research horrific and barbaric, and if he wasn't concentrating on ridding the planet of the rich, then certain scientists and 'fatties' would be on his hit-list.

He also refrained from eating too much meat, but

knew high-levels of protein were good for him.

Finished showering, he switched the water off, removed his gloves, got out and plucked a towel from off the handrail by the ridiculously small sink. He wrapped it around his neck and stepped into the main room.

It was sparse but well-maintained, and he had an agreement with the landlady that he could do whatever he wanted with the place, so long as it was returned to its original state upon him leaving residency.

When he'd first moved in, the joint had stunk.

***

"Has a plague of rats died in here?" he wanted to know.

"Look, man, don't give me shit, okay? You either want it or you don't. It's all I've got."

He turned to look at her. Cindy, who had pink hair and a fag jutting from her gob, was anorexic-thin, her cheeks sunken. She also looked doped out of her eyeballs and had track marks up her arms.

As he examined her and her shifty movements, he noticed she couldn't stop scratching and had dirt lingering underneath her fingernails.

"Two hundred a month?" he asked.

"Yeah. That's a pretty sweet deal for a room in the city, dude."

"Even a hole like this?"

The wallpaper was rotting and peeling off in parts, and the windows were grime-covered. Flies engulfed them. "I want to do my own thing."

"You mean to paint it and shit?"

"Yeah."

"So long as you put everything back the way you found it, mate." She took a couple of fast drags on her cig.

"Cindy, you actually want it kept like *this*?"

She nodded, blowing smoke.

"But I plan to strip the walls and rip the carpet up – it's waterlogged."

"That's fine, just repaper when you leave. I can live with a new carpet."

He itched; her uncleanliness burrowed beneath his skin. "Okay," he said, wanting to be rid of her. He stuffed two months' worth of rent in her hand and saw her out the door.

***

"I'll do Cindy the favour of burying her under the floorboards before I leave," he said, going to the window. He liked to dry himself before an audience.

In the heart of the city, someone *always* has their eyes on you.

As he finished towelling down, he saw the living room light in the house opposite wink out.

"My, my, what's going on – an earlier night than usual?"

He threw the towel to one side and got behind his telescope. He needed to make sure, for the sake of his plan. He watched as the husband and wife kissed and fondled each other as they made their way towards the staircase. Clothes were pulled off and scattered.

"Well, well..." he uttered, a smile stretched across his face. He adjusted the zoom as the couple tugged at each other and made their way upstairs. "You really should learn to keep your curtains drawn."

And then they disappeared out of sight, thanks to walls and arches. Undeterred, he directed his scope to their bedroom and waited for the lights to turn on.

Minutes ticked away.

His jaw tensed.

Where the—

The room at the end of his tunnel vision burst into light, and for one sickening moment, he thought they would turn down the blinds or throw the curtains closed. But they didn't. They were too engrossed in each other, their hands and mouths worked overtime.

Both parties were completely naked, and the bed was calling.

She pushed her husband onto it, and he landed with such force that he sprang back up towards her and tried for a kiss, but missed. He had a goofy grin on his face.

I'll soon wipe that away.

The wife climbed onto the bed and mounted her husband. She rocked back and forth as his hands roamed her body. He slapped her backside and raked her hair, pulling on it.

Very nice.

***

Voyeurism had become a part of his life when he was thirteen years old, which started that summer, two months after his birthday, when he'd walked into the bathroom and caught his older sister showering.

At that time he hadn't known what she'd been doing to herself beneath the cascading water, her writhing body somewhat camouflaged by the rising steam. A few months later, thanks to his biology teacher, he'd learned that Chloe, his sibling, had been masturbating.

Still, even though he'd been clueless about her activity, he'd been fascinated. He liked how her skin glistened, the way in which the water ran off her, and how she moaned, tweaked her nipples, and ran her hands through her drenched hair.

And of course, her gasps, which he'd taken for pain.

He hadn't looked directly at her, either. No. Instead, he'd watched her in the cabinet mirror, much preferring it, as though a barrier stood between them.

Stiffness had grown in his underwear, leaving him further baffled, until the lads at school had enlightened him on this topic.

"You stroke your prick until it fires white muck. I should know. I've done it," one of the boys had boasted.

He'd watched his sister until she'd finished her

show and replaced the showerhead on its hook. That night, when he lay in bed, he was kept awake by thoughts of Chloe, not that he fancied her.

Her skin radiated, he'd thought. *She looked like some kind of waterfall angel.*

***

It was from that moment on I began to appreciate the female form in all its glory, he thought, continuing to watch the lovers' rut. *And wasn't it around the same time I grew a distaste for money? No, it was a year or so after…*

He let his mind wander.

***

After spying on his sister, he found he couldn't stop, and soon it progressed to him watching his mother, and then asking for binoculars for Christmas.

"I've taken up bird watching," he lied to his parents during the build-up to the festive period. Of course, what he really wanted the glasses for was to peek on his neighbours across the street. Some of whom had teenage daughters his age.

"You'll have to wait and see. Money's always tight around this time of year, lad," his mother replied.

"Yeah, and they're thinking of making me redundant at the factory," his father had chirped in. "Christmas might be cancelled this year."

Money. There's always *cash flow issues,* he

thought.

"Sorry, mate. I can't send you on that school trip because we can't afford it," or, "Sorry lad. I can't buy you those shoes, games, and/or toys you want because we're broke."

And for this reason alone, he was constantly picked on in school. The other boys would laugh at him for wearing dated clothes that were either hand-me-downs or gear bought from charity shops.

"Where did your moth-eaten trousers come from this week, pauper boy?" the one boy, Christopher Pelt, would ask him *every* week.

"You smell funny," the girls would tell him.

"Do your parents go stripping the dead in their graves because they can't afford to dress you?" others would ask.

"God, how old are those Nikes?" someone else wanted to know.

It went on for years, and if they couldn't hurt him with words, they would beat him during and after school. His life was made a living hell.

Not that his parents cared.

They don't love me.

However, it was different for Chloe.

Chloe, being older, had already gone through her minimal troubles at school.

"Mum and Dad used to lavish me," she would tell him when they argued. And, right around the time he was having his woes, she was working at building a better life for herself. "I'm going to university to get a degree. I want to be a lawyer, and to blow this town," she'd told him, adding salt to his wounds.

Still, there had been hope for him because he was good at his schoolwork.

"You have a decent brain, young man. Try using it," his headmaster had told him.

I could have become something.

But it wasn't to be, and he blamed it on the bullying.

It distracted me.

"I'm constantly in fear, sir," he'd pleaded with the headmaster.

"Rubbish. And I'll have no tittle-tattle, boy. Do you hear me? You'll try better, understand?"

"Yes, sir."

But it didn't matter, and soon his indiscipline led to him receiving the cane across his backside and palms. Letters were sent home, which angered his father, and the man's belt would come off after too much booze.

"I do it for your own good, son. Do you want to be a worthless *nothing*, huh?" he would yell.

Like you, he wanted to shout back.

His mother would stand by every time, idly watching, with her hands buried in her pinny apron.

Chloe, true to her word, left home after securing a placement at the University of Newport. Her dreams were coming true, which ate away at his very essence, and he would have fantasies about her leaving Wales and never coming back. It perturbed him.

Ah yes, the good old days, he thought, pulling out of his thoughts as the husband and wife seemed to climax together, with her collapsing on top of him. They lay there, motionless, in a lover's embrace.

He watched on, fascinated, thinking they, too, must like being watched for they'd kept their lights on and curtains open.

They were in a rush, mind...

There was movement in the room once again.

The wife got up and walked through an open door. When she returned, the husband unmoving, she turned the lights off, killing his view.

Time to go to work.

He stepped away from the telescope, grabbed his bag of tricks, and went to the TV. As he was about to turn the set off, the chief of police came onscreen for an unofficial interview outside the police station.

"Chief, chief?!" a reporter was heard calling, and a mic was stuffed in the copper's face. "Can you tell us anything new about The Widower Maker case, sir? Chief, chief! *Please*?"

Other reporters joined in, and it wasn't long before Broadbank was jostling with the small group of paparazzi. Cameras and mics were pushed from his face as he tried to charge by them, but they were having none of it.

"Can't you give us *something*? What are the police doing to bring this psychopath to justice?" a female journalist asked.

"Are there *any* leads?" another reporter pressed.

"Can you get that thing out of my face?" Broadbank snapped, lashing out with an open hand. "We're trying to keep panic to a minimum—"

"Do you think withholding information from the

public is a great way of doing that, *chief*?" the first man asked.

Broadbank stopped, looking like a defeated man, and answered. "All I can say is that we are working round the clock to bring the individual responsible for the heinous crimes to justice."

"Is it true that the husbands have been arrested, that they themselves were involved in criminal activity?" the female asked.

"Are the killings gang related?" a new voice asked. "And is it true that Samson Valentine has been brought in to assist the police on this case?"

"Where are you people getting your information?" Broadbank looked ready to thump someone.

The Widower Maker laughed and turned the sound up.

So, the superhero P.I. is now involved? How interesting, considering I'd planned on killing him. His smile widened, and his mind worked overtime. *I could let Samson in on the next letter I send out…*

A harsh laugh burst from him, filling the room with hate.

"Just answer the question, chief. Please."

"Yes, it's true. Mr Valentine has been aiding us with this investigation. Now, please. No more questions. I'll be holding a statement tomorrow morning, nine o'clock. You'll be free to interrogate me then." Broadbank stepped into an awaiting police car, which took off before he could close his door.

But of course, the chief wouldn't reveal anything

he didn't want the papers or public knowing. The Widower Maker knew that, so, too, did the press.

Just a way of stalling them, he thought, turning the TV off. *Still, it's fun to know Valentine is involved.*

Before opening his front door, he slipped his black coat on and zipped it up to his throat. He then wrapped a scarf around his face and left.

***

The night air was biting.

He stood on the pavement opposite the family home and watched the windows. All around him, people slipped by, some of whom nudged him with an elbow. But he didn't budge, his eyes were unblinking.

They're in there, sleeping, and unknowing a predator watches over them and lurks in their slumbering shadows.

He could almost see the surprise in their eyes and it delighted him.

Not wasting another moment, he crossed the road. When he got to the other side, he made sure nobody was watching him as he slipped around to the back of the house via an alleyway. He then gained access to the home's garden by scaling the wooden fence that enclosed it.

After dropping to the soft, dew-covered grass below, he rolled along the floor and bounced to his feet. As he crept in the darkness towards the back door, his tools jangled. He slipped his backpack off and removed his lock-picking kit.

With that in hand, he set to work and unlocked the entrance within a couple of minutes. When he walked inside, he found himself standing in the kitchen. Total darkness engulfed him.

His heart hammered, his rushing blood roaring in his ears.

Such a feeling, he thought, quivering.

When his breathing came in jagged rips, he had to remain still and take deep gulps of air.

Relax.

He closed the door, removed his flashlight, and powered it on. The glow guided him through the living room and to a set of stairs that would lead him to his prize.

Before proceeding to climb, he removed his cosh. He had thought about killing the parents, but knew he'd get a bigger kick out of their suffering and pleading on nightly news channels.

The Widower Maker ascended, slowly, fearing a board would creak, but none did. Soon enough, he was at the top of the stairs and looking at the four doors around him.

The one farthest from him had coloured blocks stuck to it, which spelt out the name "Katie".

The daughter's room, he thought, shining his light on the door next to hers. The word 'Bathroom' was etched on it. *That eliminates that one.*

He turned and looked at the remaining doors, and decided to try the closest one first. When he put his hand to the handle to depress it, his heartrate kicked up several notches and sweat broke across his brow.

He pressed the handle down and pushed the door inwards. When there was enough of a gap, he put his head around it and peered inside. Thanks to the moon glow coming through the window, he saw a single bed—empty and made—a wardrobe, chest of drawers, and a small wicker chair that sat in the corner.

Pish-posh – a spare room.

He turned, walked away, and readied his cosh as he opened the remaining door, which squeaked, but not loud enough to wake the snoring occupants.

The first thing he noticed was that the curtains had been drawn.

A moment of panic trickled through him, followed by questions.

Was one of them awake?

Did this happen recently?

If so, it could mean the person who did it is lying there awake.

No, they would have seen my flashlight by now. Plus, there are two sets of snores, he reassured himself, listening.

He killed his light after locating their bed.

As he crossed from the door to where they slumbered, a board beneath his foot groaned, stopping him dead.

One of the sleepers grunted, snorted, and turned over. When they resumed snoring, he continued to creep in their direction and wasted no time at their bedside. He turned on a lamp and startled the lovers.

The husband sat bolt upright, and The Widower Maker smashed him across his forehead with his club, splitting skin, and he collapsed back onto the mattress.

"Joe?" the wife managed, more shocked than startled, and had enough time to look up at the large man standing over her. "Jesus," she gasped before the club turned her lights off.

A light spray of her blood shot up the wall behind the bed, and a tooth pinged off the bedside lamp. When she crumpled, she fell against her husband, their heads clashing.

This provoked a snort of laughter from him.

After making sure they were out cold, he checked them for a pulse, happy to find they were still alive. He then gagged and tied them. Once they were secure, he cut the wires to the bedroom phone, shut the light off, exited the room, and closed the door behind him.

Excellent.

As he proceeded towards Katie's room, he pulled a folded holdall bag out of his rucksack in readiness, and then kicked her door open. The sound of splintering wood wasn't as satisfying as hearing the eight-year-old girl scream in the darkness.

"Mammy and Daddy are gone, little bitch," he whispered.

Her wailing turned to violent sobs after he turned the light on and went to her. She tried to get off her bed, but he pinned her to the mattress by her throat.

"I don't think so," he screamed in her face, slapping her. The force was enough to render her unconscious.

He got off the bed, straightened, looked down at her, and stroked her blonde hair to one side, revealing her face. He smiled.

A fallen angel.

With the holdall unzipped, he fluffed it and placed it on the floor by the side of her bed. He looked at her and then at the bag.

Can't see there being a problem.

He rolled Katie off the bed and shoved her into the roomy camouflaged holdall.

The smile returned to his face.

She's not going to have much air, so I better make this quick. I don't want her dying on me.

He hauled the bag off the floor with minimum effort and placed the straps over his shoulder.

When he left the house via the back door, he shot down the alley and crossed the road back to his apartment with stealth. Back in his flat, all safe and sound, he unzipped the bag, removed Katie and placed her on his 'operating table'. After the ankle and wrist straps had been secured and he'd gagged her, he relaxed.

Katie was still unconscious.

He stepped back, stared at her, and thought it wouldn't be long before the muffled pleading would start.

This, to him—the snatching of an individual and the hurt of others—was *almost* sexual, even though no erection, penetration, or orgasm was required.

Chapter 10

Ice-cold water was thrown in his face, bringing Samson around with a start.

"W-*what*?!" Samson bellowed, spitting water. A lump the size of a small egg had developed above the base of his neck. He felt his eyes rolling. "Who…" His throat was desert-dry. "Wa-water," he gasped.

A glass was tipped to his mouth, his hands tied.

Samson drank greedily, draining the tumbler within seconds.

When he tried to hold his head up, it flopped backwards on its fat plinth, his eyes staring at the ceiling. "It needs painting," he coughed, wincing. "You have damp patches showing through."

"I was told you're a funny man, Mr Valentine, and I'm glad I'm going to experience it firsthand."

"You know something, if you're truly XRay, you don't sound particularly menacing. More like a love-sick hound, I'd say. You have that whole screechy, whiny thing going on, palooka. Anyone ever tell you that?" Samson raised his head. He was smiling and squinting into the darkness, trying to catch a glimpse of XRay's face.

It's no good. I can't make him out.

The women still stood beside XRay, only now there were two men at his back, and when Samson checked either side of him, he noticed thugs flanked him.

"Hatchet-men to the left of me, bozos to the right."

Smoke was blown in Samson's direction.

"Are you ready to be serious, Mr Valentine?"

"Could you not do that, please?" he asked, still smiling. "I'm trying my hardest to stay off the smokes, see, and since I don't have access to my breadsticks, you're making it difficult. Not to mention unpleasant, meathead."

Samson was smacked across the back of his head by the gorilla to his left. "Mind your manners, fuck."

"Did you sue them?" the astute P.I. asked the hired hand.

"Huh?" he grunted, putting his face close to Samson's.

"Nice gold teeth, son. The charm school, lad. Did you sue them?"

The over-sized ape growled, bared his teeth, and raised his fist. "The fuck you say?"

Samson turned from the man, unthreatened by him and his tattooed knuckles and neckline.

"What are you waiting for, dear? Hit me if you're going to."

"*Enough*!" the man from the shadows bellowed, blowing more smoke in Samson's direction.

The men behind XRay stepped from the darkness, allowing Samson to get a good look at them.

"Well, well – if it isn't Stan Laurel and Oliver Hardy. How are you, fellas? Didn't like prison food, eh?" he asked Big O and Ziggy, who looked at each other before turning back to Samson. "It amazes me how far a stack of bills will get you these days. You must have paid a pretty penny to get these goons released from the big house, X."

"My associates are of no concern to you, Mr Valentine."

"Samson, please. Let's be informal here."

"You've caused me a lot of pain and grief, Samson, in the past and of recent times. But I'm willing to set our differences aside. For now, at least."

"Well, that's sweet of you, muffin." The bruisers on either side of him shifted uneasily, and Samson expected another rap across the back of the skull, but it never came. "Care to enlighten me?"

Silence fell, but the void was filled by the music coming from the club beyond the office door. A low thud-thud engulfed Samson, making his head throb from the thump he'd received earlier. And then the compere's voice boomed, loud, yet muffled. This was followed by a hearty round of applause, wolf-whistles, and people shouting.

"Well?" Samson pressed. "I haven't got all day to waste tied to this chair, son. I have a case to crack, along with you to arrest, unless you plan on putting me six feet under?"

XRay took a drag on his cigar. "Arrest me? Whatever for, my dear sweet Valentine?"

"Don't get wise with me, bozo. I know you killed Roxie, and that you've been trying to wipe me from the face of the Earth. Don't you remember our phone call the other night, or have you taken a whack to the noggin, too, palooka?" Samson bluffed, hoping for information by throwing a couple of wilds cards at XRay.

"You've lost me," XRay said.

"All those threats you made, telling me to get out of the south and then sending a chopper squad to my flat to riddle it, and me, with bullet holes; the Tommy guns were a nice touch, by the way."

"I've done no such thing."

"Don't get smart, mister. What about the fella you had try and throttle me, hmm? You got amnesia?"

XRay laughed, his thugs and girls did, too.

"Yeah, laugh it up, wise guys, because it won't be so funny when you're picking razor blades out of your porridge." The laughter ceased immediately. "I thought that would get your attention."

"Mr Valentine, I'm not sure what you're talking about, but I can assure you I have *not* made an attempt on your life. If I had, you'd be deader than shit right now. Then again, it's not to say I didn't consider it, but a mutual friend put a stop to it."

"Mutual friend?" Samson squinted and squirmed in his chair to try and get comfortable. "What in the hell are you gnashing your teeth about?" He could feel his patience waning. "You've killed another one of my friends, clown, and I will get justice once and for all."

"Roxie?"

"Who else?" Samson's teeth ground together, and he tried to sit up. Large hands clamped down on both of his shoulders, forcing him back into his seat.

"Get off me," he told the bodyguards. "Or I'll have you for assaulting a police officer, as well as other charges."

"Samson," XRay said. "Why would I hurt Roxie? I loved her, Charlie, too."

"Don't give me that. You ruled them through fear, just like the rest of your goons."

There was a knock at the door and one of the men guarding Samson opened it.

"Would Mr XRay like any drinks?" Samson heard a woman ask.

"I wouldn't mind a Virgin Mary, doll," he called.

"No, thanks," the thug said, and the door closed.

"Our mutual friend, the person I truly suspect of harming Roxie, is The Widower Maker, Samson."

"Ha! That's rich. So now you're trying to blame your murderous ways on a serial killer? How do I know he doesn't work for you? Maybe you *are* him?"

"Don't be so foolish, Samson. Do you really think I'd lead you here, to one of my most private headquarters, if I was the person responsible for the murders? I'm as much in the dark as you and the police department are."

Samson shook his head. "I'm not buying it. You're trying to divert me with your games. But I'm on to you, and you know it, and when I get out of here, I'll have this place teeming with the good ol' boys."

"What if I told you I know who's been trying to warn you off, Samson? I could easily give you the name of the person who wants you out of the south."

"More games?" Samson laughed, excited on the inside.

Here comes the info. I've got him hooked, Samson thought.

"No."

"Then why would you want to do that?"

"Because that person *might* be trying to play us against each other, Samson, if what you're saying is true."

Trying to kid a kidder? I don't think so, he thought.

"It's not my ma, is it?" Samson asked.

One of the goons by Samson's side stifled a laugh.

XRay scoffed, blew smoke into the air above him, and shifted in his seat. "You're a testing man, Samson. I'd hate to have you hurt."

"Is it 'cause I ain't falling for your BS?"

"Your bullheadedness is a headache giver, sir."

"*Sir*? Wow, I'm honoured. Just for the fun of it, who is this mysterious person trying to rub me out?"

"A man by the name of Lovell, James Lovell."

"Never heard of *her*," he lied.

XRay dismissed the slur. "No, but you've heard of his brother. He went by the name of Alligator."

The mere mention of the cardboard cut-out mobster's name brought it all back to Samson in chilling surround sound, with clear-cut visuals, much like when Broadbank had mentioned the moniker. He heard the prehistoric reptile writhing in the mud, the snap of its mighty jaws and the disconcerting crunch, pop and rupture of Mr Barnes' bones.

Samson could almost smell the accountant's blood and fear, mixed in with a heady stench that burst from the gator's pen: a muddy, earthy reek combined with excrement.

It thrashed its tail as it rolled, crushed, and devoured.

It had taken Samson many nights to revoke those thoughts from his mind, thinking he'd never be able to banish Barnes' blood-chilling screams from his brain.

Above all else, the terror in Roxie's eyes had disturbed him the most.

The memories iced his bones, but he couldn't allow XRay to see this, and so he let his coolness do the talking.

"That fool got what he deserved. It's just a shame I couldn't put him behind bars to rot like you will, X."

"Let's try and stay on track, shall we?"

"You—"

"Lovell wants you gone, Samson. And if you *won't* go, then he'll kill you."

"Suppose you're flapping truth, why would you tell me this?"

"Because of The Widower Maker."

"What about him? I still think he's connected to you."

"He's not, and I want your help in capturing him."

Samson's mouth opened, and then he laughed the hardest he'd done in years. "You're asking *me* for *help*? You really have hit your head, haven't—"

"*Silence*!" XRay leaned forward in his chair, careful that his face never entered the light.

"Your absurdity has my interests up, son, I'll give you that."

"This killer, this Widower Maker – he's not only murdered my wife and the wives of high-powered friends of mine within *my* community, who I understand are now under arrest, but also damaged my business, Samson, and that will never do. It's bad enough the police are up to it, let alone those who sit on my side of the fence."

"Murder is bad for business? That's rich."

"As I'm sure you're aware by now, because Charlie would have blabbed, Roxie was working my strip clubs."

"Wow, hang on. What makes you think I've *seen* Charlie?"

"Come, Samson. How stupid do you think I am? It wasn't hard to have her followed, and we've been keeping tabs on her ever since; on both of you, in fact."

"I see."

"Now do you trust I'm not out to harm you? I could have had you both killed the night she turned up on your doorstep."

Samson moved his weight in his seat, his backside drifting off to sleep. "Let's say I do believe you, what of it? I can't side with gangsters, pushers, and the like. I'm Johnny Law."

"I'm not asking you to side with me, Samson. I just want a favour. And, if you're willing to do this one thing for me, I will return the gesture."

"Lay it all out for me."

"Let's go back to Mr Lovell. He wants you dead or gone, I can stop that, but *only* if you bring me The Widower Maker, Samson."

"That sounds more like a threat: do as I say or I'll have you removed. How am I doing?"

"I'm not going to sit here and pretend that some harm may, or may not come to you, but I will call him off *if* you bring me what I want. I'll even forget about you once this is all over. I'll cancel the plans I had in store for you *and* Charlie."

"And if I refuse?"

XRay took a fat drag on his cigar and blew the smoke in Samson's face. "I'll allow you to walk out of here but the mark I have on you will remain, so too will Lovell's, and I'll kill the girl, Charlie, and mail pieces of her to you from time to time."

"Good luck in finding her, pal."

"I'll also send you chunks of Alice and her parents. She seems like a sweet girl. Have you seen her in her jogging trousers? She has an arse that won't quit. Maybe I'll use her as my sex toy for a few months, before ending her."

Bile hit the back of Samson's throat and his stomach knotted. "If I wasn't tied to this chair I'd make an example out of you in front of your pretty little bunnies and bozos."

"Well, I would certainly like to see you try. So,

do we have a deal?"

"How do I know you're not lying about Lovell?"

"Good questions, P.I.," he said, stopping and beckoning one of his girls closer. "Would you bring me a scotch on the rocks, dear? Samson, would you like that Virgin Mary of yours?"

He wanted nothing more than to chew XRay's face off. "I guess so."

"Good."

"Huh, you remind me of a certain Bond villain, minus the cat," Samson said.

"Is it my ruthlessness? You know, my organisation doesn't have a name like Darkwater Syndicate or Spectre, Samson." XRay's thugs laughed. "And you won't find a Jaws or Oddjob floating around the place."

"It was more to do with your hosting skills."

"Because of a drink?"

"Next thing I know, you'll be wining and dining me, and outfitting me in a splendid white suit in your underground base before trying to kill me," Samson laughed, although he was half serious.

"What a vivid, active, and wonderful imagination you have, Samson."

The young lady dressed in bunny ears and not much else strutted towards the drinks cabinet and prepped two tumblers.

Ice clanked and then crackled as fire water drowned it.

"Reverting back to your question," he said, "Lovell and I set our differences aside months ago.

We're reasonable men, and we knew there's enough room for him to run the west and for me to get on with things here in the south. I apologised for his brother's death by sending him a large sum of money, guns, and other treasures to make amends."

"Could I get that in writing?" Samson quipped.

"Ha, yes, quite, Samson."

"So you're happy for Lovell to *think* you're in bed together? I guess there's no honour among thieves like I've been led to believe."

"He can trust me. I haven't told you anything you wouldn't have eventually figured out for yourself, and I won't hurt him or betray him in any way to get you to do as I wish. If you refuse, you know what will happen."

"So you're going to tell him off like a naughty boy? Stay away from Samson or I'll smack your botty. Something like that, yes? Who says he'll listen to you?"

"He will, unless he *wants* a war."

"This is all getting rather confusing and silly," Samson muttered. "I can't believe I'm up to my eyeballs in false gangsters once again."

"Your drink, Mr Valentine," the pretty young dancer said, holding his Virgin Mary.

"I'm a wee bit—"

"Release one of his hands, Jackson," XRay ordered one of his goons.

Samson was free to sip his drink. "Delicious," he admitted. "I can't seem to get the mix quite right myself. Do you mind?" he asked, putting his drink down and going for his coat pocket.

"Not at all," XRay said.

Samson pulled a breadstick out and gnawed on it. "They help with the cravings, see."

XRay remained silent for a moment. "You said."

"You know he's been using your name in his little scare tactics against me, right?" he lied.

Maybe I can get goon to turn against goon, he thought. *Worth a shot.*

"So you've suggested, Samson." There was humour in XRay's tone.

He knows I've been lying. Still, let's see where this goes. "I would have thought you'd want him dealt with. Isn't he belittling you? Lovell is making it look as though he's the big shot – the man who can do as he pleases."

"Come, come, Samson. Why would I go to war over such trivial matters? Do you honestly think I'd care about him telling you it was me sending hitters to your door?"

"It could land you in hot water because I've already informed Broadbank that it's *you* who wants me dead."

XRay tusked. "I'm not falling for it, Samson. Besides, this is another reason why we are having this chat. I wanted to clear my name, as it were. And, if I do find out Lovell *is* up to no good, or irritates me enough, then he will go the way of his brother. You can count on that."

"I guess this whole Widower Maker situation has you all up in the air at the moment."

"Precisely," he said, taking his drink from the bunny girl. "So, we have a deal?"

Samson finished his drink. "I suppose so. And what will you do to The Widower Maker once you have him?"

"That's no concern of yours. All you need to worry about is getting him, or her, to me and keeping yourself and Charlie alive. I shall be watching, Samson. At *all* times."

"And you're going to let me walk out of here on my own two feet? No fisticuffs or a good licking to send me on my way?"

"No. Now, be off. You have a criminal to catch. Jackson, release him."

Samson rotated his aching wrists, stood, and straightened his hat.

I could lunge at him and find out who he is. Yeah, and get a hot piece of lead inserted between my eyes. He'll keep, for now. For the time being, I have bigger fish to fry.

He walked towards the door and thanked XRay for the drink. "You boys stay out of trouble now, you hear?"

"Samson, remember. Bring The Widower Maker to me, or kiss your life goodbye. Alice's and Charlie's, too, *friend.*"

"I heard you loud and clear the first time, palooka."

"And stay away from my men and my establishments. You have no business with me, lawman."

Samson opened the door and walked through it. "Just make sure you keep your end of the bargain up when this thing's through, X." He slammed the door closed and stalked through the strip club towards the exit.

***

When Samson was outside the shopping centre, ambling nowhere in particular, he couldn't help but mentally thank XRay for all the little bits of information he'd let slip.

Does XRay really think I'm a prize fool? That I'll saddle up with him and take a lawbreaker into his arms so he can do as he pleases? What a diabolical man.

When he realised he was wandering aimlessly, he decided to head for Alice's to check on the girls before heading to Steve's. The Jazz Hole had always been a place where he could think; to map out his next moves and regroup.

I need time to mull and to take a breather.

When Alice's café came into view, he felt relieved. Not only was it a safe haven offering a hot cuppa and a slice of warm pie, but somewhere where friendly, allied faces lay in wait.

Something I need right about now. What about Broadbank? He's out of the question. If I see him at this moment, I might let something slip, and I can't tell him anything until I have this whole thing under my control.

He put his hand to the door handle and a sudden, sinking feeling devoured him. *What if the girls have already come to harm? There's no way of trusting a man who dumps bodies for a living.*

As he entered, a bell chimed above the door. There were no customers, and nobody manned the till.

Samson's guts dropped a level.

Somewhere close by, a kettle was coming to a boil, and it clicked off.

About to call out, he stopped himself.

What if there are hatchet-men here? He shook his head. *I'm being unreasonable.*

"*Sam*!" a female voice boomed, derailing his thoughts and pulling him out of the black world he'd slipped into. Colour poured into his vision as Alice appeared before him, smiling. "Am I glad to see you, palooka. Talk about a *slooooow* day."

He hugged her fiercely. "And am I glad to see you, too. Where's Charlie?" Samson was desperate to know she was still among the living.

"She's out back. You okay? Looks like you've seen a Casper."

"Something like that, muffin, aye."

When Charlie appeared at the kitchen's entrance, stepping into Samson's peripheral field of vision, he looked up and smiled at her.

"She's a good little waitress," Alice said.

Thank God she's okay. I need to get some eyes on this joint because I won't be able to watch them twenty-four seven.

He made a mental note to call Broadbank as he hugged Charlie.

I'll have to let Broadbank in on so much, he thought, *because I'm going to have to head west and sort out Lovell soon.*

Samson looked at the girls, sighed, and hoped his idea would pan out okay.

I don't want to see anyone else get hurt.

Chapter 11

He was in the kitchen frying up bacon and eggs when there was a loud knock at his door. When he'd returned home from visiting Charlie and Alice yesterday afternoon, with a brief encounter with Steve at the Hole, Samson had spent time cleaning his flat.

Must have taken me close to two hours to pick up every particle of glass, he thought.

Samson gave the wooden spoon he was using a couple of hard knocks against the rim of the frying pan, dislodging egg, before setting it aside.

His door was hammered harder, louder.

"Okay, okay, hold your horses." Samson moved from the kitchen into the living room, making sure his dressing gown was tied tight.

Who the heck could it be at this hour? he thought, noting it was a shade after eight a.m. *Hatchet-men? Give it a rest.*

Samson put his eye to the peephole and asked who it was.

"WindowMate, mate. You called us?"

Christ, I'd forgotten about that.

Before opening the door, however, Samson eyeballed the man's work fatigues, spotting his company's name stencilled on his chest.

He unclasped the chain and flipped the deadbolt.

"Hey," the man said, sticking his hand out. Samson shook it. "Name's Martin, you have a broken window?"

Samson nodded and held the door open, his eyes never leaving the much smaller man. "Several, actually, Martin. I did mean to call your company back and inform them the other day, but I forgot. Will it be possible to have them all fixed today?"

"Shouldn't be a problem—what on *earth* happened here?"

"A home warming party went awry, friend. I have to go out soon. Will you be okay to lock up when you leave?"

"Er, yeah. Not a problem. I'll need you to sign—"

"I'll do it before I leave, Martin. Now, can a man finish his breakfast in peace? Would you like a mug of coffee?"

"Please."

Samson was about to close the door to his flat when a hand stopped it. He curled his fist, ready to turn and swing some sweet chin music when the person spoke.

"Builders, matey – are you the homeowner?"

Samson eyed the man. *Got a regular crowd going this morning.*

"Name?" It had *BuildTech* written on the guy's worktop.

"Brad. Come to fix the walls. We spoke—"

"Yeah. Coffee?"

"Please."

Samson went through to the kitchen and fixed the workers their refreshments.

From top dog P.I., to head pancake tosser and

tea's maid. Maybe Alice can get me a couple of shifts down at the café. He smiled as he stirred the drinks.

"Get 'em whilst they're hot, fellas," he said, taking the coffees into the living room and placing them on the table. Thankfully, he'd moved all the images of the dead women and case notes.

I could have ended up looking like a right crazy, having to explain away such seedy pictures.

***

It wasn't long before the banging, hammering, and drilling started, which was Samson's cue to vamoose. He dumped the scrambled egg and bacon onto a bun dripping with butter, squashed it all together, and set it aside. Before he could leave the kitchen, Bogart entered with his tail between his legs, a sad look in his eyes.

"I know, boy, but this will all be over and done with today, and I'll make sure you're closed in here with plenty of food and water."

After filling the dog's bowls and picking up his breakfast roll, Samson left the kitchen and closed the door behind him.

"You chaps mind staying out of the kitchen? My pooch ain't too hot on the noise you're making, and he's not keen on strangers."

"Nah, it's fine, mate," the glazier said, throwing plastic sheets down.

"No probs," the builder replied, placing a pencil behind his ear.

Samson nodded, took a bite out of his roll and thought, *I'll pay at the gym later today for this sorry mess*. He stuffed more of the butty into his mouth and departed his flat, leaving the door ajar for the workmen should they need to come and go.

Opposite him, Samson saw two large, well-dressed men standing outside Lisa's door. One of them was wearing a trilby, and hammering his meaty, hairy fist on the wood.

"Open up. We know you're in there," he demanded. "Don't make us kick the door in, because we will if we have to."

Samson adjusted his coat and hat after devouring the last of his meal, licked his chops and rubbed his hands together; his eyes on the bozos opposite him.

They look like hatchet-men. His heart started racing. *Am I really seeing them? Come on, you've not suffered any setbacks or delusions in months*.

Sweat dribbled down the side of his face.

"Lisa!" the other man bellowed, kicking her door.

"Go away!"

Samson heard the terrified woman's plea from inside her flat.

A flicker of anger ignited in his guts, and he ground his teeth together. "You palookas lost?"

The door-kicker turned, revealing his squashed nose and the bandage that lay across its bridge. His left eye was blackened. "Help you?" he asked Samson.

His mate continued to knock on Lisa's door and threaten her, the woman becoming hysterical.

"What's your beef with the lady?" Samson asked. "She's a dear friend of mine."

"Push off, or I'll push your face in," the man warned.

He must be the muscle, Samson thought. And, judging by their looks and attitude, especially the one talking to him, Samson figured them to be debt collectors of an unorthodox nature. *It must have been the husband hounding her on the blower the other night.*

"Hey, are you listening to me?" Broken Nose asked, his tone becoming threatening. He took a few steps closer to Samson, who didn't flinch.

"I can hear you just fine, mush for brains, but you can't seem to hear me. I asked you what your beef is with my friend?"

The other goon stopped knocking. He was smaller than the brawn, but looked twice as mean.

"Who in the fuck is this guy?" Knocker asked.

"Some nosy neighbour looking for a beat down," Broken Nose answered.

"Do yourself a favour, and get gone, pal." Knocker turned back to the door and started pounding it again. "Come on, Lisa – make this easy on yourself. He just wants to know what's going on."

"You can tell him from me that he can go to hell. That pig isn't getting anything. And if you don't get out of here this instant, I'm calling the police."

"I wouldn't do that if I were you," Knocker threatened.

Samson stepped forward, but he was shoved

backwards and into the wall.

"This is what heroes get," Broken Nose smiled, coming at Samson with a right hook.

Samson blocked the man's arm in mid-air and rammed his free hand into the guy's windpipe. Broken Nose crumpled to the floor, spluttering and choking, as he tried to catch his breath.

"You son of a—" Knocker turned, swinging.

Samson brought his knee up, driving it into the guy's nuts.

"*Ooph*!" Air blasted out of his mouth, and when he tried grabbing onto Samson's coat for support, the P.I. stepped out of his way and let the goon crash to the floor.

"I suggest you clowns beat it, and if I see either of you here again, I'll bust you in a heartbeat."

Samson turned to Lisa's door and tapped on it lightly. "It's Val. Let me in, muffin."

"Have they gone?" she asked.

Samson turned and watched as Broken Nose picked himself up off the floor and helped Knocker to his feet, who was still clutching his undercarriage.

"You're going to pay for this."

"Threatening a lawman?" Samson asked.

The beaten men glared at him, stayed silent, turned and hobbled away.

"They're gone," Samson confirmed.

His response was greeted by the rattle of her security chain and the click of a deadbolt. The door was opened a crack, and Lisa's face appeared around its edge. Her eyes were wide and searching.

"Are you sure?"

"Yes, ma'am – saw them off myself."

She huffed, placed her head against the side of the door and laughed. "My hero."

"Mind telling me what's going on, Lisa? I can't help you if you don't let me in."

She stepped back and opened the door.

He chuckled. "I meant into your *life*."

Lisa huffed out another laugh and invited him in. "I know."

When she closed the door she asked, "Coffee?"

"No, I can't stay long. Work calls."

"Okay, I'll keep it brief. It's my husband. He wants money and the jewellery back he gave me as gifts over the course of our marriage."

"Gifts are gifts. There's not much he can do about that. What money?"

"It's basically a threat. Pay me to stay out of your life."

"I don't like the sounds of that. How did he find you?"

"No idea."

"If you want my help, all you have to do is ask. I can set things right for you, Lisa. I hate seeing good people getting pushed around. Was it him on the phone the other night?"

"The evening you were here?" He nodded. "How did you know?"

"I heard you, sorry. I shouldn't have been listening, but it's hard for a bloke in my profession not to stick his beak in where it doesn't belong."

Lisa put a hand to his coated forearm. "Really,

it's fine." With her free hand, she raked her hair. "How much do you charge?"

"For you? Gratis. There's nothing worse than men shoving women around."

"No, you must let me pay you—"

"I'll have none of it. Do you have a contact number for your husband?"

"Yes." Lisa walked over to a sideboard and removed a pad and pen from its drawer. She then proceeded to jot down her ex-lover's contact details, followed by his name (Derek). "I've put his office number down, too, just in case you can't reach him at home."

Samson took the shred of note paper and placed it in his breast pocket. "I'll get on it later today, Lisa, and try not to worry about anything. If it comes down to it, I'll go and see him."

"God, what a relief. That's a huge weight lifted off me, Val. Thanks."

"I haven't done anything yet, muffin."

"Just knowing you're willing to help and listen is enough for now." Her hand rubbed his arm, and she smiled.

He smiled back, tipped his hat, and turned to leave. "I'll update you this evening when I return home." He was then out the door and gone.

***

When he got outside the building, Samson stopped, took in the air and wondered what to do next. He had no real plan of attack, except for heading west, now that XRay had warned him away from his businesses and associates.

He was my big lead in The Widower Maker case. If he's out of the picture, then where in the hell do I start? He lifted his fedora, scratched his head and replaced his hat. *Just because X gave me that spiel, doesn't mean he's an innocent man. So, let's get back to knocking on known associates' doors for now; I can head west in a day or two.*

However, two things stopped him: the safety of Alice and Charlie. Samson knew XRay would have eyes on him constantly.

It wouldn't take him long to find out what I was up to and I don't think Broadbank's men could offer up much protection. The wanker has me where he wants me, unless I bring in an impostor? A stooge. Bet X wouldn't think of me doing that, and it would give me the opportunity to move freely, do what I want, and check out Lovell.

"Seems like a solid plan. Set-up a fake Samson Valentine and then blow town," he said, nodding. "I'm not going to let a well-organised goon in a monkey suit intimidate me."

With his mind made up, Samson decided to head down to the station to speak with Broadbank and to find out if there were any updates regarding The Widower Maker.

Things have been rather quiet on that front.

Samson had zero experience when it came to serial killers, but thanks to books and TV shows, he knew a lot about their habits and such.

He may not strike again for a year or so. Hell,

the hop-head may never kill again, and keep us guessing his identity for decades to come.

The P.I. had heard of some killers never being caught, such as the infamous Bible John, who killed three women from 1968-69 in Glasgow, Scotland.

The thought that John could still be out there gave Samson the creeps. He shivered, even though the day was warm.

He put the musings to the back of his mind and walked to his car.

When he got behind the wheel, a new thought hit him.

Maybe I could talk to that punk I took in the other day, the one involved with the illegal porn? The Brain. Yeah. He might be able to shed some light on known affiliates.

Samson was finding it hard to let go of the idea that XRay was somehow behind the killer/killings, and if he was, Samson was sure as hell going to bring the man to justice.

"I'll nail ya yet, Ray. You just wait and see," he muttered, putting his car into first gear and pulling away from the kerb.

***

"But why, Sam? I just don't see the point in it," Broadbank said.

"Listen to what I'm saying, fella, will ya? I ain't flapping my trap for no good health reason."

"Okay, okay."

Samson nodded. "Just give me twenty minutes

with him, yeah? Let me put some weight on him. In here, nobody can peep on me, unless X has eyes on the inside"

"Definitely not, Sam – I've picked this department clean."

"I might not turn up anything, but let me chat with him?"

"You think my guys haven't tried?"

"They're not as handsome as I am."

"That's a fair point. Come on, then, lovvie," Broadbank laughed. "Let's get you down to the cells. And, whilst you're wasting your time down there, I'll sort your stooge out. I have just the person in mind."

"Great, I can't wait," Samson smirked.

***

The Brain sat opposite him in the warm, box-sized room.

"Get the heat turned right up in there. I want him sweating and wriggling," Samson had told the plod guarding the door.

"You got it."

Within five minutes, the air in the room turned from a mild tepid to skin-sizzling

Sweat dribbled down The Brain's face and dripped off the end of his nose. He was twitching, his eyes darting. Samson didn't know if the man was scared, or had a nervous disposition.

To be fair, he didn't care either way.

"You know what they do to palookas like you in

circulation, the kiddie-diddlers, don't you?"

"I ain't touched no kids, man," he screeched, getting in Samson's face, the veins in his neck protruding. "It was merely *business*, that's all."

"You think the big cheese, XRay, gives a damn about you? Hell, son, I'm surprised you haven't had a cool blade slipped between your ribs yet. He'll see to you soon enough, I'm sure."

This seemed to get The Brain's attention.

"You *know* I was peddling porn for XRay?" The Brain asked, whispering the mob master's name.

Samson nodded. "The punks who worked with you squealed in return for protection. Are you scared these walls have ears? You should be, unless you start talking."

The Brain gulped and pulled at his collars. "Can I get a sip of water?"

"Where are your manners, kiddo? And no, not until you start blabbing. I want names, addresses and places of business. Who's The Widower Maker, Brain – one of XRay's ex-employees? Hmm? A disgruntled foot soldier with a bone to gnaw on? Talk, damn you, or I'll make you sorry you were conceived. I'll have you slung in with the big boys, and have it known you're a stoolpigeon. A blab."

"*No*."

"Then tell me what I want to know." Samson slammed his hand down on the table.

"You can't do this to me, I have rights."

"Yeah, even scumbags like you have them, but it won't stop me informing the fellas on the inside how you like to run your mouth and can't keep your hands to yourself when it comes to children." He felt ill at the mere thought of it all, but the ghost-white complexion appearing on The Brain's face was a superb stomach settler.

"Please, I'm begging you. I don't know who The Widower Maker is. Nobody does, and unless it's escaped your tiny fucking brain, the killer murdered XRay's wife. Why would a member of his organisation do that?"

"I asked you if an *ex*-employee could be behind the murders, someone you may or may not have come into contact with directly."

"Nobody crazy enough springs to mind, but you could try Four-Fingers," he muttered.

"What? Speak up, palooka. Nobody's recording this chat."

"I said you could try Four-Fingers."

"Never heard of him, Brain."

"He runs a meat-packing plant in the bay area. His real name is Johnny Marshal, but everyone calls him Four-Fingers on account of him having had a slip with a cleaver."

"You mean to say one of Xray's thugs *slipped* on Johnny's hand?"

"No, it was Four-Fingers' doing," The Brain scowled. "He was on XRay's books for years, until he grew a conscience, and I remember him letting slip to us about a guy who worked for him. Peter Lutherhead. A strange, flaky cat who liked to cut up animals and steal ladies' knickers off washing lines."

"Us? Who's *us*?"

"Huh?"

"You said us. Who were you referring to?"

"Me and a few of XRay's guys. We'd found our way over to King's Casino one evening, which is where Four-Fingers was, and we got slugging whisky. Four-Fingers, who was already drunk, proceeded to tell us everything he knew about Peter. The next day, however, he asked us to keep quiet about it, because he didn't trust the 'fucking nut job' not to murder him and his family in his sleep."

"Four-Fingers much of a talker in general?"

"Not really, no. He's a rather placid guy, who's yell is worse than anything."

"Guess he got a touch of the ol' pot-valiance," Samson said, getting up to leave. "Where can I find Four-Fingers' joint?"

"I told you, the bay area."

"Name? Or is it called Four-Fingers' Meat Packing Joint," Samson smirked.

"Marshal's Meats and Co." The Brain slumped in his chair. "You won't spread no gossip about me, will you, cop?"

"I'll think about it. For now, keep your beezer clean, and if I come back for more information, best you start spilling immediately."

"B-but—"

Samson smiled as he closed the door on the stuttering man and made his way back to Broadbank's office. *I hope that stooge is ready*, he thought.

***

"Well, what do you think?" Broadbank laughed.

Samson removed a breadstick from his coat pocket and munched on it as he eyeballed the man standing before him.

"He looks like my brother," Samson admitted. "Even the trench coat and hat appear to be the same brand, not to mention the exact same colour."

"Mike, this is Samson Valentine, who needs no introduction, I'm sure. Sam, this is Mike Haggard. He'll be your stand-in. He's my best beat officer, Sam."

"Mike," Samson said, putting his hand out. The younger man shook it. "How sneaky are you, son?"

Mike smiled. "As sneaky as they come."

"This could be dangerous."

"Mike has no wife or children. He's been briefed on all scenarios."

"You're fine playing me until this is over?" Samson couldn't believe how much Mike looked like him. Okay, so up close and personal you could tell he was no Samson Valentine, but from a distance, with the hat helping to cover his face, he'd pull it off, especially if he was overcautious.

"Definitely, and it will be a nice break from the day to day."

"Just watch your back on the streets, Mike."

"Should I go now?" he asked.

"What do you think, Sam?" Broadbank asked.

"Yeah, go on, Mike."

When the officer left, Broadbank turned to Samson. "You really think the bad guys will fall for such a stunt?"

"Here's hoping. I need him to buy me plenty of time, chief. Did you tell him to visit all my haunts and to check in with Alice and Charlie from time to time?"

Broadbank nodded.

"Good. And you informed them? Steve, too?"

"Yes. I'm a pretty decent cop, I'll have you know."

"In that case, I guess you also told him to stay away from my flat and out of the city as much as possible? We don't want Lovell's thugs getting him."

"Of course I did. Sam, stop panicking."

"I'm fine, just making sure all bases are covered. If I was being watched and followed by XRay's goons, I didn't see them, suggesting they kept a safe distance. Mike will be fine, I'm sure."

Broadbank shrugged. "Where are you going now?"

"I have a butcher to see about a weasel," Samson muttered cryptically.

Before the chief could respond, Samson was out the office door and heading towards the police station's rear exit, knowing his doppelganger had gone out the front.

***

Cardiff Bay was a clean, airy and well-lit place. It was an area Broadbank kept well policed, keeping the mayor (before he was arrested) happy and the people who reeked of money pleased. It was rare trouble brewed on these streets, where a Porsche could be found parked on every other driveway.

The homeless, drunks and druggies who happened to wander in from time to time, were immediately escorted out.

"Nobody around there wants to see the likes of them losers, Samson," Broadbank had stated after Samson had said it was a waste of money and manpower to have lots of beat cops walking the bay. "They're rich, Sam. They're entitled, I guess."

Samson had scoffed.

Now, standing close to the harbour, casting an eye over the hundreds of boats that cost millions between them, he wondered how a low-level thug like Four-Fingers had managed to set-up shop here.

Money. It talks, and any goon that is or was connected to XRay would have plenty of it.

Samson turned from where he stood and hailed a taxi. Within seconds, a black cab pulled up, and Samson poked his head in through the passenger's window. "Marshal's Meat—"

"Man, what are you wasting my time for?" the cabby stormed.

"Excuse me?"

"You want a ride to a place that's just around the *next* corner?"

Samson removed his head and looked up. As he was about to speak again, the taxi driver muttered something under his breath and pulled off.

"What a rude S.O.B." Samson raised his fist and yelled after the man, but the taxi was out of sight before he knew it.

He shook his head and moved down the street, eyeballing the wealthy who strolled around in summer wear and sandals like they were in Hawaii.

Idiots. It's hot, but not that *hot.*

When he rounded the next corner, Samson found he was standing in a street that housed mostly businesses, and that's when he saw what he was searching for.

A sign—which was much larger than the ones around it—indicated the Marshal's Meat Co. building; the neon-coloured bulbs that decorated the marker, most of which were broken or out, blinked on and off.

The closer Samson got to the joint, the stronger its smell became.

Men wearing string vests, bloody aprons, and hard hats were busy hauling boxes of freshly butchered meat out of the plant and packing them onto the backs of awaiting lorries.

Samson could barely hear himself think, thanks to the noise around him, as he entered the busy hive: workers joked, talked and laughed amongst themselves, fork trucks buzzed and whined and conveyor belts groaned as they turned out more products to be boxed and shipped.

The deeper into the meat den he stepped, Samson saw rows upon rows of men and women in white coats, hair nets, and blood-covered wellies wrapping various cuts of meat and placing them into parcels.

"Excuse me, ma'am," Samson said, going up to a

busy woman who had a fag dangling out of her mouth. As she worked, she gabbed to the young girl packing goods at her side. "I don't suppose you could tell me where I could find Joh—Four-Fingers?"

When the woman turned around, she scowled at him. "And just who in the shitballs are you supposed to be, Elliot Ness?" The workers around her laughed.

"Are you all dressed up for Hallowe'en with no place to go?" another asked.

Samson didn't bite. Instead, he flashed them his badge.

"Fuck," a young lad said. "He's the old Bill."

"That's right, sunshine. So, where is he?"

"What's holding up this goddamn line?" Samson heard someone yell.

"Here's Four-Fingers now," the young girl sitting next to the jowly woman said.

Samson gazed up and saw a man who was head and shoulders above his workers moving towards him.

What a darling, Samson thought, gawping at Four-Fingers. *He looks as though he went twenty rounds with a heavyweight champ and lost all of them.*

"Who's responsible for this?"

The workers put their heads down and frantically pushed on with what they were doing.

"*Well*?" the huge man roared.

"Here, bear," Samson said, and there was a collective gasp all around him. He could feel the workers tense when he went nose-to-nose with the butcher.

"What do you want, pencil neck? And why are you messing with my production line?"

"Name's Valentine, Samson Valentine. I'm here on police business. It's regarding a former worker of yours."

"*Who*?" he demanded

Samson knew that if he had been Joe Blogg from off the street, then Four-Fingers would have staved his head in by now. "Peter Lutherhead."

The colour drained from Four-Fingers' face. "Follow me," he said, his voice soft.

The Brain was right. His yell is worse.

Chapter 12

Even the man's office stinks of offal and blood, Samson thought, looking about the small room from the worn leather chair Four-Fingers had offered him to sit on. Four-Fingers had lots of credentials and awards to his name—which hung from the walls—even though his operation and set-up didn't look like much.

"Does XRay or any of his men know you're here talking about Lutherhead?" Four-Fingers jumped in, straight to the point.

"Why would you be worried about XRay? Are you or your business still connected to the man? Is there some sort of illegal racket continuing, Fingers?"

"You came to talk about Lutherhead, not me, right?"

Samson nodded. "True. But still. I am a man of the law."

"I'll be honest with you, Samson, is it?" The P.I. nodded. "I once had illegitimate business with the syndicate boss, many years ago, around the time Lutherhead was working for me, but not now. I'm clean and have been for years. XRay knows this, and, even though I have a lot on him, he also knows I would never squeal. I'm just an honest Joe trying to get by, that's all."

That confirms The Brain was telling the truth, then, he thought. *Good.*

"Fine," Samson said, removing the last breadstick from his trench coat. "They help with my smoking cravings," he admitted.

Four-Fingers smiled. "I see."

"I'm prepared to leave you alone, and not pick at you or your base of operations, but I want some answers."

"I've got nothing to hide, but I don't want any of this leaking onto the streets, or that you've been here to see me."

And neither did Samson, but he didn't want Four-Fingers knowing that. Before coming to the bay area, Samson had made sure he wasn't being tailed, and that nobody saw him enter the factory.

The workers paid me plenty of attention, he thought. *If someone should start asking questions*…a voice at the back of his mind uttered, but he dismissed it, thinking he'd be fine.

"My workers will be briefed to keep quiet," the butcher said, as though reading Samson's thoughts.

"Good, but we're only talking about some fella who *used* to work for you, nothing else."

"Still, do you think the monsters that hide in the shadows would believe that?"

Samson polished off his breadstick as his eyes scoured the wall behind Four-Fingers. "You boxed?"

When the man turned in his seat to look, the chair groaned under his immense weight. "Huh, that old thing," he chuckled, staring up at the Golden Gloves trophy nailed to his wall. "Many moons ago, Samson. I was a junior and senior champion, and I boxed professionally for Wales and Cardiff until I fell out of love with the sport and decided I wanted to run my own business."

"Impressive. Many knockouts?"

"Mostly all – I was undefeated. My coach told me I could have gone the distance, but I lost the hunger for it."

"I did a little bit when I was in the police force and army. I loved it – still do." Samson shook his head, smiling. "Anyway, no, I don't suppose the palookas of the night would believe what you and I speak about today, but you needn't worry. I'm not going to blab about it. I just want Lutherhead's whereabouts. Do you have a contact number or home address for him?"

"Gosh, I'm not sure. Let me check." Four-Fingers turned to his computer, started typing, and that's when Samson saw the man was missing the pinkie off his right hand.

"A slip with a cleaver?" Samson enquired.

"No, a frisky pig had his way with my paw when I first started out in this game. It took five powerful left hooks to dislodge the hog."

A laugh escaped Samson. "Sorry."

"Don't be, but if anyone asks, you tell them I told you a slicer did it, or that I slipped with a butcher's knife. Anything, just not the truth," Four-Fingers grinned. "I don't seem to have anything on my system for Lutherhead, but let me check my *old* filing system," he said, getting up from his chair and going to the only filing cabinet in the room. "I updated to the PC about two years ago.

Lutherhead, Lutherhead…" he repeated, flipping through folders. "Ah-*ha*! Here we go, Samson. Lutherhead, Paul."

Samson took the offered file and pulled it open. Inside were a few sheets of paper – one of which pertained to 'personal details'.

"This looks promising," Samson said, more to himself than Four-Fingers. "This has the whole shebang. Was Lutherhead the type of man to give false information?"

Four-Fingers shook his head. "I don't think so, but who knows? I've had my fair share of oddballs work here."

"Was he a man to be fearful of?"

"Put it like this. I don't want *him* knowing where you got his details."

"Violent?"

"More unhinged."

"Why do you say that? Did you witness anything first-hand?"

"Just the things he would say to his colleagues, about how he had rape fantasies and that he liked harming pets from around his neighbourhood. That sort of stuff, you know? None of us ever knew if it was true or not."

"Did a man by the nickname of The Brain ever work for you?"

"Yes, back when I was doing bad stuff for XRay, but as I said, that's long behind me."

"That's fine. Well, thanks for this. May I keep it?"

"Yeah, go ahead."

Samson got out of his chair and headed for the door.

"Do you mind slipping out the back?" Four-Fingers asked.

"Sure," Samson said, but he'd already planned on doing that.

When he got outside, Samson moved as far away from the factory as he could before opening the file and spying the sheet with Lutherhead's details.

Seems he lives in the heart of the apple, Samson thought, looking at the address. *A shame there's no phone number. I could have rung ahead and saved time.*

Samson's mobile started vibrating, shocking him out of his thoughts. He shoved his hand into his trousers pocket and fished the device out.

"Valentine, P.I.—Broadbank, what's the matter? You sound winded, fella? You've been trying to call me for the past hour? My phone hasn't—"

The mobile was knocked out of Samson's hand and stepped on. Before he could react, a clear plastic bag was pulled over his head from behind and he was forced backwards, his hands clawing at the restriction.

He tried to remain calm, his breath misting his vision.

A blurred face appeared before him, and for a second, he thought the punks from this morning had caught up with him.

"You don't listen too good, do ya?" the man with slicked back hair said, grinning, before laying into Samson's guts with a powerful right, left, right, left combo, stealing his air.

The bag was pulled tighter around his throat.

"When Lovell says he wants you gone, you go, vamoose, disappear, and not keep lurking around the place like a bloody pervert."

A laugh escaped the man suffocating the P.I.

Samson's eyes watered, and he realised he was wriggling like a fish out of water, worsening his air scenario by panicking.

Keep still and breathe, fool.

"This is your final warning, pal. Get out of the south or die. It's a simple choice, really."

When Samson tried to yank the bag off his head, the hatchet-man in front of him let rip with more punches to his gut, finishing off with a mighty uppercut, dazing Samson.

"Not so tough now, are you? Get out. *Today.* If I come looking for you later and find you, you're *dead.*"

The bag was removed from Samson and he was free to collapse to his knees. He held his pounded guts and strangled throat, his eyes closed.

"Hey, are you okay?" someone asked, helping Samson to his feet.

He felt like he needed to throw up, but managed a nod. "Yeah, swell." Samson winced, stumbled and braced himself against a wall. "Thanks."

"No problem. You need me to call someone?"

"I'll be fine."

And then his aid was gone.

Samson took in a few gulps of air and steadied himself. When he felt better, he opened his eyes and looked firstly for the file. It lay close by, unopened.

If they had been XRay's guys, then they would have taken that, or at least searched it, and they would have known who owns this place, he thought, bending to retrieve the dropped folder. *And they would have smoked me*.

When he unbent, a starburst flashed behind his eyes. His world slanted.

"Jesus." He put a hand over his eyes. "It's been a while since I've taken such a licking."

"Valentine? Val? Are you there?" he heard a tinny voice call.

He looked down and saw his phone, the screen cracked, the thing still working. Samson scooped it up and placed it to his ear. "I'm here, Broadbank. A couple of hoods jumped me. No, I'm fine. What's wrong? Christ, are you sure it's The Widower Maker? I'll be right there."

***

Within the hour, Samson was back at the clubhouse and standing in Broadbank's office. They were looking at the letter, and what had accompanied it, which lay in the centre of the chief's desk.

"I had a call from the *Cardiff Times* about an hour ago, Sam. They've received something similar."

"My God," Samson uttered, his gaze flitting from the detached big toe to the small pair of knickers, stained red. "You don't think…"

"Yes, I do."

"Any contact from the parents?"

Broadbank nodded. "They were on the phone after you left. Frantic and half out of their minds with worry."

"Have you notified them?"

"Not yet."

"Jesus." Samson removed the gloves from his pocket, slipped them on, and picked up the note. It consisted of a few lines.

I TOLD YOU THIS WOULD HAPPEN IF MY LETTER WENT IGNORED. I WANT THE FRONT PAGE OF THE PAPER TOMORROW, AND I WANT TO BE ON EVERY NEWS CHANNEL TONIGHT. hELP ME SPREAD THE FEAR! IF NOT, YOU CAN EXPECT TO FIND ANOTHER DEAD RICH CHILD LIKE KATIE.

The nausea was overbearing, and so Samson put the note down. "Get some of your boys in blue over to the parents' house, Broadbank. There's a pompous editor I need to have a chat with."

"Don't do anything rash, Valentine."

Samson didn't hear the chief due to the blood rushing in his ears.

***

"Jameson," he said into the intercom, his teeth grinding together. "I'm here on police business."

There was no response, only the sound of the buzzer deactivating the door's lock.

Samson ripped the heavy door open and marched into the reception area, his coat trailing out behind him.

"Mr—" the receptionist started but stopped when Samson walked past her and stormed into the press room.

Samson sought out the editor's office and thundered into the man's room without knocking. "Christ on a Christmas tree!" Jameson blurted, jumping. "You could have given me a heart attack, man. Have you seen—?"

Samson grabbed the man by his shirt, pulled him out of his chair, and rammed him against a filing cabinet. "I should have your guts for garters, *bozo*!" he threatened, yanking the man forward and shoving him again. The look of agony plastered across Jameson's mug was of little satisfaction. Samson wanted to mop the floor with him.

"Oh, God – someone, call the police," a woman shrieked from behind Samson.

"I *am* the law," Samson bellowed, ramming Jameson again. "Have I seen it? *Seen* it?" the P.I. screeched. "There's a child's toe and a pair of her underwear laying on my chief's desk, along with this very note." Samson picked up the letter from the editor's desk and fought with himself not to ram it into Jameson's flapping mouth. "You didn't get the added extras, I see. Lucky you."

"It came with a photo of a girl and a lock of hair," Jameson sputtered.

"Where? Show me." Samson threw the editor aside, who crashed off a wall and sat in his chair with a '*humph*'.

"Here, here," he pleaded, opening his drawers. He had tears in his eyes. "I was going to show you, but you didn't give me the opportunity. I'm just as disturbed by this as you are."

Samson's hands curled into fists. His knuckles cracked. "Anything else?"

Jameson shook his head, his jowls wobbling nineteen to the dozen.

"You best make sure our friend makes the front page tomorrow—give him his coverage—or we're going to have more bodies on our hands." Samson collected the evidence and left.

***

Before heading home for the evening, Samson went back to the police station with the evidence, and to find out what had happened with Katie's parents.

"So, what did Katie's mum and dad have to say for themselves?"

"The same, pretty much – that they were attacked in their sleep, and when they woke up, they were tied to their bed."

"The girl was gone?"

The chief nodded. "They never had contact from The Widower Maker, either, no ransom demands, etc. They're also pretty much refusing to believe he's killed Katie."

"Understandable. We don't know for certain it *was* The Widower Maker, do we? It doesn't fit his MO."

"No, you have a point, but you know what the letters said."

Samson huffed. "That's true."

Broadbank expelled his breath in a frustrated manner and fell into his chair. "They're going on the air tonight."

"A press conference?"

"Yeah, they wanted it."

Samson could only look at the man in disbelief. "It's too soon, in my opinion."

"That's what I thought."

"Listen, I may have a lead on who this pissant is, Broadbank."

The chief looked up. It was his turn to gawk. "You do?"

"Yeah, but don't get your hopes up, just in case it amounts to nothing. Let me do some digging first, yeah?"

"Okay, do what you must." Broadbank appeared too tired to argue the matter.

"What time are they going on?"

"Eight-thirty, nine."

"Want me there?"

"No, it's fine," Broadbank waved. "Chase that lead of yours, and get our man."

Samson said he would and left.

***

As Samson climbed the stairs to his apartment—almost asleep on his feet—it occurred to him that the thugs who'd jumped him earlier might come searching for him.

Let them come, he thought, reaching his landing.

Samson put his key in the lock, turned it, and pushed the door open. The first thing he noticed was the new windows and missing bullet holes. It brought a weak smile to his face.

Bogart barked from the kitchen as he entered.

When Samson crossed the threshold, something didn't feel quite right, as though someone had been here. Someone who didn't belong, but he shrugged it off, knowing he was being silly.

The builders, that's all.

His dog continued to bark.

"Okay, okay, hold your water," Samson said.

"Val?" Lisa's voice fluttered across the hallway.

Damn, I forgot to contact her husband. Ex-*husband*, he corrected himself. "Evening, doll," he turned, giving her the best smile he could muster.

"Everything okay?"

"No. It's been a long, cruel day. Right about now, I wish I was a drinking man." His smile faltered.

"Want to talk about it?" she asked from her doorway, her shapely hip was pressed against the frame.

He rubbed the base of his neck. "I don't know, muffin. I'm pretty beat."

"I have coffee boiling."

"You drive a hard bargain, ma'am. Okay, but let me see to my doggie first," he told her.

***

After letting Bogart out of the kitchen, Samson had taken the dog for a short walk around the block so the pooch could do his business and stretch his legs.

"I'll take you for a nice early-morning walk tomorrow, fella, I promise." With how busy he'd been of late, Samson realised he'd neglected most of his normal routine, such as visits to the gym, and not just Bogart. "Things will get better, you'll see," he told the dog.

I'll have to find him a temporary home for when I do head west. Ask Lisa? he thought. *I can't see why she wouldn't check in on him.*

When he got back to his flat and slipped Bogart inside, Samson wandered over to Lisa's and knocked, but the door was open.

"Hi," he called, entering.

"Come on in, Val."

When his sight fell on her in the better light, he noticed she was wearing a sophisticated silk nightgown that barely covered her to the knee.

"One coffee," she said, offering him a steaming mug. "I would have put a shot of something stronger in it, but I remembered you saying you're off the sauce."

"Correct, and I think if I had a whiff of it tonight, I'd end up going home and drowning my sorrows."

"So, it was a rough day at the office?"

"The pits," he confirmed, swallowing a mouthful of coffee. "Mm, delicious."

Lisa beamed. "Why don't you come over tomorrow night for some good home-made food?"

"So I can bore you to death with stories about my police work?"

She smiled. "Don't be silly."

"I forgot to say, I haven't had the chance to contact your ex-husband yet, but I will tomorrow morning. First thing."

"That's good."

"They never came back after I left?"

"No, Val."

"Wait, I *can't* come for food tomorrow evening. I'm probably going to be heading west on business. What about when I get back?"

"Sure, sounds good. How long will you be gone? Do you need a dog sitter?"

He was relieved by her offer.

"That would be great, Lisa. I don't know how long I'll be away, though, but I'll keep in touch." He drained his coffee and left. "G'night."

"Night, Val."

***

It felt good to have kicked off his shoes and showered, changed into something comfortable and to be relaxed in front of his TV with Bogart on his lap.

A Virgin Mary stood on the small table beside his chair, the glass sweating.

When Katie's parents came onscreen, a knot developed in his guts.

"Poor blighters," he whispered.

Their faces were black and blue, their eyes

swollen and sprouting tears. Husband and wife clung to each other as camera flashes lit up their distress.

Snot drizzled out of the mother's nose as she begged for her daughter's return. She then buried her face in her husband's shoulder.

"We just want Katie back. We're willing to pay, or do whatever it takes. Please, whoever you are, bring her home. Please, *please*!" the husband's voice cracked.

A knot developed in Samson's throat, and his mind diverted to Angie, remembering how badly she'd wanted children.

Samson gulped down the lead hidden behind his Adam's apple and removed his eyes from the TV. He turned his head and caught sight of an envelope hanging out of his letterbox.

It was smeared red.

His heart sank further as more memories washed over him.

Chapter 13

Samson got up from his chair, slipped over to the door, and stuck his hand out to retrieve the envelope. But he pulled his arm back with a sudden thought.

What if it's a nail bomb or something equally as deadly?

He wasn't sure what today's criminals were capable of altogether.

Behind him, on the TV, Katie's parents continued to sob and speak in between gasps.

"We just want her back," the mother reiterated.

And then he heard Broadbank bring things to a close, but the media was its usual, unpleasant self, as reporters yelled questions across the room to be heard over their rivals.

Like a zoo, he thought, his eyes on the letterbox. *If I gaze at it much longer, I'm likely to burn a hole through it.*

Samson was hesitant, but he put his hand out and wrapped his fingers around the plain white envelope that had red smudges on it. He pulled the note free with gritted teeth, expecting a blast and a face full of broken glass or rusty, germ-ridden nails and screws.

The only sound that came, however, was that from the spring-loaded letterbox as it snapped back into place.

Samson's heart scurried. There was something

lumpy within the envelope, and he wasn't sure he could bring himself to open it.

Before he tried, he turned it over and looked at the front. There was a word written there: **Valentine.**

"The Widower Maker…" he whispered, his heart almost stopping. With shaking hands, he ripped at the envelope's sealing and turned away when he saw a pinkie finger, small toe, and tongue inside. "Oh, Jesus."

He knew then, for sure, that Katie wasn't coming home.

"How are we going to tell her parents?" he muttered, turning to the TV and seeing Katie's parents through a blurred, tear-stained vision. A single fat droplet rolled over his cheek and spread across his lower lip. "The sick *bastard*!"

Seldom did Samson swear, he found it vulgar, but there was no other word for the vile creature that stalked the streets of Cardiff, preying on women. And now, as it seemed, children.

Along with the body parts, there was a note, and he avoided touching the digits and organ as he plucked it free. When he had it, he put the envelope to one side and muted the TV.

"Dear Valentine," he read, which was constructed in the same crude style as the name on the front of the envelope, and every other message he'd seen from the killer thus far. "How exciting it is to know such a high-profile individual as yourself is working my case, trying to track down little old me. How confident are you that you can catch me? I think you're capable, but not Broadbank and his team. They're too stupid, and too far behind in the game already. But not you, Samson – you're sharp, canny, and nothing will faze you. I was hoping the police would draft you in. For now, goodbye and good luck!

PS, I hope you like the gifts I included. I know how much you like such things through the post. Signed, The Widower Maker."

He went to his mobile phone.

"Broadbank, it's Sam. Give me a call as soon as you get this message."

Samson disconnected and returned the mobile to the arm of his chair.

"Now what am I going to do?"

He paced his flat and thought he should be out on the streets, trying to find the man responsible for the killings and the abduction of Katie.

I can't just sit whilst that poor child could *be suffering somewhere. The west is going to have to wait*, he thought. *I'm needed here more. Screw XRay and Lovell.*

Samson went to his bedroom and slipped into his clothes. He then pocketed his car keys, mobile, and wallet before stepping into his shoes. With his hat and coat on, he was about to unlock his door when someone started pounding on it.

"Open the hell up, Valentine. You've had your last warning, ya son of a bitch."

"Come on, we know you're in there. Don't make us kick the door in."

Damn. Samson felt like a rabbit caught in

headlights. He patted his pockets to make sure he had everything and then went to the window. Samson rolled it up and looked out at the staircase connected to the side of the building. *Thank God for these fire escapes*.

A shoulder or boot rattled his door in its frame.

Where am I heading?

He tried to form a plan in his head.

Wood creaked and then splintered.

The police station? Broadbank's? No, I need to disappear. West, that's my best bet, and cut off the head of the palooka monster causing these problems. I need to find Lovell and shut him down. What about XRay and The Widower Maker? I'll deal with them in due course. Hopefully, Mike will give them the run-around until I'm back in Cardiff.

Samson got one foot out onto the steel platform, his back turned, when hands grabbed a hold of him and tried pulling him back inside.

"And where in the fuck do you think you're going?" a man with a bottomless well-like voice grumbled.

Samson chopped at the guy's wrists once, twice, three times, hearing something click there.

"Son of a—" the attacker fell away, taking a piece of Samson's trench coat with him.

A second assailant flew at him with his arms outstretched. Samson waited just long enough before bringing the window down on the man's hands, crushing and trapping them there.

"*Argh*!" the thug screamed. "You broke my

fucking fingers!" He yanked his arms but his busted paws remained where they were.

Samson looked in at the men and considered them for a moment. He couldn't tell if they were the same pair who'd jumped him earlier.

I couldn't get a clear look at Gut Puncher's mug through the bag, he thought and didn't fancy hanging around long enough to ask. He ran down the steps, jumping the odd few.

From above, he heard his apartment window roll skyward.

"Get the bastard," one of them hissed.

Samson guessed it was Busted Fingers, who was more than likely out of action.

One down…

When he reached the bottom of the stairwell, Samson chanced a glance up and saw his pursuer a couple of levels above

Samson fled down the alleyway and into his building's car park. Once there, he went to his car and fumbled his keys out of his pocket as he dashed around to the driver's side. He wasted no time in opening up, getting behind the wheel, and starting the engine.

After locking the doors, Samson reversed, straightened, and pointed his car towards the exit. His headlights fell on the man chasing him. To his amazement, it *was* Busted Fingers.

Maybe I didn't wreck him up as much as I thought.

Samson punched the accelerator and brought the clutch up. The car darted forward and Busted

Fingers rolled onto the bonnet, where he clung on for dear life.

As they entered the alleyway, Samson saw his second attacker making his way toward a parked car close by. The P.I. jumped on his brakes, sending Broken Fingers off his bonnet and sprawling backwards.

Samson swerved around the downed man and pulled onto the main street, his car's back end sliding out and his tyres screeching, as he skidded into the night. Someone blared their horn and yelled, but Samson paid zero attention. He glanced out of his window and saw Busted Fingers hobble over to the waiting car. Soon, they would be powering after him.

A hot chase ensued throughout the outer streets of the city.

Samson took sharp lefts and rights, tracking down side streets and lanes he never knew existed, in an attempt to shake his new friends. But they kept coming.

"*This is absurd*," he said when he checked his rear-view mirror again and saw the passenger in the car behind lean out their window.

"*Is that—?*"

His back window blew out when a hot piece of lead smashed through it and drilled into his dashboard, annihilating the vents.

Samson's car veered, toppling bins.

"*Sumbitches!*"

The side of his car scraped along a wall and tore the wing mirror off.

A second bullet slammed into the passenger seat, but this time he managed to keep the car, and his nerves, straight.

Samson's Ford screeched out of another alley, cut across oncoming traffic and slipped into a new back street. He stamped on the accelerator and his head was thrown back against his headrest, making him wince, and stars danced before him.

"Where are the good ol' boys when you need them?" he yelled, shaking the daze from his vision as he looked out his windows.

Not a cop car in sight.

When Samson entered onto a main street, the men giving chase seemed to stop shooting at him. He looked in his remaining wing mirror and saw the passenger in the car behind was now back inside the vehicle.

They have some sense then, he thought, weaving in and out of traffic, trying his best to lose them. He knew it would be difficult because it was late and there weren't many cars on the road.

I can't very well lead them to the train station.

He searched in his mirror for the tailing car and noticed it had dropped back a considerable amount.

Trying not to raise suspicion, boys? A bit late for that, don't you think?

With his eyes on the road again, Samson picked out the turn off for the motorway. *I could lead them down there and then cut back into Cardiff? If those boys are from the west, they won't know the roads as well as I do.*

At the last second, he took the exit, completely

foxing his adversaries, who shot past the off-ramp. Samson heard the harsh sound of squealing tyres.

Palookas won't be able to reverse back and—

In his wing mirror, he saw them fast approaching.

His jaw slackened.

Samson sped up and joined the motorway, which was fairly busy. He raced forward, overtaking and zipping between cars and lorries, forcing some drivers to slam on their brakes to avoid a collision.

Before his pursuers could catch up to him, Samson took the first off-ramp and doubled back into the city. He was sure to use back roads, side streets, and alleys. When he pulled up outside the train station, he was relieved to see he'd lost them. Getting out of his car, he locked it and ran inside, buying a ticket for the first available train west.

The state my car's in, someone will either steal or tow it, he thought, looking at his train ticket. *What am I doing? I don't even know where to start looking for Lovell.* And then he remembered what and who he was. *I could sniff out a palooka in a tornado.*

"Next train is due at ten past ten, sir," the young lad behind the counter informed him. "Is there anything else I can help you with?"

Samson shook his head, left the booth and headed for platform one, which was deserted. The big clock found on the wall by a bank of pay phones and an elevator told him it was five minutes to ten o'clock.

Not long. Maybe I could give Broadbank a buzz

as I wait?

But Samson didn't like that idea. He had to keep his wits about him just in case the goons on his tail managed to find him.

***

At precisely ten minutes past ten, the train Samson needed pulled into the platform.

He boarded and took a window seat.

The first thing I need to do when I get to Carmarthenshire is book myself into a hotel and get organised. I'll then ring Broadbank.

Soon after sitting down, the platform guard blew his whistle, signalling the train's departure. With a two-hour journey ahead of him, Samson settled in by removing his coat and hat.

"Sir," he asked a passing conductor. "Is there a buffet cart?"

"We don't serve food at this hour—"

"No, I'm in search of a cup of coffee."

"Oh, in that case, yes. Go straight ahead," he said, turning and pointing Samson in the right direction. "It's the last carriage, sir. There's nobody working the catering car this evening, but you'll find a Clix machine that dispenses hot drinks. There's also a vendor there with snacks, fizzy pops, and bottled water."

"Thanks," Samson said, getting out of his seat and heading up the aisle to the next carriage.

***

With a coffee and a packet of nuts in hand, Samson headed back the way he'd come and was soon in his seat again. He let his mind wander as he sipped his hot drink and ate his snack.

There's not much I'm going to be able to do until morning, he argued with himself. *I'm sure Broadbank will be able to help me locate Lovell. And if he can't? The west is hardly his jurisdiction.*

Samson chewed on that for a moment, as he blew on his coffee and shovelled more peanuts into his mouth.

XRay? No, that could be fatal to Mike. If X thinks I've headed west to sort this punk Lovell out, then he'll know it's not me walking the streets of Cardiff. That's if they're even tailing Mike. Come on, they must be.

He cleared his mind, finished the last of his food and drink and then closed his eyes after putting his hat over his face.

No harm in nabbing forty winks while I can, he thought.

***

"Next stop, Carmarthenshire," the conductor bellowed.

Samson awoke with a start and his fedora rolled off his face when he sat bolt upright. "Wh-what?" he coughed, looking up at the guard who shot past him.

"Carmarthenshire *is* your next stop, people.

That's Carmarthenshire. *Next* stop," he continued to call as he made his way up the train.

With squinted eyes, Samson looked at his watch. It was a spit after midnight. He yawned, stretched and got out of his seat, taking his hat, coat and rubbish with him.

As he approached the carriage door, he popped his waste into a metal bin provided and waited for the train to come to a complete standstill. When the automatic doors beeped, hissed and parted, Samson was a little reluctant to get out.

What if the hop-heads know I'm here? The goons back at my flat could have called ahead. No, how on earth would they know where I went?

Samson put on his coat and affixed his hat atop his head.

The night was freezing, and a keen wind whipped at his chops, biting into his exposed flesh.

At least it's not raining. The cold I can stand to bear. I'd rather be shivering than sweating bullets.

Samson raised the lapels of his coat and left the station. He hailed a taxi and asked the driver to take him to the closest hotel, which was less than five miles away.

When he arrived, he paid and thanked the man.

The area, which wasn't a residential one, was deserted, and the only sound came from the neon sign that lit-up the unimpressive, sleazy-looking hotel.

Not sure what type of fella that cabby took me for, but I guess this place will have to do for tonight. I don't fancy traipsing around unknown territory in the wee hours.

Samson walked into the reception area and was greeted by the heavy smell of marijuana and bodily fluids. When he looked up, he saw a man standing in a corner, his back to Samson, with a line of urine gushing from between his feet as he sprayed the wall in front of him.

The P.I. wrinkled his nose, turned and saw a couple of punks, a man and a woman, slumped against each other on a bench. They had needles jutting from the creases in their elbows.

Small flies buzzed about Samson's head.

"Jesus," he uttered, about to turn to leave, when a voice called out.

"Help you, mister?"

Samson saw a frail-looking woman walk through a curtain of beads from behind the counter. She held something unseen in her left hand.

"Couldn't trouble you for a room for the night, could I?"

"What you dressed like that for? You're not some pervert who's going to use one of my rooms for some sick game, are you?"

The drugged punks giggled.

Samson narrowed his eyes. "No, ma'am – I'm only interested in getting an honest night's sleep."

She eyed him. "Then you better get your sorry-looking self over here, boy."

When he stepped closer, he noticed she was chewing tobacco and wielding a claw-hammer.

"These parts can get a tad unreserved at night, if you know what I mean," she continued, spitting a large wad of brown-yellow phlegm from her almost toothless gob. Strings of it graced her chin, but she didn't bother wiping them away. "Single room, do ya?"

"Does it have a phone?"

She nodded. "No long-distance calls, okay? You can pay your bill before you leave."

"Okay, great."

"Room six," she chewed, slamming the key down on the desk that had a large wooden fob attached to it; the number six was etched into it.

When he placed his hand over it, she put her free mitt on top of his. "And if you need some company during the night, sailor, you know where to find me," she winked.

Samson shivered, snatched the key from the counter and managed a weak smile. "Er, thanks. G'night."

"Room's just down the corridor there," she pointed.

He hurried down the hallway and didn't look back. When he reached his door, Samson checked to make sure he had the right room and was shocked to see a nine instead of a six.

"That can't be right," he muttered, looking at the numbers on the doors either side of his. "Five and Seven…" Samson shrugged, tried the key and turned it. The locks disengaged. Before he pushed it open, he put his fingers to the plastic number and found the six had slipped, a screw missing, turning it into a nine.

A roar of laughter escaped him. Samson shook

his head and stepped over the threshold.

The first thing he noticed was the ungodly smell here, too. It wrapped him up in its unclean paw and wouldn't let go.

"Bloody hell." Samson fanned his nose and crossed to the window. After rolling it up, he stuck his head out and gulped in clean air. A neon sign by the side of his face, which spelt out the beer Heineken, blinked on and off and was accompanied by a faint buzz. Moths butted against its filth-encrusted bulbs.

"*Ugh*." Samson pulled himself back in, but left the window open. The stained curtains billowed. "That's a tad better," he sniffed, looking at the bed.

The top sheet seemed matted, and when he tried pulling it back, he found it *was* stuck to the bottom sheet.

"Think I'll take the chair." He studied the seat in the corner of the room. "It looks to be the cleanest thing in this whole stinking joint."

He was about to cross to the phone, which sat on a dishevelled bedside table, when a rumpus in the corridor stopped him.

"You fucking slag!" a woman screeched, which was followed by the sound of glass smashing. "I'll kill you."

"*Argh*! Bitch, you cut me."

Samson grabbed the chair from the corner of the room and pushed it against the door. He then nabbed the phone and sat in the seat, confident nobody could break through and carve him up.

Unsure of Broadbank's number, he fished his

mobile out of his pocket (which had no signal since Cardiff) and searched for the digits. When he had them, he keyed them into the hotel's phone and listened as it rang and rang.

"Come on, pick up…"

Close to thirty rings in, Samson was about to give up, when a groggy Broadbank answered. "This better be good," he droned.

"It's Valentine."

"*Val*!" Samson smiled, picturing the chief bouncing up in bed at the sound of his voice. "Where are you? Are you okay? I've had boys over at your place and out looking for you."

"You *know* I was chased out of my home?"

"A neighbour reported a disturbance at yours. A Miss Dennings, Lisa."

"Oh?"

"Yeah, she reported sounds of a struggle and a possible break-in."

"Is Bogart okay?" Samson asked.

"Don't worry. I rescued the little fella. He's here with me, Sam. I found him cowering in the bathroom."

"Thanks. Can you keep him for a few days? I did ask Lisa, but since you—"

"You're not coming back?"

"Not yet. Listen, I need some information and a favour."

"Answer me, will you. Where *are* you? We couldn't locate the thugs who broke into your place."

"I'm out west, Carmarthenshire. I'm going to

track down Lovell and put an end to this madness before I end up in concrete boots or buried alive."

"So that's why you wanted a stooge, not to harass XRay's goons, but to go after Lovell."

"Bingo. Except I had to put my plan into action a little sooner than I thought."

"Okay, so what do you need from me?"

"All the information you got him, James Lovell."

"Okay, I can do that. Anything else?"

"Do you know anyone on the force out here? I'll need a contact for when I unearth Lovell's dirty deeds and run him in."

"As it happens, I know the captain, so leave it with me. Can I reach you on this number in a few hours, Sam?"

"Yeah, I'll hang around until I hear from you, but don't leave me waiting too long. I need to relocate and get the show on the road."

"Give me a few hours."

"How is Mike doing? Has he checked in on Alice and Charlie yet?"

"The girls are fine, as is Mike. He seems to think he's been giving your chaperones the run-around."

Both men laughed.

"There's something else, regarding The Widower Maker. Check on a fella by the name of Paul Lutherhead. He fits the type of man we're looking for. I didn't want to part with that name just yet, because I wanted to do more digging. Plans change, I guess."

Samson heard Broadbank scribbling. "Got it. Thanks. Is that it?"

"Yes, for now. I need to try and get some shuteye, palooka. *Don't* leave me waiting." Samson hung up and massaged his temples.

God, I need a drink.

He slapped his thighs, got up, and stretched. Samson then walked across the room to the bathroom and toed the door open. He was a little apprehensive to check in there. But, to his surprise, it was clean and smelled fresh. No backed up toilet or clogged sink. In the bath, however, a fat cockroach skittered across the ceramic base.

Samson shuddered, wrinkled his nose, and used the toilet. With his hands washed, he exited the room and turned the light off. After grabbing his hat from the coat stand, he sat back down and covered his face.

It wasn't long before sleep took him.

Chapter 14

She'd begged, cried, and pleaded for her mummy and daddy—her crotch soaked through—as she lay there strapped to his table.

"Shh," he cooed. "Mummy and Daddy *aren't* going to save you, only the angel of mercy, *if* you're lucky." Katie wailed when he revealed the large hunting knife from behind his back, which he'd sharpened to within an inch of perfection. "I will set you free into her feathery wings soon enough, child."

He stroked her hair off her drenched forehead and out of her eyes.

"Please, I want my mummy." Tears spilt down her face and slipped into her blubbering mouth.

"They're not coming, *bitch*," he hissed, slapping her face and reddening her cheek; fingerprints appeared on her skin.

"*Argh*!"

"Shout all you want, Katie. I've had this place soundproofed. Nobody is going to help you. *Nobody*. And if you keep this nonsense up, I will prolong your agony. Believe me. I have the equipment to keep you alive for a long, *long* time, no matter how much you bleed."

She whimpered—he smiled—and her tear-streaked eyes locked on to his.

He put his knife down on a steel tray by his side, which held all forms of scream-provoking implements, and picked up a pair of large scissors. He opened and snapped them closed in front of her face, and when she screwed her eyes shut, he pinched her.

"*Ow.*"

A laugh escaped him.

With his free hand, he bunched some of her hair into his fist and cut her locks off.

Katie cried further, her body quivering.

Butterflies fluttered in his guts. "Be at peace, child."

"I want to go home," she pleaded.

"Soon, I will send you home—to your maker—sweetie, I promise."

The Widower Maker replaced the scissors and looked at the knife. He had no want or desire to kill this child with such a tool, now that she lay before him. Her fright brought him all the satisfaction he needed—not to mention the sheer hell her parents will go through—and so his gaze shifted to the pillow by the blade's side.

With stealth, he covered her face with it and pressed his weight down.

"*Help*," she screamed over and over, which was muffled.

He smiled as she thrashed beneath him. "Shh," he said. "Shh, baby girl."

Soon enough, she stopped bucking and he removed the pillow.

He ejaculated in his trousers.

"Oh, Katie," he whispered. "You poor thing."

He looked down at her whitening face and her

purpling lips.

For a split second, he thought he saw something in her pupils. A flash of movement.

"Her soul departing?" he spoke softly, respectfully, making the sign of the cross. "Sleep well, child."

After muttering a considerate prayer, he snatched up the knife and set about hacking off the bits of her body he wanted to accompany his letters to the press, police, and Samson Valentine.

He whistled as he worked, and then laughed when he thought about their reactions.

"I'll bury this angel where nobody'll ever find her," he said aloud, deciding against stripping her, eating her flesh and dumping her publicly.

***

It had taken him several hours to chop the body into bits small enough to be placed in black bags. Once he'd achieved that, he'd driven the dismembered carcass out to a wooded area he knew well, and took Katie's remains deep within to bury.

After that, he'd returned to his flat to take a vigorous scrub in the shower, clean his tools, and sluice his workspace; he'd taken painstaking time in picking up all the remnants of flesh and hair, whilst making sure every drop of spilt blood was gone.

Once he was satisfied, he'd made a healthy smoothie and salad before retreating to his telescope, which is where he sat now, with the news playing out on his TV in the background.

His telescope was still trained on Katie's house, his keen eye watching her mother and father as they wept and held each other. A bottle of gin stood on the table before them, along with two full tumblers.

"What I wouldn't give to be a fly on their wall right now," he said, forking food into his mouth. After swallowing it, he took a hearty gulp from his smoothie. "Ah, delicious."

He wondered, then, if he'd ever get bored of watching their distress.

"No, I don't think so. Not yet, anyway. Besides, once I've had my fill with them, I'll have my dear Catherine to occupy my time, thoughts, and energy. And, before I'm done with her, I'm sure Hatchy will have another rich bitch lined up in readiness."

With his salad and drink finished, he burped, stood up, and collected his dirty dishes. He then deposited everything into the kitchen sink and strolled back to the telescope for one final look.

The parents were still propped against each other, crying.

A smile pulled across his face.

He walked over to his sofa and lay down to watch the rest of the news.

***

Early the following morning—after a refreshing nine hours of sleep—he set to work on filling three envelopes with the letters he'd written last night, along with the trophies he'd taken from Katie.

It was barely six a.m. when he left his flat to post

two out of the three letters. The city was still, with the sun rising over it. He looked up at the high-rise office blocks and apartment buildings in true awe as he walked, his mind pondering about whom might live and work behind the many smoked-glass windows.

With both letters deposited into a post box, The Widower Maker made his way across the city via a bus.

This one needs to be personally delivered, he thought, looking at the third and final envelope. Blood had soaked through one of its corners. Not that it mattered. He pocketed it and looked out the windows, lost in thought.

***

When he finally arrived at Samson Valentine's address—information he'd obtained through online, underground contacts connected to thugs within the city—he didn't waste time in entering the apartment complex.

How posh, he thought, studying the building's cosy interior, jazzy colour scheme, and art décor. As he climbed the stairs he gazed this way and that, enthralled by the paintings and such that clung to the walls.

And then he was brought out of his ponderings by a voice coming down the stairs, getting closer.

"No, I have to rush. I'm late for work."

When the man got near, The Widower Maker turned his head so he couldn't be recognised. He then stood still and listened, as the fella continued descending, his voice fading all the while, until he was out the main door and gone.

The building was still once again.

Before The Widower Maker could reach the floor he needed, he heard people enter the complex, which was accompanied by the sound of tools or bottles rattling.

The Widower Maker ducked into a doorway, allowing the men to pass, who looked like builders.

"A hive of activity," he breathed.

The Widower Maker stayed put for the next ten minutes or so, a little worried to move.

I'm so close to the P.I.'s flat, he thought.

Then there were more voices, followed by the sound of knocking.

He didn't know how much time had lapsed, but he was about to shift when someone came down the stairs towards him. He pushed deeper into the shadows, cowering against a door, until a man wearing a fedora and trench coat shot by.

"*Oooh*," The Widower Maker shivered, his heart fluttering.

When Samson Valentine was out of eyesight, The Widower Maker stepped from his hiding place and looked down the stairwell, watching the peeper go on his merry way.

"You're much bigger in real life, Mr Valentine," he said, staring at Samson as he slipped out the building's main door. A warmth spread through him as he inhaled, taking in Samson's trailing smell of aftershave and body spray. "We came so close to touching, connecting, Mr Valentine. A shame you'll never know."

The Widower Maker continued on his journey, and soon he reached Samson's flat, the door standing ajar. He pushed it inwards and saw a man fixing the windows, whilst another worked on the hole-ridden walls.

He breathed deep.

"*Ah,*" he whispered, expelling the air. The workers didn't notice him, thanks to the noise coming from their radio. He stepped over the threshold, after stuffing his letter in the letterbox.

He touched—after adorning a pair of latex gloves he kept for this reason—and sniffed as he snuck by the workers and found his way into Samson's bedroom, and then the bathroom. The Widower Maker avoided the closed door, thinking it was the kitchen and could hear a dog padding around in there.

After he'd contented himself, he slipped past the workers and out of the apartment. He hurried down the main steps and exited the complex.

"Jesus. What a rush," he giggled, putting his gloved hands to his face and whiffing them. He could smell traces of Samson's fresh clothes and trinkets on the latex. "He's such a proud man; a man who would undoubtedly be a lion in the animal kingdom."

***

That night, when he returned home after popping

around to Catherine's place for a quick spy, The Widower Maker showered, ate a hearty supper, and flopped in front of the TV with a diet coke and a power bar.

The news played out before him, but he was unseeing, as his mind brought up an image of Katie's dead face, her eyes staring.

And then his sister, Chloe, entered his thoughts.

They could have been twins. God, Chloe had been beautiful; full of life and optimism about her future. A resentful snort-laugh escaped him and his fingers clawed at the sofa cushions. *If I could kill her over and over again, I would.*

He took several deep breaths and thought about Chloe's face and body, and how she'd looked under the falling water in the shower.

I took great joy in destroying her and her precious future.

If he was ever asked why he did what he did, he wasn't sure he'd be able to put his finger on it. Was it jealousy? Because she had brains, a good education, and was going somewhere? Did he feel left behind? Was it the fact that she would have ended up stinking rich after graduating from university? Or was it the simple fact that his parents loved and lavished her more?

That first summer she'd returned home from her studies, she'd boasted to their parents about how amazing her marks were and that companies were already headhunting top talent from universities around Wales.

"My tutors are so impressed with me that they've

put my name forward. I could have an interview for a position in my field by the end of next year!" Chloe had squealed, clapping her hands together and jumping up and down.

"Well, at least *someone* has brains in this family," his dad had remarked, giving him a sideways glance, and smiling.

It may have been a joke, a bit of male bantering between father and son, but he hadn't liked it. The words had hurt, and it was bad enough he was getting stick at school from the other children who had now taken to calling him Charlie Bucket (from *Charlie and the Chocolate Factory),* Bucket Boy, or just plain Bucket.

"Will you have to sing for your supper during lunch break?" the children would say, adding, "Yeah, *Oliver*."

The memories reddened his cheeks.

"You want to learn to fight back, lad," his dad told him one evening after he'd returned home from school with a blackened eye and split lip. "They'll be calling you a sissy next."

But he was no fighter. He wanted social acceptance.

A reason why I never hit back, he thought, thinking they would like him for allowing them to push him around. *But that never happened, did it? If anything, it made things worse*.

The little money he received for school dinners or the odd treat was often stolen from him after a good pummelling. After years of abuse, he finally made a stand, but they ganged up on him and did awful things, such as stick his head down dirty toilets and shove him in bins, which they either rolled down a hill or beat with sticks.

When it all became too unbearable, with his parents doing nothing to stand up for him, he started skipping school. And it wasn't long before he fell in with the wrong crowd. A band of misfits who called themselves 'The Lost'; a crew made up of three boys and one girl, all around his age, who were outcasts fit for straitjackets.

***

"Who the fuck are you, chicken dick?" Benny Phils, the leader of The Lost, asked him the day they met under the railway bridge.

"My name's Chris," he lied, never telling them his real name. Not even when they became close.

"You're on our patch, brass balls," Shaun Hatch, or Hatchy as he was known to the gang, chirped. He was Benny's right-hand, and probably the fattest boy Chris had ever clapped eyes on. "Want a fucking beating, is that it?"

"N-no—I didn't know anyone—"

"Look at his poofy school uniform," Chyna sniggered. The solo girl was sat with her back pressed to one of the bridge's concrete support beams. She had her knees to her chin and a fag dangled from between her purple-covered, ring pierced, lips. She had a dirty face that was flanked by her shock of red-dyed hair and her Doc boots looked lived in. "*What,* not seen a girl before?" Her left nostril had a stud in it, and her eyes stared through him. She opened her legs, her skirt rucked up around her thighs, and flashed him her knickers.

The boys laughed, she joined in, blowing smoke in Chris' direction.

Chris thought his heart was going to explode. He couldn't take his eyes off her, and the words, "you're pretty," tumbled out of his mouth before he could bite down on his tongue or cover his gob.

"*Ha*! Oh, fuck – Chyna has a boyfriend," Paul, the third lad squealed. Benny and Hatchy brayed with laughter.

Chyna stared at Chris through a veil of smoke.

"S-sorry, I didn't mean…" he closed his mouth before he caused any more damage.

"What the fuck are you doing down here, dildo?" she quizzed him.

"I come here instead of school." He lowered his head, his chin touching his chest. "*They* don't want me there. *They* beat me up and call me names."

"What a shocker – the fucking square *is* a square," Paul ribbed.

"Just what we need – another goddamn reject," Benny said. "Is the word out on the streets or something?"

"What, that we're taking in all the rubbish and dickheads?" Hatchy asked.

Benny nodded, laughed, and stuck a fag in his mouth, which Hatchy lit.

"One more in our circus won't harm," Paul said.

"I kind of like him," Chyna admitted, winking at Chris, who blushed.

"Lose the sucky clothes, dude," Benny advised, "if you want to hang with us."

Chris nodded. "Can I stay?"

"Not looking like that. Come back tomorrow."

"Do you guys hang here together all the time?"

"Yeah, but we've got a clubhouse. We'll initiate you tomorrow, drip," Hatchy promised.

"Wow, cool. I've never had… friends," Chris muttered.

The others laughed. "Aww… Won't you guys just look at the poor baby," Chyna teased. "I think he's going to cry." She blew him a kiss which perked Chris up.

"You lot aren't just saying it, are you? If I come back tomorrow and you're—"

"Just get your arse back here in normal clothes, jackarse," Benny said, standing up and approaching Chris. "We're The Lost, and we don't act like those pricks in school, mate." The leader, who was several inches taller than Chris and wore an army jacket and combat boots, extended his hand.

Chris took a hold of it tentatively—the dirt beneath Benny's nails turning his stomach—and shook it.

"You make sure you come back tomorrow, Chris."

He has a shark's smile, Chris thought. "Okay, I will." When he turned to leave, the others yelled after him.

"Bye. See you soon, Chris."

***

That night he lay in bed with a constant tremor of excitement buzzing through him. His parents, who had no inkling of him skipping school, had resorted back to their zombie-like existence now Chloe had returned to university.

As usual, he was a ghost to them, but he didn't care. He had a new family; a family that didn't worry about his lack of wealth, social standing, and skills, intelligence and awkwardness.

However, Chris made a deal with himself to never tell them about how he liked to spy on his mother and sister. That thought made him blush.

What would Chyna think?

He then had an urge to peep on her.

I can't believe she flashed me. I wonder if she will again…

Did he even care about the lads? Was it just her he was interested in? Only time would tell. For now, he would be happy to hang with them, to act like a normal boy with real friends in the real world, and not inside his head.

I bet their den is super cool. It's probably a tree house, or something just as awesome.

***

Sleep had come in patches, but when his alarm started ringing at eight a.m., he bounced out of bed, washed, dressed in his school clothes, grabbed his school bag (which had been packed with playing clothes) and headed downstairs for breakfast.

As usual, his parents were still in bed, and so he was left to his own devices.

I shouldn't have bothered packing my play clothes, just worn them, he thought, pouring himself a bowl of cereal. *Not like they give a shit, is it? I'm invisible.*

He fetched the milk from the fridge and added some on his food.

At least they're not shouting and swearing, or hitting lumps out of each other, as is the norm lately. If things are that bad between them, why don't they end it? Who would I choose to live with?

He couldn't figure them out, not that he cared. He hated them.

His thoughts flitted back to The Lost and an urgency to get going washed over him. Chris looked down at his food and almost pushed it aside. *No, I should get something in me.*

Chris shovelled the frosted flakes into his mouth in big spoonfuls and was finished before he knew it. He deposited his dirty bowl into the sink, picked up his bag, and left the house. He gave the front door a satisfying slam as he went, thinking it would wake his parents and annoy them.

A giggle escaped him as he walked past the bus stop and gave the children waiting there the middle finger. After doing so, he was worried some of the boys would chase him, but they didn't. They seemed too stunned by his boldness.

For the first time in forever, Chris felt free; free to be who he wanted to be.

I'll be able to let my freak flag fly, he thought.

After disappearing around a corner, the bus stop now out of sight, Chris ducked down an alley and found a dark secluded spot. He stripped out of his school uniform and dressed in his plain clothes. Once he'd stuffed his school fatigues into his rucksack, he hid it there in the lane and fled the scene.

I'll come back for it later.

He ran with excitement coursing through him, and the wind tousled his hair.

"*Freeee*!" he yelled, whooping and cheering, jumping and clapping. When the school bus approached from behind, he gave it the V-signal. Some of the boys pounded the glass and others made throat-slashing signs.

It didn't matter. He wouldn't be seeing any of them ever again, and if his parents tried forcing him back to school, he'd run away.

When he got closer to the bridge, his heart sank, for he couldn't hear anyone under there.

The Lost lied to me, he sulked.

Then he realised it was still early.

Maybe they don't hook up until midday-ish? But then again, it was only nine a.m. yesterday when I got here.

Chris walked under the bridge and called out, just in case they were hiding in the shadows, or somewhere he couldn't see them.

"Guys? It's Chris."

Nothing.

The only sounds were that of water trickling from a stream close by and the roar of cars passing overhead.

He kicked a stone and pushed his hands into his pocket.

They tricked me, and I've left my school clothes and bag in that lane and missed my bus. Calm down. It's not like I would have gone to school anyway.

Chris sat on a nearby stone and put his elbows on his knees and his chin in his palms.

Now what do I do?

He let his eyes wander across the walls in front of him, noticing, for the first time, the colourful graffiti. Compelled, he stood up and walked over to where some of the brighter artwork had caught his eye. A lot of the swear words and pictures he didn't understand, but he was sure Benny and his gang could explain them, if he asked.

Lousy bastards, leaving me hanging like this.

And then his eyes fell on a series of numbers which got his heart beating faster.

"Looking for sexy girls? Then call now," he spoke aloud. Another said, "Do you like sucking dick? Then meet me here tonight."

But the one that intrigued him the most was the one that read, "Do you love to watch? Ring me, babe."

Sounds like a girl may have left that one. Damn, I wish I had a pen so I could take her *number down. Maybe Chloe wrote it? Nah, that slut has deserted me for her pish-posh studies. Haughty bitch.*

"Looking for a boyfriend?" someone called from

behind.

Chris' bladder pinched, but he turned around with a scowl on his face. "Where have you guys been? I thought you were playing a joke on me."

"Aww, did the baby cry?" Hatchy asked, squeezing Chris' cheek.

"Maybe I should change his nappy," Chyna teased.

"Piss off," he said, surprised at how easy he found his voice around The Lost.

Benny and the others laughed. "Boy got balls, I'll give him that."

"I guess we'll see just how big they are during his entry tests," Paul said.

Foolishly, Chris said, "I can take whatever you've got." Since this was a fresh start, with none of these children knowing him, he felt he had nothing to lose.

Maybe the years of abuse and putdowns have hardened me.

"Ooh, big man," Chyna joined in. "Maybe you'd like to show them to me now?" she winked and slapped Benny on his back.

"I can hear them clanging," Benny admitted, and the others broke up in fits of laughter.

Chris couldn't help but smile. *I belong with this bunch*, he thought. *It feels right*. "Come on, then, what have I got to do in order to join The Lost? Let you see me naked? Are you going to spank my arse with paddles? Make me dress like a chicken?" Chris had always been told by his parents never to use vulgar language. Once, after hearing the word ‘fuck’ in school, he’d asked his dad what it meant and he’d received his answers in the form of his father’s belt.

“If you use vile, piggish language like that again in my house, I’ll whip you raw.”

Oh, but it was fine for Chloe to talk about boys and to dress like a whore on Saturday nights. Plus, she was caught swearing plenty of times to her girl mates over the phone, wasn’t she?

He wanted The Lost to accept him, and he knew by acting big, blasé and mouthy, he’d achieve that, because that’s how the rest of them were. He could see through their paper acts.

“Well, are those the types of things you’re going to do to me?” He stood there with his arms crossed, looking at them with his best ‘I’m not terrified of you and your little tests. The Lost? *Ooh*, scary’ look. A smile appeared on his face.

“Bet you’d like a paddling,” Benny said, stepping from the pack, “but we’re no arse-bashers, mate.” He reached into his boot and brought out a slender object with a silver button in its centre. “Ever spilt blood?” Benny stepped almost nose-to-nose with Chris.

That a flick-knife? Chris thought, looking at what the much bigger lad held.

“Scared, pretty boy?”

From behind Benny, Chris heard the others laugh, and it took all the guts he could muster not to wet himself.

The blade popped out of its slender groove, the tip mere inches from Chris’ eye.

"Not going to piss yourself, are you?"

"I don't think it was the chump's balls you could hear knocking," Paul said, "but his knees."

More laughter.

"Well, pretty boy?" Benny asked, sliding the cool blade down Chris' cheek.

Chris was unsure of what to say. Would it make him look like a coward if he said yes? Would he be seen as a psycho if he said no?

"N-no," he warbled.

"He ain't so tough now," Hatchy said. "Take an eyeball for a souvenir, boss."

"Maybe I will, Hatchy. Maybe I will."

Is this a test?

"Go for it. See if I give a shit." Chris found his manhood once again. "Not the right one, though," and Chris moved the knife to his left eye. "This one, because I wouldn't be able to play with my dick as well without the other, see. Ha, *see*!"

The rest of The Lost laughed, but Benny looked annoyed, and then his face softened into a smile. "Congratulations. You've passed your first test."

"Is that it? *Pft*. Child's play." It took everything he had to calm his rampaging heart. "What chicken shit bullshit's next? Are you going to ask me to ride my skateboard without my helmet? Scary Mary."

The others laughed harder, but Benny's face darkened.

"This clown thinks he's hot shit."

Something had definitely snapped within Chris. He could feel it.

Yesterday had been the final straw, what with

that bitch going back to university to mingle with her elite friends, and my parents acting like arseholes. Fuck 'em.

Chris snatched the knife out of Benny's hand, his anger spilling over. "You don't think so, Big Ben? Huh? What if I used this little stick tool of yours to kill my sister? Would that be enough blood for you?"

The ones behind their leader fell silent.

Benny's mouth opened and closed. No words came.

"What do you say? If I do that, I'm in?"

The look on Benny's face changed. "Deal. But I want pictures, or it didn't happen."

"Yeah," Chyna said, getting up and putting an arm around Chris' waist. "I think we've found something special here, boys, alright. Chris is a Lost in the making."

"My sister's away at university until the summer, so I'll have to wait until then."

"So can your membership, in that case," Benny said. "But you can hang on to the knife until you're ready to come back here with my proof. Bye." The boss turned, gathered his troops, and led them away.

"Will you promise to be here when I come back in July?" he called after them.

"You shouldn't even need to ask that," Benny said, not turning to look at him.

Chris stood there and watched as they disappeared out of sight.

***

Jesus. That had been the longest few months of my life, he thought, still sat in front of his TV. Katie's parents were now on the news, pleading for the safe return of their daughter.

He sat up, took a drink, and watched the way in which Katie's mother's mouth moved as she begged and sobbed.

Such a breathtaking sight, he thought, his eyes transfixed on the screen.

When the charade was brought to an end by Broadbank, the parents were ushered out of the room and the screen cut back to the news presenter.

"Those were the disturbing scenes—" the anchor prattled on.

The Widower Maker retreated back to his own world.

When the summer holidays rolled around and Chloe was back in town, boy was I excited.

Before hatching a plan to execute, Chris had gone to the bridge every day (making sure he couldn't be spotted) to check The Lost still roamed there—which they did.

They'll be true to their word, and they'll never tell on me to the police, he thought. And, as that summer pressed on and he gained membership to The Lost, Chris discovered each affiliate harboured a dark secret of their own. *It was the best goddamn six weeks of my life.*

He polished off the can of Coke and deposited the rubbish in his bin. As he turned the lights and TV off, about to turn in for the evening, he noticed a corner of something poking out from under his doormat.

"What—?" He bent and retrieved the envelope. "How did I miss that when I picked up the post earlier?"

He ripped it open and discovered a card inside – much like a business one. The Widower Maker plucked it out and saw something written on it. He read it aloud.

"Four-Fingers was seen blabbing to the private eye. Signed, Hatchy."

"Mother*fucker*," he roared, booting his bin into the air, which crash-landed on his sofa. He crumpled the card in his hand and went for his hunting knife.

***

After dressing, he slipped out of his flat and boarded a night bus.

"Ticket to the bay, please," he asked the driver, smiling. His hand that remained in the pocket of his hoodie tightened around the haft of his knife.

Damn you, Four-Fingers. Damn you…

Chapter 15

Someone kicked his door and it shuddered in its frame. The doorknob, which was close to Samson's ear, rattled.

"Bloody hell." Samson jumped out of his seat, his vision blurred. "Who's there?" he demanded.

Footfalls were heard retreating in the corridor.

Samson removed the seat from behind the door and opened it a sliver, leaving the security chain on, and peeped outside. There was nobody there.

"Goddamn palookas," he muttered, locking up again.

When he stretched, he looked through the window and saw it was dawn. He yawned, scratched at the stubble on his neck, and then checked his watch. It was almost six thirty.

No point in trying to go back to sleep now, he thought.

He saw the tea's maid and pulled a face.

That thing's blacker than the ace of spades. I'll grab a coffee in town, that's if I ever get out of here.

Samson paced the room, stretching his legs and back as he thought about calling Broadbank.

Maybe he's forgotten. Hardly.

***

Thirty minutes later, the phone in his room was ringing.

Samson snatched it up. “Broadbank?”
“Yeah, it’s me.”
“What’s wrong, pip, you sound defeated?”
“Before I give you your information, there’s something I need to tell you.”
“Go on,” Samson said, holding his breath. His guts knotted, thinking he knew what was coming.
“It’s The Brain.”
“What’s that hop-head loser done now?” His apprehension ebbed.
“He’s dead.”
“How?”
“There was a riot last night, resulting in a lockdown. When the cells were checked this morning, The Brain was found shivved in his bed.”
“Holy smoke, Broadbank.”
“This is why I’m late in getting back to you, sorry, Sam. It was a scene of complete overkill.”
“What do you mean?”
“We counted at least sixty stab wounds, with five makeshift knives jutting from his body. He was pinned to his mattress.”
“Christ.”
“There’s more.”
“What, tell me?”
“The word “Blab” was found inscribed on the wall next to The Brain’s cot. It had been written in his blood. They’re on to you, Sam.”
“Have you checked on Mike?”
“Yeah, he’s fine, and I’ve filled him in on everything.”
“I think you should take him off the streets.”

"Tried, but he refused."

"Pull rank on him, then. Is anyone talking? The inmates are probably puckered up tighter than a duck's backside."

"Something like that, yeah, but we have a few candidates."

"XRay's hoods?"

"No," Broadbank said. "But I'm working on it, and when I do get to the bottom of it, the guards who turned a blind eye will be begging for mercy by the time I get through with them."

"You better get some men out to the bay. They could go after a fella by the name of Four-Fingers next."

"Four-Fingers? I've heard that name before. I'll get on it."

"You've got information for me?"

"Yeah, and it's all good, Sam. First off, the captain there, Donny Quaker, is a good friend of mine. I told him about you and your business with Lovell, and that you planned on taking the crime boss down."

"Was he fine with that?"

"Yes, and he's excited to meet and greet you, Sam. It seems Lovell is causing a lot of grief that way."

"Excellent."

"Be warned, however, Quaker is a bit of a stickler, not to mention a pain in the arse."

"I'll handle him, don't you worry. Do I go to the station this morning?"

"That would be best, yes, because I couldn't find

anything on Lovell and his operations. You're on your own there, snoop. Listen, I better get going – It's been a long night and I need to get home to the wife, who I've left in charge of your mutt."

"Ha. Yeah, you go. I'll give it a few hours and head to Quaker for a chat. In the meantime, I'm going to relocate."

"Give me a call once you've spoken with Quaker, Sam. He's a good man beneath his bullshit."

"Will do." Samson hung up and immediately felt better, even though he didn't smell the best.

He stepped from the phone, grabbed his coat, hat and key to the room and left. In the hallway, Samson had to step over two men wrestling naked in the corridor. When he looked behind him, he saw they were punching and biting each other.

No law against such pastimes, I suppose. Fools.

"It was my Barbie Doll," one of the fighters slurred.

Samson shook his head and moved down the hallway to the reception desk. He was pleased to see the manageress was nowhere in sight.

"Small mercies and all that," he uttered, placing the key on her counter. When he turned to leave, he saw the drugged-up couple still slumped on the bench. "Bloody mess."

"Leaving so soon, cutie pie?" came a voice from behind.

Samson gulped, not wanting to turn around. "Got a busy day ahead of me, ma'am," he said over his shoulder, walking towards the door. "Thanks for the hospitality."

Before she could answer, he was outside hailing a taxi.

"Where to, chief?" the cabby asked, poking his head out of his window.

"As far away from this flea-infested joint as possible, fella."

The driver laughed. "Need a new place to crash?"

Samson nodded.

"Get in and I'll see what I can do."

"You can't do any worse, that's for sure."

By nine a.m., Samson was settled in a cosy little hotel situated in the middle of Carmarthenshire. He'd showered and shaved—after purchasing toiletries from the hotel's shop—and called Broadbank with his new location and number.

He was now ready to hit the mean streets of Carmarthenshire to buy snooper equipment and a briefcase.

After that, I'll head to the police station, he thought.

***

The old marketplace that was Carmarthenshire operated on a much smaller scale than Cardiff. For starters, it was a settlement in the middle of nowhere, with no major towns or cities around it, and its minuscule police station had a force to match its size.

Cow country, Samson thought, walking through

the town's centre. *Only in such a place will you see strings of tractors at traffic lights, and farmers at road crossings with sheep.*

Samson went for the inside pocket of his trench coat and realised he was out of breadsticks.

"Damn, I'll have to get some. I'm desperate for a smoke," he muttered, looking down at the pavement.

The urge had come on strong last night, and again this morning. He'd put it down to stress brought on by the men who'd chased him, the grot bag of a hotel and its occupants, and the news about The Brain.

Plus everything else, he thought.

And then Lisa popped into his mind.

I need to try and get a message to her, to let her know I'm fine. I also need to call that lousy ex-fella of hers.

Samson searched his pockets and found he still had Derek's number.

When I get back to the hotel after this meeting with Quaker, I'll get on it.

As he passed a corner shop doubled as a stationary store, Samson went inside and bought some breadsticks and bottled water. He carried his supplies in a plastic bag until he found a place selling cases and electrical goods.

After purchasing a cheap briefcase—camera and some spare film—Samson transferred everything into it, including a pad and pen he'd picked up at the first shop.

Back on the high street, he asked for directions to

the police station from the first person he came across, finding he was less than a mile away.

"Thanks, sir," Samson said, moving away from the man.

Samson rounded the next corner and found himself branching off from the town centre. He was now strolling down a side street.

He didn't like it.

In the shadows, much like Cardiff, hoodlums, junkies and flunkies were gathered.

Samson felt threatened.

Broadbank did say they were under the hammer here. That Lovell had the place under his thumb. Well, not for much longer, if I've got anything to do and say about it.

"Hey, look at this fool," a man called from a darkened corner.

"Nice coat. You wearing anything underneath it, Flash?" a second person spoke up.

Samson kept moving.

Ignore.

As he approached the end of the street he saw more hoods; a gang of males dressed in the same colours, and who wore an insignia on their back. Samson stopped, looked at them closer, and saw they bore the name Lovell on their chests.

"What are you looking at, old man?"

The punks, who varied in age, size and creed, had been sat around a CD player listening to blaring music whilst passing booze and joints between them. When they flanked him, Samson heard the faint rattle of chains and a flick-knife clicking into place.

"Easy, gents," Samson said, putting his hands up. "I'm just passing through. I didn't mean to stare."

Christ, how on earth have I managed to run into a load of Lovell's men? If this goes south, and they report me to the man of the hour, then he'll know I'm here.

The lieutenant of the gang, who couldn't have been more than twenty, stood almost toe-to-toe with Samson.

"Is there any need to get right in my beezer, son?" the P.I. asked.

"Fool, talk English," the punk said, looking down on Samson.

The boy can't even grow a decent beard, he thought, looking at the scraggly hair that graced the youth's chin and neck.

"I'm an officer of the law, boy, so unless you want to get run in, I suggest you back off."

"*Ooh*!" one of the lad's goons mocked. "We're pissing in our pants."

"What's in the briefcase, arsehole?" a black teen asked, holding up a knife.

Samson stood up straight, sighed, and glared at the punks. "I'm only going to say this once more. Get out of my way or I'll round you up like cattle and take you to the big house. Choice is yours." Samson reached for his credentials.

"You packing heat?"

"A roscoe? What do I look like to you, hop-head?" Samson pulled his police badge and flashed it.

"That shit don't mean anything 'round these parts. You think that fat sack of noise, Quaker, runs the show?" the lieutenant asked.

"I guess you do, is that right? You, and the rest of your monkeys," Samson said, smiling and nodding at the others who stood half in and half out of the shadows.

"You say?" he shoved Samson, raising the chains he held in his hands.

A barrel-like boy of seventeen or eighteen stood by his lieutenant's side. He held the remains of a shattered bottle, and the jagged edge was thrust towards Samson's face. "Let me stick the pig cunt, Kelly, please."

How vulgar, he thought. "Did your ma and pa ever teach you about manners?" Samson asked. "You vile little specimen."

The fat boy's face twisted into rage, and had it not been for Kelly pushing the child aside, Samson would have had the bottle buried in his face.

"That's enough, Clyde," Kelly said. "This fool's Bill. We can't dust him without L's say so. You know that." And then he turned to Samson. "You best count yourself lucky today, Mr Policeman, and let's hope we won't be seeing each other again."

Samson laughed, shouldered Kelly out of his way, and walked on.

At least there's no Hitler Youth in the apple of Cardiff, he thought, glancing over his shoulder.

They were still there, watching him.

If they don't report me, a strange-looking copper, to Lovell, then I'll be the luckiest fella walking the planet.

He could just hear Kelly now: "Got some new cop in town, boss – a right weirdo in a raincoat and funny looking hat. A right *palooka*."

Well, he wouldn't use that *word,* Samson thought, smiling and drawing a breadstick from his breast pocket. *Would it matter if they called me out? That would mean Lovell would come to me?*

He pondered that for a moment.

I could go back down there and demand they take me to Lovell, shut him down this very day. No, that would be foolish. I'm going to need to play this cool. Rip him up bit by bit. The jug-head won't know what's hit him.

Samson shoved more of the breadstick into his mouth as he approached the police station.

***

It was quiet. There were no police cars parked out front, or officers roaming.

You'd normally see a bobby or two milling about.

When he entered the building, which smelt of bleach and polish, and gleamed, Samson saw the desk sergeant was on his phone, his face red.

"Ma'am, as I told you the last four times you called, I'm trying my best to get a unit out to you. We're currently stretched."

After hanging up, about to address Samson, the phone started ringing. He let it go. "Yes, how can I help?"

"Short staffed?"

"You should become a detective. You have an eye for it."

"Nice use of sarcasm," Samson said, not breaking a smile.

"Who are you and what can I do for you?" the squat, fat man asked, eyeing Samson over the top of his half-moon specs.

"I'm here to see Quaker."

"He's currently out. Who *are* you?"

"Samson Valentine. I was told he'd be expecting me."

"The private eye from Cardiff?"

Samson placed the last of his breadstick into his mouth and nodded.

The phone kept ringing.

"One moment," he told Samson. "Hello, Carmarthen—ma'am, *please* stop calling. I—he's done what? You never said he had a *knife*… Okay, okay, I'll have someone there right away. Address?" The man scribbled down the particulars, said his goodbyes, and hung up.

"Something I can help with whilst I wait for your el capitano to drop in?"

The sergeant gave Samson the once over. "No, I—can I see some credentials?"

The P.I. was only too happy to oblige and placed his cards, badge and driver's licence down on the man's desk. "You can give my chief back in Cardiff a call if you'd like. He'd vouch for me."

"I'll do just that. Can I keep a hold of these for now?" he indicated Samson's personal information.

"Yes. Where am I going? Can I take a car?"

"Quaker will have my arse if—"

"Loosen up, palooka, you'll live longer. Give me the keys to an unmarked vehicle."

The man's mouth hung open, but he didn't say anything and then gave Samson the details he'd taken over the phone. "Take car five. You'll find it parked in a bay behind the station. Do you have cuffs?"

"Of course. Is it a domestic?"

"Yeah, at first I thought it was just a lovers tiff, but it seems to have turned violent. She's locked herself in the bathroom and he's wandering around the house with a kitchen knife."

"Okay, I'll bring him in."

"Be careful, for Christ's sake, man. My head's already on the block for giving you a vehicle and handing out sensitive information."

"I'll be back as soon as I can. Does the car have satellite navigation?"

"Yes, it's built-in."

Samson turned and left. Over his shoulder, he said, "Tell Quaker what's happened."

"I'll try and get him on the radio and patch him through to your car."

"Thanks."

***

A few minutes later, Samson had the address entered into the sat-nav and was pulling out of the station's car park.

The drive would take him less than ten minutes.

As he drove around the streets, he saw multiple police officers in cars, and riot vans at various calls.

"For such a small place, they have a lot of problems, which Lovell is responsible for."

When he reached the given address, Samson found he was on a council estate—burned-out cars, fire barrels, and debris from shopping trolleys to children's toys littered the area.

"Bloody hell."

He parked the car close to other vehicles, hoping it would be safe.

At least it doesn't have 'Police' written all over it, he thought.

Samson walked across the courtyard and saw people having sex in doorways, more of Lovell's thugs, who eyeballed him, drunks, druggies and children under the age of fifteen smoking and playing cards for money.

"You don't belong here, boy," one of Lovell's hoods called, but Samson kept going.

He approached the concrete steps leading to the second floor and discovered a boy and girl kissing on the bottom step; he had his hand down the front of her jeans and she was squirming and moaning.

Is she trying to push him away? Samson thought.

And then she was raking her hands through the boy's long, lank hair.

As if sensing Samson, they stopped and looked at him.

"Are you a voyeuristic pervert?" The lad stood up and drew a large knife from the inside of his coat.

"No, Tommy," the girl said, pulling her lover back. "I don't want you going away again. Think of the baby."

Samson noticed the swell of her stomach and felt sick for her, Tommy, and the baby. The P.I. slipped by them and headed for number three-twenty.

A television, its screen busted, lay on the floor outside the house he was after. The front window was non-existent, and from the lack of glass, Samson was able to hear a man shouting (in a slurred manner) and swearing, from within.

"When you come outta there, I'm going to cut ya up, slut. You *hear* me? I'm going to feed your guts to the rats."

Samson huffed. *I've dealt with many a drunken bully in my time.*

"Hey, *scumbag*," Samson taunted through the window. "Why don't you come on out here and pick on someone your own size?"

"Who's that?" the unseen man asked, stomping closer.

Who are *these people?* he suddenly thought, fishing the paper he'd been given out of his pocket. When he'd entered the address in the sat-nav, he'd never thought to check their names. "Miss Sheds," he muttered.

There was no name for him.

Out of the gloomy interior of the smashed-up flat, Samson saw a large, shadowy figure approach. He held a butcher's knife in one hand, which dripped blood. In his other paw, he gripped a half-drunk bottle of rum.

"Fuck you want, pussy?" he staggered, jabbing the knife at Samson. "You want some? I'll gut you."

The P.I. backed away until his arse met with the landing's metal railing.

"Deaf?"

The man got closer.

Such a picture of beauty, Samson thought, looking at the guy's food-stained string vest. He didn't wear trousers, just boxer shorts. When he got that little bit closer, Samson saw his eyes were bloodshot and rolling around inside his skull.

"Easy, fella. I just want to talk. There's no need for me to take you in. Where's your girlfriend?"

"*Fiancée*, dickhead." The man tried to climb out of the window but slipped and fell backwards.

Samson stepped forward, expecting to see the guy sprawled on his back in the living room, but he wasn't there. And then the front door opened.

"You want to hope you're gone."

Samson heard the knife clatter against the rum bottle. He pulled his cuffs out and got ready to take the man to the ground. But then the man was screaming, and blood splashed across the ground in front of Samson.

"I'll kill you, you bastard. I'm not going to take any more of your shit," a woman yelled.

At Samson's back, a neighbour came out to see what was going on. "Those pricks at it again?" they asked Samson.

The P.I. turned and looked at the dumpy woman. She wore a grubby dressing gown and had rollers the size of rubbish bins in her greasy hair.

"Miss, I'm going to have to ask you to step back in—"

"Get off me, bitch." The man tumbled out of the flat with his fiancée on his back. A meat cleaver protruded from his shoulder, and blood pissed down his chest. With a lucky shot, he managed to slam her in the face with the butt of his elbow.

Samson heard the woman's nose crunch.

"I'm calling the police," the female next to Samson said.

"Relax, I *am* the police." He gave her a quick flash of his badge and stepped in to apprehend the fella. Before the man could regain his composure, Samson palmed the knife out of his hand and snapped a cuff around his wrist. He then clicked the matching bracelet to the landing's railing. "Stay put, friend."

Samson stepped inside the flat to find the woman in the kitchen. She was lying on her back with blood pumping out of her nostrils. As she tried to speak, more blood gushed out of her.

"Did—I—ugh-*uch,*" she choked, trying to brace herself up on her elbows but failing due to the blood pooling beneath her. When she collapsed, her head struck the kitchen floor with a sickening crack. "Did-*uch…*"

"Shh," Samson soothed, using her house phone to call for an ambulance. He wasn't sure how much blood the man had lost, but it wasn't looking good for him.

After being told a medical unit would be with

him within five minutes, Samson hung up and knelt by the woman's side. He took her hand in his. "You're going to be okay, miss."

"Tha-that was the last time he was going to lay his f-fucking—*uch*—hands on me."

"He's your *fiancé*?" he asked, not believing the drunk. She nodded. "And your name's Sheila?"

"Yes," she gargled.

"What's his name?" Samson remembered from his first aid course back when he was on the force that you should always try and stay with the injured person.

"Keep them talking and make them comfortable," his instructor had said.

"P-Paul…" she spat, which seemed to take everything she had to answer.

Blood spattered Samson's face. "Surname?"

"Lu-Luther-Lutherhead," she gasped.

Samson's jaw slackened. Could it be the same Lutherhead Broadbank would be searching for in Cardiff?

"Did you say *Lutherhead*?" He spelt it out for her.

"Y-yes."

Where's that ambulance? God, I hope she hasn't killed him. "Are you going to be okay by yourself? I need to check on him."

"Don't let him get me, please." Tears slid from her blackened eyes.

"Not going to happen, sweetheart."

"T-thanks."

"You're *sure* you'll be okay?"

She nodded. Samson got up and peeled his hand away from hers.

Outside, Samson noticed more neighbours had gathered. Some were taking photos of the blood-soaked Paul Lutherhead, whilst others whispered and pointed.

"About time someone did something about that piece of woman-beating scum," a man voiced his opinion from the crowd.

"Please, can you all take a step back," Samson ordered, hearing sirens in the near distance. A vehicle came to a screeching halt below. "Mr Lutherhead, can you hear me?" Samson put a finger to the man's neck. There was a faint pulse. "Don't you die on me, palooka. Don't you goddamn dare."

Doors slammed.

Voices called out.

The next thing Samson knew, there were paramedics rushing towards him.

"This fella's seriously hurt, and there's a woman inside."

"Thanks. Are you a relative?"

"No. I'm with the police."

"Fine, but we'll take it from here, sir."

Samson backed off after removing his cuffs from Lutherhead and he leaned on the banister. *Paul Lutherhead.* He couldn't believe it. *That's if it's the* same *Paul Lutherhead. But it has to be, right? How many Paul Lutherheads are running around the place*?

He pushed off the railing, his head swimming, and he noticed for the first time the blood over his hands, coat, and suit. The paramedics pushed by with Lutherhead on a stretcher—who was awake and mumbling something—but Samson couldn't make it out.

"Can I accompany him in the ambulance? I have questions—"

"No, sir," he was told by one of the medics. "He has a serious wound that needs urgent treatment en route."

"Which hospital?"

"Carmarthenshire General, sir, but you won't be able to ask him anything for a while."

Samson conceded defeat and watched as the ambulance personnel navigated the concrete steps at a slow pace. "What about his girlfriend?" he asked, but they were gone.

Damn, now what? he thought. C*hat with Quaker, pronto, that's what.*

Chapter 16

"You come storming into my jurisdiction like some cowboy on a power trip with a sparkling badge and start giving *me* orders? Look, people, it's big bad Valentine, riding into town." Quaker's jowly face turned red, then purple. The veins in his neck protruded and his nostrils flared. "Have you any idea how much *shit* you could land me in? What if you'd crashed that car? Or if those punks from the streets had caught up with you?"

"I didn't storm into anywhere. You were told I was coming. You were expecting me, Quaker. Also, I was careful, *sir,*" Samson defended himself, sat across from Quaker in the man's office.

Quaker was on his feet—a chunky cigar in his mouth—his hands pressed flat on his table, propping him up. He blew smoke in Samson's face. "I told Broadbank I was happy to assist you, not to loan you patrol cars so you could help us with every whipstitch of a case. You think we're incompetent, is that it?"

"Your streets would suggest so, yes," Samson dared.

A cloud came over Quaker's face. "I—"

"Look, I'm sorry," Samson cut him off. "I thought I was doing the right thing. Your man on the desk seemed under the cosh, and I wanted to help out. Besides, it was a good thing I did. Paul Lutherhead is important to my case in Cardiff.

He *might* even be The Widower Maker. If he isn't, he'll know who is."

"Is that so?" Quaker softened, lowering himself into his seat. "I thought you were here to try and nab Lovell? Broadbank told me you're the best P.I. to walk God's green Earth."

"He's kind. But, yes, I am here for Lovell. That fella has been trying to kill me by sending hitters to Cardiff. I need him out of the picture if I'm going to catch The Widower Maker."

"If Lutherhead is as important as you say, then you may kill two birds with one stone, whilst you're here," Quaker sighed. "I'm not sure how easy capturing Lovell will be, friend." Quaker's chair groaned when his large frame relaxed into it. "We've been trying to get dirt on him for the past twelve months."

"Any leads on his operations?"

"Nothing."

"What's he into? Drugs? Guns? Pro-skirts?"

"We think drugs, but we're unsure of how he's getting them in and out of the country, if he is."

"We're not far from the sea?"

"It's a possibility, and it's one we've been covering, but nothing."

"Did he pick up right off where Alligator left things?"

"Pretty much, yes. He breezed into the west and took charge of things before we could smooth things out. He brought with him a small army from the north of Wales, which he still has control over."

"Is there any part of this land of ours that isn't

run by scum and blood money?" Samson asked himself, more than Quaker.

"It wouldn't seem it. Look, I can give you the low-down on Lovell, his bases of operations, his top thugs, and everything else you may need."

"That's good. Will you make sure someone watches over Lutherhead for me? Not that I think he's in danger."

"Consider it done, even though I'm short on manpower."

"I'll need full access to him, too."

"That's fine."

"Do you want me to come back later to pick up the info on Lovell?"

"Shouldn't be necessary," Quaker said, prying himself out of his chair and going to his filing cabinets. "I have it all right here." He opened a drawer and pulled out two large files. "Got everything from transcripts to photographs – you'll find everything you need."

Samson opened one of the folders and took a quick look over things, nodding as he did so. "This is great."

"Do you, er…"

Samson looked up at Quaker. "What?"

"Plan on, you know," Quaker rubbed at the back of his neck. "Changing into something different whilst you're here? His thugs will spot you a mile off."

Samson laughed. "The punks who stopped me on the street earlier seemed as bright as a broken bulb. No, I won't be. Now that I have everything, nobody will see me unless I want them to. That includes you and your men, sir. I'll be a ghost; a lonesome presence in the shadows." Samson stood up to leave. "I think that's everything, for now. You have my number at the hotel, should you need me."

They shook hands. "I sure do."

"One more thing before I go, may I keep the car I was assigned?"

"Yes. I'll file the paperwork for you."

"Thanks, Quaker. Broadbank was right, you are a good guy."

As Samson left, Quaker apologised for yelling and insulting Samson. "I'm glad to have you here, believe you me."

"Thank you."

***

Before Samson made his way back to the hotel, he checked in at the hospital to see how Lutherhead was doing. Samson was told the man had lost copious amounts of blood, but was out of danger.

"No interviews for now," the doctor added. "Come back in a few days."

***

When he reached his room, he felt relieved. It had been a long, strange day, and all he wanted to do was report in with Broadbank, kick off his shoes, and mull over the notes Quaker had provided.

I need to get a game plan together, he thought,

turning the key in the door to his hotel room. When he entered, the lights came on—courtesy of the sensors—and so he placed his files down on the sideboard close by.

"Thank God," he muttered, stepping out of his shoes as the door behind him inched shut, locking into place. Samson removed his hat and coat and hung both on the stand by his side. "Just in time, by the looks of things." He loosened his tie and stared out the window; fat droplets of rain started to bombard the glass. "Ugh, ugly weather."

When he turned to place his tie, he heard footsteps from behind.

His heart leapt into his mouth and his arms remained suspended in midair.

Had he heard the click of a gun's hammer? No, he didn't think so.

Samson felt paralysed.

How did they track me? I made sure no one had been following me.

Did someone blab? Broadbank? Quaker? The goons from the street?

His mind was a derailing freight train of thoughts, spilling its cargo and flooding his brain.

"Samson," she said.

His breathing became constricted, his throat narrowing. Samson closed his eyes—he didn't want this to be true—he'd hoped he'd been wrong about her, that the nagging thoughts and feelings had been way off the mark.

"Lisa," he sighed, turning to face her. She didn't have a gun pointed at him.

She forced a smile.

He couldn't.

"You're dressed like a grieving widow," he shot at her, trying to ice his tone, but giving her the benefit of doubt. "Did I know him?"

Lisa raised the veil attached to her hat and revealed the tears spilling down her cheeks, that left dirty mascara tracks in their wake. She tried to speak, but couldn't.

"Well, aren't you going to explain yourself? And no more lies, yeah? I knew there was something off about you from the start."

She stepped closer to him and raised a hand.

Samson took a step backwards, his arse connecting with the coat stand, wobbling it.

"I'm not going to hurt you," she said, her voice barely audible.

"What are you doing here? How did you find me? Who are you working for? Tell me, gal. Do you plan on killing me? To shut me up? Is that it?"

"No, not at all…"

"Don't give me that. Why else would you be here?"

She sighed, collapsing into the only seat in the room. "Mind if I smoke?"

"Carry on," he said, shrugging his shoulders. He didn't take his eyes off her or her hands as they plunged into her bag.

"Nice and slow, Lisa, please."

"You think I have a gun? God, what kind of person—"

"Can it, lady. I'm not buying what you're selling.

Start talking, or I'm going to get upset, and you won't like that."

"Give a girl two seconds." He saw her hands were shaking as she placed a cigarette in her mouth, and it took her three attempts to light it. She took a long pull on the fag, dipped her head back, and expelled smoke into the air above her. "I've been keeping tabs on you. I was hired to do so."

"By who?" Lisa looked away. "Come on, *who*?" He slammed his fist down on the sideboard and the cups next to the kettle rattled. A spoon fell to the floor. He wanted to grab her by the shoulders and shake it out of her. When he took a step closer, she blurted her answer.

"XRay."

Samson stopped dead. "*What*?"

She jumped and then looked down at her feet. "You heard. XRay."

"Holy moly, woman – you're on his *books?* As a spy? Moll? *Enforcer*?"

"I guess you'd call me a spy. I'm used mainly to infiltrate opposing gangs for his organisation."

"He put you in that flat across from me?"

"That was all me. I was given you as my job – told to keep eyes on you – and so I set myself up there and watched you. I put a tracker on your car."

"You—unbelievable. Why are you here?"

"I wanted to come clean."

"Is this some game? Think before you talk, because I'm a human lie detector, Lisa. *Lisa*," he scoffed, "if that's even your *real* name."

"It is. I promise you. I wanted to be honest with

you because I felt like we clicked that first night we had dinner. That wasn't meant to happen, Sam."

"Don't spin me that one. This is all part of your diabolical plan. I'm just surprised you didn't try poisoning me, or doing something equally as unpleasant."

"I'm being upfront with you, Sam, for Christ's sake. I take my assignments deadly seriously, but you caught me off-kilter. I was touched by what you told me about your wives and not having children. I saw softness in you, Sam."

"Well, well – a compassionate member of the black masses. It must have made you feel pretty good about yourself, hoodwinking me like that? And tell me, who would I have been speaking to had I contacted your husband? We both know that's a smokescreen."

"One of XRay's men."

"I see. And who is the elusive XRay?"

"I don't know. I work through his hierarchy."

"Of course you do. Well, you have moxie for showing up here and feeding me this rubbish. But then again, no doubt, it's all part of your plan."

"It really isn't, Sam. I've been meaning to make a fresh start for a while now, and when you came into my life, you made that urge stronger. Hell, I've put myself in danger by coming here to tell you this, he's already annoyed with me because you beat up his thugs after I told him I wasn't willing to dupe you any longer."

"Those goons outside your flat the other morning?"

Lisa nodded.

Sam scoffed out a laugh. "Okay, let's for a moment pretend I believe you. What's your end goal?"

"To help you and get myself out of the business. I don't want that life anymore, Sam. I'd also like to continue getting to know you."

He almost laughed. "I don't lay with the enemy, doll."

"I'm not the *enemy*. I came here to prove that, and I have enough dirt to help you put XRay and his ilk away for good. I'm also willing to infiltrate Lovell's gang to get you what you need. I'll even wear a wire or whatever. You have to believe me."

"And what would you want in return?"

"Protection would be good."

"How do you know Lovell?"

"He and XRay are partners."

"Does the name Paul Lutherhead mean anything to you?"

Her face turned white. "You've *found* him?"

"Yes," Samson admitted, feeling a little more relaxed around her. *I don't think she would have been so loose-lipped if she wasn't telling me the truth.* "Would you like a coffee?" Samson put the kettle on to boil.

"Please." Lisa remained in her seat as he prepared their drinks. "Thanks," she said, receiving her coffee.

"I ran across Lutherhead today, but I'm not sure how much I can tell you at this point. I'm torn because I don't completely trust you. You might have a solid poker face, muffin."

"What can I do to gain your confidence?"

"For starters, I want to know *everything*."

"I have nothing to hide, not anymore."

"Who is Lutherhead?"

"He used to work for XRay. They grew up together and it's to my understanding they were like brothers."

"And?"

"Something happened between them. A row, I think, but I'm unsure. XRay drove Paul out of his organisation, and the last anybody ever knew about Lutherhead, was he was still in the city and working for a small-time thug who used to be in XRay's pocket."

"Four-Fingers," Samson said.

"I see you've done your homework."

"The butcher seemed disturbed by Paul and gave him the sack, suggesting he headed this way. Would Lutherhead work for Lovell to annoy XRay?"

"Definitely not, Sam."

"Then is he from Carmarthenshire, originally? Does he have family out this way?"

"Not that I'm aware of, but I could be wrong. I don't know everything. Most of what I do know has come from the grapevine."

"Okay, right. Look, I want to get on the inside of Lovell's gang and rip it down from the centre. You're willing to help me do that, right?"

She nodded. "Yes."

He tried not to get ahead of himself. "Well, I guess we'll see who's telling porkies and who isn't, won't we?"

"I know XRay wants Lutherhead found as soon as possible. There's a massive reward on his head."

"Oh?"

"Again, I don't know all the ins and outs, but I think he's somehow connected to The Widower Maker."

Samson's guts flipped. "What did you say?"

"Lutherhead. I'm sure he knows who the killer is."

"Hmm, yes, I suspected so. I had a chinwag with the glorious XRay a few days ago, and he seemed awfully desperate to be getting his hands on the killer. He even wanted to work with me, for me to deliver The Widower Maker to him personally. Is there a chance he, too, knows the murderer stalking the streets of Cardiff? If so, why doesn't he get him himself, or at least tell me who it is?"

Lisa shrugged. "So many questions, but as I said, I'm happy to help you if that's what you want?"

"I'm curious to know if you're blowing smoke or not."

"I'm not, so you're just going to have to take a chance on me, Sam."

"Fine. Tomorrow morning I'll get you fitted with a wire and send you into Lovell's den to see what you can do. Whilst you undertake your duties, I'm going to press Lutherhead's fiancée."

"Sounds like a plan."

Lisa finished her coffee and set her dirty cup down by the kettle. She then put her hands on Samson's arms.

"Please, don't touch me."

She withdrew her hands with a wounded look in her eye. "I understand."

"Where are you staying, because my couch isn't up for the taking?"

"I have a room in this hotel."

"My, you are a sneaky snake."

"I deserve that."

"And more. Much, *much* more." Samson went to the door and opened it. "Now, if you don't mind, I have things to be getting on with. I'm sure you have to report back to HQ and fill XRay in on my whereabouts. Should I start running?"

"Goodnight, Sam." She stifled a sob. "I'll prove I'm not lying."

"I'm sure you will. G'night." He closed the door on her and placed his chair up against it by stuffing the top of its back beneath the handle. He then put the flats of his hands and forehead against the wall and expelled air through his nose.

Samson felt giddy.

Bile rose in his throat, burning, bringing tears to his eyes.

He swallowed it and shook his head.

I need to call Steve, he thought. *God, he's going to just love me. But it needs to be done. I have to put a safety net in place in case Lisa* is *telling the truth.*

He picked up the phone, but decided to call Broadbank first. The chief answered his mobile after the second ring.

"Broadbank?"

"Hey, it's Samson. I just wanted to check in."

"We're up to our neck in this Widower Maker mess. The press is calling for our guts, wanting to know why there haven't been any arrests yet."

"Did you release the news about Lutherhead?"

"No, why?"

"Keep it under wraps, for now. I don't want XRay and his goons knowing I've got my claws into him. In time, I'll want you to tell the papers, but not yet."

"Okay, not a problem."

"I have it on good word that Lutherhead is connected to XRay and possibly The Widower Maker. I've yet to establish it, though. However, if it turns out to be the case, then it may rattle The Widower Maker into doing something stupid if Lutherhead is mentioned by the police or the press."

"Not sure how long I can sit on it, Sam. The powers that be will be screaming for my head."

"Just hold off for now, pal. It could be worth it."

"Okay. I'll put my trust in you. How long will you be out west?"

"A few weeks, I'm not sure."

Broadbank huffed. "Fine, do what you need to. You will anyway. Plus, I fully trust you, Sam."

"Thanks, sweetheart," Samson smiled. "That reminds me. How is Mike doing? Is he safe?"

"Mike is doing just fine, Sam. Nobody's on to him. However, if he keeps calling me 'palooka', 'hop-head', or any other of your silly tags, I swear I'm going to punch him on the nose."

"You mean beezer. I'll be in touch in a few days,

Broadbank. Oh, one more thing. How's Bogart keeping?"

"Spoiled rotten by the missus," Broadbank laughed. "The little fella is eating better than I am."

Samson chuckled.

"Hell, Doreen speaks nicer to that mutt of yours than she does me, Sam. But, yeah, hurry up and get home, and stay safe."

"Will do." Samson hung up and readied himself to speak with Steve. "Come on, it's not like I don't know the guy. Still, it's a big favour, and with what happened to him…"

Samson went to pick up the receiver, but didn't.

Stop being foolish. Foolish? *I promised the man I would never get him involved in anything, ever again. This is different, and I'm sure he'll understand.*

When Steve picked up, Samson heard the familiar raucous of the Jazz Hole in the background, making him a trifle homesick.

"Steve? It's Samson. Have you got five to talk?"

"*Sam*! Where have you been all my life? Course, let me turn the jukebox off."

Before Samson could speak again, he heard Steve set the phone aside and it wasn't long before silence filled his ear, the music cut off.

"That's better," Steve said. "You still there, Sam?"

"I'm here, pal. How's tricks and trade?"

"It's been a slow few days. Hey, how come you're not here? It's been a while since I saw you."

"I know, but I'm out of town on business. Listen,

I need a favour."

"Oh, no... When Samson Valentine needs a favour, heads start hurting and businesses go up in puffs of angry grey smoke," he chuckled.

Samson didn't know how to respond. A silence stretched out.

"Sam, I was kidding."

Samson huffed out a laugh. Sweat had broken across his brow. "I need you to post me the keys to your cabin." As soon as he'd said it, he thought he'd made a dreadful mistake.

What if Steve's phone is tapped? No, why would it be? XRay may figure I'll go to Steve for help at some point.

He shook his head. It was a ludicrous thought. Besides, it was too late now, and so it was a chance he was going to have to take.

But what about Steve? I'm sure he's bug-free.

"Not this again. Are you having me on? Am I safe to be talking to you on the phone?" he asked, as though reading Samson's thoughts.

"I know, I know, and I'm sorry. I said I'd never put you in such a position again, but I need a good hiding place, and your cabin is the best I can think of."

"Am I *safe* on this line?" Steve pressed.

What am I meant to say? "I'm not sure friend, but I can't see why you wouldn't be. Besides, it'll be me they're after. And if they come asking, tell them where I am, but warn me."

Steve huffed. "Doesn't sound like I have much choice, does it? Where are you? Can I get an address?"

Samson relayed the hotel's information. "Send them recorded delivery. We don't want them going walkies, do we? Not only that, I may need them ASAP."

He heard Steve scribbling. "I'm on it. And Sam, try not to let the place get wrecked. I recently had it refurbished, which cost me a bomb."

"I'll be careful, I promise." Samson hung up, grabbed a file from off the sideboard, and lay down on the bed.

By lamplight, he pored over Lovell's notes.

"This meathead's not going to know what's happened to him."

Chapter 17

Samson was up and treading the boards early, with a busy day ahead of him. After calling room service to have someone collect his clothes for cleaning and pressing, he'd shaved and showered.

Now, as he towelled off, there was a knock at his door.

"Who is it?"

"Room service, sir – we have your clothes."

"Great," Samson muttered, opening the door and taking receipt of his things after wrapping the towel around his waist.

"If you could just sign here, please, sir." Samson took the pen from the man and scribbled his name. "Thanks. The charge will be added to your bill. Please enjoy the rest of your stay with us, Mr Valentine."

And then he was gone.

Samson closed the door, drained the last of his cold coffee, and finished preening himself. When Samson was dressed and looking sharp, he left the room and went down to reception to get Lisa's information.

"Could you tell me which room Miss Dennings is staying in, please?" he asked the young girl stationed there.

She looked up, flashed him a smile, and was only too happy to help. "Sure." She turned to her computer and entered a series of letters. "Miss

Dennings is in room three-five-five, sir."

"Okay, great."

"Is there anything else I can assist you with this morning?"

"N—actually can you put a call through to Miss Dennings' room for me, please? I'd like to know if she's awake or not."

"Of course, sir. Who shall I say is asking?"

"Samson, her friend."

"Very good." She turned from him, picked up the phone and dialled. "Hello, Miss Dennings, this is Susan from front desk. Your friend Samson is here. He wanted to know if you were awake. Yes, right away. Bye." Susan replaced the phone and smiled at him. "She asked you to go up."

"Thank you."

"Are you aware breakfast starts in twenty minutes?"

"I am, thanks," Samson confirmed, and then headed upstairs to collect Lisa.

***

A couple of minutes later he was rapping on Lisa's door.

"Just a minute, Sam."

When she opened up he was glad to see she wasn't adorning the grieving widow's veil. "I'd like to escort you down to breakfast so we can talk things through."

"Our plan of attack?"

"If that's what you'd like to call it, yes."

"Sounds good. Let me grab my coat and I'll be right with you."

***

When they walked into the dinning hall, they noticed they were the only guests there, and a strong smell of bacon and eggs wafted from the kitchen.

Samson's stomach rumbled.

"I'll let you choose our seating," he said.

Lisa picked a small table with two seats facing each other, which was situated close to the kitchen's doors. Samson pulled her chair out for her to sit.

"Thank you," she smiled, scooting herself closer to her place mat. A modest white vase with a single red rose in it stood at the table's centre. It was flanked by the salt and pepper shakers, two menus, and their cutlery – which lay wrapped in pristine napkins.

"Pleasant," Samson said, sitting. He unrolled his knife and fork and laid his napkin across his lap.

"Are you ready to order?" a young, dapper lad asked, taking a pad and pen from the breast pocket of his waistcoat.

Samson removed his hat and placed it on the table. "Lisa?"

"Oh, I'll have the pancakes, please."

"Syrup?"

"Yes, thanks."

"Anything else?"

"No, thank you."

"Very good. And for yourself, sir?"

"The full English, please."

"Okay, that's it?" he smiled at them. Samson nodded and Lisa flashed a smile. "Do help yourselves to cereal, tea, coffee, and fruit, which can be found at the front of the restaurant. Enjoy."

***

Lisa and Samson chewed the fat as they ate. "So how much do you know about Lovell?"

Lisa shook her head, finished her tea, and replaced the dainty cup before answering. "Only the generic stuff: that he's in bed with XRay, and his brother used to run this part of the world."

"Does he know of you?"

"I don't think so. Why?"

"How do you plan on getting inside if they know who you are and what your speciality is?"

"Wouldn't matter if they did, Sam," she said, pushing her empty bowl aside and picking up her cup. "Excuse me while I go for a refill. Would you like one?"

"Please." He offered her his cup. "No milk or sugar, thanks."

"You got it." Lisa put a hand to his shoulder, but he shrugged it away. "Sorry, I—" Lisa walked off to get their drinks.

"What do you mean, it wouldn't matter?" he asked as she returned to her seat, placing their cups down.

"Employees come and go between the organisations all the time, Sam, now that XRay and

Lovell are partners."

"Okay, fine. So what's your plan?"

"To get close to Lovell by seducing him."

He gulped. "Sleep with him?"

Lisa looked away. "It wouldn't be the first time I've slept with the enemy to get what I, XRay, or a past employer has wanted. What? Why are you looking at me like that? You think just because I'm a woman I can't use what's been God given to me to get my own way? Jesus, you really are a dinosaur."

"I—"

"You're just like XRay and the rest, but in a more polished, refined way. Guys like that don't like women having their own mind, either. You think I should be hobbled and left chained to the kitchen sink, right?"

"Damn *you*!" he said, slamming his napkin down on the table. The cutlery rattled and their tea and coffee sloshed, tarnishing the peach-coloured tablecloth. The saltshaker fell over. "How dare you speak to me like that after I find out how much you've lied to me? You're clearly an untrustworthy scoundrel, capable of cheating and deceiving. You're a poor excuse for a woman, when I think of the decent ladies I've known. You're a disgrace, and when this is all said and done, I don't want to see you again. My hands will be washed of you. Now, let's get on with the matter at hand, and leave what we think about each other out of it. What do you say?" He fixed her with a cold, hard glare. His neck and cheeks were flushed.

Lisa's mouth hung open. Tears glazed her eyes, with one escaping. "Yes, quite. And for what it's worth, I'm sorry. I didn't—"

Samson waved her words away. "Stick to business and save your crocodile tears, sorrow, and sorrys for the palookas on *your* side of the fence." He went back to cutting his food. "Tell me, what's your first move? Do you know where to go?"

Lisa took a moment. She wiped her eyes and pushed her tea away. "I was hoping you'd have a starting point for me."

"I pored over Lovell's police reports last night. It seems he has a lucrative business down on Fishguard's docks."

"You think it might be a front for something?"

"They could be shipping guns or drugs out of there."

"To Ireland?"

"It's possible. Have you heard about the biker wars going on over there at the moment? Those guys are killing each other left, right, and centre."

Lisa nodded. "You want me to check it out?"

"No, I'm going to go down there with my camera and do some snooping. I want you here, in Carmarthenshire, where it's safe. He has a few businesses set up around town. Why don't you see if you can get yourself a job at the pub he owns; the Boar's Head?"

"Sounds like a half-baked idea, Sam. Wouldn't it be better if I tried getting into his circle?"

"You would be, Lisa. The Boar's Head is the jewel in his crown, and from what I can gather, his main base of operations. He's likely to be there most of his time."

"I'll do that, then."

"We'll finish up here and I'll take you to the police station. I want to get you hooked up with some recording equipment." He drank the last of his coffee, set his cup aside, and looked at her. "Are you sure you want to do this? You came to me, remember?"

"I'm one hundred percent sure, Sam. I want out of this."

"Good. Then let's get moving."

They left their table and walked outside to Samson's car.

"I just thought of something. What if they're not looking for staff?"

"I already checked that, Lisa. They have a couple of positions going."

"You really are prepared."

"Of course, in my trade you have to be ready for anything and everything." He placed his hat on his head, straightened it, and unlocked his car. "Get in," he told her.

He got behind the wheel and drove off.

"What have you told them about me at the station? Am I going to get a load of black looks? Do they want to put *me* behind bars?"

"I haven't told Quaker, the captain, anything yet. We'll do it together when we get there. You'll be fine," he told Lisa, looking over at her. And then he felt guilty about how he'd spoken to her over breakfast. "I must apologise for my outburst earlier.

It's unforgivable."

"Nonsense." She placed her hand on top of his, which rested on the gear stick. He didn't pull away. "I disappointed you."

"You could say that," he said, trying to stay composed. "But it doesn't matter, truly."

"If you say so, Sam."

***

Ten minutes later and they were standing in Quaker's office, with Samson relaying everything to the captain. The rotund man didn't remove his quizzical glare from Lisa the whole time the P.I. spoke.

"So, you're looking for redemption? This isn't a church, miss. Somewhere you can come to repent your sins."

Lisa looked down at her shuffling feet. "I don't want forgiveness or sympathy. I just want to help put things right for my own sake and sanity."

Samson put a hand to her shoulder. "It's okay, Lisa."

"I can get my tech guys to set her up, Samson, but she's *your* responsibility."

"I'd like all of this to stay between us, captain," Samson said. "Don't tell anyone on your force."

The captain looked at him and removed the cigar from his mouth. "Throwing orders around *again*?"

Here we go, Samson thought. "Sorry, I didn't mean for it to come across like that. I just don't want our position compromised, sir. That's all."

"Do you think I have rotten apples in my force? This isn't your precious *Cardiff*, lad."

"Understood, but you have to see it from my point of view."

The captain waved his hand. "It's fine. I didn't plan on saying anything to anyone anyway, and I'm only too happy to help as much as possible, especially if it gets my town cleaned up. You know, going back a few years, before Alligator got his claws into the west, people used to leave their doors unlocked. Now folk are too scared to walk the streets after five p.m. And parents won't allow their children to play out on the streets in case they are snatched, offered drugs, or sold to sex rings. I feel powerless, Samson, and if I seem a bit impatient, arrogant, or annoyed, it's because of that."

"We'll get this sorted between us, sir. I'm sure," Samson said.

"We shall see." Quaker got out of his chair. "Miss Dennings, if you could follow me, please. You too, Sam."

***

After Quaker's tech team had provided Lisa with surveillance paraphernalia – pocked-sized cameras, recording equipment, wiretaps, and had shown her how to use it all – Samson had driven her into the town's centre.

"Want me to wait here whilst you go in and inquire about a job?" he asked, pulling up outside the pub.

"That won't be necessary," she said. "I need to do a spot of clothes shopping first."

Samson looked down at her. "What you're wearing is fine, surely?"

"Not if I want a bar job and to catch Lovell's eye."

"I see."

"Why don't you swing by here around midday, Sam? We could grab a coffee and chat about things."

"Sounds good. I'll need a few hours to get to Fishguard docks, check it out, and to get back."

Lisa got out. "Be careful," she warned.

"You, too."

After she closed the door and he drove off, Samson's thoughts became a worried and scrambled mess.

God, I hope she'll be okay.

***

It took him forty-five minutes to drive to Fishguard and then a further ten to locate the docks that were a hive of activity.

"Where in the heck do I start?" Samson wound his window down and stopped a passing worker wearing mud-caked wellies. "Where can I find Lovell's Fresh Fish Company?"

"Lovell's?" The man looked at him.

Oh, no. Have I asked the one person on this dock who works for the man? "Yeah, I think I have the name right," he lied.

"You do, but you're way off, mate. Lovell's is around the other side, a couple of miles away."

His heartrate backed off. "Around that corner?" Samson asked, pointing.

"Yeah, mate. And drive straight. You can't miss it. It's a huge building on its own."

"Thanks," Samson said, driving off and leaving his window down. The cool air relaxed him.

He took it easy as he went. Worker bees, fork trucks and lorries lined his path. The noise was deafening. The farther he went, the quieter it became, until he thought he'd driven away from the docks completely.

But then a huge wooden structure came into view with a mass of seagulls encircling its rooftop. A dozen fishing trawlers were docked out front.

Samson stopped his car, killed the engine, and watched.

Nothing about the joint seemed out of place.

Fishermen worked the boats and rushed around with boxes, transferring to and from the building.

Samson turned and reached behind him, grabbing his camera off the back seat, along with some spare film. When he faced front, he started reeling off snaps.

"I could do with being closer," he muttered, capturing a few more images. "If I drive down there, someone might get suspicious."

Samson lowered his camera and looked around. He spotted towers of metal containers to his left.

I could park my car behind them and walk to the fish factory, he thought.

Liking the sound of that idea, Samson started his car and tucked it out of sight. Happy, he got out, locked it, and strolled closer to the building. When he was nearer, he hid behind stacks of creates and reeled off more shots.

"Are they customers?" He put his camera to one side and scrutinized the men and women who wore plain clothes and milled around. Some appeared to have wrapped goods under their arms. "Question is – *what* have they been buying?"

After taking a few more photos, mainly of the 'customers', he hid his camera in his coat and broke cover.

Let's see if I can get inside for a poke around.

He walked past the workers, who paid him no attention, and strolled inside the wooden structure. Employees were busy boxing, packing, and wrapping. Nothing appeared out of the ordinary.

When Samson saw he was approaching CCTV, he turned his head and lowered the rim of his fedora.

"They have the best fish," he heard a woman say.

"I know. A little pricey, but what can you say? It's direct from the sea."

Samson didn't look up. Instead, he kept his eyes on what was going on around him. And then he came to a locked door with 'authorized personnel only' written across its middle. Samson plunged the handle.

Locked.

He tried forcing it with his shoulder. Nothing. It didn't budge an inch.

"Wouldn't mind seeing what's behind there." Samson looked up and saw a string of blacked out windows. He squinted. "They do their *true* business up there. This place is definitely a front for something. I can smell it, and not just the fish."

Movement to his right caught his attention. Three men dressed in black suits, with visible bulges beneath their jackets, patrolled the factory floor.

Can't let those palookas see me.

Samson strolled away from the door and hid behind a tower of boxes. He gave it a couple of minutes before moving again. When he saw the men had their backs to him, he made a beeline for the toilets that were close by.

He entered and walked into one of the cubicles, closing and locking the flimsy door at his back. Samson discovered a large window there, which was locked.

"Perfect," he mouthed, unlocking the bolt that kept it in place. He then stepped onto the pan, pushed the window open, and poked his head outside. From where he stood, Samson overlooked the backend of the dock, which was empty, apart from more crates.

I'll come back tonight when the place is closed and slip in through this window. Hopefully, nobody'll notice it's unlocked.

He stepped off the loo and pulled the window shut. Samson then walked onto the factory floor and slipped out the exit. Before he left the site completely, he managed to take a few sneaky photos of the men in suits.

“What are you fellas protecting?” he wondered, looking through his camera lens. He saw they wore earpieces and carried clipboards. “You won’t get one past ol’ Valentine.

“Can I help you?” someone asked.

Samson almost dropped his camera as he turned to eyeball the man standing behind him. The worker wore an apron splattered in blood and fish guts; some had even splashed across his boots.

“I was told I could buy fish here?”

“You don’t look like a regular to me. Are you from around here? That accent suggests otherwise.” He brought a blood-encrusted knife up and jabbed it at Samson like an accusing finger.

“No, I’m not, but my sister lives this way. She told me you guys have the best products in the west,” Samson smiled.

The man eyed him. “There’s nothing for *you* here.”

“I guess I’ll be off then. Thanks for—” The man had already turned his back. “Charming.”

“For your sake, I hope nobody saw you taking those photos,” the man said over his shoulder.

“But I was only testing—”

“On your way.”

Samson didn’t need telling a third time, and he didn’t look back as he made his way to his car.

Tonight, he thought. *Under the cover of darkness*.

***

The drive back to Carmarthenshire took less time than it did to get to Fishguard, but he was still late when he arrived outside the Boar's Head, and Lisa was waiting for him. When he tooted his horn, she looked up and waved.

After parking across the road from her, he got out and met her behind his car.

"How did it go?" he asked.

"Come on, Sam, I'll tell you over a coffee. It's all rather exciting, and I don't want us seen together."

***

Sat opposite each other at a minute table in a greasy spoon two streets away from The Boar's Head, Samson noticed for the first time how Lisa was dressed, and his cheeks coloured.

Did she catch me looking?

The dress she wore—which had a plunging neckline and exposed most of her cleavage—sparkled under the café's strip lightning. A pendant in the shape of a heart hung around her neck.

His eyes flicked back up.

No, she's too busy stirring her coffee, he thought, inspecting her face. *Her lips seem fuller, redder.*

A rich, sweet smell emanated from her.

Samson examined Lisa further and noticed her eyelids were covered in a smoky grey-coloured eyeshadow and that her cheeks were rouged.

When Lisa spoke, she broke her spell over him, and he quickly gazed down at his drink.

"So, Lovell was there. He actually interviewed me, Sam. Can you believe that?"

"He was serving?" He then realised how stupid that question sounded, but he was still dazed by her appearance.

"Ha! No, he was sat in the corner doing some paperwork when I walked in and spoke to the girl behind the bar."

"He must have liked the cut of you, Lisa. Did he recognise you at all?"

"No, I don't think so. I'm sure he would have said, otherwise."

"And he was happy to give you a job?"

"Got my first shift tonight. How's that for quick work?"

"It's good, but I don't like the thought of you being in his den. It's dangerous."

She smiled. "Don't let my concern for your safety give you mixed signals. After your lies, I could never forgive you, but it doesn't mean I wish harm to come to you."

Lisa hung her head. "I know, Sam. I know. Listen, I'll wear my wire tonight and see if I can start gathering information. Maybe we shouldn't see each other now until I'm ready to break cover and get the hell out?"

"I think that's a great idea. I'm heading back to the fish factory this evening to see what I can gather. I'm sure there's something illegal going on there."

"Okay, good." Lisa finished her drink. "Did you speak with Paul's wife?

"Not yet."

When Lisa got up to leave, Samson looked away when he saw her tug her dress down, which barely covered the tops of her thighs. He blew on his coffee. "Ring me at the hotel if you need me."

"I will. Bye," she said, leaving.

***

Samson had stayed at the café and ordered himself some food. When he finished, he made his way back to his hotel room to check in with Broadbank.

"Everything's going as well as can be expected here, Sam. I have teams of officers walking the streets around the clock, and helicopters doing nightly patrols."

"About the best you can do, sir. Has there been any further word from The Widower Maker?"

"Not a damn thing. The case has gone cold. Have you managed to speak with Lutherhead yet?"

"No, he's still out of it. I will though, and after I do, you'll be the first to know."

"Fine. Speak soon, Sam."

"Bye." The P.I. hung up and decided to get forty winks ahead of tonight's adventures.

***

At two a.m., Samson's alarm started blaring, but he was already up and dressed. He crossed to his nightstand and switched the noise off.

"That's enough," he muttered

With his hat, coat, and shoes on, Samson took his key card from off the dresser and made his way out into the corridor. It was deathly quiet, apart from the buzz coming from the fire exit signs.

Hotels, for this reason alone, always gave him the spooks.

Samson took the lift to the bottom and bade the night worker on reception a "Good evening" as he walked by. The wind was biting and it flapped his coat as he strolled towards his car.

***

Within thirty minutes, Samson was at Fishguard docks, thanks to the roads being deserted. He parked his car where he had done earlier that day and walked to the rear of the building.

To his amazement, the window had gone unchecked.

Before entering, he switched on the flashlight he'd brought from his car.

Samson then dropped down onto the pan below and exited the toilets. He wasn't worried about the cameras, because he would be removing the tapes.

I'll be able to locate them in the office, he thought, waving his beam this way and that. *I just hope there isn't a dog or security guard in here.*

He doubted there was, though, because the whole place was in complete darkness.

Samson, with caution, weaved his way towards the door he'd seen earlier. When his light fell on it, he felt relieved. After trying the handle and finding it locked, he removed his lock-picking tools from within his trench coat and set to work. In seconds, he bypassed the bolts and had the door open. Beyond it was a set of stairs, leading up.

He took them two at a time, not wanting to waste a second. At the top, Samson saw several closed doors along the landing.

"One at a time, ol' chap," he muttered.

The first room he checked was a toilet, the second, a canteen.

When he entered the third, he was stood in a huge office, and the hum of computers assaulted his ears. At the far end of the space was a large wooden desk, and the nameplate that stood on it told him the office belonged to J. Lovell.

A grin spread across Samson's face.

"Got ya, but I'll come back," he said, leaving to go in search of the surveillance equipment.

The final room at the end of the corridor housed the building's recording setup. Without taking a chance, he removed all tapes and pocketed them. He then closed the door and made his way back to Lovell's office. Once there, he pulled open drawers and filing cabinets alike, taking photos of anything he thought might come in handy.

"I need to find something big. None of this would hold up—wait a minute…"

He discovered a locked drawer in a bureau that stood in the corner of the room, with a laptop and a lamp sitting on it.

"*Interesting…*"

Samson got his lock-picking tools out and

worked the drawer, but it gave him problems, and it took him close to thirty minutes to open it.

"Pesky thing."

Inside, buried beneath files, Samson discovered a diary. He pulled it out and took it over to the desk.

"And what do we have here, then?" he said, sitting down and opening the hard, heavy book. "Could it be a little black ledger of women?" Samson chuckled, shining his light on the first page.

He whistled. "I think I've hit the jackpot."

Before him, written on fine paper with tight margins, was a list of meetings and contact numbers next to certain dates and times. Samson kept flipping the pages, bringing the diary closer to today's date. Throughout, he saw schedules for shipment plans, dodgy dealings, merchandise exchanges, money sums, and various notes. He took his time and plenty of photos.

However, a lot of the information appeared coded.

"It wouldn't take much to crack them, I'm sure," the P.I. said.

When he saw there was nothing planned for Lovell on this day or the next, he kept going until he came across two important dates in a week's time.

The first one was marked 'Dispose of TR the rat'. There was a memo underneath it which read: "This will have been ample time for T to suspect we're not coming for him."

Lovell means to execute one of his dogs? Samson thought. *A squealer? I wonder if Lisa can get Lovell to talk about this – it would be good to have dates, times, etc... this could be big.*

The second entry regarded a possible shipment arriving at Fishguard docks. *If it is, it seems it's coming in early*, the P.I. thought, deciphering the three a.m. drop off. There was a note below this entry, too: "Make sure I go along. This one's important – *no* fuck ups."

Samson took pictures and wrote both dates and times in his pad.

Just in case the pictures don't come out too clear, he thought. *I need to get Lisa on this. Pronto.*

As he progressed through the book, he found other dates and meetings which seemed to have significance, but they were far into the future, and he couldn't crack their meanings.

I can't stick around here too long. He made sure to take plenty of photographic evidence. *I can pore over the snaps later.*

When he felt he had enough, Samson replaced everything the way it was, locked all doors and drawers, and made his way back to the toilet window. Outside, he heard voices.

Samson pressed his back to a wall and listened.

"You heard as well as I did, Leon. They said they saw someone skulking around out here."

"Come on, Patrick. It's almost four in the morning, and it's freezing."

"Are you afraid of the dark, pussy?"

Samson edged his way to the nearest corner, poked his head out for a quick look and spotted the two men heading in his direction.

"Piss off, Pat. I'm no pussy. I just don't like

being sent out on a wild goose chase."

"If we let this slide and it turns out someone is robbing the place, then Lovell will sink us to the bottom of this fucking dockyard. You hear me?"

"Yeah, yeah – I've heard the stories."

"And they're not just told to scare us, man. They're a warning."

Samson crept to the other end of the building and peered around the corner. He was just in time to see Pat and Leon disappear behind the building. When he looked over his shoulder, he saw their torch beams sweep over the area he'd been standing in only moments ago.

These jug-heads are hardly stealth on legs, Samson thought, continuing to creep away from them. *I just hope they don't discover the window. Then again, would it matter? Nobody'll know the contents of Lovell's diary have been spied on.* He patted his camera and smiled.

When he heard the men get closer, he rushed from the building and took cover behind some nearby boxes. Samson eyed the guards as they continued circling the factory.

"Think we should go inside, Pat?"

"Nah, I don't see the point. It's quiet here, man."

Samson ducked into the shadows when he heard a crackle of static burst from their radio, which was followed by the sound of a voice a second later. "Squad two, what's your status?"

"God, Wade is such a tool," Leon said.

"Agreed, man," he said, unclipping his walkie. "Copy, Wade. All clear here."

Samson watched as the men walked away, the darkness swallowing them. "*Phew*," he said, removing his hat and mopping his brow with his kerchief. "Too close a shave."

Samson got moving and fast-walked over to his car, got in, and drove off after ten minutes of waiting to make sure nobody else happened by.

Upon leaving, he prayed nobody had spotted him and taken his plate number.

***

When he got back to his room, he called Lisa and told her about what he'd found and asked her to try and find out what she could with regards to a suspected execution and a large shipment.

Chapter 18

The next day, Samson was told by the man working the reception desk that he had mail; Steve's key had arrived and so Samson placed it on his bunch. After a light breakfast and checking in with Broadbank, Samson decided to go to the hospital, where good news awaited him.

"Mr Lutherhead is awake and able to speak with you, Detective," a matron-type informed him.

"Do I need to wait until visiting hours, because this is a matter of emergency?"

"No, you can go right ahead."

"Excellent."

***

Samson entered the private room where Lutherhead was kept and was surprised to see the man sitting up in bed—his TV playing—and eyeing Samson.

"What do you want, pig? Have you arrested that fiancé-killing bitch of mine yet?"

"Shut up and listen, palooka," Samson said, grabbing a chair and placing it by Lutherhead's bedside. He switched the TV off.

"Hey, I—"

"Your muffin is no killer, pal. You're still ticking, aren't ya? And from what I've seen, you're no future husband material. Or man, for that matter."

Lutherhead scrunched his face and for a moment Samson thought he was going to cry.

"You're no cop, are you?" he spat, looking at Samson through squinted eyes. "What, and who, the *fuck* are you?"

"I'll ask the questions, son. You know, you're in a heap of trouble. I got people looking all over Cardiff for you."

Lutherhead gulped and shrank away. His puffed-out chest deflated. "I ain't been there in years, you got nothing on me," he pleaded. "Honestly."

"*Honest*? That's cheap."

"Look, I've got nothing to tell you."

"So you don't know a fella by the name of Four-Fingers, who, I'm told, was connected to the biggest crime lord in Cardiff – a jug-head by the name of XRay?"

"N-no…" Lutherhead's face lost its colour.

"Well, that is strange, because I have it on good word that *you* worked for Four-Fingers, which ties you to XRay. Not that you need tying to him, because you grew up together. You were friends. Like brothers, weren't you? I've also been informed that you *could* be The Widower Maker. What have you got to say about all that?" Samson settled in his chair, his eyes fixed on Lutherhead, who started holding his shoulder.

"I don't feel so great." Lutherhead reached for the call button.

Samson snatched it from the man's reach, stood up, and pressed his hand against Lutherhead's wound, digging his fingers into it whilst clapping his other paw over the guy's mouth.

Lutherhead's eyes bulged and he screamed beneath the P.I.'s shovel-like hand.

Samson drove the man's head into the pillows and got closer to his ear.

"Shut up and listen, or I'll make it hurt worse." Lutherhead stopped squirming. "Are you going to behave and tell the nurses what they want to hear if they come in here?"

The man's eyes made frantic movements and he nodded.

"Good. Now, I'm going to take my hands away, so you better keep your flapper shut, unless it's to answer my questions. And you are going to, aren't you, buttercup?" Samson dug his thumb deeper into the man's shoulder, causing blood to seep through his hospital gown.

"*Argh*!" Lutherhead's cry was muffled and tears slid down his face. He repeatedly nodded and whimpered.

"That's great. I'm much more agreeable with co-operating folk, Paul. May I call you Paul?"

Lutherhead kept nodding.

"You want to watch your noggin doesn't fall off, friend."

"Is everything okay in here?"

Samson removed his hands and turned around. A nurse stood in the doorway.

"Just fine, ma'am. Isn't that right, Mr Lutherhead?"

"Y-yes," Lutherhead choked.

"Not too long, mind, Detective."

"Not at all, miss." Samson tipped his head as she backed out the door. He turned to Lutherhead. "Good lad."

Lutherhead pulled the sheets up to his chin and glared at Samson. "You're just lucky I'm laid up and out of action."

"I'm sure I am. Now, no more threats or clamming up on me, or I'll make you pay. We understand each other, don't we?"

"I suppose we do," he pouted.

"I'm happy to give you a free pass, Lutherhead, because my gut tells me you're no killer. You might like to beat women and torture defenceless animals, but you're no murderer."

Lutherhead's cheeks flushed, and he turned his head, not bothering to deny it.

"However, I do happen to think you *might* know the killer, or have an inkling as to who it may be. I'm sure you know a lot of shady people, Paul."

His head snapped in Samson's direction. "I don't—"

"Before you rush to deny things, let me make this clear. If you don't give me something, then I will force other, more sensitive information out of you, like who is XRay and what does he look like."

"Why don't you ask Four-Fingers?" Lutherhead's bottom lip poked out.

"I would have, but I happen to think he's a man of integrity. He's trying to do well for himself. He doesn't want any part in your world any longer, and it would be wrong of me to put him in danger. You, on the other hand, are scum."

"You've got me wrong, cop, or whatever you are. I'm not like that and haven't been in a long time. It's a reason why I came out west – I wanted to escape that life."

"Did they come looking for you?"

"They tried, but I buried myself. You were one lucky son of a bitch to stumble onto me the way you did."

"Someone would have found you, sooner or later."

"Yeah, how do you figure?"

Samson leaned forward. "Because you can't keep your hands clean, or to yourself, and I'm guessing the police have been out to see you on a few occasions."

"They have a fake name for me…" He couldn't meet Samson's eyes. "If someone from Cardiff *does* find me, I'll never be seen again."

"Who did you annoy, Paul? Do you know who the killer is?"

"No, but I have an idea and a name for you. That person could probably tell you. I know I'm not a good man, but maybe I can redeem my soul."

"I wouldn't count on it, pal."

"Is it true what they said on the news, that he killed a little girl?"

Samson gulped down the knot in his throat and pushed aside the images of the trophies he'd received through his letterbox. "Yes, and if you don't stop wasting my time, more bodies are going to stack up."

"He pushed me out of his syndicate, you know?

After promising me he never would."

"Who did?"

"XRay."

"Because people found out you liked cutting up animals in your spare time?"

Tears slipped down Lutherhead's cheeks. "I can't help it. I've always had a thing for doing it, ever since I was a little boy. XRay knew that."

"Tell me about when you grew up with XRay."

He looked Samson in the eye. "You do know my life won't be worth shit if I give up every piece of information, right?

"Is it worth much anyway, now that you've started blabbing? Also, you're already hiding in the shadows like a damn rodent."

"If I give up *everything*, will you promise to help keep me hidden?"

"How am I supposed to do that?"

"Aside from Sheila, you're the only one who knows my real name. And that bitch is too scared to tell anyone. Unless you've told the cops?"

Samson nodded. "I have mentioned you." Lutherhead gasped. "But I'm sure you could persuade me to tell them I got it wrong."

"Okay. And I promise never to beat my wife or hurt animals, ever again. I'll get help, I swear it."

"I'll hold you to that."

"It's been a long time coming. I told myself I'd seek professional help years ago." Lutherhead wiped the tears from his face. "Is Sheila okay? How badly did I hurt her? I don't hold this against her," he said, indicating his shoulder.

"The headshrinkers fixed me," Samson said, unsure why he'd tell Lutherhead such a thing.

I guess everyone deserves a second chance. A lifeline, he thought.

Lutherhead looked him in the eye.

Samson nodded. "Hard liquor, ghosts, and a failing business almost got the better of me, but then I managed to change things. I turned the tables on my fortune, Paul, and I'm willing to help you as much as I can. But I want what's needed first. Hell, I'll even talk to the nurses for you."

The man sobbed. "Why?"

"Why would I want to help you?" Samson asked. Lutherhead nodded. "It might be hard for you to believe this, but I *like* helping people."

"Thank you. But I'm sure some would argue that you're doing it to get the information you want."

"Those palookas can assume what they want."

"XRay knew I liked to hurt animals, as I said, and it's what attracted me to him back when we were children."

"Go on."

"It was when he formed his first ever gang. The Lost."

"The Lost?"

"Yeah, short for The Lost Souls of Society. There were five of us in total, four for many years, until a boy by the name of Chris came along. I can't remember his surname, though, it's been too long."

"Okay."

"Benny ran the show. He was a big boy for his age. When he and I got kicked out of school for fighting one summer, Benny decided he would start The Lost and recruit me as his first member."

"Benny?"

"That's XRay's real name."

"Okay. But why recruit you – you'd been hitting each other?"

"Yes, but he liked the fact I held my own. I got a lucky punch in and bloodied his nose."

"Why the fisticuffs?"

"It was rumoured I killed, gutted, and fucked kittens. The latter wasn't true."

"Just the former, right?"

Lutherhead nodded. "I told Benny that, which he seemed to believe, but I don't think he cared. He just wanted to make himself look good in the yard. That day we were expelled, and we never returned to our homes. Instead, we found a bridge close to our street on the outskirts of the city and set up base there."

"Were the other members of the gang children from your school?"

"Yes, Shaun Hatch was."

"What's his story?"

"Hatchy was Benny's right-hand man, and between us, I think Benny was terrified of him."

"But he was just the bodyguard, right?"

"Hatch was too stupid to see how much of a threat he posed. He could have been our leader any day of the week. Then again, Benny had a way with words, and he could make you fear him with a quick turn of phrase. And don't get me started on his stare. Fuck. It was ungodly."

“Hatch have killing potential?”

“You’re thinking he could be The Widower Maker?”

“That’s exactly what I’m thinking.”

“He liked playing with fire and looking at photos of dead people. He also had a hand in the killing of Chris’ sister, but I don’t know all the details.”

“I’d say that makes him a prime candidate, Chris, too. Tell me more about *him*.”

“He was a strange one and had a massive chip on his shoulder about his sister, who he wanted dead. A plan he carried out to cement his place within The Lost.”

The Hillside Stranglers, Samson thought.

“How did he do it? Was there proof?”

“There was, I think, photographic evidence shown to Benny.”

“They sound like they could be my culprits, Paul. Do you know if either is still close to XRay?”

“I couldn’t tell you.”

“Whatever happened to The Lost?”

“We disbanded some five years after Chris entered the fold.”

“And you don’t know if Chris, Hatch, and Benny, or XRay, stayed close?”

“No, man.”

“Did an argument flare up within the group?”

“Not that I was privy to, but I would have known.”

“How so?”

“Because there was nothing really to row about – anything and everything pretty much went."

"What do you mean?"

"There was only ever one rule to live by if you were a Lost: never rat out a fellow member.

"And you're positive that's the only thing that would have caused a rift?"

"Most certainly."

Samson nodded. "Anything else you can tell me about Chris?"

"He was beyond a bad apple, Samson. From the very first day I met him, even with all my bravado bullshit, he gave me the willies. I didn't show it, though—none of us did—but I don't think I was alone in being chilled by him. Not Benny, though. Benny saw promise in Chris."

"Was there an initiation, by any chance?"

"Only for Chris. Why, I don't know."

"What was it?"

"To shed blood."

"Human?"

"It was never specified, not that it mattered, because Chris admitted to us about his sister."

"And you can't remember his surname? Was Chris even his real name?"

"No, and I'm not sure he ever told us his surname."

"XRay welcomed anonymity?"

"Yes. We all had fake names."

"So is Paul your real name? I'm assuming not."

"I'd rather not tell you, if that's all the same to you, Samson."

"I suppose not, so long as you keep spilling. If

not, I will find out, and I will see you behind bars. Do we understand each other?"

Paul nodded.

"Is Benny XRay's real name?

"N-no, and it's been so long now that I can't remember it."

Samson glared at the man.

"It's the truth, I swear."

"I will find out if you're lying."

"I'm not, and if it does come back to me, I'll let you know."

"You do that, Paul, and give me a bell," Samson said, handing him one of his business cards. "Okay. So what happened after Chris went through with his plan?"

"We were all sworn to secrecy, not that any of us would have said anything anyway. We were all too scared of Benny."

"How did you feel about that? You must have been a pretty cold person on the inside to know—"

"You have no idea how long I've been holding on to that, and the guilt and shame I've felt, Samson. I couldn't say anything to anyone because they would have stoned or beaten me to death. It ate away at me until it drove me over the edge and I became hooked on drink and drugs. When The Lost fell apart, I thought it would be good for me, but I had no one. I was out on a limb and too scared to open up to anyone."

"Benny could see your self-destruction?"

"Thinking about it now, he did, or sensed it more than anything. I was okay with being around people who did bad shit. I mean, I was no saint, cutting up animals and that, but humans? I drew the line. I felt unsafe, so I started to distance myself by hanging out on my own at different locations."

"This annoyed Benny?"

"Not to begin with, no. I kept him at arm's length by telling him I was going through some emotional stuff—that my past was haunting me—and that I needed space."

"How long did that go on for?"

"I drew it out for months, until Benny cornered me one afternoon when he saw me out on the streets. He was alone, and I didn't need anyone to tell me he was pissed. Benny came at me, got in my face, and called me a deserter. He said that I'd be punished if I didn't step back in line. And then he came out with it."

"With what?"

"He told me I was scared over what Chris had done. That it had broken me and got under my skin. He wanted to know if I planned on telling. I said no, of course not, but he didn't believe me. The trust and bond between us fell apart that day, and I believe that if The Lost hadn't disintegrated, Benny and the others would have eventually killed me."

"Or set Chris onto you?"

"More than likely, yes."

"What happened on the day the posse broke-up, Paul? Was there a meeting?"

Lutherhead was shaking his head. "No. A day or so after being persuaded back into the fold by Benny, I went to the bridge to find him alone.

Hatch, Chris and Chyna were—"

"The final member was a girl?" Samson cut in.

"Didn't I already say that?"

"This is the first you've mentioned of her."

"We loved Chyna like a sister, and would have done anything for her."

"Was she like the rest of you?"

"What do you mean?"

"A menace to society?"

"No, she was a good girl."

"Then what was she doing with a band of misfits?"

"She had daddy issues, and ran away from home."

"What type of issues?"

"Do I need to spell it out for you?"

"He was—*touching*—her?"

"Give the man a goldfish. Yes, he molested and sodomised her until she had the courage to break free – to run and never look back."

"She could have blown the whistle on him."

"Chyna told her mother once and earned a black eye for it."

"From her *mother*?"

Lutherhead nodded. "The old bitch wouldn't have a word said against Chyna's dad, who had meant to be a victim for Chris, but, as I said, the gang split."

"Chyna…Was that *her* real name?"

"As far as I was aware, no."

Samson dug his notebook out and scribbled in it. "*Any* idea where I might find Hatch or Chris?"

"None at all, but I wouldn't be surprised if the creepy bastards still lurked under the old bridge from time to time."

"Where can I find it?"

"It crosses over from St Jude's Street to the park on Cathedral Road."

"By Harkin Square?" Samson quizzed.

"That's the one, yes. Start there. Other than that, try some of XRay's associates."

"I've already done that."

"Then the bridge is your best bet. It was our home."

Their home. *How sad*, Samson thought, looking at the seriousness in Paul's eyes. "Is there anything else you can think of?"

"I guess you could try some of our other hang-outs, if they're still there."

"Go on," Samson said.

Lutherhead reeled off various buildings within the city that had once been derelict, or disused for many years. "Some, if not all, have probably been knocked down by now. However, I'm willing to wager you'll find Hatch lurking somewhere, that's if Benny hasn't killed him for something or other. Same stands for Chris."

Samson got up and replaced his chair. "Thanks for your time and co-operation, Paul. You've been a great help, and you've got my number should you think of something."

"You will—er—keep up your end of the bargain, right?"

Samson patted the man's arm. "Of course I will.

On my way out, I'll see a nurse about getting you help, too. Just don't disappoint me and revert to your old ways, or I *will* come back for you, pal." Samson straightened his coat and was about to leave, when something occurred to him. "Hang on. If this Chris bozo *is* still out there, and he *is* the killer, then wouldn't XRay have a clue to that, especially with Chris' track record?"

"I'm not sure what you're getting at?"

"Before I came to Carmarthenshire, I had a meeting with XRay, who asked me to take The Widower Maker to him when I had the killer under arrest." The vacant look on Paul's face told Samson the man wasn't getting it. "Why would he do that? If he thought Chris was behind the killings, why not go after him himself? Get his hop-heads and sewer rats on the streets to sniff him out."

"I'm not sure, but Chris could be dead, remember? Also, he might have moved, and if not, and he is still alive and in the city, he's probably a ghost with Hatchy's help. *If* Hatch is still breathing."

"But that doesn't answer my question, does it?" Samson pressed.

"If it is Chris, and he's taken in for questioning by the police, then he could finger XRay."

"Of course. X wants to shut him, and me, up. If I take The Widower Maker to XRay myself, then he'll be able to kill us both without anyone knowing. It's all making sense, now."

"There you go. And he'll silence me, too, if he finds out where I am."

"I bet you anything he's been looking, too."

"Definitely."

"Thanks once again for your help, Paul," Samson said, leaving.

And, as good as his word, Samson stopped at the reception desk to fill in the nurse on Paul Lutherhead, and how he wanted professional help after leaving the hospital.

"Can you make sure to get him started and on the right track, nurse?"

"Of course, Mr Valentine – we'll take good care of your friend."

Samson left the hospital feeling pleased with himself.

I may have saved a palooka's soul whilst gathering case-cracking information.

Outside, Samson checked the time and saw it was still relatively early. Lisa was working a day shift today and had arranged to meet with Samson later on.

"I have some info pertaining to the execution and shipment at Fishguard," she'd told him over the phone last night. "Meet me at the greasy spoon tomorrow afternoon. Three o'clock. I'll be waiting for you."

"Excellent," he'd wanted to say, but she hadn't given him the chance to respond.

The line had gone dead.

I could go back to my room and read through more of the notes Quaker gave me? he thought.

But decided against it.

Think I'll have a mooch around town, take in the

sights, to hell with it. When does Valentine ever get a break?

Before taking off on his stroll, Samson put in a call to Broadbank and told him about Benny, Chris, and Shaun Hatch.

"At least you have one surname to go off, Sam, fake or not. It might help us track Benny and Chris. I'll put someone on it immediately and see if we can dig up details on Shaun Hatch."

Samson didn't tell the chief where the information had come from, and that he had it wrong about Lutherhead.

"A case of mistaken identity – I had the names mixed up, Broadbank. I was so sure it was him."

Broadbank had bought it. "We win some, we lose some. I'll get people looking for him here, Sam."

After the call, Samson walked into town and mulled things over.

***

At five to three, Lisa walked into the greasy spoon smiling.

Samson waved at her as he stirred his coffee with his other hand.

A couple of minutes later, with a mug of tea in her hand, Lisa weaved her way through the seated people towards Samson.

"Punctual as ever," she said, setting her drink down.

"How was your shift?"

"Good, but not as great as last night's."

"Oh?"

"I got cosy with Lovell."

"That didn't take you long," he said, picking up his coffee and looking across at Lisa. She seemed wounded. "Sorry, I didn't—"

"It's fine, honestly. I knew what you meant. I'm too damn sensitive for my own good, sometimes, Val. Anyway, tell me how it's going with you first?"

"I think I have what I need to crack The Widower Maker case. Lutherhead opened up and spilt his guts like a good stool-pigeon."

"No barter?"

"I promised to keep his identity secret. You know, after we're finished here, it might be an idea for you to lay low." Samson placed the key to Steve's cabin on the table after removing it from his bunch.

Lisa picked it up and turned it in over. "What's this?"

"It belongs to a remote cabin in Canaston woods. A friend of mine owns it. Once I have enough dirt to flush Lovell down the pan, I plan to take you there, out of harm's way."

"For how long, Sam?" Her bottom lip quivered.

He put his hands on hers. "I'm not sure. Six to twelve months. Longer, maybe. I'll clear it with my mate, don't you worry. If XRay finds out what you've been up to, he may try and grab you and extract information from you. You've got to trust me."

She gulped and gave him a stiff nod.

"I'm not going to tell you any more about Lutherhead, either, because it's for your own good. Forget the name."

"Okay. Makes sense, Sam."

"So, spill? What have you got for me?"

"Well, Lovell came into the pub early last night and he was in a foul mood. I thought maybe there was something wrong within his organisation, so I lent him an ear."

"Didn't he think that odd?"

"No, because I've been getting closer and closer to him over the past few days – he's taking me to dinner tomorrow evening."

"Right, okay. It sounds like you have him eating from the palm of your hand."

"Oh, I do, Val. He doesn't suspect a thing."

Samson smiled. "What was he grumpy about?"

"Well, for starters, you are right about that note you found – there's a shipping deal going down between Lovell and the Irish, who don't trust him."

"Why?"

"Something about them being screwed over by Lovell in the past, so they want to air their issues before handing over more of their money. This deal is huge, Val. A lot of people are going to get rich."

The side note in his diary regarding the deal makes sense now. "Are they pushing drugs, guns, or both?"

"Both. Women, too."

"Women?" Samson asked.

Lisa nodded. "It seems Lovell has been picking

up ladies off the streets and selling them in bulk."

"Sex slaves," he uttered, blowing on his coffee.

"Yeah, and he told me there were two hundred females being thrown into this deal with the Irish to sweeten it for them, which stands to make Lovell a cool ten million. More, maybe."

Samson whistled. "Not shy in bumping his gums around you, is he?"

Lisa shook her head. "I don't think he would have been so loose-lipped if he'd been sober. Also, he was really annoyed about having to show up at that meeting. I don't think he trusts the Irish—"

"Not to smoke him?"

"That's the impression I got."

"He'll go to that meeting in force, then. Did you get all this on tape?"

Lisa nodded. "Yes, Val. Also, you know the planned execution?"

"Yeah, what about it?"

"The man in question is Tony Regan – he's an undercover police officer out of the Carmarthenshire police force. Special branch, I think."

"Why didn't Quaker tell me?"

"Maybe he didn't want his man put in jeopardy?"

"I suppose so. I need to talk to him."

"Lovell is sending his best men out to the woods to see him off."

"He must know a lot. How did they find out about him?"

"They caught him reporting back."

"And the poor guy doesn't have a clue?"

Lisa shook her head. “You have to put a stop to it, Val.”

“I plan to. You get that recorded also?”

“Yes.” Lisa made sure there was nobody looking, pulled the recorder and wires from under her blouse, and gave it to Samson. “I’m not going to need that now. You have all you want. God, he was awfully chatty, and I’m starting to worry he might put his hands on me soon. He thinks I want him.”

“Give it a few days and I’ll get you to that cabin.”

“Why so long? What if he finds out I’m a mole?”

“He won’t. Look, as soon as I’ve got the evidence to Quaker and we have a plan, I’ll get you to safety. It’s going to look suspicious if you leave right away.”

Lisa thought about it. “What if I give it until the execution has been stopped? I’m sure I can shrug off his advances until then.”

“That would be perfect. The shipment deal is two days after that, so you could phone in sick.”

“Okay.” Lisa drained the last of her tea, got up, and started to leave. “I’ll call you on your hotel phone in a few nights, Val, so we can make the last of our arrangements.”

“Sounds good to me, muffin.”

When she was gone, Samson pocketed the audio equipment, finished his drink and left. Before heading to the station, he went back to his hotel room to listen to the recordings.

***

Samson yawned. He'd been sat in Quaker's office for five hours. When he'd arrived at six that afternoon, he thought he'd have been in and out within two hours.

"So, what do you think?" Samson asked as Quaker stopped the recording for

the fifth time. "Is there enough to go on, along with my photos and whatnot?"

Quaker relaxed in his chair, which squeaked, and relit the cigar resting in his ashtray.

"God, yes, and we'll have a stronger case again after we pick up his boys during the execution."

"I'd like to tag along for that, Captain, and for the bust at the docks."

"Don't trust us not to mess it all up, eh?" Quaker eyed him through thin trails of cigar smoke.

"It's not that, Quaker, and you know it. I just want to see them go down."

"Fine, do as you please. I'm sure you will anyway. From what Broadbank has told me, you're a hothead when you want to be, and that you have a mind of your own."

"What adult doesn't?" Samson asked, allowing his mouth to run away with him. He smiled at the sobering look on Quaker's face. Before the man could answer, Samson jumped in. "What's your plan for the execution arrest?"

It took the captain a moment to reply. "Well, I'll get a wire on my man and hopefully he'll get them to talk about why Lovell wants him dead. That way, we won't have to extract it from the gunmen when we bring them in."

"You'll have an armed team ready and waiting?"

"Of course."

"Okay, good. I'll be in there with them."

"As you wish, Sam."

"What about the shipment at Fishguard?"

"I'll hit that with everything I have, Samson, which I'll start planning with my team tomorrow," Quaker said. "I can see you're worried, but I'm a capable police officer. I know about Davis. We're not *all* the same. Look, leave it with me and get yourself ready for the woods next week. Have a wee break—take things off your mind—and I'll ring you in a couple of days, okay?"

Samson sighed. "Fine."

"You're a man who likes jazz, right? There's a classy joint in town that showcases the best blues in Carmarthenshire."

"I am, but I've been off the liquor for close to two years."

"That's fine, head on down there anyway. They have a great non-alcoholic cocktail menu." Quaker checked his watch. "And they'll be opening their doors right about now. Tuesday nights are when they host their new talent."

Samson's interests heightened. "Whereabouts?"

"Right in the heart of town. A little place called Toots."

Samson got up, grabbed his coat and hat, and headed for the door. "Don't forget to call me."

Quaker laughed. "I won't."

"And call if something pops up in the meantime,

okay? If you can't reach me at the hotel—"

"Call your mobile, I got it. Now, go and take it easy, will ya?" Quaker blew smoke in Samson's direction. "That's an order."

Samson closed the captain's door without another word. He didn't feel like relaxing. *I should be back in Cardiff, getting things tied up there*, he thought. But he knew he couldn't return until Lovell was taken care of. *He'll just keep coming for me, time and again.*

"Talk about being caught between a rock and a hard place," Samson muttered, walking out of the station.

At least Broadbank hasn't called me, and I'm sure he would have, if The Widower Maker had struck again.

That thought seemed to ease him as he flagged a taxi, got in, and asked to be taken to Toots.

It's going to be a long few days, he thought, the taxi pulling away.

Chapter 19

The Widower Maker got off the bus and inhaled deeply.

He hated the bay area.

"Fucking reeks of money," he muttered and a woman walking her poodle close by turned and shot him black looks. "What are you glaring at, you piggy-whore?" he snarled, flicking his tongue at her.

She pulled her coat tighter around herself and scuttled off.

"Ha!" he bellowed, arching his back. He felt alive. *There's definitely something about being out at night that gets me going*, he thought. *I'm one of those nyctophiliacs.*

He took another deep breath and then crossed the road. He knew exactly where Four-Fingers worked (which was where he lived, too) as he'd once been employed by the man.

Not that Four-Fingers paid me much notice. I was invisible, unlike Hatch and Paul, who got too close to him, he thought. *Yeah, and as soon as he knew how crazy Paul was, he got shot of him. Got spooked, didn't ya, Four-Fingers*?

The weight of his ten-inch buck knife that lay in the pocket of his German army combat jacket felt good.

I'm going to cut you up like the fat pig you are, Fingers. Make you squeal.

The Widower Maker shot down a side street and found himself adjacent to the meat-packing company. There was a single light burning in a window located on the second floor.

He smiled, put his hand in his pocket, and stroked the blade's cool steel.

After a quick pull of a smile and a lick of his lips, he crossed to the building and snuck around its back.

No point in trying to take him head-on. The man's built like a fucking fortress. Plus, he can box. Well, we'll see how well he can shadow dance with a blade stuck in the small of his back.

A throaty laugh escaped him.

The backyard belonging to the meat plant was deserted, apart from the delivery vans and lorries that were parked in a neat line and locked for the night. A glow came from a solo spotlight affixed to the building's rear wall.

"Goddamn smell," he muttered, covering his nose and stepping closer to a window with a broken pane. As he did so, he failed to spot a puddle filled with washed out blood and stepped in it. "Great."

He forced his large frame through the gap and lowered himself to the floor on the other side. *You really should think about getting that fixed, Fingers – you have no idea who could be lurking at night. You think The Widower Maker is* only *interested in rich women? Think again, pig boy.*

A cloying stench of meat and blood assaulted his nostrils—even though a hand covered his face—as he made his way through the dark factory by using the glow of a few internal lights.

I didn't think this through. Rage makes you blind and empties your mind. Not that it matters. I can see well enough, and I remember where his office and sleeping quarters are.

When he got to the back part of the warehouse, he was able to see better because the lights on the second floor were fully on and shining down.

He heard a muffled cough from above.

Still awake, then? You're probably counting your coins like the greedy boy you are. I wonder if you still watch the cameras as religiously as you did. Didn't like anyone stealing bad cut-offs, did you? How many did you sack for that, Fingers? This will be payback for them.

He climbed the staircase to the floor above and crept along the corridor. He didn't bother checking any of the rooms around him, knowing Fingers would either be in his office or living room.

Unless he's on the pan, and that's something we could all do without seeing.

As he got nearer to a door that stood open at the end of the hallway, he heard sounds of movement, muttering, and coughing.

He wrapped his hand around the knife and got ready to charge in there.

But then a board creaked underfoot.

Shit.

The noise from within the room ceased.

The Widower Maker stopped walking and held his breath. Time seemed to stand still.

When Fingers started shifting around again, The

Widower Maker began his approach until he heard a clicking noise that sounded much like the hammer of a gun.

"Okay, shithead, show yourself," Fingers snarled. "Come on, step into the open where I can see you. That way I can give you both barrels of buck."

Since when did he own a firearm? He used to talk about how much he loathed—

The crack of gunfire tore the air apart, stinging The Widower Maker's ears, and chunks of flooring before him was splintered and thrown around the place.

"Still think I'm fucking with ya?"

The Widower Maker took a step back when he heard the gun's barrel being broken—the spent cartridge hitting the deck—and a fresh shell being loaded.

"Plenty more where that one came from, pal, and I guess I'm going to have to come out there and get you, huh?" The sound of his voice was followed by that of his footsteps.

The Widower Maker looked to his left, saw a door, and dashed towards it, trying to make as little noise as possible. When he turned the handle, he found it to be unlocked, and he slipped into the darkened room beyond.

Out on the corridor, he heard Fingers make his slow approach.

"Where did you go? Playing hide-and-seek? I know this building like the back of my dick."

The Widower Maker hid behind the door with

his knife clutched to his chest.

I don't want to kill him, not yet, he thought.

A door was thrown open, its back hitting a wall.

"You in here, weasel?"

Another door was flung open, followed by a third.

"Where are you? You can't fool me."

When The Widower Maker looked down, he saw shadowed feet beneath the door he was hiding behind. The handle was rattled.

"And what do we have in room number four?"

The Widower Maker bit down on his breath and watched as the door inched open. A light popped on.

"Come out, piggy."

The sawn-off shotgun's barrel entered the room bit by bit, until The Widower Maker saw the back of Four-Fingers' hand. He raised his blade and brought it down, slashing at the exposed flesh.

"*Argh*!" Four-Fingers dropped his weapon.

The Widower Maker kicked the shotgun across the floor, away from them, and then, with all his weight and force, he rammed the door closed on Four-Fingers, shoving the bigger man off balance.

When he pulled the door fully open, he saw Four-Fingers holding his hand as he crawled away from the room.

"Leaving so soon?" The Widower Maker asked, smiling.

Four-Fingers looked over his shoulder. "W-who are you? What do you want? Get. *Out*! I called the police."

"No, you didn't. I heard every move you made. However, I would like to talk about the police, Fingers, and you're going to tell me everything I want to know, or so help me God I'll gut you like one of your pigs. Do we understand each other?"

Four-Fingers continued to crawl away, leaving behind him a bloody snail-trail. "Fuck you!"

"No, fuck *you*, Fingers." The Widower Maker slashed at the back of the butcher's legs, cutting criss-crosses into him.

Blood squirted and splashed his face and lips, which he licked clean.

"Mm, you taste divine."

"Ugh-*argh*," the ex-boxer screamed. "Leave me—"

"What did you tell Valentine? Was it something about Lutherhead?"

"Huh?" He looked back at The Widower Maker again. "What did you say?"

"The P.I., Valentine. You were seen talking to him by a close friend of mine, and we want to know what you told him. A fair question, don't you think, considering it could get me and my mate into a lot of trouble?"

"It-it's you, isn't it?"

"Excuse me?"

"The whack job they've been reporting about on the news. The Widower Maker – it's you."

"Why did you have to go and say that?" he smirked. "I considered letting you live, Fingers, but not now. Still, if you give me what I want, I'll promise to make it quick. If not, I'll draw it out until you're begging for the end."

"You're fucking crazy."

"Probably, but I've never been evaluated. Now, tell me, what did you and the P.I. speak about? Was it Lutherhead? Do you know where he is, Fingers? I should have come to see you a long time ago."

"You know as well as I do, Lutherhead is dead."

"That's the word on the street, Fingers, which was probably started by Lutherhead before he disappeared, the little fucking cat killer pussy that he is. I never did trust him." The Widower Maker slashed at the felled man some more, cutting patchworks across his back, tearing his shirt asunder. "Answer my fucking question. What did you talk about?"

Fingers laughed. "Fuck you, you prick."

The Widower Maker raised the knife again, its haft and his hand covered in gore, but he resisted striking. He swallowed his rage and took to the man with a few hefty boots to his ribs.

His cracking bones brought a smile to The Widower Maker's face.

"Tell me," he insisted, continuing his torture.

Fingers coughed up blood. "I'm afraid you're going to have to kill me, friend. Bigger and better men have put the hurt on me more than you have or ever could, princess."

The Widower Maker kneeled by Fingers' side and punched the knife through his hand, pinning it to the floor.

"*Bastard.*" He scrunched his face and flashed his blood-soaked teeth. "If I get up, I'll beat—*argh*!"

The Widower Maker wiggled the blade back and forth, irritating Fingers, who gritted his teeth and screwed his eyes closed.

"All this will go away if you tell me what you told the cop. Did you talk about Lutherhead?"

"He's dead. *Dead*, you shitstain – XRay killed him."

"You're a goddamn liar, Fingers, because they were friends. XRay would have only killed Lutherhead if he'd opened his trap about certain things. Why are you protecting Valentine? Are you prepared to die for Lutherhead?"

The men locked eyes. "Do you work for XRay? Is this a hit? All this shit about Lutherhead is a smokescreen, isn't it? Just kill me, if that's what you're here to do."

"Did. You. Talk. About. Lutherhead?" he asked, punctuating each word with a kick.

Another rib popped and a piece of bone splintered Four-Fingers' skin.

"Sweet Jesus!" Fingers cried, holding his side. "Yes, alright, I told him about Lutherhead, but all I said was he used to work for me, and that I don't know where he is. That's the truth. Please, just let me live. I don't know you and I'm not going to say shit."

"How did he know about Lutherhead?"

"I'm not sure, but I'm guessing one of XRay's boys blabbed. Was it Hatchy who told you about my meeting with Valentine?"

"What the hell did you say?" he kicked the man in his face. "How do you know he's still around these parts? We put the word out that he and I had skipped the country."

With annoyance, The Widower Maker ripped the knife out of Fingers' hand.

"*Argh*! I know who you are, *Chris*!" Four-Fingers rolled onto his back and glared at The Widower Maker. "You and Hatchy thought your tracks were covered, didn't you? He's been looking for you, you know? He's never stopped."

"*Nobody* knows Hatchy and I are in the city. We've been keeping a low profile. How did you know, tell me?"

"Fuck you, Chris. You can stay as hidden as you want, but it won't make a difference, because he knows, and when he finds you, he's going to rip your fucking guts out. Think he'll let my death go unpunished?"

The Widower Maker laughed. "You need a better poker face, Fingers – I know you don't work for him any longer. He's not your biggest fan, and he probably keeps tabs on you. In fact, I'll be doing him a favour by killing you."

The look on Fingers' face excited him.

He knows his end is coming.

"Did you tell the P.I. about me?"

Fingers shook his head. "No, I swear. I would never have remembered you."

"You were quick to recall my name just then."

"It's *only* because I've seen you."

"Convenient, don't you think?"

"Please, don't do this to me."

"That's what my sister said, right before her ride

blew up," he smiled, feeling himself slip back to a time he'd *never* forget, and the smell of burning petrol and bodies was all around him.

"You sick—"

The Widower Maker cut him off by slashing the serrated steel across the butcher's eyes, ripping his vision away.

Fingers howled and rolled about the floor.

I don't think I would have got much more out of him, he thought and then plunged the blade into the man's side. When he retracted it, he aimed for the chest and then the groin, face, neck, throat, back, legs and didn't stop until the knife was buckled beyond use.

He stood—chest heaving and face drenched red—and looked down at the twisted, tangled mess of Four-Fingers.

As a final insult, he opened Fingers' mouth and yanked his tongue out.

"I'm told the tongue of a tittle-tattler is delicious." He wrapped the savaged organ in a piece of cloth and pocketed it.

He stepped back, giddiness enveloping him, and his mobile phone buzzed in his pocket a series of times before going quiet. He reached for it and pulled it out. When he flipped it open he saw it was a message from Hatchy. He read it aloud.

"Sorry about the card through the door, but I had no way of contacting you as my burner phone is broken. This is a new one. Also, I didn't want to hang around your flat too long, just in case someone saw me, us, and put two and two together. I've had

The Brain taken care of. He was our snitch."

The Widower Maker smiled. "Excellent," he said, typing his reply. "Fingers is also dead. I've silenced him. I hope to snatch Catherine tomorrow night. Do you know of any other rich bitches I can have?" He signed off with a smiley face before taking some photos of Four-Fingers.

He replaced his phone and put his back to a wall, sliding down it. He was spent.

It really was something, he thought, *watching Chloe burn up. Her skin and hair had been so fine.*

He closed his eyes and let his mind wander.

***

Staying away from his new friends was hard, but he was determined to until he'd done what was expected of him.

"I'll show them," he muttered, sat in front of the TV one afternoon as he dreamed up ways of killing his sister.

I could shove her down the stairs? Drown her in the bath? Poison her? Cut her up with Dad's chainsaw? The latter idea made him smile. *No, that would be too noisy and messy.*

And then it came to him.

I should wait until she's ready to go back to university and do it then. Mum and Dad will drive her... I could get them all in one go by cutting the brakes on the car.

But then he wondered how he would get his proof.

Follow behind? How? I'm too young to drive.

His excitement dwindled.

"I wonder if asking for help is against the rules?" he blurted, sitting up from his slouched position. "Hmm. I could always ask Benny if one of The Lost could drive? I'm sure he, Hatchy, and Paul can, illegally of course. Still…"

Chris checked the time, saw it was still pretty early, and left the house.

***

"I didn't think I'd be back here so soon," he muttered, getting closer to where The Lost hung out. He heard them talking and laughing, and then he saw their shadows dance on the walls, which were thrown by the firelight coming from the barrel they used.

Chris gulped. It had been a few weeks since he'd last seen them.

"Hey, guys," he said, entering their domain.

"Hey," Hatchy called. "If it isn't the killer." The rest of The Lost laughed.

"So, you got something to show me?" Benny asked. "By the look on your face, I'd say no."

"I haven't, no."

"What did I tell you?" Paul said. "He's not fit to be a Lost, Benny. He's a liar and a shithouse."

"Actually, *Paul*, I've come to ask for a favour, so I can carry out my plan."

"You want someone to hold your hand when you do it?" Benny asked.

Hatchy laughed.

“No. I need someone who can drive.”

“Why?” Benny pressed, and so Chris revealed what he had up his sleeve.

“I’ll be free of them all after they’ve crashed and burned.”

Benny laughed. “You really are crazy.”

“Will one of you help? Once my parents are dead, their house will become mine. I can either sell it, or we could use it as our base.”

“Hmm, now that is interesting, and I guess you won’t need photographic proof, either, if one of us is there to support what you’ve done. How about Hatchy helps you?”

“I’m cool with that, but it won’t be for a couple of weeks yet, as you know.”

“That’s fine. Come back when you’re ready, Chris.”

At that moment, Chris felt he’d gained a lot of respect from Benny, who looked at him proudly, with a smile on his face. “You bet I will, Benny.”

***

The fortnight following the brief hook-up under the bridge dragged, and Chris feared his day would never come.

Nights spent around the dinner table with his parents and sister were near unbearable, and it took all the false smiles he could muster to get him through it.

The day before he planned to cut his dad’s

brakes, Chris went back to the bridge and asked Hatchy to be at his house late the following evening.

"I'll meddle with the car once my family is in bed."

"Okay. What time and where?"

"Wait outside my house, in the bushes, around midnight."

"You better not be fucking him, or us, around," Benny warned.

He hadn't bothered arguing that he wasn't. *They'll soon see*, he thought, smiling.

***

The next night, as planned, Chris snuck out of bed at ten minutes to midnight and crept downstairs. He went outside and found Hatchy leaning against a vehicle he didn't know.

That doesn't belong here unless it's a neighbour's friend's car, he thought, approaching Hatch.

"I thought you were going to hide in the greenery?"

"Couldn't be arsed," Hatchy confessed.

Chris shrugged. "Yours?" he asked, indicating the car.

Hatch nodded. "You haven't cut the brakes yet, have you?"

"No, but I've unlocked the back doors so we can get in. Come on, let's do this."

"Cool. So, you're really going through with it?"

Hatch asked, grinning.

"Of course, why?"

"Brilliant. I can't wait."

Chris smiled. "You're sick, just like me, aren't you?"

The boys giggled and threw their arms around each other's shoulders.

"Definitely," Hatch said. "From the moment we first met, I knew we were going to be good friends."

***

Chris and Hatch entered Chris' parents' house via a door attached to the garage, and turned the lights on.

"You sure someone won't spot us?" Hatch asked with a tremor in his voice.

"Hell no, nobody's awake inside and this street's deader than shit. Not scared, are ya?"

"Piss off," Hatch said, laughing.

Chris giggled, opened the bonnet to his dad's car and raised it skyward, clicking it into place. It took him less than ten minutes to do what he had to, having asked his dad loads of questions about the vehicle three days prior.

"He always checks her over before a long trip," he informed Hatch, putting the bonnet back in place.

"That's it?"

Chris nodded. "Piece of cake," he said, dusting his hands off. "You saw me do it, right?"

"Yeah, course."

"What are your plans now, Hatchy?"

"I was going to sleep in my car until we were ready to go."

"Nah, you can stay in my room for the night. Nobody'll notice."

Hatch smiled. "Great. What time will everyone get moving in the morning?"

"Early. Eight-ish."

***

The next morning, Chris and Hatch were awake and ready to roll. They'd sat in Chris' room listening to his parents and sister moving about as they got ready to go.

Nobody had bothered to knock on Chris' door to inform him that they were leaving.

"I told you, didn't I? They don't give a shit about me. They'd be happy if I didn't exist," Chris told Hatch.

When the front door closed, Chris and Hatch raced downstairs and exited the back door. By the time his parents had rolled out of the garage, down the drive, and onto the street, the boys were in prime position to rush to Hatch's car.

"Let's go, let's go!" Chris ordered, dashing across his lawn.

Hatch got behind the wheel of his car and caught up with Chris' dad within seconds. "This is going to be good. I'm so excited." In time, Hatch would come to tell Chris how much of a sexual kick he got out of death and murder. Something he thought he'd never tell anyone, not even Benny.

"Who taught you to drive, Hatch?" Chris asked, not taking his eyes off his dad's car.

"My shitbag of a father. About the only decent thing he did for me."

"You must have been young."

"Oh yeah, about eleven, I think."

"Jesus."

"He was a drunk, and he didn't know what he was doing half of the time."

The boys laughed. "I hope my family get out onto a faster road before the brakes go completely."

"Me, too," Hatch admitted. "I'd like to see them take others down with them."

The boys didn't get their wish, however, for Chris' dad lost control of his car on a deserted lane, smashing head-on with a tree. His mother flew through the windscreen and died on impact with the road, her head coming apart like a ripe pumpkin.

"Holy shit, did you see that?" Hatch asked, close to orgasm, and pulling his car to one side. "Come on, let's have a closer look."

Chris' dad was screaming. The front end of his car had crumpled in, pinning him where he sat. His face was torn to ribbons, with bits of glass embedded in his cheeks and eyes.

"Get me out of here!" Chloe pleaded from the back seat, unseen.

The engine made a funny '*whoomph*' sound, and flames licked from beneath the bonnet. Fluids splashed against the asphalt.

"We better step back, Hatch," Chris said, taking as many photos with his Polaroid as he could. And then Chloe popped into his lens, just as the car burst into flames.

"*Help*!" she begged, stretching her arm out her window towards Chris.

"This is what happens to rich bitches," he told her as the car detonated.

Heat fanned the boys' faces and shrapnel bombarded them.

"Goddamn," Hatch brayed with laughter.

Chris joined in.

After watching the wreck burn for a while, they gathered up the snaps and headed back into town, to the bridge where they knew the others would be waiting.

***

That night, they celebrated with a few boxes of stolen beer as Benny, Chris and Hatch pored over the demented photos; Chyna and Paul were uninterested. Chris had never felt happier. He was now a member of the crew. A Lost.

"Now that you're fully fledged, you won't have to worry about a thing. We've got your back," Benny told him, putting an arm around Chris' shoulders. "We're brothers for life, Chris. For. *Life*."

They clinked their beer bottles together and smiled.

"To us, Chris. The Lost."

"The Lost!" Chris cried and the others joined in.

***

"Except it didn't work out like that, did it, Benny?" he muttered, opening his eyes and looking at Four-Fingers. "No, not at all. You became more powerful, gaining contacts within the underworld and leaving us behind, apart from Chyna, who you treated like a queen. That is, until you put her to work on the streets like a dog."

How long after that night? Five years? Six? he thought, getting to his feet, his eyes remaining on Fingers. *Once you wormed your way in with the big boys you left us high and dry. Sure, you gave us jobs within your organisation, such as working for this sack of shit, but what good was that? You were better than us, or so you thought, and you let us know it.*

"Bet I made you feel vulnerable when I killed your precious Chyna, Benny," he continued talking to Fingers. "No, *not* Chyna. What did she change her name to? Rona? No, *Roxie*, and if it hadn't have been for that meddling P.I., I definitely would have killed her a lot sooner. God, how Hatchy had longed to see her innards splayed out in front of him."

Sirens. He heard them in the distance.

Can't be coming here.

"At least by pushing us all out, you allowed me and Benny to form a strong bond. We shared all our secrets, and it wasn't long before I got the nerve to start murdering the filthy rich and sending the photos to Hatch. We have a nice little thing going. Him scouting, and me killing and then sending him the photos of my victims."

The sound of the blues and twos got closer until the corridor he was standing in became drenched in their lights.

"*Shit*! How? Why? Fuck. Someone must have heard the gunshot."

From outside, he heard car doors slamming, followed by the sound of police officers talking. The Widower Maker went to a window and saw two police cars and four officers; one of whom was giving orders.

"You pair, around back," he told the two women coppers, before addressing his partner. "We'll take the front. Come on."

"I need to get the hell out of here, fast." The Widower Maker found his knife and made his way downstairs. When he got to the factory floor, lights burst on all around him.

Get to the back. If it comes to it, the women might be easier to slip by, he thought, entering a long, thin hallway that led to a fire exit door. There was no sign of the female officers. *I might just make it yet. Maybe they've entered via the side entrance? Either that, or something has distracted them. The broken window?*

He smiled and reached his hand out to the door's push bar. From behind, he heard the male officers shifting around, getting closer to where he was.

"Losers," he mouthed, depressing the bar, opening the door, and slamming straight into one of the female coppers.

She jumped, as did he, but he was quicker, and

had his knife jammed under her body armour and into her belly before she could react. She gasped, dropped her flashlight and grabbed a hold of his shoulders as he tore his blade sideways, spilling her innards onto the floor.

She began slipping away until she crashed to the ground with a hard smack. Her radio crackled and spat static voices.

"Looks like someone has been here – I've found a broken window, over," came a female voice.

He peeped around the side of the building and saw the second woman.

I'm going to have to nail her, too.

The Widower Maker waited until she faced away from him before sprinting at her and ploughing his knife into the small of her back. Before she could scream, he covered her mouth and eased her to the floor.

Not wasting time, he fled into the night, sticking to the shadows and backstreets, aware he was covered in blood.

***

When he got to his apartment, his heart jackhammering and sweat pouring down his face, he whooped and beat his chest.

The exhilaration was almost too much to stand.

Images of the women's blood jettisoning kept flashing through his mind.

A buzz ripped through his body.

After a quick shower, a bite to eat, and a drink,

he sat down in front of the news and couldn't stop smiling until a photo appeared onscreen.

His blood turned cold and a breath hitched in his throat.

"What the—?"

He turned the sound up to discover the second cop had survived his attack.

"No, no, no, this can't be happening." He looked at the artist's sketch again and calmed down. It wasn't a great likeness. "How did she see me anyway? It was dark and she had her back to me."

"We believe this is the face of The Widower Maker," a spokeswoman said. Camera flashes exploded all around her.

He felt as though he'd been kicked where it hurt.

His phone buzzed.

It was a message from Hatch: "Have you *seen* the news?!?!"

"We're fine. It looks *nothing* like me. We'll have to lay low for a while," he replied and set his phone aside.

When his mobile jangled again, he didn't bother looking at it. "*Fuck*!" His lungs burned.

He picked up the TV remote and launched it at the set. It exploded into hundreds of pieces when it connected with the screen, which cracked. Sparks flew and smoke puffed. The Widower Maker put his feet up on the sofa and he huddled himself into a ball.

"No, no, no," he repeated. "No, no, no…"

Chapter 20

It was cold in the woods. Dark, too, but neither bothered Samson as he crouched in some bushes close to a few dead trees and a massive stump. All around him, Quaker's men lay in wait, with two armed officers on either side of him.

They'd arrived in Rose Garden Woods three hours prior, wanting to make sure they were set up long before the attempted execution took place.

"We can't have any surprises, Sam. That's my man out there," Quaker had said.

Samson had been worried at first that they had the wrong spot, but no, he knew they didn't. *I listened to that tape ten times or more to make sure*, he thought, recalling Lovell's voice on the recording.

"We have a spot in the woods marked out for such occasions, right where a house used to stand," the crime boss boasted.

Before him, Samson spied the remains of a large cottage. The roof was missing, the door, too, and the entire set of windows on this side were smashed. An unkindness of ravens was gathered on what remained of the chimney stack. To an average person passing the condemned structure, the joint wouldn't stir much interest or suspicion in being a graveyard-cum-killing ground.

The cottage would have fooled Samson, too, and every other cop who happened across the ramshackle place, but he knew of the secrets it held at its centre.

***

“Why take them there?” Lisa asked the oblivious Lovell.

“Because, my dear, it has an undisclosed underground passageway, with a hatch built into the kitchen floor. All my men have to do is drop a body down there and it’s gone for good. *Poof*! Just like magic.”

The thought of multiple dead bodies down in the darkness had given Samson the creeps when he’d first laid eyes on the cottage. And, after venturing inside to unearth the hatch and opening it, he’d never felt fear quite like it when he gazed into the blackness beyond the trapdoor.

“That *smell*!” someone blurted.

“We’ve been dumping bodies down there a while…” Lovell’s words echoed in his mind.

He really can’t keep his flapper closed. What a shmuck, Samson thought. *I’m surprised Lovell has lasted this long.*

“The man can’t be this thick,” Quaker pointed out. “He’s an underground warlord, and he hasn’t got to where he is by spewing out information to some random woman who works for him.”

“Hey, when you’ve got the gift, you’ve got it,” Lisa winked at Quaker. “He trusts me with his life.”

“How do you know?”

“I just do.”

"I'm not sure what you've promised this palooka, but he seems to be comfortable in chatting to you."

"I've got him wrapped around my little finger."

"It would seem that way," Quaker said.

"Have you called in sick yet?" Samson asked.

"Yes."

"Good. After we pinch his men in the woods, I'm taking you to safety."

"Okay, Sam. I'll be ready to blow town on your return."

***

That thought pleased him, but didn't settle his nerves or stomach.

I'll be glad to get this over with.

"Smoke?" someone asked Samson, tapping his arm.

He turned his head to his left to see Special Officer Peters brandishing a pack of cigarettes.

"No, thanks," Samson said, holding up his hand. "Those things will kill ya, didn't you know?"

"So will this job," Peters quipped.

Even though Samson had only been in Peters' company a few hours, he liked him a lot. Samson snorted. "You're not wrong, pal. I've been in enough scrapes to last me a lifetime, and one of these days the job *might* just catch up with me, but not today."

Peters laughed, lowered his weapon, and stuck a fag in his mouth. After lighting it and taking a drag, he spoke again. "How much longer do you think we're going to be out here, Sam?"

"Not long, I hope. I need to get home, back to Cardiff – I have a case to close."

"The Widower Maker?" Peters asked.

Samson nodded, and then there was a voice inside his head, thanks to an earpiece given to him by Quaker's tech team.

"Targets are approaching the area. I repeat; targets are approaching the area."

Samson and Peters looked at each other in a knowing way, and then hunkered down, out of sight. It wasn't long before they heard the snapping of twigs underfoot and the sound of voices in the distance.

The P.I. readied himself. Not that he thought he'd see any action with armed coppers around him.

This should be a simple swoop. Grab the palookas and save the good guy. I just hope they talk and give us something. At the brief, Samson had aired his concerns to the captain, who'd promised him that the men would squeal when brought in anyway.

"Heavy pressure will be applied to them, Sam," Quaker had said.

Fingers crossed.

When Samson parted the foliage in front of him, he saw three men lumbering out of the woods towards him. They were laughing and joking and as they drew closer, he saw Quaker's man standing in the middle.

"Okay, bozos, time to get yours," Samson

muttered, looking over at Peters, who had his gun ready. "Remember, we need them alive."

Peters nodded.

Samson turned back to the parting in the shrubbery in time to spot one of the hatchet-men producing a handgun. Samson clutched his torch and got ready to surprise him.

"Hang on," one of the brunos said.

"What is it, Eric?" the second thug asked.

"I'm sure I heard something. Didn't you?" Eric asked Quaker's man.

"Can't say that I did."

This is it. They're getting ready to plug him, Samson thought.

Samson was about to spring from where he was crouching and cover them in torch glow, but a voice boomed from close by, stopping him.

"This is the police. You are *surrounded*!"

"Holy shit, Eric – there are cops all over," the second thug said, holding his gun up. Moments later, he started blasting.

A bullet whizzed past Samson's head and smashed into a nearby tree.

Then the first heavy was shooting. Return fire was given.

"Cease fire!" Samson tried, but it fell on deaf ears. "Christ."

Samson saw Quaker's man jump for cover, appearing unharmed.

"Let's get the hell out of here, Geoff," Eric said, continuing to shoot blindly.

Both men ran in Samson's direction, and he got

ready to pounce. As he did, Peters lunged from his spot and tackled the bigger goon to the floor.

"Geoff!" the hatchet-man cried out as he wrestled with Peters.

Eric turned, about to fire on Peters, when Samson brought a hefty stick down across the man's arm. "*Argh*!"

Bone and wood cracked.

Eric didn't go down, much to Samson's surprise, and swung his good fist at the P.I., who managed to avoid the blow by inches.

"Bastard," Eric said. "I'll kill you." He went for his dropped gun, giving Samson the opportunity to bring his knee up hard, connecting with the man's chin. His mouth snapped shut and broken teeth sprinkled the leaf-scattered floor.

This time Eric did go down, dropping to his knees, and holding his busted mouth together.

Samson pushed the man onto his stomach and snapped his cuffs on him.

"You're under arrest, palooka. It's time for you to visit the big house."

When he looked over to see if Peters was okay, he found the firearms officer had Geoff cuffed and was pulling the goon off the floor.

"The inside of a cell is too good for scum like you," Peters told Geoff, shoving him. "Get walking."

Within seconds, Samson was flanked by what seemed like a hundred officers.

"Freeze!" someone called.

"Police!" yelled another.

"We've got this under control," Peters shouted. "Come on – let's get them in the van, Sam."

Samson followed Peters out of the woods by dragging his man behind him. Minutes later, both hoods were placed inside a police riot van and taken away.

That was far from smooth, but we achieved what we set out to do, he thought, searching for Quaker among the officers. When he spotted him speaking to Peters, Samson went over to him.

"Well, I hope it goes better at the docks," Samson smiled.

Quaker gave him a dry smile. "I thought it was a huge success. We got the bad guys and saved my man."

"Yeah, a roaring achievement that almost got me my face blown off," Samson said.

"Look, Valentine—"

"Save it. Just make sure your men get the information required to put Lovell away. Or do you need assistance on that, too?" Samson knew he was stepping over the line, but the lack of authority in the woods had rattled him.

"You've got some balls and neck on you, matey," Quaker said, jabbing a fat finger in Samson's face.

Peters snorted a laugh and walked away.

Quaker glared at the firearms officer's back whilst answering Samson. "I'll get what we want out of them, don't you worry, because it will mean getting *you* out of *my* town."

"Good." Samson tapped the man on his back and

walked off. “I’ll be at my hotel if you want me.”

Samson heard Quaker mutter something under his breath and he smiled. When he got to his car he turned back and saw the captain staring through him. The P.I. waved.

“Clown,” he said, getting behind the wheel of his vehicle and driving off.

***

Two nights later, hidden behind a bunch of crates on Fishguard dock, waiting for Lovell and his thugs to appear, Lisa crossed Samson’s mind again.

***

“You’ll be fine, I promise,” Samson told Lisa, escorting her into Steve’s cabin. “Nobody knows you’re here.”

“It’s so quiet and isolated, Val. You’re sure I’ll be safe?”

He chuckled. “As houses, Lisa, and you’ve got my number should you need me. I know I’ll be a drive away, but I’ll be here in a flash.”

“My white knight,” she said, placing a hand on his arm.

Samson pulled away, but gave her a warm smile. Earlier that morning, Samson had whisked Lisa out of town, not wanting to take any chances.

***

"That was Quaker on the phone," he informed her as they ate breakfast at a café before departing for Steve's cabin. "It seems Lovell's men have cracked under questioning and spilt their guts about everything."

"That was fast."

"It's a good thing we got an early start. Come on, let's get out of here."

***

"You're much better off here, Lisa. It won't take Lovell long to put two and two together, no matter how much of a dope he is."

"Be careful in Fishguard, Val, please, and come back to see me once you've arrested him, yeah?"

"I'll try, but I can't promise anything. I have to get back to Cardiff."

"I understand. You know that, right?"

"Of course, muffin."

"Can't you take me with you, Val?"

Samson shook his head. "Definitely not, Lisa – it's too hot for *anyone* to be in my company, especially you. Please, stick it out here, okay?"

"I am sorry for lying to you."

"Forget it. You're not the first red herring, sweetheart," he said, winking at her. "Now, go in and lock the door behind you. It's going to be dark soon. I'll ring you later."

"Okay." Lisa closed the door.

Before driving off, he watched as a light burst to life within the dwelling, and he couldn't help but wonder what she was doing. He shook his head, started his car, and left.

On the trip back to Fishguard the next day, Lisa had entered his mind and stayed there.

***

Good God man, she's a grown woman. She'll be dandy, he thought, looking about him. The sun had started to set over the docks, but workers continued to buzz about the place: most were operating fork trucks, cranes, and getting lorries into position to help unload a ship that was docking.

Amongst the workers were copious amounts of Quaker's men and women, dressed to blend in, and ready to swoop on command. Samson looked over his shoulder and up at the roofs of the buildings close by. He knew there were armed men up there somewhere, snipers, along with Quaker and a couple of other high-ranking officers and superiors from the Fishguard police department.

"This will be the biggest bust carried out in West Wales, Samson," Quaker had affirmed.

"And the second biggest in Welsh history, I would have thought," the P.I. shot back.

"Your little stunt with the nuclear codes being the first, no doubt." Quaker gave him a mocking smile.

Don't like having your toes stepped on, do ya, Quaker? Samson smiled as he listened to the chatter across the police radios via his earpiece and poked his head out from behind the crates once more.

“Aye, aye – and what’s this then?” he said, raising his binoculars.

“Looks like mother hen has landed,” a female officer said in Samson’s ear.

Directly across the shipping yard from Samson, a slick black limousine pulled up, close to where the ship marked with an Irish flag and Gaelic writing had docked.

From the front of the vehicle, much to Samson’s surprise, stepped a huge man brandishing an Uzi 9mm.

“Jesus, those things are highly illegal. And where in the hell did he get it?”

The voices across the police band went crazy.

From the opposite side of the stretched car stepped another ape, also wielding serious hardware.

“These guys aren’t fucking around, Captain,” a male voice came over the airwaves.

“Snipers – get ready on my command,” said another.

If someone gets nervous out there, a bloodbath could *ensue*, Samson thought, rapping on the bullet-proof vest which Quaker had so kindly offered him. *I hope it can stop rapid machine gun fire.*

He kept his binoculars trained on the man with the Uzi, who stepped to the back of the car and opened the door there. Out stepped a tall, broad, and dapper man. His suit looked expensive and pristine; his shoes were polished to a military gleam.

He doesn’t impress me much, Samson

thought, *with his silk scarf and designer beard. Lovell looks soft. I don't think his jaw could take much.* Samson cracked his knuckles.

The man from the other side of the car joined Lovell and Mr Uzi, exposing the AK-47 he carried.

"Chinese issue," Samson muttered. "I've seen those things cut men in two."

Three more musclemen crowded around Lovell, each one packing iron.

The six men stood around the limo talking and throwing nervous glances towards the ship.

After a while, Samson shifted his gaze to the left and saw a gang of men depart the ship and walk towards Lovell and his gorillas. The man leading the Irish had a machete over his shoulder. He wore a white wife-beating vest and dirty torn jeans.

The polar opposite, Samson thought, turning his attention to the seven men at their leader's back. Most of whom appeared to be bare-knuckle fighters or boxers, as their hands were wrapped in protective cloth; they didn't seem to be holding a weapon of any kind, apart from two of them, who had vicious dogs on heavy-duty chains.

Samson feared them more than the well-dressed, cardboard cut-out gangsters.

They'd chop you up for dog food as soon as look at you. Between the eight of them, they had enough tattoos to fill the walls of an outsized tattoo parlour. *They're walking with a purpose, and the looks on their faces will tell all who behold them that they mean business.*

"We'll let the deal take place before we make

our move," Quaker said. "And Samson, just remember, you're an *observer* here. No goddamn heroics like in the woods. You hear me?"

If I hadn't taken control, palooka, then some of your people, and our suspects, might have been killed, he wanted to say, but grinned and bared it. "It's your party, Quaker. I'm just the guest."

"Good, I'm glad we're on the same page."

Samson turned his mic off. "Jug-head."

In a way, he was glad to be out of harm's way.

I don't much fancy getting riddled with bullets, he thought, raising his binoculars to see the Irish step up to the Welsh mob. Machete seemed to be doing all the talking, his knife hand animated. Still, the blade never left his shoulder by more than a few inches.

He's awful twitchy, Samson thought. *I don't like it.*

But then Lovell and the Irish leader shook hands, and four large suitcases—hauled from the boot of Lovell's limo—were handed over to two Irishmen.

"Team one, are you in position?" Quaker asked.

"Yes, team leader, over."

"Teams two and three, are you in position?"

"This is team two – we are."

"Team three is also on the mark, over."

"On my command, I want you all to move. Snipers, get ready."

"Copy, sir," came a chorus of voices.

Samson couldn't take his eyes off Lovell. And, even though his heart hammered and sweat broke across his brow, he felt elated.

Takes me back to my heyday, he thought, wiping his moist palms on his trouser legs.

As the Irish walked away, backs turned to Lovell's men, Quaker bellowed over the radio: "All teams. *Move*!"

Cracks of gunfire followed, and Samson watched as the men holding the Uzi and AK-47 hit the deck, one after another.

Panic ensued, and Lovell's men started shooting.

Bullets pinged and whizzed.

Three teams of ten armed men and women encircled Lovell, his men, and the Irish – none of whom were going quietly.

Bodies hit the floor from all sides, but it was the police who seemed to be taking the biggest number of casualties, with a lot of their support pinned down and unable to help.

Through the gun smoke, Samson lost sight of Lovell.

"Damn. Where did you go?"

He swept his binoculars back and forth, scanning the entire dockyard.

"Quaker, where did Lovell go?"

"Keep out of this, Valentine, and get off the airwaves."

"Goddamn palooka," he said, pulling the audio equipment off him and breaking cover. He weaved between towers of steels containers, fork trucks, and stacked boxes as he drew closer to the action.

When he took cover, bullets tore up the ground before him, showering Samson in chunks of concrete.

"Christ," he spat, sitting down hard.

All around him, people were screaming.

The rattle of gunfire from nearby reverberated in his ribcage, and the stench of cordite hung thick in the air and stung his eyes; muzzle flashes lit up his peripherals.

He took a chance and peeked from behind a fork truck he'd used as a shield, and caught a glimpse of Lovell. The boss man was being covered/escorted back towards his limo, whilst the rest of his boys laid down gunfire.

Samson turned to look in the direction of the ship to see the Irish were dead.

I've never seen such carnage. The P.I. shook his head as though trying to clear the mist of a bad dream, but the shootout was real, and bullets continued to ping off various objects around him. *If I don't get to Lovell soon, then he's going to get away. God, I can't believe this bloody mess. Goddamn Quaker.*

Samson held onto his hat and made a beeline for a stack of containers, close to where the limousine was parked. From there, he took another glance, noting it was only Lovell, a guy with a handgun, and the driver left, who got in and started the car.

Bullets flicked off the vehicle's bodywork, leaving zero damage.

It's a bloody mobile fortress.

"Get in, get in!" the guy with the gun yelled, holding the door open for Lovell, who jumped it. When Handgun Guy slammed the door closed, a sniper's bullet took his face off.

The limo's wheels spun, kicking up smoke and laying down rubber marks. When the car lurched forward, the shooting from all around Samson stopped, and so the P.I. broke cover again and launched himself onto the vehicle's bonnet as it swerved close to him.

What the Christ am I doing?

The car weaved, which indicated the driver couldn't see, and so Samson clung on for all he was worth.

But then his stunt started to pay off, as the car slowed down.

I've got you, bozos.

A hand holding a small bat shot out of the driver's side window. When it was swung at Samson's head, he managed to avoid it, almost losing his grip on the bonnet as he did so. Wood connected with steel, setting Samson's teeth on edge. The weapon was brought back at his face, but again he managed to dodge it, only this time one set of his fingers dislodged.

"*No*." Samson took his eyes off the bat, which was brought down on the joint of the arm still holding on. He gritted his teeth.

Then a loud popping sound occurred and the car started to veer violently, slowing its progress and tossing Samson free. The P.I. hit the ground with force, coming to rest on his back.

A deafening crash filled his ears and the sound of twisting metal and shattering glass engulfed Samson; the car's horn blared non-stop.

He turned to look and saw the limo had collided

with an iron girder. The reinforced support beam had jousted through the windshield and popped out the vehicle's back window. Blood and gore dripped from it.

Samson—his coat cut to ribbons, his hat lost—staggered to his feet and held his right arm. His face was covered in dust. The knees in his trousers were ripped and bloody, but he didn't seem to notice, as he hobbled over to the car and looked in through the back passenger window.

"Jesus," he muttered, turning from the carnage and smelling and hearing fuel leak from the vehicle's petrol tank.

Men, including Quaker—who had a face like thunder—stormed towards him.

"Get back, she's going to blow," Samson warned.

Samson moved as fast as he could, grimacing with every step he took, and then dived for cover. A second later, the car blew, and hunks of metal and chunks of other debris landed all around him.

It was over. Lovell wouldn't be sending any more goons Samson's way.

I didn't envision it ending like this, he thought, getting to his feet and brushing himself down.

Samson looked at the burning wreck and saw the bodies inside. His guts flip-flopped, and a hand landed on his shoulder. He was spun around.

"What in the blue balls was that John Wayne bullshit, Valentine?"

"Get your damn hands off me, Quaker. If you weren't so bloody inept, this mess could have been avoided. You're a damned fool, fella."

"I'll see you're struck off for this, pal. You'll never work in law again, do you hear me? Don't you—"

Samson turned and landed a punch on the man's chin, sending him into the arms of one of his men. "I'll take this up with Broadbank," he said coolly, picking up his fedora and placing it on his head as he walked away, back to his car.

"You're finished! *Finished*!" Quaker continued.

Chapter 21

When he arrived at his apartment block on foot—his bullet-riddled car missing from outside the train station—Samson stopped and looked up at his flat window.

"Thank God," he yawned. "I never thought that journey would end." Samson glanced at his watch and saw it was a few minutes to two a.m. He stood there for a moment longer—enveloped in the cool night air—and listened. Nothing stirred. The city seemed at peace. Not even a car zoomed by or idled.

"I could get used to this," he muttered.

After leaving Fishguard docks late yesterday afternoon, Samson had been tempted to go back to his hotel, check out, and head straight for Cardiff after dropping the loaned car back at Carmarthenshire police station. But Lisa had continued to occupy his mind, even though he'd argued against it until his better judgement lost. And so, before heading to the hotel, Samson had gone to the cabin.

***

When Samson arrived, knocked, and announced it was him, Lisa opened up.

"You scared me half to death, Val. I wasn't expecting to see you again. Well, not so soon, anyway. What happened to you?"

"Things have changed slightly. Lovell is dead," he blurted.

"Oh… You better come in, then. I've just boiled the kettle."

"I'll stay for one drink."

"Okay," she said, opening the door further.

As they sipped their teas, Samson relayed what had happened at the docks.

"Sounds like something out of a film," Lisa admitted. "It's scary to think that those types of people are walking our streets with such hardware."

Samson nodded, as though deep in thought. "I would take you back to Cardiff, but I still don't think it's safe for you. I'm sure XRay will be out for your blood, too."

"How would he know what's been going on here, Sam?"

"The fella has spies everywhere, Lisa."

"Yes, you have a point, so I won't push the matter."

Samson drained his tea. "Good. Do you know if the phone here is working?"

"No, sorry, but you can use my mobile if—"

"I'd rather use a landline for the call I need to make." He got up and crossed to where he knew the cabin's phone was. Samson picked it up and smiled at the sound of the dial-tone.

Good old Steve.

"Broadbank, it's Samson. Listen, I haven't got long. I need you to send stakeouts to these locations," he said, reeling off hotspots The

Widower Maker might be lurking, thanks to the information Lutherhead had given him. "I think we might find The Widower Maker at one of those hangouts, pal. I forgot to give them to you the other day."

"Got 'em, Sam. I'll get men onto it immediately. Hey, one thing, I had a mighty pissed off Quaker on the phone earlier."

"Oh yeah? Did he tell you how much of a screw-up palooka he is? The jug-head damn near messed everything up. *Twice*."

Broadbank chuckled. "I've got your back, don't worry."

"Thanks. How is Mike and everything else?"

"Things are as good as you'd expect them to be with a serial killer running amok. You've stopped the bad guys there, then?"

"Just, no thanks to Quaker. Have you got any new info regarding The Widower Maker?"

"Nothing, even though I have teams sweeping the city day and night. However, now that we have these locations, we might hit the jackpot."

"If you catch him before I get home, don't beat him up too badly. Leave some for me."

Both men chuckled.

"When will you be back, Sam?"

"I should be home around one a.m."

"I'll try you at home then, and give you an update if there is one. And don't worry – I won't ask where the information came from," Broadbank said, hanging up.

Samson replaced the phone and said his

goodbyes to Lisa. “We should have the whole Widower Maker case wrapped up pretty soon, so I’ll give you a call in a couple of days.”

“Will I be able to return to Cardiff after that?”

“Yes, because I hope to nab XRay in the process.”

“And if you don’t?”

“You could always go back north, Lisa, to where you came from.” He didn’t mean for it to sound as harsh as it did, and he winced. “I’m—

“It’s okay, I know what you meant. And yes, I could do that.”

“Don’t think about it now. We’ll work something out.” Samson put on his hat and coat and left.

***

You did the right thing, he thought, climbing the stairs to his flat. The inside of the complex was silent, apart from a TV playing somewhere close by. *A bit late to be up*, he shrugged. *Then again, who am I to talk*?

Samson arrived on his landing, flicked the light switch on, and the bulb blew. *Every damn time it happens to me*. He felt for his door key and found it without an issue. After opening up and stepping inside, Samson saw his answering machine blinking.

God, I’ve probably got hundreds of messages, he sniggered, throwing his keys to one side before heeling the door closed. He switched the lights on and crossed straight to the phone, about to hit play

a thorn in my side, get it? I needed him out of the way in order to carry out my investigation. You could have called him off and saved your pal, partner and ally, *friend*."

"And where would the fun have been in that?" XRay laughed. "I love watching you squirm."

The P.I. gritted his teeth. He wanted nothing more than to slam the phone down, but he knew he had to hear XRay out. "You're crazy, bozo, and your time will come. I'll see to that."

"Would you like to know how mad I am, Valentine?"

"Proof isn't required at this juncture."

"Well, it's too late for that, I'm afraid. Tell me, did you think you could keep me fooled with a stand-in Valentine? I mean, I have to admit, we were none the wiser, but sooner or later you must have known I'd figure out?"

"Guess I didn't take you as being the sharpest tool in the box."

"Yes, and it's that lack of respect that's dropped you in hot water."

"What are you talking about, X? It's too late for riddles."

"Have you not reacquainted yourself with *Mike*? He's right *there* with you, Samson…"

Samson felt a chill slip down his body. His flat suddenly felt alien to him. Swallowing what felt like a marble, the P.I. reluctantly turned around.

"The suspense is killing me," XRay said, the receiver still pressed to Samson's ear.

The crime boss started laughing.

Samson gasped when he discovered his easy chair was facing the wrong way, its back to him. "You've been here?"

"*Personally*."

He put the phone down on the sideboard and moved closer to his seat. When he was able to see over its back, he spotted a slumped figure in it, wearing a hat just like his.

"*Mike*?"

Samson darted around the chair—almost slipping in a pool of dried blood—and went to Mike's side. He lifted the officer's head up, causing the man's body to tip backwards into the seat, and stared into his vacant eyes. Mike's face had lost its colour and his lips were purple. Running the length of his throat was a slash mark.

"Oh, Jesus."

Samson ran his eyes down Mike's body and saw he'd been stabbed multiple times in the chest and guts. His hands and legs were tied, execution-style.

Probably gave him a good working over, too.

Samson snatched up the phone's receiver. "You *bastard*! You'll burn in hell for this, *Benny*." The P.I. put a hand over his mouth, bolting the gate after the horse had split, and cursed himself.

"Well, well, well. That's a name I've not heard in many years. Tell me, was it Lutherhead who told you that? I assume you know Four-Fingers is dead, right?"

"Yes." Samson thought his teeth would shatter due to the pressure he was applying to them. His jaw clicked.

"Another victim of The Widower Maker, Sam? Seems a bit odd, though, don't you think? He hardly fits the profile."

"Maybe he fancied a change."

"Don't be coy, Samson. We both know what's going on. Fingers' death has pretty much sewn it up for me."

"Chris," Samson said.

"Exactly, Sam."

"If you knew this all along, why didn't you hunt him down yourself?"

"Oh, I have been, don't you worry about that. But I could have been wrong."

"So you thought you'd come to me and get me to help track down one of your rabid bulldogs? You're scared he's going to yap about you when he goes down, aren't you?"

"Something like that, yes. He could do a lot of damage if he's allowed to open up."

"Well, now that you've killed Mike, and Lovell's out of the picture, I don't see what you've got left to play? The Widower Maker's *mine*."

"Ah, but that's where you're wrong, Samson. Before your friend in the chair died, he gave up quite a bit of information."

"What?"

"Before I get to that, let me put this to you. Would you want to see any harm come to Lisa, Samson?"

His guts dropped like an elevator with cut brakes. "Oh, no…"

"You honestly thought the cabin was the best

hiding place? *Really*? I mean, even if I didn't have spies, I still would have gone there looking for someone close to you, Sam, because I know she's not the *only* one you care about."

The P.I. didn't like where the conversation was going. A tingling sensation shot through his guts.

"Have you checked on Alice and Charlie lately? No? Doesn't matter, because I can tell you they're doing fine. Do you want them to stay that way?"

Samson had no words.

"Cat got your tongue? That's a rarity, I'll bet."

"What do you want?"

"Not *what*, Valentine, but *who*. You know, you're very lucky I'm warranting a second chance. However, you only have forty-eight hours to deliver The Widower Maker to me."

"Where?"

"The strip club."

"Where you ambushed me?"

"The very one, Valentine."

"Is Lisa okay?"

"She's unharmed, as of yet. My men at the cabin are awaiting my orders."

"You—you—"

"Would you like me to make it twenty-four hours?"

Samson bit down on his tongue. "Are Alice and Charlie okay?"

"Forty-eight hours, Samson, and the clock started ticking five minutes ago."

"Just tell me—"

The line went dead. "God*damn* it!" Samson

smashed the receiver into its cradle. "So help me God, I'll kill him." He snatched up his keys from the sideboard, looked at Mike one last time, and was about to head out the door when his answering machine caught his eye.

He hit the play button.

"Hey, Sam, it's Broadbank. Give me a call when you get in. I have tried. I'm worried about Mike – he seems to have dropped off the radar. Bye."

The machine beeped. Nothing followed.

Samson patted his clothes down and found his mobile phone. He pulled it free and dialled the chief's number as he rushed downstairs to grab a taxi.

By the time he'd hailed one, he'd informed Broadbank of Mike, and what was going on.

"The psycho will kill them all if we don't find The Widower Maker."

"Where are you now?"

"In a taxi, headed to the car pound to retrieve my battered Ford. I take it your boys picked it up at the train station?"

"Go to the police station and get an unmarked car, Sam. I'll have it authorised by the time you get there."

"Thanks," Samson said, ending the call.

***

Once he had a car, Samson headed towards Alice's café to get the girls and her parents out of there.

"Please, God, let them be okay. Please."

His mobile jangled, startling him enough to make his car zigzag.

"Samson," he said, answering it.

It was Lisa. "Th-there are men here, Samson. Outside the cabin," she sobbed.

The line wasn't the best, but he could hear her. Samson pulled his car to one side and gave her his full attention.

"Lisa? Are you still there? Have they hurt you?"

"They're sat outside in their jeeps with their lights on full beam. I'm so scared. I don't know what to do, Sam. Who are they? Lovell's men?"

"XRay's. Look, he knows, but he's promised not to harm you."

Lisa screamed.

"Lisa?"

In the background, Samson heard men shouting, accompanied by loud bangs.

The line cut out.

"*Lisa*?! No, *no*!"

He hung up and rang back. The line was engaged. "This can't be happening." Samson hit redial and got the same result. When he tried a third time, there was nothing, not even a ring. "Her mobile has either died or been switched off."

Samson contemplated driving west, but he knew that was a foolish idea.

I'd be too late to do anything, anyway. Besides, what about Alice and Charlie? I could take them with me? No, I have to sit tight. If he's giving me forty-eight hours, then he won't hurt Lisa. He's trying to put the spooks on me, that's all. Yeah, and it's working.

"Also, if he does have peepers on me, he might kill Lisa before I can set foot in the west. Damn it."

Samson thumped the steering wheel and restarted the engine. After releasing the handbrake, he eased his car away from the kerb and continued on his journey.

***

Parked opposite Alice's coffee shop, he saw no cause for panic.

The lights were off, and all around the building nothing seemed to stir.

Samson undid his belt, got out, closed the door and crossed to the other side of the street. He stood outside the joint's door and listened. He couldn't hear anything but the slow, steady whip of the wind that flapped his coat's lapels.

When he put his face to the window—flanking it with his hands—he could see movement inside. Shadows danced across the walls, thrown by a backroom light.

"Alice! Charlie!" he called, hammering on the glass. Samson went back to the door and pushed it, thinking it would resist, but almost fell through as it opened for him. "Christ."

He stumbled over the threshold and into the café, colliding with a bench.

"Alice? Charlie?"

Samson heard something shuffling around.

"Hello?"

A muffled sob rang out.

Somewhere on the street, tyres screeched, and Samson turned to see a car zooming away. He was about to run outside when a shrill cry stopped him.

"Help! He's bleeding to death. *Help*!"

"Where are you?"

"Upstairs. Quick, please. Call an ambulance."

Samson rushed around the counter, tripping, his hands searching for the phone he knew was there. Somewhere. "Come on, come on…" he muttered.

Items crashed to the floor and then his paws fell on the landline. He picked it up and thumbed in nine, nine, nine.

"Ambulance, fast – I have someone bleeding out." After relaying his whereabouts, Samson replaced the receiver and staggered his way towards the back room.

Once there, thanks to an upstairs light guiding him, he was able to rush up the blood-stained steps with his hand on the sticky banister for balance.

"In here! Jesus, help me. He's dying," the woman wailed.

Samson went from room to room, searching for the distressed lady, finally finding her in a front bedroom.

He'd never seen quite so much blood. On the floor, with her husband clutched to her chest, was Alice's mother. He had a knife sticking out of his guts.

"What happened? Where's Alice and Charlie?"

"Men—" she hiccup-sobbed. "Three of them.

They pulled us from our beds, stabbed Peter, and threatened me."

"Why did they do this to your husband? Did he resist?"

Peter was, although not the tallest of men, burly; his forearms had always reminded Samson of Popeye's, minus the anchor.

He wouldn't have let any palooka take his daughter without a fight, Samson thought.

"Yes," Maria said. "I begged him to do as they asked, but you know my Peter." She stroked his hair.

"I'm so sorry," Samson said. He felt sick.

"Don't be."

Blue lights from outside illuminated Samson, Peter, and Maria.

He clutched her hand. "I'll see them in and make my way. Do you have any idea where they may have taken the girls?"

Maria shook her head.

Samson stood, balled his hands into fists and stormed out of the room.

"Someone's going to pay with their damn teeth for this," the P.I. muttered, running downstairs to let the medics in. "Upstairs, front bedroom," he told them.

Samson took a look up at the window before jumping in his car to leave.

***

He drove at speed, the city flashing past in a blur of

neon.

I'm coming, girls, he thought, gripping the steering wheel tighter. *Thinks he can push me around? Be his little pet? I don't think so. I don't do tricks for any man.*

Samson arrived in the city centre in record time, and then showed little regard for parking laws as he pulled up outside St David's shopping centre.

He got out and rushed inside the building, not bothering to lock the car. Samson dashed up the escalator to the second floor and sought out XRay's strip club. The shopping centre was dead, apart from the odd security guard roaming, but the club itself was jumping. Multi-coloured lights lit-up its windows, and music thundered.

As Samson approached the flashy joint, he heard the raucous cheer of men as the MC announced girls onto the stages.

Never saw the appeal, myself.

Samson pulled the saloon doors open and stepped inside.

Every fibre of his body was tingling, and a slow burn ignited in his guts.

If he had them taken somewhere, here would be the best bet.

Samson stalked over to the bar and shouldered a number of men out of his way as he did so.

"What's it to be?" a tall, broad, and grinning man sporting mutton chops asked. Through the barman's thin shirt, Samson could see a bulky frame. "Well?" he pressed.

"Where's Ray?"

The expression on the man's face changed, and he turned his head to look behind him. Samson followed the barkeep's gaze and picked out a photo of him pinned to the wall above the till.

The barman's head snapped back in Samson's direction. "It's *you*!" He grabbed a walkie-talkie from behind the counter, but he wasn't fast enough speaking into it.

A surge of rage flicked through Samson, along with the innocent images of Charlie's and Alice's faces. A red mist befell the P.I., and before he knew it, he'd grabbed the man by his ears and slammed his face down on the counter once, twice, three times.

Teeth rattled across the bar like spent peanut casings tossed by a barfly. The barman went slack, blood pooled across the countertop, and the music stopped.

"Oh, Jesus!" a young girl from behind the bar gasped, picking up the phone.

"Don't," Samson warned, letting the man go.

A fist drilled into Samson's back and he was spun around.

There were two of them. One he knew. It was Big O, and he was holding a baseball bat with the word Kansas etched across the wood.

The same one? Samson thought, taking a robust fist to the face from O's sidekick.

Samson slammed against the bar but refused to go down.

"Try this on for size," Big O said, swinging his bat into Samson's guts.

"*Ugh*," the P.I. groaned, doubling over.

The other man grabbed Samson by his elbow. "Come with us."

Samson snatched his arm back and drove an uppercut into the man's jaw, snapping his mouth shut. The blow propelled the lump of a bloke backwards, and he rolled over a table, smashing glasses and spilling beer as he went.

"Come on, palooka," Samson enticed Big O, putting his fists up.

Big O came at him with his bat raised, but a yell from behind brought the fight to a stop.

"That's enough."

Samson looked up to see a man standing at the back of the room. He was shrouded in darkness—plumes of cigar smoke rose from him—and six men flanked him.

"Everybody out," he demanded. "*Now*."

It took less than five minutes for the punters to clear out and for the girls to rush backstage. By then, the man Samson had slugged over a table was back on his feet. So, too, was the fella from behind the bar, but he wasn't going to be much use to anyone: his mouth had swollen to the size of an apple.

"You need some ice for that, meathead," Samson advised, turning back to face XRay. "Why don't you cut the dramatics and release the girls, Ray? If you do, that's the end of it. This doesn't have to go any further."

"I told you what I want, and until I get it, the girls stay with me. I suggest you get going, Samson.

Time isn't on your side."

"You—" he tried lunging across the room but he was pinned down by Big O and the other guy. "I *will* take you down."

"The next time we meet, which will be very soon, of that I'm confident, we'll both get what we want. Until then, goodbye, Valentine."

"You—you—"

"Take him outside and say your farewells, boys," XRay ordered.

Samson was dragged to a side door, escorted down two flights of steel steps, and thrown through a pair of double-doors out onto the street. Rain started falling.

The P.I. rolled onto his back and looked up at the faces towering over him. "I got the message, fellas—*ugh*!" he cried, as a flurry of kicks laid into his ribs and guts.

After what felt like an eternity, the brutality was brought to a close by Big O. "That's enough. He's going to need to walk, drive, and function. We don't want Ray pissed at *us*."

The thugs with him grunted in agreement, and they all disappeared back inside, leaving Samson where he lay. The steel doors were closed with a bone-jarring slam.

Samson rolled over, got to all fours, and flopped down onto his stomach. His head came to rest in a neon-lit puddle. Blood trickled out of his mouth and nostrils.

***

Ten minutes later, Samson found the strength to pick himself up and to stagger-hobble to his car. He crashed against it as he found the right key and slotted it home. Before getting in, he threw up in the gutter.

"That's better," he wheezed, wiping his chin.

He folded himself into his car and drove off, after sitting there for a few minutes.

Now what? I need to find him, *that's what, and I'm not going to rest until I do.*

***

For a while, Samson drove around aimlessly, the girls and Lisa flooding his mind, and then the list of 'hangout spots' Lutherhead had given him came to mind. *It's worth a shot,* he thought, parking and digging his notebook out. *Is it? Broadbank has men at each of these spots and he would have contacted me if something had turned up. Still, it's better than doing nothing.*

"I'll work my way down the list," he muttered. "Hmm, most of these places are here in the centre of town."

Samson found a decent parking space, locked his car, and started out on foot. His first port of call was an abandoned powerhouse. *It's about time I ended this,* he thought, punching his hands into his coat's pockets as he disappeared into the night.

Chapter 22

It had taken him until the following evening to move from the ball he'd rolled into on the sofa and read the text from Hatch.

"I think we need to meet and chat about things. But not yet – the streets are too hot."

He hadn't bothered replying immediately, even though he'd read, and re-read the message several hundred times in the past few weeks.

And now, as he read it again, he couldn't help but think of its menace.

He means to kill me. He's not going to want me to get caught in case I talk, and it's not going to make a blind bit of difference if I try to reassure him, The Widower Maker thought, continuing to stare at the message. *What if I take him an offering? That might defuse the situation.*

He liked that idea.

"I could take him Catherine, alive, and he could watch me cut her up and get his jollies right there and then, but only if he promises to let me walk away. I'll persuade him that I won't talk *if* I'm caught," he thought aloud, his thumb hovering over his mobile's keypad.

In the last few weeks, since he'd been lying low, the police were none the wiser. There were no new leads.

They haven't got a clue as to who I am. I knew that photo wouldn't help – it looked nothing *like me.*

Well, maybe a teeny-tiny bit. I panicked for nothing. Damn it. I really should have messaged Hatch back straightaway. He's going to know shit isn't right, that I might suspect he'll try something.

"Sorry for not replying sooner, but I didn't know what to do. I'm up for meeting – how about tomorrow night?"

He put his phone down on the table in front of him and gave it some time. No sooner had he relaxed back into the sofa, than his mobile was vibrating, the screen flashing with Hatch's name.

"Okay, here we go," he muttered, and read the message aloud. "That's good by me. Where? What time?"

Surely if he'd wanted to hurt me he would have come here and done away with me by now? Maybe, or maybe he'd like to do it in a dark, unseen spot. Like...

"How about our old home, friend, the bridge?"

"That works for me. Time?" Hatch came back with, complete with a smiley face.

See, I'm being paranoid. "I'm thinking the wee hours. Three a.m.?"

A second later, there was a response. "See you then."

He set his phone aside, relaxed, and thought about how he was going to work things.

I think the easiest thing to do, is to drive to Catherine's house, snatch her, and throw her in the boot. If it's late enough, like it will be, I shouldn't have a problem.

The only obstacle he foresaw was the police.

The piggies have been out in force recently. He'd also seen on the news how they were carrying out random checks by stopping motorists and people walking the streets at odd hours. *They even have a chopper in the sky, so taking the car could be risky.*

But what else could he do?

Hatch would need appeasing if he was going to wiggle his way out of danger.

Does the car need fuel? He couldn't remember. *When did I drive it last*?

***

It took him close to an hour to find his car keys – which were hidden at the bottom of his fruit bowl. After discovering them, he decided to go outside to his Honda and start it. He was pleased to see the petrol needle flip up to the halfway point.

"Excellent," he muttered, killing the engine and locking up.

On his way back to his flat, he saw police officers milling around.

They're everywhere, trapping me.

In an ironic twist of fate, it was now he who was fearful of the city around him.

"Huh, I'm still in control. *I'm* The Widower Maker, and tomorrow night, Cardiff will once again feel the tightness of my cold grip," he muttered, entering his home.

***

Happy with the car, and his plan for tomorrow evening, he was able to eat and drink something before settling in front of the TV for an hour. After that, he turned in early, knowing he had a big day ahead of him.

***

After several hours of creeping, peeping, searching, spying, nosing and sneaking around the dodgier, seedier sides and underbelly of Cardiff, Samson decided to call it quits.

He was in a panic.

What am I going to do? He wiped the sweat from his forehead. The sands of time were running out on him. *Maybe Broadbank has heard something*?

Samson fished his phone out of his pocket and was about to hit dial when he noticed a coffee shop worker opening up for the day.

"Excuse me, miss?" he called, attracting the attention of the young blonde barista.

She turned to look at him with a fearful look on her face, and he realised that he had not changed, washed, or shaved in a couple of days.

"W-what?" she asked.

"Could I grab a tea, please? I know it's early, and I look like hell, but I'm not going to hassle you. I'm with the police," he assured her, finding his credentials. "I've been up more hours than I care to think about. I just need something to help keep me going."

She relented, smiled, and held the door wide for

Samson. “Come on,” she said. “I’ll fix you something.”

Samson dragged himself inside and heard the door being closed and locked.

“We’re not supposed to let anyone in before nine—if someone found out, I’d get the sack—but I’m acting manageress today,” she informed Samson, passing him.

“This is very kind of you.”

“Please, take a seat at the counter.”

Samson sat and watched as she affixed her nameplate and adorned an apron. Within minutes, she had the kettle boiling.

“Would you like something sweet to eat – there’s cake left over from yesterday? It’s only going to go in the bin,” she said, turning to face him from behind the counter.

And that’s when he spied her nametag.

“That sounds lovely, Sophie. Thanks.”

She returned his smile. “No problem. It’s coming right up.”

“Thanks. I just have to make a quick call.”

“Sure.”

Samson yawned, got up, stretched and dialled Broadbank’s number. The chief answered after a few rings.

“Any news on your end, Broadbank?”

“Nothing, Sam.”

“Damn it. We need to do *something*.”

“Where are you?”

“I’m out in the city, which is where I’ve been all night.”

"Doing what?"

"Lurking around The Widower Maker's 'known spots'."

"I'm sure my guys would have radioed if they'd seen something."

"I guess I'm grasping at straws."

"You know, we could take the girls back by force, Sam. Do you know where they are?"

"If we try and do that, he'll kill them."

"Then you suggest we sit tight and hope?"

"Pretty much, yes." Samson expelled air through his mouth noisily, whilst removing his hat with his free hand and dropping it onto the counter. He ran his hand through his moist hair.

"Try not to panic just yet. You might be able to buy more time if you do some sweet talking."

"Maybe, Broadbank. Maybe. I'm going to get a hot drink inside me before hitting the apple's streets again. See if I can't dig something up. Speak later." Samson hung up and took his seat at the counter.

As he sipped his tea and picked at his cake, he tried to think about his next move, but realised he didn't have one, apart from getting back out there.

***

He'd willed yesterday away, eager for time to pass, and now that tomorrow night was finally here, The Widower Maker wasn't sure he wanted it to be.

I just got to keep it together for the next few hours and everything will be okay again.

His thoughts switched to Catherine, and he

smiled.

I've been waiting a long time to cut her up. Too long. After checking the time and seeing it was almost one a.m., he decided it was time to start getting ready. *I need to be rolling in twenty,* he thought, making his way to his bedroom to dress in all black clothing.

When he was done, he gathered up his 'kit', grabbed his keys, headed out the door to his car, and left for Catherine's.

***

Parked opposite her house, he used a small pair of binoculars to spy on the place, which was shrouded in darkness. The curtains were closed.

He poked his head out the driver's side window and looked to see if he could see any police in the area or neighbours on neighbourhood watch duty.

Not that I'd see them, he thought. *Okay, there's no point in messing about.*

He set his binoculars aside, picked up his bag of tricks, got out, locked up and scuttled across to the house and hid in the shadows. As he caught his breath, he pricked his ears.

Nothing, and there appeared to be no movement on the street.

A smile brightened his face and drove his fears to the back of his mind.

He turned to the house and saw the outline of the back gate—thanks to the moon—and proceeded towards it as quietly and as quickly as possible.

Before reaching for his lock-picking tools, he tried the knob to the back door, just in case it was unlocked, and laughed when it opened.

"And people wonder *why* there's so much crime," he muttered, pushing the door until it was fully open, exposing a kitchen beyond.

With his torch in hand—which he'd taken from his bag—he swept its beam around the room. He didn't hang about to admire the view as he marched through the room and into the living area. After locating the stairs to the second floor, he took them two at a time, wanting this part to be done with.

Do I disable the children? What's the point when they're only young? It's not like they're going to be able to stop me, is it?

At the top of the stairs he was met by three doors.

If my memory serves me correctly, their bedroom is located at the back of the house, which would make it this door here, he thought, pointing his light to the right.

He crept in its direction and placed a hand to its handle. With ease, he depressed it and pushed the door inwards, hoping the hinges were good. As it opened, he held his breath, but it didn't squeak.

Sweat beaded his brow.

Before entering the room, he popped his balaclava on and removed the cosh from his bag. He gripped it tight, about to cross the threshold, when a light from above burst on, illuminating the entire landing.

"The fuck?!" a voice from behind The Widower

Maker called, startling the killer further.

He was almost too scared to turn around, but he did. At the other end of the corridor stood a teenage boy with bed hair and morning wood.

Who the hell? *No, no – this can't be right.* His thoughts came so fast that they smashed into the tail end of the previous one. *Catherine and her husband have two* young *children. They don't have—he looks like the father…*

Neither the lad nor The Widower Maker moved.

"Josh?" a groggy voice came from the master bedroom. "Is that you out there, honey?"

Catherine, he thought. *I'm in a whole heap of shit here.*

Bedsprings groaned, and her husband continued to snore.

"Are you okay?" she yawned, her feet shuffling closer.

Josh opened his mouth to speak, but no words came.

The Widower Maker turned back to the room to see Catherine step towards him whilst wiping the sleep from her eyes. She walked into his cosh as he brought it down on her head.

"*Bastard*," Josh growled and then charged towards The Widower Maker.

"*Wh*-what?" Catherine's husband called from their bed.

I don't fucking believe this, The Widower Maker thought, turning in time to club Josh across his face. The blow sent the youngster sideways, and The Widower Maker watched in awe as the boy tripped over his own legs and somersaulted over the banister.

He hit the floor below with a sickening crunch.

The Widower Maker smiled, turned, and entered the bedroom to shut the father down. He jumped onto the bed, surprising the sleepy man, and repeatedly pounded his skull until it was staved in. The sheets became saturated, and blood splashed his balaclava.

The Widower Maker got off the bed, breathless.

"Mummy?"

He snapped his head in the direction of the doorway, spotting Catherine's daughter.

"Get back to you room, you little bitch, or do you want some, too?"

The girl started crying, turned, and fled.

He went to Catherine, grabbed her by her feet and then pulled her down the stairs as fast as he could. Above, he heard the daughter talking on the telephone.

"Yes, police..."

I don't have time to deal with her now, he thought, lugging Catherine off the floor and carrying her outside to his car, risking everything. *Fuck, fuck, fuck...*

He threw her limp body into the boot and then quickly scanned the streets.

"I don't think anyone saw me."

Sirens blared in the distance.

The Widower Maker started his car and floored it.

After taking a series of turns, he parked for a few

minutes to see if he was being tailed, but there were no police cars onto him.

"That was beyond lucky." He checked the time and saw it was still early. "I've got another thirty minutes before I need to meet Hatch." He drummed his fingers on the steering wheel and thought about ditching the car once this was over. "I could burn or drown it. Either way, it has to go."

When he thought the streets were safe, he pulled off and made his way towards the bridge.

***

Fifteen minutes later, he arrived at his destination, parked up, lugged Catherine's body under the structure, and laid her close to the water's edge.

He checked the time again.

03:05.

"Where is he?" When he spoke, he saw his breath. The Widower Maker looked about him and stamped his feet whilst rubbing his arms.

Minutes ticked away, and he got the feeling he was being stood up, but then came the sound of footsteps.

He stopped all movement and pricked his ears.

Over the sound of trickling, gurgling water, he heard the footfalls draw closer. He wanted to call out, but remained silent from deep within the shadows. From where he stood, he had a good view of the path a person would need to use to get down here.

With squinted eyes, he watched with bated

breath.

"Come on, come on…" he whispered. "Show yourself."

A large figure appeared at the foot of the dirt path.

"Chris?" It was Hatchy's voice.

"I'm here, Hatch."

"Where?"

The Widower Maker stepped from the shadows and into the moon's beams that had managed to find their way under the old structure.

Hatch stepped up to him and they stood almost nose-to-nose.

"It's been a while since we were under here together," the bigger man said and smiled. "Hang on, what's that?" he pointed over The Widower Maker's shoulder.

"A present."

"For me?" Hatch's smile grew wider.

The Widower Maker nodded. "Yes, and I'll let you watch me destroy her, but on one condition."

"Anything."

"I firstly want your word, Hatch."

"My word?"

"That you won't try anything – that you'll let me on my merry way after this 'chat' is over."

Hatch eyed him and then revealed to The Widower Maker what he'd feared all along. "Can I trust you not to say anything if the police catch up to you?"

"You shouldn't even need to ask me that, Hatch."

"That's all I needed to hear."

"Then why bring me here for that?"

"So I could look you in the eyes, Chris."

"Are you happy?"

Hatch nodded. "Very. Now, will you rip her open for me? This will be much better than the photos…"

The Widower Maker produced his buck knife. "It would be my pleasure, Hatch."

***

After walking around for hours on end, Samson had given up the ghost and headed home. He had no leads and no hope; he began to fear the worst for Alice and Charlie.

There's only one thing left to do, he thought, looking at the card with XRay's number on it.

Samson got up from the dining room seat he was sat on—unable to look at his blood-stained easy chair—and crossed to his landline. He picked up the receiver and punched XRay's number into the keypad. After a few rings, there was an answer. "Hello, Ray?"

"Ah, Mr Valentine, you're burning the midnight oil," XRay said.

In the background, Samson heard the rowdy sounds of the mobster's strip joint. "I need more time."

"Forty-eight hours was the deal, Valentine."

"Look, palooka, in case you hadn't noticed, Cardiff is a big apple, and our killer could be hiding under any old rock. Hell, he might not even dwell in this grand old city of ours."

XRay chuckled. "What a pickle you're in. I'd love to see the look on Alice's parents' face when you tell them she's not coming home, and that she's working the streets as a hooker for an unscrupulous man."

Samson wanted to smash the man's beezer in with the heel of his hand.

"I'm asking for a few more days, that's all."

"Time is wasting, Samson. I suggest you get back out there and work your magic."

"But—" Samson's mobile started ringing in his pocket. He fished it out and saw Broadbank's name flashing on the screen.

As XRay went off on a tangent in his ear, the P.I. faded him out and answered his phone.

"Broadbank?"

"Sam, I *may* have something for you. I've had reports from a man who thinks there's someone up to no good under the old bridge on your watch list."

"Where are your men?"

"They're not answering."

"Leave it to me – I'll get right over there."

"Okay. Shall I send backup?"

"I'll let you know. If it *is* our boy, I don't want to spook him."

"Sam, please be careful."

"I will, chief."

He ended the call and put his mobile in his pocket. Samson then went back to the other phone and listened, but only dead air came at him. XRay was gone.

***

She was awake and screaming, her cries muffled due to the strip of silk nightgown he'd torn from her body and stuffed in her mouth. In fact, most of her garment lay in tatters—which he'd shredded to make ties for her wrists and ankles—exposing almost every inch of her flesh.

"Do her, Chris. Do her in the pussy – fuck her with the knife," Hatch panted in his ear.

Catherine looked at The Widower Maker's blood-coated blade as he brought it close to her face. She shook her head, her eyes bulging.

"No, no, no!" she begged, the words stifled.

Both men laughed.

"This is going to hurt, I won't lie," The Widower Maker whispered, about to rip her stomach open, when footfalls from behind stopped him.

"What was that?" The Widower Maker asked. "I thought you said you'd taken care of the cops?"

"I did," Hatch argued.

More steps.

"There's more than one person, Hatch."

"How can you tell?"

"Listen for yourself."

He watched as Hatch turned from him.

Do you think I'm an idiot, old friend? The Widower Maker thought and slammed his blade into Hatch's back.

"*Urgh*!" the fat man cried, collapsing into the

water with a splash.

The Widower Maker watched as Hatch floated downstream. "Bye, comrade Hatch." He turned to the woman. "Looks like you'll be saved, Catherine – the police—"

Three shapes appeared before him.

"Hello, Chris – how many years has it been?"

"B-*Benny*?" The Widower Maker blurted. "How did *you* find me? What's going on?"

XRay stepped out of the shadows, removed the cigar from his mouth, and blew smoke in The Widower Maker's face. "It wasn't easy, Chris. I've been searching for you ever since this whole Widower Maker thing began. Why did you kill Roxie? I would have been happy to let you go about your business if you'd left her alone."

"Because I wanted to hurt you like you hurt me and the rest of The Lost. You threw us away like rubbish. It was unforgivable."

XRay sighed. "I grew up and moved on to bigger and better things. Why would you hate me for that? And why did you kill Hatch?"

"Maybe if you'd taken us to the top with you, none of this would have happened, but you knew I had a thing for Roxie, didn't you? You knew I wanted to make her mine, and you couldn't stand that."

XRay huffed. "It doesn't matter now," he said, producing a gun.

The Widower Maker froze. "Wait. Please, Benny. It doesn't have to end like this."

"Ah, but it does." He raised the shooter, about to

fire, when XRay's men cried out.

"What's this, a party for prize palookas?" Samson asked, stepping over the men he'd floored with a police baton he'd taken from a dead officer above. "Did you kill them good ol' boys, Ray?"

"I was hoping you'd get here on time, Samson," XRay said, avoiding the question. His eyes remained fixed on The Widower Maker.

"Is that so?"

"Yes. Now you'll know for sure the streets are safe again." XRay pulled the trigger, and a bullet smashed through The Widower Maker's left eyeball, splattering the pillar behind him in gore.

The mobster then turned and trained the gun's smoking muzzle on Samson. "It appears we're at a stalemate once more, Valentine."

Samson heard the thugs at his back groan as they gathered themselves up off the floor. He held his hands above his head. "Just give me the girls and you can walk."

XRay scoffed. "Do you really think you're in a position to barter or threaten me, Samson?"

"Please. This, us, it can be saved for another day. As far as I'm concerned, you've done the city a favour tonight," Samson said, trying his best to defuse the situation and win the girls back. "And, if it wasn't for you overhearing me on the phone to Broadbank, you never would have known to come here and catch The Widower Maker."

"Yes, you get points for that, Samson, but still – you didn't deliver, did you? However, for your efforts, I will spare Lisa's life for another forty-eight hours. That should give you enough time to get to her, right? How's that? Sadly, though, Alice and Charlie will remain in my care, and if you argue or try any of your games, I will mail them back to you in pieces."

"You can't do that."

"Oh, but I can. Call it payment for the millions you've cost me over the last few years."

"Those girls have done nothing to you. *Nothing*."

"Charlie was *my* property, Samson. Mine."

He felt helpless, and then XRay's goons grabbed him and pinned him to a wall. This allowed XRay to slip past, his face hidden amongst the shadows. "This was another excellent game, Samson."

"This isn't over, XRay, and as soon as your boys let me go, I'll be coming for you and the girls."

XRay laughed as he disappeared up the dirt track and called back over his shoulder. "I'd be highly disappointed if you didn't, Samson, and if you can find and rescue them, I won't come after you for it. But I will kill you if I catch you trying."

"You swine, X."

"Goodbye, and good luck, Valentine."

"This isn't—*ooph*!" the P.I. doubled over as a fist rammed into his guts once, twice, three times. His body went limp in the arms of the men that held him in place, his head lolling, leaving his chin open to a powerful knee.

His world turned black.

Epilogue

After regaining consciousness, Samson kept his promise to XRay and began searching for Alice and Charlie after untying Catherine and getting her to safety. His first port of call was St David's shopping centre. However, when he got there, much to his surprise and dismay, the strip club was gone. The space where it had been was unoccupied and boarded up.

"I'll tear the city apart," he'd bellowed.

Early morning shoppers looked at him as though he was crazy. He certainly looked and felt it, with his bedraggled clothing and days' old stubble.

Samson stalked out of the shopping centre and pounded the streets.

"I won't let you down, girls, I swear. As God is my witness, I will find you..."

***

In Samson's haste upon leaving the bridge, he'd failed to spot the wounded Hatch crawl out of the water and collapse into nearby shrubbery.

"*Argh*, you bastard, Chris," he hissed with clenched teeth. Hatch placed his hands around the knife's entry wound and applied pressure, suppressing the blood loss. "Got to get to a hospital..." he grunted, staggering to his feet.

When he got to the streets above, he fell into the

road and almost got run over by a car pushing the speed limit. Its tyres screamed and smoked.

"Christ alive, I could have killed you," the driver protested.

"Help. Me," Hatch begged, holding a gruesome hand out. "I'm dying."

"Holy shit." The man escorted Hatch into his car and drove him to the nearest hospital.

***

After surgery and a mouthful of lies, Hatch slipped away into the night, vowing to settle the score with Benny, once and for all.

It may not have been Benny who plunged the dagger into me, but it was him who spooked Chris enough to do it, making him think I had double-crossed him. Oddly enough, he felt no hatred towards the man dubbed The Widower Maker. *After all, I had planned to kill him under the bridge if I'd seen a lie in his eye.*

***

The only winners were the good people of Cardiff. When it hit the news that The Widower Maker was confirmed dead, the city seemed to release a collective sigh of relief.

It was over for them, at least, but not Samson.

For Samson, things were only just beginning, who, after twenty-four hours of tearing the city apart for the girls, was now headed west to

Carmarthenshire to rescue Lisa.

"I swear to God, if they've harmed one hair on her head, I won't be responsible for my reactions," he said from behind gritted teeth as he drove through the night…

The End

Also from Red Cape Publishing

Anthologies:

Elements of Horror Book One: Earth
Elements of Horror Book Two: Air
Elements of Horror Book Three: Fire
Elements of Horror Book Four: Water
A is for Aliens: A-Z of Horror Book One
B is for Beasts: A-Z of Horror Book Two
C is for Cannibals: A-Z of Horror Book Three
D is for Demons: A-Z of Horror Book Four
E is for Exorcism: A-Z of Horror Book Five
F is for Fear: A-Z of Horror Book Six
G is for Genies: A-Z of Horror Book Seven
H is for Hell: A-Z of Horror Book Eight
I is for Internet: A-Z of Horror Book Nine
J is for Jack-o'-Lantern: A-Z of Horror Book Ten
K is for Kidnap: A-Z of Horror Book Eleven
L is for Lycans: A-Z of Horror Book Twelve
It Came from the Darkness: A Charity Anthology
Out of the Shadows: A Charity Anthology
Castle Heights: 18 Storeys, 18 Stories
Sweet Little Chittering

Short Story Collections:

Embrace the Darkness by P.J. Blakey-Novis
Tunnels by P.J. Blakey-Novis
The Artist by P.J. Blakey-Novis
Karma by P.J. Blakey-Novis
The Place Between Worlds by P.J. Blakey-Novis
Home by P.J. Blakey-Novis
Short Horror Stories by P.J. Blakey-Novis
Short Horror Stories Vol.2 by P.J. Blakey-Novis
Keep It Inside & Other Weird Tales by Mark Anthony Smith
Everything's Annoying by J.C. Michael
Six! By Mark Cassell
Monsters in the Dark by Donovan 'Monster' Smith

Novelettes:

The Ivory Tower by Antoinette Corvo

Novellas:

Four by P.J. Blakey-Novis
Dirges in the Dark by Antoinette Corvo
The Cat That Caught The Canary by Antoinette Corvo
Bow-Legged Buccaneers from Outer Space by David Owain Hughes
Spiffing by Tim Mendees
A Splintered Soul by Adrian Meredith

Novels:

Madman Across the Water by Caroline Angel
The Curse Awakens by Caroline Angel
Less by Caroline Angel
Where Shadows Move by Caroline Angel
Origin of Evil by Caroline Angel
Origin of Evil: Beginnings by Caroline Angel
The Vegas Rift by David F. Gray
The Broken Doll by P.J. Blakey-Novis
The Broken Doll: Shattered Pieces by P.J. Blakey-Novis
South by Southwest Wales by David Owain Hughes
Appletown by Antoinette Corvo
Nails by K.J. Sargeant

Art Books:

Demons Never Die by David Paul Harris & P.J. Blakey-Novis

Children's Books:

The Little Bat That Could by Gemma Paul
The Mummy Walks at Midnight by Gemma Paul
A Very Zombie Christmas by Gemma Paul
Grace & Bobo: The Trip to the Future by Peter Blakey-Novis
My Sister's from the Moon by Peter Blakey-Novis
Elvis the Elephant by Peter Blakey-Novis
Grandad, Where's Your Hair? by Tony Sands

Follow Red Cape Publishing

www.redcapepublishing.com
www.facebook.com/redcapepublishing
www.twitter.com/redcapepublish
www.instagram.com/redcapepublishing
www.pinterest.co.uk/redcapepublishing
www.patreon.com/redcapepublishing
www.ko-fi.com/redcape
www.buymeacoffee.com/redcape

Printed in Great Britain
by Amazon

30654799R00225